MAGITECH RISES

MAGITECH RISES

EXCEPTIONAL S. BEAUFONT™ BOOK 3

SARAH NOFFKE

MICHAEL ANDERLE

DISRUPTIVE IMAGINATION

LMBPN Publishing
PMB 196, 2540 South Maryland Pkwy
Las Vegas, NV 89109

First US Edition, January 2020
Version 1.05, June 2021
eBook ISBN: 978-1-64202-714-3
Print ISBN: 978-1-64202-715-0

THE MAGITECH RISES TEAM

Thanks to the JIT Readers

Angel LaVey
Billie Leigh Kellar
Dave Hicks
Deb Mader
Debi Sateren
Diane L. Smith
Dorothy Lloyd
Jackey Hankard-Brodie
Jeff Eaton
Jeff Goode
Kathleen Fettig
Larry Omans
Lori Hendricks
Micky Cocker
Misty Roa
Nicole Emens
Paul Westman
Peter Manis
Veronica Stephan-Miller

If we've missed anyone, please let us know!

Editor
The Skyhunter Editing Team

Once again and a thousand times more, for Lydia.

— Sarah

To Family, Friends and
Those Who Love
to Read.
May We All Enjoy Grace
to Live the Life We Are
Called.

— Michael

CHAPTER ONE

The gravel slipped under Sophia's fingers, sending her sliding another inch. She gasped and bit her tongue, tasting blood.

She kicked and tried to secure her footing on the side of the crumbling cliff where she dangled. The dirt fell away, granting her no reprieve from her precarious situation.

Don't look down, Lunis calmly warned in her mind.

Sweat dripped into her mouth as she shook her head.

Why did you have to say that? Now I have to look down, she answered, hardly able to hear her own voice in her head over her heavy breathing and racing heartbeat.

The fall to the bottom of the ravine was several hundred yards. *Sophia wouldn't survive it.*

And I can't rescue you, Lunis reminded her for what felt like the dozenth time.

I know. Sophia grunted. She tried to claw farther up the rocky wall. Her fingers were numb from the cold, making it harder. She'd started the climb halfway down the cliff wall. Just another few inches and she'd be safe at the top.

Looking down, she shuddered. That, or she'd die a painful death.

1

Finding a root with her boot, Sophia secured her foot, grateful not to have to use pressure to keep her position on the wall.

You're almost there, Lunis urged. *Don't give up.*

I'm not giving up, she complained. *I'm breathing.*

You can breathe when you get to the top.

Sophia's hand shook as she reached for a hold a few inches up. A wind sent by the devil nearly blew her off the wall.

She cinched in tighter and pressed her face to the rock, her teeth chattering from the cold and adrenaline.

"Angels above!" she yelled. The winds had been unrelenting since she started, but now they seemed to have a special vendetta against her.

The wind is a dragonrider's friend, Lunis explained.

"With friends like that…" Sophia muttered.

It's meant to make you stronger, Lunis stated.

"Is that what friends do?" Sophia asked, surprised she had the energy to laugh as the wind howled past her ears.

Yes, he answered simply.

"No wonder I never made friends growing up," Sophia joked, daring to take one of her hands off the wall, her fingers climbing a few more inches as she pulled herself up.

You're turning away from the wind, Lunis observed.

"Yes, that's my attempt not to get blown off the side of this cliff," Sophia told him.

If you embrace the wind, you'll find more often than not it propels you in the right direction, instead of the wrong one, Lunis told her, a sage-like quality heavy in his voice.

Sophia allowed his words to wash over her. She wanted to make a joke, but deep down, she knew there was great wisdom in what he was saying. She felt it at her core, and as if unlocked by his words, Sophia felt a rush of wind glide underneath her to push her up a few inches. Given that momentum, Sophia's hands began to move, her feet following.

Her fingers came over the edge of the cliff and found the top. She scrambled for a hold, but the surface was smooth grass and dirt.

You're almost there, Lunis urged.

Sophia could feel the heat of her dragon close to her hand. He wasn't helping her, though. Not now that she'd come this far. It was strange to have him so close and be all on her own, but that was the lesson of the exercise. Something she hadn't expected to get out of it was the realization that she had to make peace with the wind, but that would take time.

Sophia pushed with her legs, remembering a woman's strength as a climber was in her thighs—not the upper body like a man. It might have been a bit late in the trek to remember, but the timing might have just saved Sophia.

She hiked up her leg, slid her knee over the edge as she kicked off, and scrambled firmly over the side. Rolling away from the edge, Sophia lay flat on the earth, grateful to be horizontal after the long climb.

Her dragon swung his head around and looked down at her from only a few inches away. *You made it.*

Through hyperventilating breaths, Sophia said, "Barely."

"In battle, there is no victor who barely wins," Lunis stated. "There is only life and death. You lived, and that's what counts."

Sophia turned her head to the side and looked out at the clear blue skies of Scotland and the landscape spread out beyond the crumbling cliff. She couldn't help but appreciate the green hills right then or the gentle breeze which wrapped around her forehead beaded with sweat.

Returning her attention to the blue dragon, Sophia smiled up at him. "You would have saved me if I fell, right?"

He shook his head. I let you with no

She rolled her eyes as she pushed up to a sitting position, making him retract his head. "It's just a training exercise."

What we do in training will determine whether we survive the battles to come, he informed her. *If you train always thinking you have a safety net, then you'll surely fail when the time comes to face real danger.*

Wilder strode across the Expanse, closing the distance between them, a proud smile on his face. He extended a hand to Sophia. "You've earned a shot of whiskey."

3

She wrapped her fingers around his and allowed him to pull her to standing position. Her legs quivered under her, fatigued. "I could use two shots, actually."

He gave her an impressed grin. "You haven't even had breakfast yet."

"So?" she argued.

Shaking his head, Wilder said, "I swear, you might have Scottish blood in you after all."

"Do you need some porridge before your morning whiskey?" Sophia teased.

He laughed. "A real Scotsman brushes his teeth with Scotch Whiskey, my friend."

"That's surprising," Sophia remarked. "I didn't know you even brushed your teeth."

He flashed her a smile. "There's a lot about us that will surprise you. Speaking of surprises, you beat Evan's time when he first did the climb." He indicated the cliff she'd just scaled.

Sophia scoffed at him. "Why are you surprised? Because I'm a woman and Evan has more upper body strength than me?"

Wilder smirked. "Yes, actually, but you're quickly dispelling all my stereotypes."

Sophia stretched her neck and felt the tension start to roll out of her muscles. The next phase of her training was to focus on building her strength, agility, and speed. According to Wilder, she couldn't just rely on Lunis for these things. Individually, Sophia needed to be strong enough to withstand obstacles without her dragon. He'd told her that before pushing her over the side of the cliff where she fell quite the distance before catching herself on a thick root. She'd been forced to climb back up, her heart nearly beating out of her chest from the scare.

"What if I hadn't caught myself on that root?" she asked Wilder. She had the urge to punch him in the face for the assault.

He winked at her. "I knew you'd catch yourself."

"What if I hadn't?" she challenged.

He strode off for the Castle after giving an appreciative nod to Lainis. "Well, then you'd be dead, wouldn't you?"

Sophia shook her head at her dragon as she hurried after Wilder. "One of these days, I'm going to get you back for that stunt."

Wilder flashed her a crooked grin. "I have no doubt, Sophia."

CHAPTER TWO

"You realize weapons of mass destruction are not my specialty," Alexander Drake said to Thad Reinhart as the pair strode through the top-level-security facility. They halted in a room with viewing windows into the other research areas.

The billionaire stopped, his usual expression of annoyance covering his scarred face. "I simply asked you to look into the matter since you installed the weapons for Ember 2.0."

"Is that really the name you're going with?" Drake dared to ask. "I mean, it's not really a machine and not really—"

"Do you not value your position here?" Thad replied.

Drake straightened, used to the threats. "Of course, and I figured you'd prefer my honest feedback rather than—"

"I don't care about your opinions," Thad interrupted. "What I care about is whether the magitech you recently installed could be used on a larger scale system?"

Drake combed his fat fingers over his equally thick chin. "In theory, it makes sense. Something like that could be enough to wipe out an entire country. Is it something you really want to do?"

Thad's eyes fluttered with annoyance. "None of that should be your concern."

Drake pursed his lips, his beard twitching. "Thing is, I live on this planet too and would like to see it continue."

"When did you start caring about this world?" Thad challenged.

Blowing out a breath, Drake ran his hand over his bald head. "I was aware you had ambitious plans, but..." He swept his arm at the many compartmental rooms lining the hallway. "I was under the impression you needed my help with dragon genetics and technology connected to them. And that alone won't maim the world. What you're talking about—"

Thad sighed. This was happening more frequently as his plans progressed. The scientists and engineers were okay with the research and technology until they realized he was going to use them. It's like they didn't take it seriously, and thought it was all a hobby project.

Like most, they didn't have the gall to do what needed to be done when the time came. Or maybe it was because people like Drake had a sentimental attachment to this place called Earth.

They wouldn't if they knew what Thad did. None of it mattered. He'd lived five-hundred years and couldn't find any true meaning in the world. Nothing made it better. What was the point in making things better anyway? Life was about taking. Getting. Having. Even after all that, it was pretty meaningless. He figured he'd be doing this planet the biggest favor by destroying it and the people on it since they mostly just complained and were leeches on the world.

Thad yanked up his arm, his suit jacket sleeve pulling down to reveal the device on his wrist. It didn't tell time or make phone calls, but it did listen to his thoughts and respond with incredible accuracy. Magitech was brilliant, once the bugs were worked out.

A red dot appeared on the center of the face of the watch-looking device. It grew bigger as Thad turned and strode for the thick metal door on the far side of the room.

"Sir," Drake called after him. "Are we done? Don't you want me—"

"*You're* done," Thad said simply. He yanked the door open and stepped through to the other side. He didn't offer Drake a last look before sealing the door into place, turning the latch and locking it shut.

A moment later, a detonation rocked the room he'd exited, killing anything inside. There had been only one person in there, and now Drake and his conscience weren't a problem for Thad Reinhart.

He sighed as he realized he'd have a lot of paperwork, trying to find a replacement for Drake. Glancing up at the ceiling, Thad smiled to himself, glad he'd had the last scientist install small explosives that could be dropped down based on a single intention from Thad.

Of course, the CEO had to learn some restraint since it made getting rid of troublesome employees incredibly easy. Then Thad realized, just like any other time in his life, restraint wasn't really all it was cracked up to be. Like in his days as a dragonrider, Thad gave in to his desire to do as he wished.

Hiker Wallace might think pillaging the world was a sin, but Thad didn't believe such things—which had always been the rub between the two.

The time to settle their lifelong dispute was coming to a head. If Hiker loved this planet so much, then he could die for it. There would be little other option for him, Thad thought, appreciating that everything he'd worked for was finally coming together. Soon it would be time to exact the revenge he'd been planning all these centuries.

CHAPTER THREE

"We wish you a Merry Christmas," Sophia sang, swaying to the music in her head.

Hiker Wallace had his feet stretched out and his boots resting on the ottoman in front of the fire, the day's newspaper spread open. "Bah, humbug." He turned the page, not even glancing at Sophia when she twitched her mouth to the side.

"*Rudolf, the red-nosed reindeer,*" she began to sing.

He lowered the newspaper and blinked at her. "Reindeers are nasty creatures who leave their droppings all over the place. And they can't fly."

She sighed. "Fine, I don't like that song anyway since it's about how people bully the underdog until the moment they need them for something."

Hiker tilted his head to the side and squinted at her like the light in the sitting room wasn't bright enough. "You take quite the literal sense to these repugnant songs."

Sophia sighed, slumping. "Seriously, why can't we have Christmas at the Castle?"

"Because we're dragonriders," he answered at once. "We're not little rosy-cheeked children with thoughts of sugar plums in our heads. Well, most of us aren't. You are."

"Just because we ride dragons and fight with swords doesn't mean we can't enjoy a bit of Christmas cheer."

Hiker straightened out his newspaper and tried to refocus on the print. "That's exactly what it means."

"I just don't get why we can't have a few decorations," Sophia complained, indicating to the fireplace. "Just imagine how great the mantle would look adorned with stockings and greenery."

The Castle, as it often did, indulged Sophia, attaching seven stockings of varying shapes and colors to the mantle and decorating the top of it with pine needles and red bows. Each of the stockings had the name of a resident in the Castle: Hiker, Mahkha, Evan, Wilder, Ainsley, Quiet, and of course, Sophia.

She smiled, enjoying the cheer the décor had instantly created.

Hiker grunted. "What are those?"

"Stockings. They are for our presents," Sophia said, narrowing her eyes at Evan's stocking. She slipped her hand into the long sock and pulled out a piece of coal. A laugh fell from her mouth.

Hiker nodded appreciatively. "At least the Castle got something right. Now go ahead and get rid of those."

A second later, the stockings and decorations disappeared.

Sophia slumped again. They'd been going back and forth like this for the better part of an hour. The Castle would indulge her by throwing up a Christmas tree or garland, but as soon as Hiker told the Castle to take it down, everything disappeared. Apparently, even though the Castle tortured Hiker by taking his books and rearranging his office, it still thought of him as a boss and wouldn't keep up anything Christmas related without his approval.

"How about just a small snow globe collection?" Sophia asked, her tone laced with persuasion.

On the side table at the frosty window, a set of varying sized snow globes appeared, flurries dancing around inside them like they'd just been shaken.

Hiker eyed them. "How about no?"

The snow globes vanished.

Sophia thought for a moment. "What about a bunch of Christmas dragons? We can have a little snow-covered village with dragons roasting chestnuts and keeping the villagers warm with towering bonfires."

Right on cue, the miniature village Sophia described appeared on the side table, complete with a small version of Lunis and the other dragons wearing Santa hats.

A squeal of delight fell out of Sophia's mouth as she admired the Castle's work.

Hiker dropped the newspaper in his lap. "Seriously, can I get my books back?"

The Castle made zero replies to this request.

"Okay, but will you get rid of that monstrosity?" Hiker pointed at the little village, and it disappeared at once. He sat back in his armchair, looking mostly satisfied.

"It was adorable, not a monstrosity," Sophia complained.

"Bell was wearing a fuzzy scarf," Hiker spat.

"Well, maybe her neck gets cold," Sophia reasoned.

"She's an ancient dragon, who breathes fire and can waste an entire village if she so desired," he fired back.

"Still, she might like a few accessories," Sophia argued. "Have you asked her?"

"I'm not sure I'd survive the conversation." Hiker pushed up to a standing position. "Shouldn't you be training? I believe Mama Jamba said you getting your wings was of supreme importance."

Sophia nodded. "Yeah, I was going to throw myself into it tomorrow."

"Because today you have to thread popcorn and frolic in the snow, making a snowman?" Hiker asked.

"No point in making decorations you won't let me keep up," Sophia grumbled. "And if I made anything out of snow, it would be a Snow Viking, and then I'd pelt him with snowballs."

Hiker looked down his nose at her and shook his head. "You realize I'm not a Viking, right?"

13

She shrugged. "If you say so. Maybe I just see you as one because of your temper."

"Your training, Sophia…"

She nodded. "Yes, I'm going to get to it, but I need to take the magitech Gordon used on Lunis and me to Liv to see if she can offer insights."

He rolled his eyes and looked at the ceiling. "Of course, because you're obviously in charge and get to do whatever you want."

"Oh, well, in that case, how about some candy canes—"

"It was a joke," Hiker interrupted.

"Fine," Sophia stated. "You don't want me to try to get a lead on Thad Reinhart? Would you rather I stay and train and send one of the guys to research the magitech?"

Hiker seemed to think about this. "No, it needs to be you. They don't know what they are doing with that stuff well enough. When you return, you're going to need to focus on training full time."

"I totally will," Sophia said. "All the way up until Christmas dinner when Ainsley roasts us a special goose."

"There will be no Christmas goose," Hiker disagreed. He shook his head at her.

"Christmas Spam?" Sophia asked.

"I don't know what that is, but the answer is still no," Hiker answered. "We've never done Christmas in the Castle, and we're not about to start. The sooner you get used to the idea, the better."

"Because any cheer would hurt your cold, dark heart?" Sophia asked.

"Because we are dragonriders who train, eat, sleep, and arbitrate. We don't sing carols and make Christmas lists."

Sophia blew out a long breath. "Yeah, fine then. No Christmas spirit. No fun. Just a nonstop mission to save the world."

She dragged herself toward the door.

"Is that a problem for you, Sophia?"

She turned and gave him a reluctant expression. "No, not at all, sir. Just thought it might be fun to do things a little differently."

"We don't do things differently, Sophia," he stated. "We do them as we always have, and that keeps us alive."

Sophia nodded. "Of course, sir. My apologies." She pivoted and strode for the stairs, wondering why Hiker Wallace was simultaneously one of the best men she'd ever met and also a huge pain in the ass. She could never shake the feeling he was hiding something, but she knew if anyone was aware of his secrets, it was the sentient being all around her.

CHAPTER FOUR

Gliding her hand over the walls of the Castle, Sophia hummed to herself, noticing the artwork had changed. She wasn't entirely sure how or why the Castle underwent interior design but suspected there were many factors involved.

The corridor had changed too. It was wider in places, narrower in others. There were windows where there hadn't been any and a skylight. She was pretty sure there were several stories on top of this one, although it was hard to tell how many.

Ainsley swore there were at least five stories to the Castle. On one occasion, Sophia had found the fifth floor but had been unable to do it a second time. From the outside, there were only four stories. Apparently, there was a basement, but Sophia hadn't found that either. She was pretty certain she'd barely scratched the surface of exploring the Castle.

Checking over her shoulder, Sophia ensured she was alone. The last thing she needed was Ainsley sneaking up on her and telling her what she was about to do was a bad idea. Maybe it was Sophia's conscience more than anything else talking to her. Ainsley had warned her not to make a deal with the Castle, stating it wouldn't live up to its end of the bargain. Sophia didn't really know what other options she had.

She reasoned it was all about how she positioned things. Clark often said it was more about how things were said, rather than the actual words used. Most people implied meaning if things were kept brief. Still, outsmarting the Castle was a tall order, especially because she sensed the words used would be limited. This meant Sophia needed to think the right thoughts—which seemed a bit more complex than negotiating using words.

"So…." Sophia began.

In response, the Castle walls warmed under her fingertips. She halted when she noticed the flames in the chandeliers overhead grow brighter. "Do you know what I want?"

Sophia figured she could launch into an explanation, but what was the point? The Castle was clued into everyone's head some way or another. She hadn't figured out how to keep it out or had a good enough reason to do so. Maybe if she was Hiker and hiding things, like the fact Thad Reinhart was once a dragonrider, then she'd have a reason to do so. However, so far, having the Castle in her head only ensured most of her desires were met and things prepared for her well before she anticipated needing them.

It was like staying at a five-star resort when she got out of the shower to a fresh, warmed towel. Or when she found her bed turned down at night, the specific types of books she wanted to read just under her pillow. The Castle had served up hardcover books on those occasions, not making her use a Kindle to read like it was trying to force Hiker to do. That made her hopeful for the request currently sitting on the top of her mind.

"So, what do you want in exchange for *The Complete History of Dragonriders?*" Sophia asked aloud. *There,* she'd said it. She was offering an exchange. She'd do something for the Castle if it gave her something. She'd just have to figure out how to shake on it, which seemed complex when talking about making a deal with a building rather than a person.

A window ahead in the hallway glowed, and Sophia picked up her pace. She halted in front of the glass. It was distorted in places with bubbles and thicker parts like most of the glass in the Castle.

At first, she tried to squint through the windowpane, but then it began to fog up like someone was breathing on it. She realized the Castle wasn't trying to show her something out on the Expanse, as she'd expected.

Once a thick coating of condensation had fogged up the glass, an invisible force began to draw in the residue, creating a picture Sophia quickly recognized.

"That's the House of Fourteen," she said aloud, identifying the intricate design of the layered house being depicted like an architectural building cut away to see the inside.

It was the only way she would know the structure anyway, since it appeared like a modest, closed down palm reading shop from the outside. The Castle showed the House as she was used to seeing it in her mind, which made sense to her since it was how it had known about the place where she'd grown up. She clearly saw the many levels with the residential wings and the library, which was vast.

"You want something from the House of Fourteen?" Sophia guessed, watching as the Castle continued to etch more details, seemingly making a masterpiece before her very eyes.

At her back, a creaking sound stole her attention. Thinking Ainsley had snuck up on her, Sophia spun around to find a slender door opening at her back.

She tensed and squinted at the darkness on the other side of the door as it opened. Sophia glanced tentatively at the picture of the House of Fourteen, watching as the light illuminating the window dulled. Peering over her shoulder, she noticed light began to fill the small door.

Not remembering seeing the door before, Sophia took careful steps in its direction. When she peeked in, she was surprised by what she found. It was a plain closet cramped with hanging clothes and boxes.

Sophia yanked her head out and glanced at the window. The

drawing had disappeared. She turned back to the closet, trying to put it all together.

"You want me to find a closet in the House of Fourteen?" she asked.

The flames of the candles lining the hallway grew in intensity. It seemed like a yes from the Castle.

"Okay," she said, drawing out the word. "Can you be more specific and tell me which one?"

The flames all shrunk in response.

Sophia's shoulders slumped. "That's your way of saying no, isn't it?"

Again, the candle lights flared.

She sighed. "Great, we understand each other. There are probably a few hundred closets in the House of Fourteen. It's hard to know. I've hardly visited many of the apartments, and most are off-limits to anyone who doesn't live there."

The candle lights remained unchanged.

"So, you don't have any tips on which closet you want me to find in the House of Fourteen?" Sophia asked, turning her attention to the window, hoping another picture would appear.

Nothing happened.

"So, I'm supposed to search the House of Fourteen for a specific closet?" she questioned.

The flames grew an inch.

Sophia nodded. That was progress, at least. "And how do I know when I find the right closet?"

No response.

"Okay," Sophia muttered. "And any indication of what I'm supposed to do when I find this mystery closet?"

She knew these open-ended questions weren't going to work. The Castle was mostly answering yes and no, but she had to try. It had painted her a picture on the glass, so she was staying hopeful.

"Fine, you want me to search the House of Fourteen for a closet," Sophia began. "I suspect I'll know it when I find it, is that right?"

The candles flared.

Sophia nodded. "And I'm guessing I'll also know what to do when I find this closet."

Again, the flames grew in intensity.

"Great," Sophia said mostly to herself. "And you promise when I find this closet and do whatever you want, you'll give me *The Complete History of Dragonriders?*"

There was a delay which made Sophia hold her breath. Just when she was about to complain, the candle flames all brightened more than before. Sophia squinted from the sudden brightness.

Sophia let out a long breath, feeling strangely victorious, although she realized she had quite the task ahead of her. The House of Fourteen was as convoluted as the Castle, constantly changing, with many locked doors. Exploring it would be a challenge. Finding this mysterious closet? Well, that would be interesting, to say the least. More intriguing was what the closet was for and why the Castle wanted her to find it.

She sighed. If it got her *The Complete History of Dragonriders*, she was hopeful it was worth her time. For some reason, Sophia believed the text held answers only a few knew, and one man was definitely hiding.

CHAPTER FIVE

S ophia was deep in thought, wondering where to look for the mysterious closet first when she came down to breakfast. That's why she nearly tripped over Evan lying in the middle of the floor in front of the long dining room table. He was staring up at the ceiling, a bewildered grin on his face.

Halting suddenly, Sophia glanced down at Evan and backed up to avoid trampling him. "What are you doing?" she asked him. She watched as he squinted up at the ceiling as if he was trying to make out a complex code.

He pointed up toward the rafters. "I'm staring at the beautiful stars."

Following his gaze, Sophia looked up at the ceiling to find the same stone she was used to seeing up there, punctuated by large wooden support beams. "So, these stars you're seeing…"

"Aren't they pretty?" Evan asked with a dreamy quality in his voice. "Will you help me count them?"

"They are something else. And no, I think I'll skip the counting," Sophia answered. She gave Mahkah, the only other person at the dining room table, a tentative glance that said, "What the hell is going on?"

He shrugged good-naturedly and returned to shuffling his eggs around on his plate.

Stepping over Evan, Wilder casually strode into the dining hall. "I see the young lad has gotten into Ainsley's pantry again."

Mahkah nodded and picked up a piece of toast from the top of a pile and started to butter it.

Wilder glanced back at Evan lying on the stone floor and shook his head. "When will you learn? You can go after the dried fruits and nuts but stay away from the confections. Ainsley knows those are your weakness, so she spells them."

"How can I resist them?" Evan asked, clasping his hands to his chest and looking longingly up at the ceiling.

Sophia shook her head as she joined the guys at the table. "Ainsley did this to him for breaking into her pantry?"

"I sure did, S. Beaufont," Ainsley sang, buzzing through the swinging door, carrying a breakfast tray. "And I'll do it again and again until he learns."

Wilder cast a thoughtful stare at Evan. "I'm not sure it will ever happen, dear Ainsley. He wasn't chosen as a dragonrider because of his brilliance."

"Well, then he'll lose a day to hallucinations each time," Ainsley answered.

Her head perked up at the sound of footsteps in the entryway, and she quickly shapeshifted into the form of Quiet, dropping the tray onto the table. She appeared almost exactly like the squatty gnome with his rugged appearance and red nose, save for her trademark small scar on the side of her head. She pulled Quiet's cap down low, covering the scar as Hiker Wallace marched into the dining hall.

He halted abruptly. His face turned red at the sight of Evan laid out on the floor. "Damn it! Ainsley! You've done it again!"

The leader of the Dragon Elite looked around for the housekeeper before his gaze went to the door to the kitchen. "Where is that woman? She knows damn well I told her to stop spelling Evan when he broke into her pantry!"

Wilder and Sophia exchanged tentative glances. Mahkah continued to appear placid as he chewed.

Ainsley, in the form of Quiet, simply shrugged.

Hiker shook his head and walked to his normal seat at the head of the table. "For the love of the angels. Don't I have enough to do trying to manage things? Now I have a dragonrider who is good for nothing for the better part of the day."

Quiet muttered.

Mahkah nodded.

Evan said, "The stars are so pretty, sir. Staring at them can't be wrong when it feels so right."

Hiker grunted and tucked a napkin into his collar. "When will you learn, boy? Stay out of that woman's pantry." He looked around the table. "Where is that elf anyway? Where is my coffee?"

Ainsley, in the form of the groundskeeper, hurried off for the kitchen just as the real Quiet materialized in the entryway, his face windswept from being on the Expanse.

Hiker realized what had happened and narrowed his eyes. "I should have known." He gave Wilder and Sophia punishing looks, apparently not thinking Mahkah should be given a scornful expression for not confessing the truth. "You lot didn't feel like telling me that woman was in disguise?"

Wilder glanced at Sophia. "Oh, was that Ainsley? I just got in here."

Sophia busied herself with scooping eggs onto her plate. "Me too, sir. I don't even know what's going on here. Why is Evan lying on the floor?"

"Because my housekeeper is a horrid woman who doesn't understand disciplining dragonriders isn't in her job description," Hiker answered.

Quiet mumbled something as he took the seat next to Sophia.

Hiker shook his head at the gnome. "I don't know what you said, but I'm certain I disagree with it." He banged his fist on the table, making the saucers vibrate. "Where is my coffee?"

"Coming right up, sir," Ainsley sang as she came through the door, carrying a cup of coffee and a platter of food. She laid both down in front of Hiker and gave him a pleasant smile.

He narrowed his blue eyes at her. "What did you do? Explain yourself."

She sighed. "Evan knows if he messes with my pantry, then he's going to get into trouble. I have to remain consistent and can't make exceptions, or he'll never learn."

He shook his head. "No, I mean, my coffee and food? Why are you bringing it out individually?"

"Would you believe because I want it to be fresh?" Ainsley answered innocently. Mama Jamba walked into the dining hall, wearing a starched pair of white jeans and a matching jean jacket like she was going to pop off to a summer concert after breakfast. Sophia couldn't help but think the woman looked like spring with her fresh appearance and bright eyes. It was a nice sight on the frigid winter morning.

"No, I wouldn't believe it," Hiker said, lifting the coffee and sniffing it. "What did you do to this?"

"I didn't do anything, sir," Ainsley said, taking the now empty tray of eggs.

Hiker took a sip. "It tastes weird."

"It shouldn't," Ainsley answered. "Caffeine doesn't make coffee taste any differently."

Hiker peeled back from the cup and shook his head. "This is decaf? Why would you do that, woman?"

"Well," Ainsley began, "I figured with all the stress of the goings-on, you should cut back on the caffeine. We don't want you kicking the bucket, do we?" Ainsley looked around, expecting an answer from the others. When no one said anything, she shrugged. "Okay, maybe some want you to kick the bucket, but can you really blame them?"

"Ainsley…" Hiker said, holding the cup of coffee out. "Fix this."

"Fix it how, sir?" she asked. "Are you going to start taking it with sugar after all these centuries? I think a little sweetener could do you good. Maybe sweeten you up."

"I want you to caffeinate it," he said tersely.

"I think Ainsley is right. Too much caffeine can't be good for your heart, Hiker," Mama Jamba said in her beautiful Southern accent as she glanced over the breakfast options. "Ainsley, are you going to serve anything not vegan?"

Hiker pushed back from the table like his food was toxic. He looked over his breakfast platter of sausages, beans, toast, and mushrooms. "Vegan? What does that even mean?"

"It means none of this has a face," Wilder supplied. "Or at least it didn't used to have a face. That's how I understand veganism." He looked to Sophia for clarification.

She nodded. "Yeah, that seems about right. No animal products."

"What is the meaning of this, Ainsley?" Hiker asked the housekeeper.

"Well, Mahkah liked the eggs," Ainsley argued, pointing an arm in the stoic warrior's direction.

Mahkah nodded, digging back into his eggs.

Sophia thought the eggs appeared different and now saw it was because they weren't actually eggs but just a yellow gelatinous material.

"Ainsley!" Hiker bellowed. "What are you up to?"

"Well," Ainsley began. "I was going to dust the Castle after breakfast, but it depends on how it's feeling. It was quite ticklish yesterday, and I'm not sure of its mood now. And—"

"You know what I mean," Hiker interrupted.

She sighed. "I don't read minds, sir. I really don't know what you mean."

"Ainsley!" Hiker repeated. "I want real food! Stuff that once had a face. What are these sausages even made of?"

"You don't want to know," Sophia muttered.

"Fine, be that way," Ainsley said, picking up his untouched plate. "I just thought we could try something new. I mean, I don't want you to live terribly long, but I don't want you to die anytime soon. Not before I find a new position. With your stress because of the new situation and all, I figured a vegan lifestyle and a cut-back on caffeine would help."

"Would you kindly get me and my riders some real food?" Hiker asked tersely.

Mama Jamba nodded. "Yes, I would really love some pancakes with real butter and all the good stuff."

Ainsley nodded and left for the kitchen.

"So, you don't support the vegan lifestyle?" Wilder asked Mama Jamba curiously.

She smiled at him good-naturedly. "Oh, you thought because I created all things on Earth, I'd want to preserve it, don't you?"

He blushed, his dimple on his right cheek surfacing. "Well, it's just that..."

"It's a good assumption, Wilder," she said with a wink. "But I also respect the circle of life, which vegans love to graze right over, just like sheep."

Everyone laughed at this, Quiet and Hiker included.

Sophia tensed and gave the leader of the Dragon Elite a strange expression, which he caught.

"What?" Hiker questioned. "That was funny. I didn't even know what vegans were until now. I'm guessing you, Sophia, have something to do with teaching Ainsley about this?"

"She wanted to watch some cooking shows," Sophia explained.

Ainsley returned a moment later with another cup of coffee and a platter of pancakes.

"Would you get—"

"I'm working on it," she interrupted Hiker, turning back for the kitchen. "Mama Jamba first, then you, sir."

Mother Nature smiled and pulled the platter of pancakes in her direction.

"Sophia, why don't you tell Mama how you aren't training this morning," Hiker said, lifting his cup of coffee to his mouth and giving her a rueful smile.

Sophia pushed her plate away. She thought she might choke on her last bite and then remembered she hadn't really had one while she'd been consumed with watching the normal and yet unique antics of breakfast at the Castle. "Oh, I want to train. It's just, I was thinking I also needed to do some investigating based on this new magitech I've found."

Mama Jamba looked at Quiet, who had his attention on Ainsley as she set a fresh platter of meat and fried eggs in front of the group. "What do you think, Quiet, my dear? Is it okay if Sophia takes a side quest?"

"What?" Hiker interrupted. "Why are you asking him?"

Everyone ignored Hiker.

The gnome was about to reach for a piece of bacon when his attention snapped to Mother Nature. He pursed his mouth and deliberated before reaching for a pastry. Finally, the gnome muttered something inaudible.

Mama Jamba nodded appreciatively. "That's what I thought."

"What is what you thought?" Hiker asked, looking between Quiet and Mama Jamba.

Quiet shook his head and smiled, a rare sight on the gnome's face. He whispered something that almost sounded like "Soon but not yet."

Sophia leaned forward. "What did you say, Quiet?"

He stuffed a pastry into his mouth, his eyes bulging.

"He said, you should go on this magitech mission," Mama Jamba stated as she buttered her pancakes.

"He did?" Hiker and Sophia said in unison.

Mama Jamba smiled wide and winked at the pair. "That was cute. And yes, he did. We're not ready for Sophia to continue training and definitely not ready for her to finish it."

"What?" Sophia questioned.

"What does that mean?" Hiker asked. "Why is my groundskeeper in charge of this decision?"

Mama Jamba daintily cut into her pancakes, relishing the first bite. "Oh, it's nothing. It's just it would be good if Sophia did something else for a bit."

"I thought you said there was nothing more important than her training," Hiker argued.

"I did," Mama Jamba said, through a bite.

"So, what's changed?" Hiker asked.

"Nothing," she answered. "It's just there is a season for everything, and right now we are in winter."

"And?" Hiker questioned.

"I think it would be better if..." Mama Jamba looked to Quiet, expecting him to supply an answer. He gave her a pointed glare. "Yes, it would be good if Sophia finished training later in the winter. Maybe closer to the start of spring. Yes...spring would be good...maybe."

Hiker gave her a strange expression. "What are you up to, Mama?"

"Nothing," she answered, but there was definitely a hint of mischief in the old woman's voice.

He shook his head as he looked between the woman and the gnome. "I don't know what you two are up to, but I'd like to be in the know."

"And you will, dear Hiker," Mama Jamba answered. "But really, there's nothing to tell. Quiet doesn't think the Expanse is in ideal condition for training, and I think this magitech Sophia has is worth investigating. Let's delay training a bit longer. It can't hurt."

"You thought training was all Sophia should be doing, and now you're changing your tune," Hiker argued.

"Well, a woman can change her mind," Mama Jamba sang. "Can't she?"

"She can," Hiker said skeptically.

"Yes, she can," Mama Jamba added, taking another bite.

Hiker blinked at her, not convinced as he took his first bite of food. "Anything else?"

Mama Jamba smiled. Winked at him. "Yes, you have eggs in your beard, dear."

CHAPTER SIX

The warm Santa Ana winds were a stark contrast to those that had nearly knocked Sophia off the crumbling cliff in the Gullington in Scotland. It felt strange to shed her layers as she made her way to John's Electronics Repair shop, where she expected to find her sister, Liv Beaufont.

She wadded up her cloak, missing the cold where she'd just been. All her life growing up in Los Angeles, she had never questioned this city was her home, but it didn't give her the same fond feeling it used to. She wished it was colder since the warm air didn't feel very holiday-like.

As she passed display windows covered with fake snow and garlands, Sophia began to miss the decorations she'd had at the Castle. They hadn't lasted, but they were far better than any of the ones on this street in West Hollywood.

"Whoa, did you just get finished jousting at the Renaissance fair?" a man asked at Sophia's back.

She halted, immediately knowing he was referring to her. She glanced down and thought she should have changed before her field trip. Even though she was in West Hollywood, where everyone was strange, she managed to stand out with her silver and blue armored top and riding boots. Inexorabilis was strapped to her side, where it usually was when she left the Castle, and her roughly braided blonde hair hung down her back, windswept from her early morning ride on Lunis.

"I think you left your horse back there on Melrose," another guy said with a chuckle.

Sophia let out a breath and thought it was better just to keep walking and leave the mortals alone. Then she asked herself the one question that would no doubt lead to trouble. "What would Liv do in this situation?"

Without hesitation, Sophia turned to find two hipsters sharing the same ridiculous smile as they ran their eyes over her. They had their jeans rolled up like they'd just gotten finished wading in the Pacific Ocean. One had his collar popped, and the other had the brim of his hat sticking straight up.

"I ride a dragon, not a horse," she remarked, her hands on her hips.

The guy with a popped collar and a bad skin problem smirked at her. "Yeah, right, sweetheart. You're capitalizing on the new rumor dragonriders are back."

His buddy slapped him on the arm. "I've heard there's this whole group in Topanga Canyon who are welcoming any of the riders if they want to seek refuge with them."

"Yeah, like riders want a bunch of dumb crystals from hippies," his friend replied.

"I am one of the dragonriders you've heard about," Sophia dared to argue, wondering what the point even was in trying.

"I heard there's not many of them left," Popped Collar said to the other guy as if he hadn't heard a word Sophia said.

"Yeah, and I heard they are super old magicians," his friend replied.

"They definitely wouldn't look like you," the first hipster said, pursing his lips at Sophia. "I'll buy that sword off you if you'd like."

"It's not for sale," Sophia said bitterly.

Remember you're supposed to protect the mortals, Lunis said in her head, having witnessed the exchange.

She nodded and let out a breath. *Shouldn't that mean taking out the dumber ones, so they don't bring down the rest?* she replied.

Good logic, Lunis offered. *Maybe just put them in their place if it comes to it. I'll let you know.*

Or point them to the closest community college, Sophia added. *These guys desperately need some life skills and fashion advice.*

I'm not arguing there, Lunis said just as the guy with the hat pointed to her sword.

"Seriously, I'll give you like twenty bucks for that piece of junk," he said with a laugh.

"Twenty bucks!" his friend exclaimed. "That's a steal, girl. He'll have to melt it down to get his money back."

"The sword isn't for sale," Sophia repeated and started to back away, thinking it was best for their health.

"Hey, where are you going?" Popped Collar asked. "We're just messing with you."

"Yeah, it's not every day we meet a fake dragonrider," his buddy said.

"I'm not a fake dragonrider," Sophia said through clenched teeth, wondering why she was letting these Jack Fruits get to her.

"Man, this one is delusional," Hat said to the other dude. "I mean, even if you didn't have the fake sword, who is going to believe a girl is a dragonrider?"

And there it is, Lunis said in Sophia's head. *You have my blessing to rearrange their faces.*

Sophia stretched her head to one side and then the other, working out the tension in her neck. "The age of dragonriders has changed."

Popped Collar laughed. "Sounds like it's going downhill if they are letting girls ride."

All Sophia's restraint evaporated. She pulled out Inexorabilis in one swift movement, earning wide-eyed expressions from the pair. They didn't even have a chance to react before Sophia brought the blade around. If she had used her full speed, she would have easily decapitated the two, but that wasn't her intention. She didn't even want to harm them, just scare them out of their wits so they never again underestimated a female.

"Oh shit!" Hat yelled, grabbing his friend by the shirt and yanking him down to the concrete as the sword passed overhead. They dropped clumsily as Sophia struck in a low lunge.

The guys stumbled back on their hands and feet, crab walking on their bums as they tried to get as far from Sophia as possible, fearful looks on their faces.

She twirled her sword, doing some fancy work that wouldn't harm anything except a few horse flies, but it looked rather intimidating.

"Dude!" Popped Collar exclaimed.

"Who the hell is that?" his friend exclaimed, nearly rolling into the street to put distance between Sophia and them.

"I think she's an actual dragonrider," his friend replied.

"Yeah, that's exactly who I am," Sophia said, her chin down and eyes full of intent. "And instead of kicking your ass, I'm going to save it for the next time a danger nearly takes you out. What do you say, boys?"

The dudes clumsily stumbled to their feet.

"W-W-We're sorry," the first one stuttered.

His friend slapped his arm. "I think she meant for us to say thank you."

"Thank you!" the other yelled. Both boys tucked tail and hauled themselves down the sidewalk, easily intimidated by the small dragonrider before them.

CHAPTER SEVEN

L iv was standing with her arms crossed and her boot tapping the tile floor when Sophia entered the electronic repair shop.

The dragonrider halted and studied the amused expression on her sister's face. "What's up?"

"Just watching an interesting display in the streets," Liv replied and pointed to the large display window at the front of the shop.

Sophia glanced in that direction and saw it gave her sister the perfect vantage point to see the whole incident which had just taken place. "Oh, well, those guys—"

"Are Laffy Taffies who not only can't dress or put logical words together to form coherent ideas but are constantly getting on my last nerve putting up posters advertising their dumb podcast," Liv stated, interrupting Sophia.

"Oh, yeah, that all seems about right. So you've met?"

"Unfortunately," Liv answered. "What I don't get is why you didn't give them haircuts or shred their clothes, so they had a reason to go down to the thrift store and buy things their grandfathers threw out decades ago."

Sophia shrugged. "I just wanted to scare them. They are harmless."

Liv nodded. "You have more restraint than I do."

"Well, my job is to protect the mortal world," Sophia stated.

"And mine is to keep the magical one in check," Liv added.

The sisters smiled at each other. "We are pretty cool counterparts," Sophia said.

"That we are," Liv said with a smile. "Too bad Clark is so lame and doesn't have as cool a position as us."

"He's the book nerd, so we all have our roles," Sophia stated proudly.

"Yeah, we are a pretty cool bunch," Liv offered.

"That we are." Sophia smiled, feeling the familiar euphoria take over when she thought of her siblings. *"Familia Est Sempiternum."*

"What brings you here?" Liv asked, giving her a sideways skeptical glare. "Did you miss my famous nacho recipe?"

Sophia giggled. "You cover chips in way too much cheese. There's not really much of a recipe to it."

"It's about the approach," Liv stated. "Well, then you came to give me your Christmas list?"

Sophia shook her head. "I don't need anything for Christmas. Well, having it at the Castle would be nice, but the angry Viking won't allow the boys to have electronics, the housekeeper to express herself, or me to have any Christmas traditions."

The light expression on Liv's face dropped. "You're coming home for Christmas, right?"

"Well, I hadn't really planned on it," Sophia answered and immediately regretted it. "I mean, I want to, but I might need to work, and we don't really do anything."

Liv recovered and nodded. "I get it. We don't really get holidays off at the House of Fourteen. I'm not sure what I was thinking. In case I do see you, what do you want for Christmas, little sister?"

Sophia thought for a moment. "I don't know. I mean, I have you and Clark and Lunis and pretty much everything I want."

Liv yawned loudly. "Come on. You can do better than that. You have to want something."

She sighed. "I want dragons not to be extinct."

Liv gave her a sympathetic expression. "I get it. No luck on that front?"

"No, it appears most of the lone dragonriders were hunted down and taken out by Thad Reinhart," Sophia explained. "It's unclear if there are any lone dragons out there, but so far, it doesn't appear hopeful."

Liv thought for a moment. "Have you considered looking into genetic testing?"

The laugh that popped out of Sophia's mouth surprised her. "I can't even get Hiker to use a Kindle device. I'm absolutely certain he's not going to allow genetic testing to manufacture dragons. Is it even possible?"

"Well," Liv began, "remember Adler Sinclair?"

Another laugh spilled out of Sophia. "You mean the evil man who killed our parents and siblings, made it so mortals couldn't see magic and almost destroyed the magical world? Yeah, I seem to recall him slightly."

Liv gave her a subtle smile. "You were young, that's all. Just ensuring I didn't relate things from before your time."

Sophia rolled her eyes, tired of being treated like she was born yesterday. Magic might have accelerated her growth, but that shouldn't matter. She was every bit as mature if not more than any other eighteen-year-old. Actually, the chi of the dragon had put years of experience into her that made her well beyond her years. She liked to think she was more mature than Evan, who was over one-hundred years old, but that wasn't saying much.

"Yeah, so what about Adler?" Sophia asked.

"Well, I'm not sure if you remember he had a small dragon," Liv told her.

Sophia blinked, memories rushing back. "Indikos, right? That's right!"

Liv nodded. "That's right. From what I understand, he was a result of cross-breeding and magical genetic engineering. He was very rare, but couldn't the same possibilities apply to real dragons?"

Sophia thought for a moment. "I don't know. I want to say no since there's the collective dragon consciousness that connects them all. It's not like they can be manufactured. There were only ever one thousand of them. They are unique, like the souls of humans."

"So you can't just create one because it has to come from somewhere, you mean?" Liv asked.

The complexity of this was enough to make Sophia's head burst. "Yeah, I think so, but if all else fails, I guess we could look into it. Whatever happened to Indikos?"

"Oh, I gave him to Hawaiki," Liv answered, pointing to Inexorabilis on Sophia's hip. "The maker of your sword. She was the right fit, and when the small dragon needed refuge, it just made sense. The last I checked, the two are enjoying island life together."

Sophia smiled. "I'm glad he got a happy ending after everything."

Liv nodded. "Yeah, it just shows no matter how we come into this world, no matter who thinks they own us, the story can always take a turn."

A tired sigh fell out of Sophia's mouth. "I'm not sure if that's the way it will work out for the dragons, but that's why I'm here. I was hoping you could help me look into some magitech that seems to destroy the connection between dragons and riders."

"I'll try," Liv answered. "The real magitech expert is in the back grooming the chimera."

"Do you ever listen to the things you say out loud?" Sophia asked, withdrawing from her cloak the magitech gun she'd gotten off Logan that severed her connection to Lunis, at least momentarily.

Liv stepped back at the sight of the device, her eyes widening, her hands in the air. "Whoa, that's not any normal magitech."

Sophia went to hand it to her sister, but Liv took another step back. "You shouldn't be touching it, and neither should I. That thing isn't safe."

Using magic, Liv withdrew the magitech from Sophia's hand. It hovered for a moment before it glided to a workstation and rested with a clunk.

"I know it's dangerous," Sophia explained. "It was used on Lunis and me. It's horrible."

"Then why do you have it, and why did you bring it here?" Liv asked. "I know an abyss that empties into the pits of hell. Do you want me to throw it down there for you? I'll just need a mortal to offer the demons so we can use their trash receptacle." She peeked out the window and pointed to the street. "I think one of those hipsters will do nicely."

Sophia laughed, loving how her sister always had that effect on her. "No, I know it's dangerous and probably unstable, but it's the only real lead we have right now. I was hoping you could examine it and give me some information. Maybe tell me where it came from or who created it or something."

Liv studied her sister, seeming to look into her soul. "You all are pretty lost, aren't you?"

Sophia's mouth twitched. "Yes. Thad Reinhart has the upper hand and always seems to be one step ahead of us. We can't get close to him, and even if we could, we don't know where to look. And with technology like this, we really shouldn't risk getting close until we figure out how to combat it."

"So you also need a way to fight this?" Liv asked.

Sophia nodded in reply.

"Don't worry about him having the upper hand," Liv consoled. "That's how it always works with all my enemies. I'd get really concerned if I went into a fight with the advantage."

"Yeah," Sophia related. "I guess it's that upper hand that makes us so relentless."

"No, it's the Beaufont blood." Liv took several steps backward and poked her head through the swinging door at the back. "Alicia, can you join me up here when you get a chance?"

"Of course," a woman said, her voice cloaked in an Italian accent.

A moment later, a beautiful woman with long brown hair and a chiseled face strode through the backdoor, her brown eyes smiling at the sight of Sophia. Behind her came John Carraway carrying his terrier, Pickles.

"Oh, if it isn't my favorite little dragonrider," John said, hugging Sophia into him, making her suddenly feel small.

She patted Pickles on the head and smiled up at the owner of the electronics repair shop. It was John who had given Liv her second life when she'd abandoned the House in favor of a simpler way. She'd abandoned her magic too, wanting nothing that reminded her of their parents and their death. That felt like eons ago and had proven to Sophia that people change and then change again.

"You say 'little dragonrider' like Lunis is a toy she flies around on," Liv said with a laugh.

Pickles licked Sophia's face before John pulled him back. The little dog wasn't a normal terrier by any standards, but a timeless chimera meant to protect the Mortal Seven. Sophia was glad he wasn't in his chimera form right then because it was quite overwhelming and usually resulted in objects being tossed around when his tail, a serpent's head, swung around.

"She'll always be little Sophia to me," John said fondly to her sister.

"Well, this little dragonrider has brought in one of the darkest pieces of magitech I've had the misfortune of seeing." Liv pointed to the gun on the workstation. "I haven't examined it, but just being in the same space, I can feel the magic and sinister vibes rolling off it."

Alicia cut her eyes to the device. She was an expert with magitech, which worked out perfectly since John was an expert when it came to mortal electronics. Together the pair had revolutionized the shop, now catering to both mortals and magicians, helping both worlds to manage their electronics better.

"Oh, I thought I sensed something," Alicia said, eyeing the device. "I thought it was just Liv going off on those hipsters again."

John chuckled. "She does bring a lot of negative energy into the shop when she berates those guys."

"They deserve my wrath," Liv grumbled.

"Then there was yesterday when she had that zombie accidentally follow her in here," John related to Alicia, sounding amused.

The scientist nodded. "Yeah, there was a lot of negative energy around that fellow."

"It wasn't an accident," Liv explained. "I needed some parts for a project I was working on but wanted to be close to a freezer first."

John grimaced. "I'm not sure I want any more information on the subject."

"I'm certain you don't," Liv answered. "Also, if you look in your freezer, the stuff in the blue Tupperware isn't leftover casserole."

John shivered. "I think I'll go and shop for a new freezer at the junkyard."

Alicia nodded. "Good idea."

The shop owner winked at Sophia as he made for the door. "Good seeing you, little Soph. Take care and try not to get yourself into too much trouble."

"She rides majestic dragons for a living!" Liv called to him.

He waved. "Still, she's just that little magician to me. Always will be."

Liv shook her head as John left. "It must get pretty tiring when no one takes you seriously, Soph."

"It can be, but then again, the look on people's faces when I kick ass is worth it," Sophia said with a laugh.

"So, this magitech…" Alicia gave the device a tentative look. "It's going to take me some time to investigate."

Liv came over to Sophia's side and elbowed her. "Don't you love that? It will take her just enough time until Thad is about to take over the world and destroy it. Then Alicia will conveniently figure out what you need to know and deliver the information, giving you just enough time to step in and kill the bad guy who had the upper hand right up until then."

Alicia shook her head and smiled. "I really wish I could be fast with this one, but I've never seen any magitech like this."

Liv whistled. "And she's seen it all."

"Well, I'll take whatever I can get," Sophia said, trying not to sound disappointed.

"Actually, I think I might be able to offer a bit more," Alicia began. "Magitech like this has a strong frequency it gives off."

"As we've discussed," Liv added.

"Exactly," Alicia answered. "Now that I know what I'm looking for,

I might be able to find a way to track other magitech that shares the same frequency."

"Which could lead me to Thad Reinhart himself," Sophia said, growing excited.

"I can't promise anything," Alicia amended. "Magitech of this caliber is incredibly hard to disguise or hide."

"A magician like Thad Reinhart will have top-level security," Liv said.

"He does," Sophia stated, remembering when she broke into his facility north of the Gullington.

"I might also be able to help with foiling security measures," Alicia stated. "Like I said, I need to investigate this fully. You can understand a lot about a magician based on the magitech they create. It tells you how they operate, what brand of magic they use, and a whole host of other crucial information."

Liv draped her arm around her sister's shoulder. "Aren't my friends excellent?"

Sophia nodded and laid her head on her sister's shoulder. "Yeah, and you're pretty great too. Thanks for the help, ladies."

Alicia smiled. "I'm happy to help. And if you're working on getting rid of the person who created this, then my efforts will be well worth it. Whoever is behind this is thoroughly evil."

"Okay, so I'll check back in with you?" Sophia asked the scientist.

"I'll ping you," Alicia answered.

Sophia nodded. The expert of magitech didn't need her phone number or any other contact information. She'd find her. "Okay, then I'll leave you to it." She pulled herself off of Liv and smiled at her sister. "3D printer," she said simply.

"3D printer what?" Liv questioned.

"You asked what I want for Christmas," Sophia said with a smile. "I want a 3D printer so I can freak out Hiker. He'll totally think it's some devil tech magic and stomp around the Castle for weeks bellowing about it."

Liv nodded proudly. "You are my sister." She tossed a sideways look at Alicia. "I think we can manage a 3D printer, don't you?"

The scientist smiled wide. "Consider it done."

"What do you want for Christmas?" Sophia asked her sister.

Liv leaned forward, brushing Sophia's hair out of her face. "Just world peace, my dear sister."

Sophia's eyes fluttered with annoyance. "Seriously, you can't offer me anything a bit less complicated? Like new snow boots or a grappling hook?"

"Ohhh," Liv said, looking impressed. "Yes, to a new grappling hook. Wait, no, I just got a new one on Amazon. It came next-day because the fairies who run that place are freaking amazing. Anyway, I'm good with my grappling hook for a bit, at least until the next troll tries to throw it into Crater Lake."

Sophia laughed. "That seems like a story I need to hear."

"It's not that entertaining," Liv said dismissively. "He cried when I threw him in after it. I cried too because that dude wasn't light. But yes, just world peace. If anyone can give that gift, it will be the very Exceptional S. Beaufont."

CHAPTER EIGHT

At the entrance to the House of Fourteen, Sophia hesitated. She worried she wasn't using her time wisely. Maybe she should turn back and leave. She should be back at the Gullington training, she told herself. However, Mama Jamba had said the timing wasn't right to complete training, which she didn't understand at all. Then again, maybe she should be working an adjudicator case for Hiker, she reasoned just before pushing the door open to the House of Fourteen.

Deep down, she knew finding *The Complete History of Dragonriders* was crucial, without knowing why. Liv always said things you felt, "deep down" were worth paying attention to.

"If we learn to live in the 'deep down,' we have a lot less confusion in our lives," Liv had once told her.

"So I need to do this," Sophia said, pushing open the door to the House of Fourteen to find the long corridor glowing with statues and the arched ceiling overhead. The ancient symbols of the founders on the walls greeted her, dancing around in different directions.

"Only you will know what you need to do," a warm voice said at Sophia's back. She spun around, having not realized anyone was behind her.

She relaxed at the sight of Hester DeVries, a Councilor for the

House of Fourteen and also a healer. Her short gray hair was covered in water droplets like she'd just come through a rainstorm, although it wasn't raining on the boardwalk in Santa Monica outside the House of Fourteen.

The older magician shook her head, dispelling the rain droplets as she shrugged off the wet cloak she was wearing.

"Oh, you heard me," Sophia said, blushing at the woman. "I was just…"

"…trying to convince yourself you're in the right place at the right time," Hester offered. "I feel like that's most people, most always."

Sophia sucked in a breath, used to having these strange conversations with the healer, and not really minding them. Hester's sister, Trudy DeVries, was a seer, although few knew since it wasn't something safe to be, even in the magical world. This meant Hester was usually privy to things most didn't know, and she often slipped little tidbits into conversations with Sophia.

One of the last times they spoke, Hester had run into Sophia when her heart was breaking. Thinking she'd been kicked out of the Dragon Elite, she hadn't realized Hiker Wallace threw people out willy-nilly. Hester had told her then the pain she felt would get worse. She'd followed this up with, "I only tell you this so you learn how to shoulder the pain. It won't kill you for your heart to ache, but it can ruin you if you're not careful."

Sophia had turned the advice over in her mind ever since and hadn't made sense of it. Knowing there was more heartbreak on the horizon shouldn't have surprised her. That was part of life. She'd lost her connection to Lunis after, which had left scars on her heart. Since then, she'd tried to process things, so any pains she did feel didn't ruin her. Deep down, Sophia felt Hester was referring to something very specific. A pain Sophia couldn't avoid, but if she could, she'd do anything to deter it.

"I was just trying to rationalize being here when I have other obligations," Sophia explained to the healer after a long silence.

Hester nodded. "That's the story of my life. I think we often feel torn, not knowing how best to use our energy or time. Those really are our most valuable assets at the end of the day. All you must ask yourself is what you want most."

Without thinking, the response fell out of Sophia's mouth. "Answers," she said at once.

The smile that flickered to Hester's mouth made her gray eyes light up. "I dare say, the House of Fourteen is full of those and ways to get them."

"Oh, I suppose you're right," Sophia said, her eyes drifting off as she thought of where she should start her investigation. The number of closets that could potentially be in the House of Fourteen was simply overwhelming.

"Incidentally," Hester said with a wink. "Only families belonging to residents can enter their apartments here. Or that's the way it was supposed to be set up."

Sophia turned her head to the side, wondering where this strange tidbit came from. She remained silent.

"I accidentally learned a spell to allow me to get into any residence I wanted as long as my intent wasn't for nefarious purposes."

Sophia continued to stare at the strange magician before her, a curious expression on her face.

Hester held out her hand. "I'm guessing your motives would be anything but nefarious. So, if any of this interests you, then here you go." The healer then blew on her palm.

To Sophia's surprise, she didn't jump back in alarm. As the sparkling dust hit her face, she simply blinked and let it wash over her, spilling a spell of sorts into her brain.

She shook her head when Hester backed up, a victorious expression on her face. She flicked the sparkles off, brushed her hands and looked around. "Well, it seems I better be off."

Sophia, not feeling as disoriented as she thought she should be considering the last few moments, simply looked at Hester as she hurried down the corridor, leaving her alone without even saying goodbye.

CHAPTER NINE

It was strange, but Sophia had never learned a spell the way Hester had just given it to her. She'd mostly learned from books. Some from instructors, but never by way of pixie dust blown in her face.

The spell was clear as day in her head. She repeated it with ease, knowing everything she'd need to do it right. This was how she'd get into apartments belonging to others in the House of Fourteen. Otherwise, she'd only be allowed into the Beaufont residence, which would do her little good since she had been in every closet in the apartment. Also, she knew the Beaufont residence was empty since Clark had moved in with Liv and Sophia. Well, and she now lived at the Gullington.

To try to keep things easy, Sophia tried all the closets in the common areas. More than a few times, she got strange looks for sliding out of closets in the kitchen, hallways, and dining areas. The staff and other resident magicians didn't stop her when she would exit a closet with a defeated expression, but they gave her questioning looks.

The good news for Sophia was she was at the House of Fourteen, which abounded with eccentrics who often did strange things. At the

Gullington, there was a much more prescribed way of acting, although Ainsley defied that with every action.

Magicians for the House of Fourteen were often expected to do the unexpected, and that was good for Sophia. What wasn't good was she'd been in over two dozen closets and only found magical cleaning supplies, cloaks which hid large things and erased small things, and fairies who didn't like sharing their small dark compartments with Sophia.

"I'm leaving," Sophia argued when the last fairy sought to kick her out of their spot.

With a defeated sigh, Sophia realized she was going to have to actually enter the residential areas to explore closets. She wasn't looking forward to such trespassing.

She kept her head down as she climbed the stairs she'd passed hundreds and thousands of times. It wasn't unnatural for her to avoid eye contact on this trek. That had been normal during her childhood since she was the strange child who didn't talk to the others.

The families always spoke about Sophia, because they thought she was antisocial. No one suspected the truth: she was special. At age four, she'd had the powers of an adult magician and a family of siblings who had encouraged and taught her how to use those powers.

Reese, her sister, for all her eccentricities, had been very excited to teach Sophia spells she shouldn't have learned until she was much older. Ian, for as practical as he was, also recognized Sophia's talents should be nurtured and taught her many things only advanced magicians knew. And Clark, for as careful as he was, fostered Sophia's talents, teaching her how to decode and decipher spells well beyond her years.

During those early years, she hadn't known Liv since her sister had abandoned the House of Fourteen after their parent's death. The things her sister taught her when she did return filled up more pages in Sophia's mind than from anyone she'd ever known. No one measured up to what Liv had taught her, which were mostly matters of the heart.

When Sophia came to the first residence, she halted and checked the area around the hallway. It felt wrong to enter someone else's residence, even if Hester had given her the spell to do it. She eyed the family crest next to the door and smiled with relief. This made it a little easier. It was the DeVries family residence, which would be occupied by Hester and Trudy. She suspected neither was in the place currently.

Reciting the spell she'd just learned from the healer Sophia watched as the magic wrapped around the lock and then sent the door back a few inches, magically opening it.

She pushed open the door and found the first closet easily. When she stepped into the space filled with traveling cloaks, she wasn't sure why she wasn't surprised there was no strange magical switch or whatever else she expected.

As Sophia entered each of the closets, the mission became ridiculous to her. She didn't even know what she was looking for, and entering other people's closets was wrong. That's where people kept their secrets, right? That's where their skeletons were buried and where their demons lurked. That's where they kept the teeth of their enemies; the bad things they didn't want others to know about. The shopping purchases they were trying to hide, at the very least.

To Sophia's relief, there was nothing that bad in any of Trudy's and Hester's closets. There was also nothing to give her any clues or lead her to what the Castle wanted in return for relinquishing *The Complete History of Dragonriders*. She exited the residence, sealing the door back as if she'd never been there.

If she had been a bad magician, up to no good, then with that kind of access, she could have done a lot of damage. The most powerful magical families in the world were located in the House of Fourteen. All Sophia wanted was to find a closet, although she still didn't know what she was looking for as she slipped into her dozenth residence, checking to ensure there was no one in there. To her luck, most families were still out at work, lessons, or afternoon errands. Not many returned to their residences until after dinner, which gave Sophia the opportunity she needed to do her searching.

This residence was filled with many strange artifacts Sophia spent too long studying on her way to the closets. She hadn't spent much time with these family members, but that wasn't saying a lot. The Mantovanis were relatively new to the House of Fourteen, not founder families like the Beaufonts.

Sophia knew the Mantovanis weren't the nicest magical family. Bianca had inherited her parent's superior attitude. Her brother Emilio was trying to reform, but some things were hard to change. How the Mantovanis had gotten into the House was beyond Sophia. She reasoned it had something to do with when the Sinclairs were controlling things.

Sophia stopped to both admire and gawk over a crossbow displayed as being responsible for the death of "thousands of giants." She was certain Wilder could tell her the truth about what the weapon had done. She didn't want him to have to experience that brutality, but strangely, she wanted to know if what the placard beside the weapon boasted was true. Sophia didn't have a chance to investigate anymore because precisely then, someone entered the apartment, sending her to the recesses of the darkened closet, where she should have been headed in the first place.

CHAPTER TEN

"Get in here before someone sees you," Bianca Mantovani said, her voice a tight whisper.

Sophia pictured Bianca wearing her usual pursed expression on her pale face, black hair tightly pulled back into a bun, and the collar of her black lace dress buttoned all the way up. Her appearance never really differed, and one could count on Bianca to always have her brown eyes narrowed, judgments scrolling through her head as she picked those around her apart.

"Your hospitality is overwhelming," Lorenzo Rosario said in a sarcastic voice, a shuffling sound marking his footsteps as he entered the residence.

He was a Councilor for the House of Fourteen, and according to Liv, his voting history was questionable at best. Liv had never had a firm reason to distrust Lorenzo but had been skeptical of him since the beginning. Unlike Bianca, he didn't seem to vote according to how he was told by the corrupt Sinclairs, but he did seem less interested in justice and keener on what would benefit magicians over other magical races.

Sophia pressed herself farther into the closet as the pair walked by the door, which was open a few inches, a bit of light streaming into the dark compartment. On her trip backward, she knocked into something and reached down just in time to grab the umbrella before it clattered to the floor and gave her away. There would be no way to escape the two magicians if she alerted them to her presence. There was no portaling inside the House of Fourteen, and many of the combat spells didn't work either.

Holding her breath, Sophia held the umbrella, afraid to lean it back up against the wall and potentially make noise.

"You don't need to sit," Bianca said in a chastising voice. "You won't be here that long."

"Again, your civility leaves a lot to be desired," Lorenzo said dryly.

"We both know this isn't a friendly visit," Bianca stated. "We merely have a mutual goal. Do not confuse this as a friendship. Now let's get down to business. What have you learned?"

Sophia's attention perked up, and she dared to lean forward and press her ear closer to the opening of the closet.

Through the crack in the door, Sophia noticed the tall, lean figure of Lorenzo Rosario stroke his short, black goatee, a studious expression in his dark eyes. "Although the House's favor has increased among the other magical races with the expansion of the council, I don't believe that will hamper what we're seeking to accomplish."

"Yes, we now have the support of the elves," Bianca said bitterly. "That isn't a good sign."

Lorenzo sighed. "I agree. I did everything I could to ensure they didn't approve of the House's rule."

"And Olivia Beaufont did everything to ruin your efforts," Bianca retorted.

"That is what she does," Lorenzo commiserated. "Even gaining the support of the elves, gnomes, and giants, I think there's still a way to upset the new structure of the council."

"Good," Bianca said with relief, "because sharing a seat with those mortals and other magical races is making my skin crawl. This wasn't the way the House was meant to be."

"I realize you were a supporter of the Sinclairs," Lorenzo said, starting to pace, his soft-soled shoes making note of each step. "You will have to hide your disdain for the current structure; it could ruin everything. We are up against many liberal thinkers who believe they have control over the House."

"They are the problem!" Bianca yelled, her voice shrill, making Sophia grimace from the high-pitched wail. "The Sinclairs might have been too powerful in the end, but the God Magician had it right. Mortals don't belong in the House, and definitely not other magical races. Magicians should be ruling the House on their own. It is having all this influence from other sources that's disrupting the balance."

"You know I won't argue with you there," Lorenzo said matter-of-factly. "We have to be careful how we manipulate things. If anyone suspects we're trying to revert things to how they used to be, there will be hell to pay. We could both lose our positions."

"I don't plan on going anywhere," Bianca stated with confidence.

"Yes, you were able to dodge a bullet when the Sinclairs fell," Lorenzo admitted. "But I don't think you can do it again."

Sophia's breath remained shallow as she listened intently. Liv had been instrumental in reforming the House after mortals were allowed to see magic again. She incorporated the Mortal Seven back into the structure, expanding the council to the Fourteen they were once intended to be. She didn't stop there though, lobbying for the major magical races to have a vote on the council as well. Now the House was a menagerie of magical races and influences which would obviously do a better job of serving the world than when it was partisan with only votes from magicians.

"Adler was the most powerful magician in the House," Bianca argued, making a clanking noise. It sounded like she was moving crystal glasses around. "No one suspects me. We were all following his rule."

"Not all of us," Lorenzo corrected. "Hence the reason he fell from power."

"He got sloppy, is all."

"Why yes, I'll take a drink," Lorenzo said smugly.

"I wasn't offering. You won't be staying long enough for one," Bianca replied.

He sighed. "My point is if we aren't going to share the same fate as the Sinclairs, then we have to be more strategic. They were bold, changing the structure of the House. I think it would be better if we let the new structure implode on itself. Then we will be standing victorious at the end, ready to put things back together with the vision only the old structure will work."

"And how do you propose we do that?" Bianca asked, setting her glass down with a clinking noise.

"We have good reason to oppose the diversity of the House," Lorenzo began. "It doesn't work for the simple reason multiple races shouldn't be in charge of world affairs."

"You're not telling me anything I don't know," Bianca quipped.

"If you'd let me finish," Lorenzo snapped. "I think the best way to fix this problem is to accelerate it. Currently, the House is stalling on inviting the Dragon Elite to have a seat on the council."

Sophia nearly gasped at the mention of the Dragon Elite.

"Well, for good reason," Bianca argued. "There aren't very many of them, and they are so out of touch they really can't offer perspectives of any use. Having the gnomes and giants on the council is bad enough since they are so poorly educated. Having the Dragon Elite on the council would really set us back."

Bitterly, Sophia clenched her fingers into a fist, wishing she could punch Bianca in the face.

"Exactly," Lorenzo exclaimed victoriously. "They can't even successfully do their jobs as adjudicators, and they are allowing a madman to run rampant. What if we encourage them to take their place on the council?"

"I'm not following you," Bianca said, her tone tentative.

"The Dragon Elite," Lorenzo said, drawing out the last word, "are supposed to protect mortals. We are currently swimming in too many on the council who have votes that outweigh ours, two to one."

"A ridiculous rule that should have never been made," Bianca said bitterly, taking another drink.

"I agree," Lorenzo stated. "Fighting it is useless when our goal is to get rid of the mortals. So why not pit them against the Dragon Elite?

We invite Hiker Wallace to have a vote and give him enough rope to hang himself on the council. It's only a matter of time before his dragonriders screw up something which impacts mortals, putting their population in danger, maybe even killing hundreds of thousands of them. I haven't really worked out the specifics, but—"

"It's perfect!" Bianca cheered, interrupting Lorenzo. "We orchestrate something, the Dragon Elite fail and the mortals will reject them. Then the council will momentarily fall into chaos as the magical races choose sides, and bickering is the ultimate result. You and I will be the voice of reason and state too many votes will only create problems and imbalance."

"And the House will return to being comprised of only magicians," Lorenzo said, a pleased tone in his voice.

"This plan will take some instigating on our part," Bianca warned.

"I understand, but I think it won't be enough to ever come back on us," Lorenzo agreed. "We just have to get the ball in motion because inevitably, the current model would never work. That's why the Sinclairs had the good sense to do what they did."

"Maybe we will even be lucky enough to debunk some magician families from the House in the process," Bianca said, glee in her voice. "I know Olivia will do just about anything for those pesky other races. Maybe she'll die for them."

Sophia had to restrain herself. It took everything she had, but she remained hidden in the dark closet.

"That would be ideal," Lorenzo agreed. "She really has a way of grating on my nerves."

Bianca's heels clanked against the floor as she passed the closet on her way back to the entrance. "Okay, well, let's meet again."

"When I have updates," Lorenzo said, following her out, a promising tone to his voice.

Sophia waited until the two left before she let out a hot breath, her mind reeling with anger. She hadn't found the right closet, but she'd discovered something of great use. What to do with it was the question. She had to be a lot more strategic than Lorenzo and Bianca if she was going to bring them down, her new goal.

CHAPTER ELEVEN

L ost in thought, Sophia found herself wandering through the House of Fourteen. She didn't notice when she passed magicians on the stairs, and she suspected they didn't notice her, even if she was angrily muttering to herself.

That snobby Bianca Mantovani thought the Dragon Elite only "needed enough rope to hang themselves" was infuriating. Hiker might have some challenges assimilating back into the modern world, but he wasn't a moron. They were making a difference in the world as adjudicators. It might be taking time, but there were only a few dragonriders. And Thad Reinhart had an advantage, but that wasn't going to last forever.

Sophia felt like she was trying to dispel all the reasons Bianca and Lorenzo had stated, which only made her feel what they were trying to do might actually work. If they pitted the Dragon Elite against the mortals and something catastrophic happened, the dragonriders would be blamed.

The Dragon Elite didn't have the reputation they once did. There was nothing to point at to explain how important they were to the mortal world. Right now, they seemed like a liability at best.

Sophia's heart began to ache as she realized Bianca and Lorenzo's plan could actually work. The ultimate result would be disintegrating everything Liv had worked for. The structure of the House would revert to what it once was and magicians would rule the world, which meant only their interests would be considered.

That wasn't what Sophia's parents had wanted. She hadn't known them and didn't remember them, but she knew that much, and she believed in what they wanted. Even as a magician, she didn't want the absolute rule of the world. She wanted the power to be balanced. She wanted the influence of the other magical races and of the mortals, who without, there would be no magic since that's the element they governed.

On autopilot, Sophia was surprised when she awoke from her daze to find herself standing in the middle of her old family home. Her legs must have led her there, or maybe her heart.

All the furniture was covered in white sheets, the place having been closed up after Clark officially moved out. The residence still belonged to the Beaufonts in case they ever decided to return. And since Liv didn't want the stuffy old furniture, it had remained here, covered up, waiting for a second life.

This wasn't the apartment where her parents had lived. That place was much larger, with enough room for all six Beaufont children. Of course, there had only been five since Sophia's twin, Jamison, died at birth. Still, the residence had been allotted for them.

When Sophia's parents, Guinevere and Theodore Beaufont, had died, Ian had moved them to this place. Maybe it was to escape memories. Or maybe he was just being practical, as was his nature.

Sophia's earliest memories lived in the small apartment where she currently found herself. She remembered pretending to fall asleep on the couch so Clark would carry her to bed at night. She remembered when she came into her magic and set fire to Reese's dress. Her sister had simply laughed with delight. After putting out the fire, she'd lifted Sophia and swung her around, her eyes dazzling because no one expected a four-year-old to have magic. And then her brothers joined, and they danced around the living room, celebrating a Beaufont child. It was something incredible. She wondered what Ian and Reese would think about her becoming the first female dragonrider in history. She smiled to herself, knowing they'd be proud.

Sophia brought her eyes up, feeling overly sentimental as her gaze ran over the family motto, sketched across the wall.

Familia Est Sempiternum.

The words her parents had said to their children almost every day, according to Clark and Liv. They had insisted, no matter what, their children remember what was important in the world.

"It's easy to forget who you are when your job is maintaining justice," Liv had recounted their father saying. "However, we can't fight for anyone if we don't remember what's most important—family. That's why we do what we do."

Sophia was surprised when the tear edged out of her eye and rolled down her cheek. She wasn't crying for the father she couldn't remember, or the siblings she'd lost that she could remember. She was crying because she was afraid the Beaufonts were on the edge of losing. It had been a miracle they'd held onto this much for this long when threatened, but what if it was the end? What if Liv and Clark lost their positions in the House of Fourteen? What if the Dragon Elite failed and she lost her position as a dragonrider?

The tears fell more rapidly and she allowed it, knowing a good cry would make her stronger when the time came.

Footsteps at her back put her straight into warrior mode. In a fluid movement, Sophia withdrew her sword and whipped around, brandishing the blade inches from her brother's throat.

CHAPTER TWELVE

Sophia's chest was rising and falling with great rapidity as she ran her eyes over Clark's fearful face. He was pale in the darkness of the apartment, his hands reflexively in the air.

"Soph, it's me," he said, his voice shaking.

She felt she should be shaking too, with her cheeks fresh from tears and her heart aching, but to her relief, the hand holding her sword was steady. She lowered her arm. "I'm sorry. I didn't expect anyone. What are you doing here?"

Clark gave her an uncertain expression. "Soph, what are you doing here? I work in the House of Fourteen. I come up here between breaks to unwind."

She nodded. It made sense. "I-I have business that brought me here, investigating."

He gave her a scrutinizing expression. "Business. Do you want to expand?"

There was no reality where Clark was going to like her breaking into other people's apartments and investigating their closets. She shook her head. "It's nothing. Just a way to find out more about the Dragon Elite."

She felt good about the explanation because it wasn't lying. Telling

Clark the truth would only make him worry unnecessarily, and he already did enough.

"Have you been crying?" Clark asked, concern springing to his voice as he stepped forward.

She sheathed Inexorabilis before rubbing the backs of her hands against her cheeks. "I'm fine. It's just being back here...well, it brought back memories."

He nodded, looking around. "It does it for me too."

Letting out a weighty breath, she turned to face her brother head-on. "I need to tell you something. And I need you to listen with objectivity and an open heart."

Clark gave her a skeptical look before nodding. "Yes, of course, Soph. What is it?"

Sophia told her brother what she'd heard Bianca and Lorenzo say. When she was done, she was unsurprised to find his face lined with stress.

"Are you sure you heard this right?" he asked her three times.

"I'm certain," Sophia stated.

"And they don't know you heard them?" he asked.

She hadn't expanded on where she was when she overheard the conversation, and he didn't seem to need more details. "No, they don't know I heard. But Clark, you have to believe me. I know you want to believe the council members are all good but—"

"There is no one I believe more than you," he interrupted. "It's true I want to believe my fellow councilors are good-hearted, but after the Sinclairs, I don't have delusions anymore. Liv has seen to that."

"They are trying to set up the Dragon Elite," Sophia argued.

He shook his head. "It won't work, though."

"But it could," Sophia stated. "I'm sorry to be the one to say this, but the Dragon Elite don't have their act together. We are on the brink of extinction. Our leader is struggling. We are up against an enemy even Mother Nature doesn't want to face and thinks will be the Earth's demise. It's not far-fetched to think we could be set up and then ruined. Clark, their plan could work."

He chewed on his lip. "So you don't join the House."

She shook her head. "That won't work for long. And we'll just look weak. We have to figure out how to not fail mortals. We have to hold the House together when everything falls apart. Because if it all goes to hell, then Bianca and Lorenzo will be able to state everything failed because of the inclusion of other magical races."

Clark nodded. "Things will go back to how they were. I can't say I haven't seen this coming. Even those who were in favor of diversity are struggling. We are constantly arguing among ourselves, the mortals bickering with the magicians. The representatives from the other magical races are constantly butting heads. It's hard to even have a conversation without issues, let alone a straight-up vote." He threw his arm out at the room. "Why do you think I come up here? It's to think."

"You still agree diversity is the way, right?" Sophia questioned.

He nodded at once, making her feel better. "Of course, I do. It's harder, yes. That's the way of progress, and we have to be patient with it. But I could see how Bianca and Lorenzo would position the chaos in their favor."

"What do we do?" Sophia asked.

He combed his hand over his chin. "I need time to investigate. To try to figure out something. We just need to stall. If they invite the Dragon Elite into the council, just tell Hiker he needs to wait. When he actually joins, hopefully I'll have everything in place to keep anything bad from happening."

"What else can I do to help?" Sophia asked, feeling desperate.

"You have to take down Thad Reinhart," Clark said darkly. "I know that's a tall order, but his dominance is specifically what will degrade the Dragon Elite's reputation. It's what Bianca and Lorenzo will use to discredit you all. There will be other things to threaten mortals, and I'm sure Bianca will unearth those for her own advantage, but if you can get rid of Thad Reinhart it will put you ahead."

"Okay," Sophia said, feeling a heavy weight on her chest. "I feel better having your help."

Clark stepped forward and took her hand. "I'm always here to help. I only wished you would ask for it more often."

She gave him a pained smile, not really knowing what to say.

"It's so weird to see you all grown up," he remarked. "I'm still not used to it."

Sophia giggled. "Even after I just held a sword to your throat?"

Clark joined her, laughing too. "Yeah, even after that. I think I've just been waiting for the day when you held mom's sword and rode off on dragons, without knowing the specifics of it. You don't watch a young child come into magic at an unprecedented age and not expect her to go off and do great things."

Sophia's mouth twitched from the tenderness of the moment. "I'm only who I am because I had you."

He returned her look, emotion in his blue Beaufont eyes. "Can I interest you in a cup of mulled wine? The stuff is flowing like…well, wine around this place right now due to the holidays."

Sophia was grateful for the relieved smile that crossed her mouth. It had been nice to stroll through the House and see all the Christmas decorations. "I would love that."

Clark held out his arm, offering it to Sophia. "Shall we?"

She took her brother's arm and allowed him to lead her to the doorway. "Hey, I have a question. What do you think Liv wants for Christmas?"

He gave her a look. "Besides world peace?"

"Yes, besides that," she stated.

"Well, you know, I've been thinking about it, and there's something, if I could get my hands on it, that would be perfect for her," he answered.

"Oh?"

"Yeah, our father had this journal where he kept all these notes," Clark explained. "It had all the sage-like things he always said in it. I remember seeing it often. He used to keep it in his desk in his study. Ian forgot to clean out the contents when he got rid of many of their possessions."

Regret filled her brother's face as he fell silent.

"Ian was overcome with grief and was just trying to clear out the things that brought back memories, wasn't he?" Sophia asked.

Clark nodded. "I think so. He was overwhelmed, taking care of us and taking on his new position for the House. The desk traded hands before the book was collected. There wasn't really anything else of use in the desk. Just maps and books. But that book...well, it was Dad incarnate. His words. His teachings. His wisdom. I can't think of anything that would mean more to Liv, or actually to me, to have than the book. You're busy with so many things. It doesn't even seem right to ask you to look for it."

"Of course, I'll look for it," Sophia argued. "There's nothing more important. *Familia Est Sempiternum.*"

He smiled. "I've tried to find the desk, of course. It was moved out of the House of Fourteen. The best I can determine, it was given to a magician family, but then the lead dried up there."

"Leave it to me," Sophia said, thinking this was a job for her fairy godmother to help her with. "I'll find Daddy's book."

Clark hugged her in tightly as they descended the stairs. "If anyone can, it will be you, Soph."

CHAPTER THIRTEEN

Sophia felt much better after a warm glass of mulled wine and a relaxed conversation with Clark. She left him at the Chamber of the Tree and decided to keep exploring the House of Fourteen, hoping to find this mysterious closet the Castle had sent her after. She didn't think the Castle's motive was to have her overhear an evil plan being hatched by Bianca and Lorenzo. That had just been a side benefit.

She climbed the stairs and tried to think which residence would be the best to try next. Many residents were down at dinner, so it presented a good opportunity for Sophia to sneak into places, although the guilt was starting to get to her. She consoled herself with the fact she was doing this for the Castle so she could get hold of the only copy of *The Complete History of Dragonriders*. She had no idea why the book was so important, but deep down she knew it was, and that was enough of a reason.

"I have a message from Subner for you," a voice popped up next to her.

Sophia looked around until she found Plato standing next to her in the hallway. She knew they were alone if the lynx had appeared and was talking to her.

"From Subner?" she asked, confused why Father Time's assistant would have a message for her.

"Yes, he wanted me to tell you to tell Wilder he needs to come and see him," Plato related.

Sophia grimaced. "What? Why wouldn't he just tell Wilder himself? He's supposedly working for the Protector of Weapons now. This seems very inefficient."

"Actually, Subner told Papa Creola, who told Liv, who told me who is telling you to go get Wilder," Plato explained.

Scratching her head, she gave him a confused look. "Again, why couldn't Subner just send a message to Wilder?"

"He's busy," Plato answered. "And so was Papa Creola and Liv, which was why I was sent on the errand."

"Well, if Wilder is the one who needs to go to this meeting, why don't you go and tell him yourself?" she questioned.

"Because firstly, I don't talk to just anyone," Plato answered. "And secondly, most people, even old magicians, are reluctant to talk to a lynx. We're seen as untrustworthy."

She gave him a curious look. "Oh, I wonder why."

"I do, too," he fired back at once. "We are devilishly helpful when we want to be."

"Which is when?" Sophia asked.

"About as often as a blood supermoon," Plato answered.

"That's like the rarest of eclipses," Sophia stated, having brushed up on things related to the moon since it impacted Lunis so much.

"Yes, so maybe not even that often."

"Fine," Sophia offered. "I'll tell Wilder to go meet Subner, but in the future, he should ping his own people."

"Well, he wants you to come too," Plato purred.

"For what?" Sophia asked, wondering when she was going to find time to go on an adjudicator mission or train or do this new side mission to find the closets. Not to mention now she needed to find this desk with her father's book. It was a lot, but she'd just have to give up sleeping because it was all-important.

"I wasn't told the reason," Plato began. "As someone who values privacy, I don't dig into others' business."

"Yeah, but you know just by virtue of being you and knowing everything, right?" Sophia asked, her hand on her hip.

"Maybe," he said, drawing out the word, a hint of mischief in his voice.

"Fine," Sophia said with a sigh. She looked around the hallway to figure out which residence to try.

"Also, about this closet you're looking for…"

She turned and scowled at the lynx. "I'm not even going to ask how you know about that."

"Good, because I'm not even going to tell you," Plato replied. "However, you might consider abandoning this mission for the moment."

"Because I need to be a messenger service for Subner?" she asked.

"Because I'm not sure you'll have much luck finding this closet," Plato offered.

"Because there are a billion closets in this place, and I have no idea what I'm actually looking for?"

"Because we're playing the 'because' game, it's because the closet you're looking for is here, but what you're looking for can only be found at a different time in history," Plato answered.

Sophia reeled back several inches. "Say what?"

"And you say I'm never helpful," Plato said proudly. "The next bit of advice I give you won't come until after the next blood supermoon."

"Different time?" Sophia asked. "Like I need to find the closet in the past?"

Plato shrugged, lifting his paw and casually licking it.

She sighed. The lynx had been uncharacteristically helpful. He had a track record lately for giving her information, but it was usually confusing and altered to have some sort of agenda.

"I really don't know how I'm going to visit the House of Fourteen in the past," Sophia muttered, mostly to herself.

"I know, you'd need a time machine or access to someone who owns the balance of time or something…"

Sophia lowered her gaze and gave the lynx a proud smile. "Guess I'll need to pay Papa Creola a visit when I deliver Wilder to Subner."

"I guess…" Plato said, ambling back the way he'd come.

"Thanks, Plato. This might have actually been helpful."

He nodded. "I hope it's worth the steep price you'll pay when I come to collect for all my helpful advice one day."

"What?" Sophia asked, realizing the lynx could be proverbially charging her for the advice. The cost could be something as great as her soul.

Before she could argue, he winked and said, "See you soon." With that, the lynx disappeared.

CHAPTER FOURTEEN

Sophia slipped out of the saddle on Lunis and tumbled through the sky, falling toward the ground fast.

Free falling was not in the least freeing. It was terrifying.

The wind blasted her in the face, tangling her hair and obscuring her view. She was mostly okay with that since the ground was getting closer, promising to be her end.

The sea of green around her was quickly approaching. Out of the corner of her eye, she spotted a clip of blue rushing toward her.

As if they had planned it, Lunis slipped under Sophia. Her hands found the saddle knob, and she slipped back into place as if she'd never tumbled free of her dragon. He picked up speed, racing away from the Earth, which had been close to being Sophia's demise.

That was fun, he said in her head.

Fun, Sophia replied. *You* do *own a dictionary, right?*

I don't have that app on my phone, so no, he joked.

That was terrifying, she related.

Well, then next time, don't fall out of the saddle, he offered.

Then warn me before you go into a spiral, she ordered.

Where's the fun in that? he asked.

And I'm steering, she argued. *How come you can do that if I'm in charge?*

Our relationship is a partnership, he answered. *I'm not your vehicle. I do still have free choice, you realize.*

Which I'm totally in favor of unless you throw me off with an unexpected turn, she said.

Well, this is all part of the training, Lunis offered.

I get it, Sophia said, feeling the exhaustion tunneling in her brain. She'd come to train with Lunis immediately after returning from her trip to the House of Fourteen. The lack of sleep could be responsible for her slow reflexes, she thought, wondering when she had slept last.

Speaking of slow reflexes, Lunis said, privy to her thoughts.

Yes? Sophia tensed, sensing she might get tossed off his back again.

Look up, he said.

She jerked her head up and caught sight of Evan on Coral. They were in a nosedive, plummeting in the direction of Sophia and Lunis. She whipped her sword out, holding on tight to the reins with her other hand.

This time when Lunis spiraled, she was ready. She pulled her weight down low to him and brought Inexorabilis around just as Evan nearly collided with her.

His loud cackle and the whites of his teeth were all Sophia processed as their swords clanged against one another. Their dragons rotated around one another as Sophia held her position, not allowing Evan to knock her off. He gave it all his effort, throwing his shoulder into her when he knocked her sword off his.

She didn't let up even when Lunis pulled into a steep dive. Instead, she brought her blade around low, making Evan have to jump to a standing position if he hoped to avoid getting cut as the sword came all the way around.

He plopped back down on the saddle, landing so hard his crotch took the brunt of the impact. His brown eyes bulged, and he keeled over, holding onto Coral as she veered away.

"Sorry," Sophia called after him. "You're going to want to put some ice on that."

Lunis pulled out of the dive, snickering with laughter. *He was just doing what you told him to*, Lunis stated.

I told him to help me with flight combat, not to come out of nowhere when I wasn't expecting it and nearly lopping my head off, she complained.

Your enemies don't ask for permission to charge in battle, Lunis argued. *What Evan did was helpful.*

Really? Sophia argued. *When we were on the Expanse earlier, I asked him if he'd help me with training. He said he was too busy, and then he darts out of a cloud and nearly throws me off you again.*

But he didn't, Lunis countered. *Good reaction and thinking about disarming him.*

Thank you, Sophia said proudly. As they headed back toward the Expanse, Evan was already on the ground, limping away from Coral. His ego was bruised, along with other parts of him.

CHAPTER FIFTEEN

"I t feels like we're missing something in here," Sophia said, sitting at the dining table, a pointed stare lodged in Hiker's direction.

He took a sip of his water and pretended not to notice her.

"More ice," Evan groaned. "That's what we're missing." He bent over the table, lying his face on his plate.

"You're a dragonrider," Hiker warned. "Act like one."

"I don't even feel like a man after what happened," Evan complained.

"You need more training and real-world experiences," Hiker said just as Ainsley came through the kitchen door, holding a large platter.

She set it down in front of Hiker, a proud smile on her face.

He pointed to the mound of gray on the platter. "What's that?"

"It's haggis," she said, her hands on her hips.

"No, it's not," he argued.

"Of course, it is," Mama Jamba said, leaning forward and sniffing. "It's just not the haggis you're used to."

Quiet muttered something besides Sophia.

"You can say that again," Ainsley said with a laugh, waving at the gnome.

"He'll have to for any of us to know what he said," Wilder commented.

"Ainsley, what did you do to the haggis?" Hiker asked, not appearing at all in the mood for this.

"Does it really matter?" Ainsley asked. "It is not like you lot ate the haggis before."

"I tried," Wilder stated.

"You always do," she said to him fondly.

"It looks weird, and I don't think it's safe to eat," Evan groaned.

"It's completely fine." Ainsley pointed to the platter of haggis. "This one is even safer. It's vegan."

Quiet looked to be trying to shuffle out of his chair as he muttered something.

Ainsley clapped her hand on his shoulder and pushed him back down. "You don't have to go and let the sheep out. They don't get let out."

He mumbled something.

The housekeeper rolled her eyes. "It's not too cold for them. They are sheep. They are literally wearing wool. And you're going to try my vegan haggis and love it."

"Why?" Hiker growled. "Why are you making vegan fare?"

"Well, I just thought I'd try something new," Ainsley sang. "You all throw your noses up at my food all the time, so what's the difference?"

Mama Jamba scooped a large bit of haggis on her plate, giving it an uncertain expression. "It sure has an interesting texture."

Evan flipped his head up from where it had been resting on the table. "I think it needs some bacon bits."

"That defeats the whole vegan idea," Ainsley argued, storming off for the kitchen.

"Would you bring out some sides?" Hiker called.

"Neeps and tatties," Wilder stated.

"Amen, brother." Evan pointed to the bread bowl on the other side of Mahkah. "Can I get some. I'm starving."

"Why?" Hiker questioned. "You didn't do anything today besides nearly get knocked off your dragon by a…" He glanced at Sophia, who had her own gaze narrowed at him.

"By a what?" she grilled. "By a girl?"

"I was going to say by an inexperienced rider who hasn't completed her training," he stated.

"Fair enough," she said, eyeing the haggis, which seemed to be changing shape.

"Tomorrow, you will all need to get back to training," Hiker stated.

"Shocking," Evan said blandly. "We're training again tomorrow, guys. Real change to the schedule." He patted the table in front of Mahkah. "Training, bro. Get ready for something completely different."

Mahkah managed a smile as he handed over the basket of bread. "I've got a mission, actually."

Hiker nodded. "Yes, so Sophia, you'll need to work with Evan and Quiet on dragon-training."

"Actually," Sophia said, drawing out the word.

This drew Hiker's attention, making him lower his chin. "Actually, what?"

"Well, I've got an errand I need to run outside the Gullington," she explained.

"Doing what?" he asked, his voice tense.

"I'm not certain, but Father Time is involved and requested I stop by his shop," she said.

"Lovely man," Mama Jamba stated. "If he needs you, you have to pay him a visit."

Hiker gave Mother Nature an annoyed expression. "But her training."

Mama Jamba was having a chore of chewing the vegan haggis. After quite a bit of effort, she swallowed, washing it down with a gulp of water. "Quiet, about Sophia's training. Are we ready yet for her to go full steam ahead?"

The gnome mumbled for a long bit, buttering his roll with a huge pat of butter, shaking his head as he did. When he was finally done,

Sophia looked around the table, wondering if anyone understood a word he'd said.

"Well, there you have it," Mama Jamba said, pushing away from the table.

"Have what?" Hiker asked. "What did he say?"

She shook her head. "Clean out your ears, dear. Quiet said we aren't ready for Sophia to complete training, so there's no point in her pushing to get it done just yet."

"And why aren't we ready for her to complete training?" Hiker questioned. "What are we waiting for?"

Mama Jamba gave Quiet an uncertain expression. "That's a secret."

"Damn it, woman," Hiker said, standing at once and throwing his napkin on his plate. "How can you have secrets from me about my own riders?"

She simply smiled good-naturedly. "It's a surprise, my love. No spoilers."

Hiker shook his head at her as Ainsley came through the door carrying the tray of sides. He took his seat once more, interested in what she'd brought.

"Oh, Ainsley, the haggis was really well seasoned," Mama Jamba said, striding away from the table.

"Then why didn't you eat it?" Ainsley asked, looking down at the unfinished meal.

"Because I don't think there's enough time left on my Earth to chew that," Mama Jamba said with a laugh.

"Well, I have the sides," Ainsley said, uncovering the potatoes. "Don't you want some of this?"

Mama Jamba shook her head. "Oh, no. I have a bag of butterscotch candies and a box of chocolate upstairs and a Nicholas Sparks novel. I'm going to turn in and indulge. I've been looking for an excuse to eat candy for dinner."

"You're literally the queen of this world and can do whatever you like," Evan said. "Do you really need a reason to eat candy for dinner? You could be eating ice cream for breakfast or whatever else you like."

She shook her head at him. "Oh, you think just because I created everything on this Earth calories don't count?" She clicked her tongue. "Dear, you have a lot to learn. Just because we have the power to create, doesn't mean we can change the rules. I have you all as my children, and I can't make you all do a thing. Free will and rules always apply."

Evan shrugged. "Yeah, I guess. When I have children, I'm going to make them do whatever I say."

"If you don't ice your injury, you're not having children," Mama Jamba said, indicating Evan's crotch.

He groaned again, lying his head back on his plate.

After Mama Jamba had left, Hiker turned his attention to Wilder. "Well, tomorrow, I want you to train with Evan. I'll have adjudication missions soon and want you both ready."

Before Wilder could answer, Sophia cut in. "Actually, about Wilder…"

Hiker lowered his chin again, giving her an annoyed expression. "What?"

"Well, my appointment at Father Time's shop involves him," she said in a rush. "Subner, who Wilder now works for, requested his presence."

"Thanks for letting me know," Wilder said with a laugh.

"Hey, Wild, Subner wants to see you," she stated dryly.

"Cool," he chirped. "I'll just need to clear it with my boss." Wilder looked expectantly at Hiker.

The leader of the Dragon Elite stood from the table, not having eaten anything. "What does it matter if I give my permission? The groundskeeper is dictating Sophia's training schedule. Mama Jamba is keeping secrets. And Father Time is now stealing my riders."

"You still have me, sir," Evan said, batting his eyelashes at Hiker.

He shook his head. "Great. The Dragon Elite is totally doomed."

CHAPTER SIXTEEN

"You don't know what this is about?" Wilder asked Sophia after they stepped through the portal to Roya Lane.

The magical street was decked out for Christmas with garlands covered in ornaments hung along the rooftops. At first, Sophia thought it was lights twinkling along the perimeters of the buildings, but as they drew closer, she realized it was tiny fairies.

"I don't know what this is about," Sophia began, navigating around a bunch of drunk gnomes who smelled like hot cider. "I don't know why I'm supposed to accompany you or why Plato has turned into a messenger service."

Wilder paused at a food cart run by a fae selling caramel covered apples. Sophia grabbed him by the shirt and hauled him forward.

"Don't you know not to eat anything made by a fae?" she warned in a whisper.

He blinked at her, confusion heavy in his blue eyes. "No. Why is that?"

"Because firstly, most of them are incompetent and their food tastes like rubbish," Sophia stated. "And secondly, it's most certainly laced with drugs that will alter your ability to make decisions, since their inevitable goal is to get us to unknowingly enter into a contract.

Don't ever agree to something from a fae. There will always be strings attached."

"Oh, your friend, Rudolf," Wilder said, glancing over her shoulder briefly.

Sophia nodded. "King Rudolf is an excellent example of Laffy Taffy you shouldn't trust. He once conned Liv into a lifetime of servitude. She got out of it, but just barely."

Wilder shook his head. "No, I was literally referring to the actual fae." He pointed over her shoulder.

Sophia sighed and turned to see none other than the king of the fae. He wore a wide smile as he jostled in their direction, his arms full of packages wrapped in brown paper.

She looked around, searching for a place to hide. "Do you think he's seen us?"

Wilder laughed. "Since he's trying to wave and shouting your name, yeah, I think so."

The fae had dropped a few packages attempting to wave at them and was now yelling, "Sophia Beaufont! It's me! King Rudolf. Wait up!"

She lowered her chin and stepped behind Wilder. "Are you sure? Maybe he will think he's seeing things."

"I don't think so," he said over his shoulder, still laughing at her attempts to hide behind him.

"Just play it cool, and he'll get distracted by something shiny and forget," she offered.

"Hey, King Rudolf," Wilder said cheerfully. "Can I help you with your packages?"

Sophia sighed with defeat. "What part of cool do you not understand?"

"Absolutely, kind sir," Rudolf exclaimed, dropping the packages into Wilder's outstretched hands as Sophia came out of hiding behind him.

The king smiled wide at her. "There you are. At first, I thought I was seeing things and had mistaken someone else for you."

Sophia cut her eyes at Wilder. "See. It would have worked."

Rudolf bowed to Wilder, offering a curt nod. "And so we meet again, Neil."

"My name is Wilder," he said, managing the packages Rudolf had been bumbling with ease.

"I know that," Rudolf replied. "I can't call you by that awesome name because it makes me feel inadequate, so you'll be Neil from now on when we speak."

"You do realize you're the king of the fae and shouldn't feel inadequate based on someone's name, right?" Sophia questioned.

"And yet I do," he said sadly. "It's a lot better than it used to be. The year when no one wore clothes was probably my lowest."

"What year was that?" Wilder asked, curious.

"I don't remember," Rudolf answered. "Actually, I don't remember a lot from that year. I spent most of it drunk and finally moved up to Canada, telling people I'd become a Communist."

"You realize Canada has never had a Communist government, right?" Sophia asked.

Rudolf nodded. "I only moved there because it's cold, and even during the nude year, people in Canada wore clothes."

"Oh, right," Sophia said, drawing out the words, realization dawning on her.

"Now, if you will just deliver those to the Cosmopolitan in Las Vegas, Neil," Rudolf said, waving Wilder off. "My lovely bride, who is in labor, is expecting those things."

"Wait, Serena is in labor?" Sophia questioned, shock covering her face.

He gave her a look of surprise. "Of course. Didn't you get my message? I thought that was why you were here. To help me shop."

"I have so many questions," Sophia muttered. "Firstly, how did you send this message?"

"Via telepathy, obviously," Rudolf answered.

Sophia pursed her lips and glanced at Wilder.

He laughed. "Obviously, Soph. Gosh, don't you know anything?"

"Apparently, no," she said dryly. She returned her attention to

Rudolf. "And what are you shopping for when your wife is in labor with your triplets? Don't you think you should be there with her?"

He reeled back, covering his chest with a hand. "My Gods, woman. What kind of witchcraft are you into? A husband can't be with his wife when she's birthing. Watching the children come out of her is something I can't unsee, and I need to be able to find my wife desirable after this whole ordeal."

"You do realize..." Sophia shook her head. "Never mind. It's probably best if you allow her to handle this on her own."

"Yes, and Bermuda says I have a whole three to five days before I have to return," Rudolf stated.

"Three to five days?" Wilder questioned, still holding the packages.

"Yeah, the fae have an incredibly short incubation time compared to other mammals," Rudolf explained. "However, the labor process lasts exponentially longer."

"Your kind is all sorts of screwed up," Sophia muttered, mostly to herself.

"Anyway, my next objective is to find something for the babies to eat when they arrive," Rudolf said, looking around at the various shops.

"How about milk?" Sophia offered.

He shook his head, dispelling the idea at once. "Nope. That won't work. The children will be vegan."

For a moment, Sophia thought her head was going to explode from the strange thought. "Yeah, I guess vegans can't breastfeed."

Rudolf giggled nervously. "You said 'breast.'"

"Oh, for the love of the angels." Sophia sighed. "I didn't know you and Serena are vegan."

He gave her a surprised expression. "Oh, we're absolutely not."

"Then why, if you two aren't vegan, do you think your children will be?" Wilder asked, sounding amused.

Rudolf took the packages back from him. "Because they are progressive."

"Obviously," Sophia said, shaking her head at the fae.

"Well, since Neil is as unhelpful as he is attractive," Rudolf began, juggling the assortment of packages, "I'll take these back to the casino myself. When I return, Sophia, I want your help picking out a good hemp formula for Captain, Captain, Captain, and Captain."

She rubbed her head, the familiar headache she got when around Rudolf starting to pinch her brain. "I wish I could, but I've got to go see Papa Creola."

"Oh, and he takes precedence over me?" Rudolf questioned.

"He's the father of time, so yes," Sophia answered.

Rudolf smiled. "Yeah, that's probably a good call. I literally have zero authority over anything."

"You're in charge of the fae," Wilder offered.

"True," he sang. "That mostly means I have to oversee a lot of laws regarding the sexual display of affection and incest."

Sophia let out a long breath. "It's really a wonder the fae don't get taken more seriously."

"I know, right," Rudolf said, nodding. "Okay, I'll message you when the triplets are born so you can stop everything you're doing and help us with the children's education for the next several years. We've elected you, Sophia, as the one who will teach them about unicorns."

"Why is that?" Sophia questioned.

"Well, because you're a unicorn rider," Rudolf answered.

"Yeah, Soph," Wilder said with a sigh.

"Right," Sophia said, shaking her head. "Just be sure to send that message like you've sent all the others, so I get it."

Rudolf tapped the side of his head. "I absolutely will. Nothing more reliable than our telepathic link."

CHAPTER SEVENTEEN

Wilder laughed the entire way to the Fantastical Armory. Sophia pretended to roll her eyes at him, but she was really very amused by the whole interaction with Rudolf, per usual.

"What's your unicorn's name?" he joked.

Her eyes fluttered with annoyance. "Well, Neil, if you knew anything about unicorns, you'd know they don't have names."

"Oh?" he asked, sounding curious.

"No, you call them using a melody," she answered.

"That's inherently false," Subner said when they entered his shop. He was leaning over the counter, inspecting a knife with an intricately carved handle. His stringy brown hair was partially covering his face.

"Yes, I know," she said dryly. "It's a joke."

"You take after your sister," he said absentmindedly, his attention on the weapon.

"Thank you," she stated proudly.

"That wasn't a compliment," he muttered. "I never know what that Warrior is actually saying or if she's serious or not. Sarcasm is a very confusing device that is also incredibly ineffective."

Sophia turned her attention to Wilder. "You've got two uptight bosses. Good luck with that."

Wilder gave her an uncomfortable expression. "Subner, you paged me? What can I do for you?"

He lifted his gaze, peering at Sophia, an impatient glare in his eyes. "You'll have to leave before Wilder and I can meet."

Her annoyance was palpable. "Are you serious? You made me tote him here, and now you're kicking me out?"

"I'm not a purse," Wilder argued, a smile dancing in his eyes.

"And I'm not kicking you out," Subner stated, standing from his stool.

He was wearing a t-shirt that said, "Certified Organic" over his cut-off jean shorts. Sophia still couldn't get used to him in his hippy form, but she guessed she would in time. He and Papa Creola had apparently been gnomes for several hundred years before they were "rebooted" as hippy elves. Barring any catastrophic situations that put Father Time at risk, they'd stay in these forms for another few hundred years, at least. Sophia was looking forward to when they became fae. The pair would be extra grumpy. They liked being gnomes because it suited their no-nonsense personalities. Being hippy elves was harder for them. Being fae would be painful.

Subner pointed to the door at the back of the shop. "Papa Creola wants to see you."

"Oh?" Sophia asked, curious.

"Yes and no. I don't know what it's about, but apparently you do, or you should," Subner noted.

Sophia nodded and headed for the door. "Of course, I should." She waved to Wilder as she entered the area that led to Papa Creola's office. "Have fun with your secret meeting. Can't wait to hear all about it, Wild."

"He won't be telling you a thing," Subner said dryly.

"It's a dragonrider thing," she replied, looking over her shoulder to the hippie elf. "He has to tell me, or he gets kicked out of the Dragon Elite."

Subner didn't appear amused, and he waved her through the door. "Why do the Beaufont children have to be simultaneously the most irritating magicians while also being incredibly skillful and necessary?"

She winked. "It's a gift."

CHAPTER EIGHTEEN

It took much longer than Sophia would have expected to descend the stairs to Papa Creola's office. She'd heard about this space from Liv and heard it was what felt like a hundred stories down in a dark basement. Things must have changed since then because Papa Creola's office wasn't how Sophia's sister had described it. Instead of being warm and dark, it was…hippy-ish.

A few large bean bags were arranged in a circle. Incense was burning, making Sophia's nose twitch. The sound of chiming music could be heard overhead. Sitting cross-legged in the middle of the bean bag circle was none other than Father Time. His eyes were closed, and his hands were resting on his knees as he sat in lotus position.

Where Liv had described a fireplace on the far wall was now a Buddhist shrine of sorts. Over it was a large hourglass attached to the wall. Sophia studied the space for a moment, wondering if she should clear her throat to get Papa Creola's attention.

She stood uncomfortably, alternating putting her weight on either foot.

"Why don't you take a seat," Papa Creola said, his eyes still closed.

Sophia looked around. "On one of the bean bags?"

"That's entirely up to you," Papa Creola answered.

Since there weren't really any other options, Sophia ungracefully slipped into the bean bag chair directly across from Papa Creola, making way more noise than she should have. This particular chair was a lot less firm than the pink one she had in her room in the Castle, and it made her really have to engage her core to sit upright.

When Papa Creola opened his eyes, the blue of his piercing gaze made Sophia sit up. He appeared alert, a certain knowing in his stare.

"Thank you for joining me," he said, looking around.

"Well, I didn't really have a choice," Sophia said casually. "Subner kicked me out of the shop upstairs. He said I was needed down here and totally knew what it was about, although you may be surprised to find out I don't."

"You do, but your mind is overwhelmed," Papa Creola stated. "Do you want me to sage the place for you? Do you think that would help?"

She scowled at him. "Is that a result of your new hippy persona?"

He nodded, guilt covering his features. "Sorry. Liv is trying to help break me of it, but it will take some time. I'm afraid I'll say other really repugnant things without meaning to."

"Like how children should name themselves and vaccinations are ruining the modern world?" Sophia asked.

He nodded, stretching to a more relaxed position. "Yes, I'm afraid so. It's just a part of who I am now. I'm aligned with the elfish ways, so when I respond, I pull from their well."

"Which is a sparkling spring full of hippies bathing with mud masks," Sophia joked.

He nodded. "That is very accurate."

"So I should know why I'm here," Sophia mused to herself.

"You do," he stated. "Just relax your mind and it will come to you."

"Then you'll offer me the answers I seek?" she asked.

He shook his head. "No, then I'll offer you an unhelpful riddle that will make you wish you had never visited me, and it will make you more confused than before you started."

Sophia pursed her lips and nodded. "That seems about right."

So much had been going on for Sophia with training and Thad

Reinhart. She racked her brain to remember what other missions she could be turning to Papa Creola for. He was devilishly helpful when he wanted to be, but the keywords were "when he wanted to be." He was much like Plato in that regard, and apparently, the two were made of the same stuff—the oldest and most powerful magic in the world.

"I'm looking for a desk..." she muttered. She tried to process the last few days, which were all running together.

"That's not it," Papa Creola said, sounding terse.

"Okay," she said, drawing out the word, thinking. It suddenly hit her. Sophia couldn't fathom how she'd allowed it to escape her memory. She had too much going on for sure. "Papa Creola, I'm looking for a certain closet in the House of Fourteen."

"There you go, sunflower," he said, nodding.

"Say what?" she asked, confused by the nickname.

"Sorry," he said, shaking his head. "Ignore that part or anything else hippy-ish, I say."

"I'm sorry, but I won't be able to do that," she teased.

He shook his head. "You are your sister's sister."

"So, the closet. That's what I need your help with," Sophia began, thinking. "Plato, your bestie—"

"Nope," Papa Creola interrupted.

"Okay, fine." Sophia laughed. "But Plato said the closet I was looking for could be in the House of Fourteen, but at a different point in time. Does that make sense? Is that possible?"

"It is," he answered simply.

Realizing Papa Creola wasn't going to expand on his own, Sophia tried to pick her questions carefully. "How can I get to the right closet in the House of Fourteen at the right time?"

He let out a long breath. "You can't. But I can."

She perked up, leaning forward. "Oh! Will you?"

"No," he answered simply.

She slumped. "Dude, this isn't going well."

"I think you know, Sophia, I'm not going to hand-deliver you the solutions you seek," he said, sounding sage-like.

"Cool, but deliver me something I can work with," she asserted. "There is a way to get to the closet on another timeline. Can you give me a clue about how to find that? Something really confusing I won't understand that will make me want to knock my head against the wall, but still give me an option?"

He thought for a moment. "We live in the present moment."

"Some of us," she observed, looking at his tie-dye pants.

"Well, for my example, we technically live in the present, regardless of my attire," he amended. "But in some cases, the present isn't gone and lost like it should be."

"Not at all following you," she stated.

Papa Creola held out his hand and a snow globe appeared in the center of his palm. In it was a figurine of the House of Fourteen, snow fluttering all around it, which had never happened in Santa Monica. "The past is meant to be a lost reality. Once it passes, there's no more revisiting it, except in your mind."

"Or if you know Papa Creola and he'll grant you access to things to turn it back like when you allowed me to bring the Phantom back to life so I could kill it again."

Papa Creola sighed dramatically. "And here I thought Liv was a pain in the ass."

She smiled. "You want me to shush it so you can make a point, don't you?"

He nodded, still holding the snow globe, an expectant expression on his face.

Sophia waved him on, urging him to continue.

"The past is meant to be gone," Papa Creola began. "That's the way I created it so others couldn't tamper and change things. There are rare occasions where I made exceptions to preserve the world."

Papa Creola paused, ensuring Sophia was still following him.

"You have my attention," she said, her eyes big.

"When the Great War broke out and mortals were made to not see magic, I had to make a really fast judgment," Papa Creola explained. "I froze the House just before mortals weren't able to see magic. It was a quick decision, but it was the only course I saw to save everyone if your sister Liv didn't fix things. That was what the timeline told me, but it is never completely accurate. I needed to have a backup. A way to save things if no one else did. If that happened, if things went to hell, then I could reset the timeline from the save point."

Again, Papa Creola paused. He gave her a studious expression like he was trying to determine if this was computing for Sophia. It hardly was. This was more than confounding.

"So you created a reboot in a way?" she asked. "A way to restart everything from a certain save point if things didn't get better?"

"Yes, as I said, I saved things just before the war broke out and mortals couldn't see magic," Papa Creola said. "And since then, I've kept that save point just in case we ever needed it. It so happens, this timeline still exists inside the House…and also the Castle."

"It does?" Sophia asked, shocked. "Are you telling me the closet I need to find is on the other timeline?"

Papa Creola simply nodded.

"You could send me to this same point in the House of Fourteen, and I can find the right closet on the other timeline?" she asked.

"No, no, no," Papa Creola said with a dry laugh.

Sophia gave him a peeved expression. "Hah. Hah. Hah. Obviously, you can't."

"You know I can't send you anywhere," Papa Creola stated.

"I know you won't," she countered. "But I get how this works. You need me to do something. Is that right?"

"I protected the save point using a token of sorts," Papa Creola explained. "A monster guards it and—"

"Of course, it does," she said, laughing.

"This monster," he continued, "has done its job for entirely too long and has grown a bit restless. I fear it will abandon its mission to guard the token unless it's slaughtered."

"You need someone to kill this monster," Sophia guessed.

"Yes," he answered. "And they would need an ancient creature to help them."

"If only I had a dragon…"

He smirked at her. "If only."

"Where do I find this monster, and what is it?" she asked.

He crossed his arms across his chest. "I really wish I could give you information, but unfortunately, that's not something I can do."

She lowered her chin, scowling at the most powerful man on the Earth. "I know you can, but that's not how this works. I have to figure it out on my own."

He smiled at her fondly. "You are much quicker than your sister at learning this stuff."

"Fine," Sophia said. "I find this monster and kill it. Then I have to take the token it's guarding. That will help me to get to the other timeline, right?"

"Yes," Papa Creola confirmed. "But then you'll have become the keeper of the token until I have to replace you. It must be supervised at all times since the other timeline can't be erased and needs to be preserved in case anything happens to this one."

Sophia nodded slowly and wondered if what she was agreeing to was as momentous as it felt. "Okay. I'll guard it until you decide otherwise."

"I'm not certain when that will be," he answered, an ominous tone to his voice. "It depends on you. When you grow restless with your job or slack in your responsibility as a supervisor, you'll be replaced."

Sophia's eyes enlarged, realizing what the word "replaced" meant.

CHAPTER NINETEEN

"Yeah, Papa Creola totally told me about your mission with Subner," Sophia said to Wilder as they strode through Roya Lane, the smell of peppermint strong in the air and bells rattling from seemingly everywhere.

"Did he?" Wilder questioned, a pursed expression on his normally cheerful face.

"Well, he said nothing about it, but I think he meant to," she amended. "You go ahead and fill me in, and then I'll tell you about what I'm working on."

Wilder shook his head. "Not only can I not tell you what I have to do for Subner, but I'm certain if you're doing something that involves Papa Creola, you can't tell me."

She sighed, looking longingly at a cart with fresh pretzels. "You're kind of the worst, Wild."

He nodded. "I know. I'd love to know what your mission is, but I know I can't, and you won't tell me, will you?"

She shook her head. "There's no way I can divulge that information."

"Then you understand my position," he confided.

"Yeah, unfortunately, I do." She gave him a long sideway expression. "It's not something dangerous or anything, right? I mean, it's not like I'd worry about you, but if I did, this wouldn't make me worry more?"

"No," he said dismissively. "You know how Subner and Papa Creola work. They send us on missions that are perfectly safe and never full of dark, mysterious monsters."

"Yep, totally," she said, worry starting to creep into her being as she wondered what Subner was sending Wilder to do.

CHAPTER TWENTY

Hiker was pacing his office, which had shrunk even more, when Sophia and Wilder entered. Sophia stopped at the threshold and backed up slightly, wondering where she would stand if she entered.

Evan was laid out on the couch, his hands behind his head. "Oh, look who has decided to join us while the boss and I have been holding down the fort."

"Shut it, Evan," Hiker ordered, halting in the narrow pathway he'd made between his desk and the tiny, only remaining window in his closet-sized office.

Sophia leaned against the doorway and gave Wilder a hesitant expression. He returned it as he leaned on the other side of the door-way, trying his best to look comfortable.

"Thanks for holding down the fort, Evan," Sophia said. "It looks like it's been a tough job."

"Totally draining," he said yawning.

"Good, now you two are back—"

"Actually, sir," Wilder interrupted, making Hiker straighten. "I have a mission I need to leave on right away. It's for Subner, and you understand I couldn't refuse, right?"

Hiker swallowed as he tried to assimilate this information. After a moment, he nodded. "Of course. Subner. Your other boss…"

"Yes, sir," Wilder said, his eyes low. "You understand I wouldn't abandon missions you'd assign me to, but…"

"You have other obligations," Hiker stated. "I get it. What is it that will take you away?"

Wilder's eyes skirted to the side. "The thing is, sir—"

"You can't tell me," Hiker guessed.

Wilder nodded.

"Fine," Hiker acquiesced. "I get it and realize this won't always be the case. For now, it is fine. I'm sure Sophia can handle the mission I had for you."

"The thing is, sir," she said, her tone uncertain.

The leader of the Dragon Elite growled. "Don't tell me…"

She backed up a step. "Okay, I won't."

"You've got a mission?" he asked, anger rising in his voice.

Evan rose to a sitting position, looking between the two with interest.

"Yeah, so I have to go and do a thing for Papa Creola," she explained meekly. "I wouldn't do it, but…"

"He's Father Time," Hiker grumbled. "You have to. I get it, but I wish it wasn't taking two of my riders away when we are trying to build our reputation as adjudicators."

"But, sir, you have me," Evan offered.

Hiker sighed and nodded. Then he shrugged. "Oh, yeah. I have you."

"I'm going to need you to be a bit more enthusiastic about the dragonrider who is remaining loyal to you in the middle of all this rider-pillaging," Evan said, his tone jovial and bringing a much-needed lightness to the otherwise tense conversation.

"When will you two return?" Hiker asked.

Sophia looked to Wilder, who seemed to share her feeling of uncertainty. They both shrugged.

"Sorry, sir," Wilder explained. "It's hard to know. We will report back when we can and make your missions a priority as soon as we are able to."

Hiker began pacing once more. "Yeah, I guess, I understand."

"I think you should fire them, sir," Evan offered.

"I'm not going to fire them," Hiker said tersely. "Yet. Maybe later."

"Well, at least give them a good talking to," he suggested. "Yell at them. Call them names. I have a few for Sophia."

"I have a few names I've been wanting to call you," Hiker said to Evan, making him shrink back down on the sofa.

"Sir, I'm going up," Wilder stated. "I've got to get up early for…"

"The mission you can't tell me about," Hiker finished his sentence. Wilder nodded.

"Yeah, I have to go too," Sophia stated, backing away with Wilder and following his lead.

"Fine," Hiker said, sounding thoroughly defeated.

The two turned and made for the stairs just as Evan raised his arms, casually pinning them back behind his head. "Okay, sir, let's talk about our future plans for the Dragon Elite. I'm here to help."

"Angels above, why do you torture me," Hiker groaned, despair heavy in his voice.

CHAPTER TWENTY-ONE

Sophia didn't feel bad about abandoning Hiker for her side missions. Finding *The Complete History of Dragonriders* was important. And there was finding her father's book for Liv for Christmas. That one was especially time-sensitive. She had more questions about both cases than answers, which meant she only had one option to find helpful information.

When she stepped through the portal to Mae Ling's shop, she was momentarily disoriented, wondering if she got the location wrong. The last time she'd visited her fairy godmother of sorts, the nail shop had been under construction. She had thought it was going to be remodeled, but it appeared to have been leveled. In its place was a huge shop that ran the length of the shopping center.

The donut shop, optometry office, and kickboxing studio were all gone. In their place was a giant nail salon with a large sign that read: "Mae's Beauty Emporium."

Through the glass, Sophia could see the salon was filled with people. She strode through the door to a cacophony of women chatting excitedly at nail stations. The line to the hostess desk was nearly out the door, but Sophia managed to edge into the front area to put her name on the list.

She worried she wouldn't be able to find or meet with Mae Ling. Sophia was counting on her to give her information on the desk and the monster guarding Papa Creola's token. If she couldn't talk with her fairy godmother, she really didn't know how she'd find the answers she needed.

When she came to the front of the line, Sophia smiled politely. "Hello," she said to the receptionist sitting behind the desk. "I'd like to see Mae Ling."

"You and everyone else," the lady behind the desk said, smacking her gum and appearing bored as she scrolled through Instagram on her phone.

"Oh, well, can I get an appointment?"

"Yeah, sure," the receptionist said, not glancing up. "What's your name?"

"Sophia Beau—"

"Oh!" the lady exclaimed, jerking her head up. "Sophia. You don't need an appointment."

"I-I-I don't?" Sophia stammered.

"Of course, you don't," Mae Ling said from behind Sophia. She turned to see the short Asian woman. "And what did I tell you about stuttering?"

"Not to?" Sophia guessed.

Mae pushed her glasses up on her nose and turned. "Follow me, love. We'll go to the back where it's quieter."

Sophia followed the woman through the crowded salon until they came to a station in the corner removed from the other bustling areas.

"You sit," Mae ordered, pointing to the other side of the desk.

Sophia did as she was told. She laid her hands on the surface of the table and prepared to get her nails done.

"Oh, we're not going through the formalities this time," Mae said, taking a seat on the other side of Sophia and waving her hands away.

Sophia sank back, feeling silly. "I'm sorry. It's just in the past you've ordered me to have manicures and pedicures."

Mae nodded. "Because that was a part of the experience, but

you've come with a tall order this time, and I have to do some research to supply the answers you need."

"Oh," Sophia said with surprise. "You know why I'm here?"

"I know why, but not enough to help you," Mae explained, pushing her glasses up on her nose, the chain anchoring them around her neck making a gentle clinking sound. "Now, you'll have to look into my eyes for me to figure out where your father's book is."

"Wait, how is it you know that's one of my questions?" Sophia knew it was probably ridiculous to question how this magical being knew so much. It never mattered how much of the strange and amazing magical world she saw, it always amazed her. Maybe that was the point. Magic was meant to keep everyone on their toes. She thought the moment this all became normal for her was when she needed to bow out and have a regular life. She hoped that never happened.

"It's a fairy godmother thing," Mae said, leaning forward and looking deep into Sophia's eyes. "I always know what questions you have, but I don't always know how to help you with them. That's the case now."

"Why are you looking into my eyes?" Sophia asked, feeling like she was having a strange eye examination.

"Because you know the answer," Mae stated matter-of-factly.

"I do?" Sophia asked, blinking rapidly, her eyes watering from holding them wide.

"Well, of course, you do," Mae stated like it was common knowledge. "You were there when the desk was sold. You saw the whole thing happen."

"I was?" Sophia said and straightened. "You can see that in my eyes?"

"Not if you don't remain still, I can't," Mae admonished. She grabbed Sophia's hand and pulled her forward. "Now stay still. I've almost got it."

Sophia didn't so much as breathe while Mae looked intently into her eyes, studying something deep within her. "Oh, yes, that's very curious. Going to be quite the ordeal for you."

"What?" Sophia questioned as Mae released her, sitting back in the seat. "What did you see? Where's my dad's desk? Is the book in it?"

"First things first," Mae said, waving her off. "You need the location for the monster guarding the save point token, but I don't have it."

"Oh, really?" Sophia muttered, disappointment edging into her tone. "I guess there are other places I could look."

"Don't worry, child," Mae said, taking off her reading glasses and smiling at her. "I don't have the location yet. That one is a bit tougher. I love a good challenge. The animal has been off most radars for a long time. And the save point token is of great value. I agree with Papa Creola. You'd be the best keeper of it. Defeating the monster, well, that will probably give you some scars."

"What is the monster?" Sophia asked.

Mae shook her head. "All in time, child. I don't have the answer to that question yet. But I will, and when I do, I'll send it your way." She removed a receipt pad from the apron around her waist and wrote something on it. "In the meantime, you can busy yourself by going to this address. That's where you'll find your father's desk. The book is stuck in the top of the middle drawer, which is why it wasn't removed with the other contents."

Sophia went to grab the piece of paper, grateful for her luck. "Really? This sounds easy. I'm very excited, and Liv will love this."

Mae pulled back the piece of paper and gave Sophia a look of warning. "Please don't mistake this straightforward information for the idea this mission will be easy. You may know where to find the desk and where to find the book, but getting to it will be a challenge. I think you'd rather face an evil unicorn again than enter this house."

CHAPTER TWENTY-TWO

Sophia thought there should have been more sounds emanating from the swampland around her. Even though night was falling, she thought a bird should be making noise or a cricket chirping or the water at her back trickling or gurgling or something.

She turned, noticing the way the shadows from the tall trees created eerie shapes on the surface of the water. She refocused on the house in front of her. It rose two stories up from the marshland, making it look like an island in the middle of a strange lake.

This was the house Mae had sent her to. The location of her father's desk and his prized book. The house once stood on a successful plantation in the South. Now, the marshlands had overtaken it, making it a part of the landscape, rather than the monument it once was.

Sophia had briefly researched the house. It had once belonged to an affluent family. They owned most of Louisiana but had lost their wealth after a series of strange business dealings. It was only five years ago they bought Sophia's father's desk. And yet, so much had changed for the family during that time. It was strange to her how fast things turned. Dry land had become soaked with water and an affluent family fell into despair, abandoning their house.

I don't think they abandoned it, Lunis said in her head, having seen what she'd seen and learned even though he was still at the Gullington.

The history records weren't clear, Sophia offered.

I believe you were supposed to read between the lines, Lunis remarked. *The father went crazy after losing all their money in assorted unorthodox investments.*

The records say the family left for Europe, though, Sophia mused.

But no one has seen any of the Peters since, Lunis argued. *And soon after, the property flooded and since has been unusable.*

So, what are you getting at? Sophia asked him.

The house is obviously haunted, he explained.

Just then, Sophia felt an icy wind coast over her shoulder, tangling her hair around her face. *Haunted, but ghosts can't hurt me, right?* she asked.

It depends, Lunis answered. *If they are really emotionally charged, they absolutely could.*

Like they lost it all in bad investments and murdered their family, she asked.

I'm not going to pretend to know what Luther Peters did, but that's pretty much the commentary I read between the lines from the history records, Lunis stated.

Cool, Sophia said, pretending to be casual. *I'll just waltz into this house and grab the book. I'm sure Murderer Ghost Man won't mind.*

Maybe he won't even be home, Lunis offered.

Yeah, maybe he popped down to the store for ghost supplies, Sophia interjected.

The wind howled over the marsh, making the surface of the water ripple.

Soph, Lunis said after a moment of silence.

Yes, she answered.

Ghosts don't need supplies.

She sighed. *Thanks. I sort of knew that.*

Do you want me to come over there for backup? he asked.

Sophia shook her head, studying the house as the sunlight waned.

The timing of entering the haunted house couldn't be any better, and by better, she meant worse. Soon it would be dark with no lights. They were miles from anyone or anything except trees and swamp.

Thanks, Lunis, she answered. *However, you can't fit into that house, and I'm not sure what you can do to help. Being in my head is about the best thing.*

Well, I'm definitely here for you, Lunis consoled. *Don't you worry, I'm not going anywhere.*

Sophia smiled, grateful wherever she was, she always had Lunis, no matter what.

CHAPTER TWENTY-THREE

Wading through the ankle-deep water took a little longer than Sophia had expected because of the mud and the many squirming things that slithered around her feet.

You've literally fought evil unicorns and battled magical robots, Lunis teased. *But you're scared about some tiny snakes.*

You didn't see that snake, Sophia argued. *It had black eyes and no soul.*

They are more scared of you than you are of them, Lunis offered.

Not that one, she stated. *It wanted to eat me. Thanks to a handy dandy spell, it is now in snake heaven.*

I don't think snakes go to heaven, Lunis joked.

Because they are soulless? Sophia asked.

Because they are snakes and snakes would totally mess up heaven for the masses, he answered. *Could you imagine sitting up on a cloud, enjoying your free Wi-Fi, and all of a sudden, a snake slithers over and curls up at your feet? That would totally ruin the experience.*

You need to get out more, Sophia said as she climbed the stairs to the large plantation house, grateful to have her boots on a solid surface not covered in water.

Yo—don—kno—

What? Sophia asked, halting a few feet from the door.

Yo—break—up, Lunis said in abbreviated words.

Lunis, I can't hear you, Sophia said, her breath growing faster.

The ghost... he said, the rest of his words falling away.

What about the ghost? she asked, panicked. The last time her connection with Lunis had been severed, it had broken her heart. She didn't want anything like that to happen again.

Soph. Lunis broke through, his voice clear and loud in her head. *I think the cosmic field created by Luther Peters is breaking into our psychic connection. I can't keep this up much longer. You'll have to go in without me.*

But Lunis!

I know, he said, empathy in his voice. *You can do this. I can see everything you can. I'm here, even if you can't hear me. You aren't alone. You will get in there and get out with the book.*

Sophia nodded and looked at the large door in front of her. A hogshead on the front with a ring through the nose was the knocker. She wasn't planning on knocking.

Okay, I'll be home soon, Lunis, Sophia said, taking a step forward.

Good, he said. *And just remember the one thing you must never do in the presence of an angry ghost.*

She froze. *Wait, I don't know what that is. Tell me!*

You must never—

Lunis, Sophia exclaimed in her head. *You cut out. I must never what?*

Her head was silent except for her own racing thoughts. She stood frozen on the large porch for a full minute, waiting for Lunis to chime in her head again, but his voice never came, and Sophia knew she was alone and on her own.

CHAPTER TWENTY-FOUR

I *must never what*, Sophia worried as she pressed down on the handle for the Peters' front door.

It was locked.

She had no idea what Lunis was going to tell her or what she must never do in the presence of ghosts. There was an obvious gap in her education when it came to spirits. She knew they were mostly harmless, but Lunis was right. If they were emotionally charged, they could be extremely dangerous, controlling power fields and all sorts of energy. The fact Luther Peter's energy broke through her connection to Lunis made Sophia really worried.

Still, there was nothing more important to her than her family. She needed to get the book. For Liv. For Clark. For her. Sophia wasn't backing down from this challenge even though it had gotten complicated.

She held up her hand and flicked her wrist, unlocking the door with a simple spell.

Okay, these ghosts couldn't keep her out. That was a good sign. Maybe they weren't so powerful.

She pushed back the door, peeking her head through and finding a long hallway cluttered with broken furniture. It definitely appeared like a struggle had happened in the Peters' house before it was locked up.

An object soared straight at her head, and Sophia ducked just as it crashed into the open door. Glass shattered and rained down on her. She covered her head and darted into the house, even though she thought running outside was the smarter option.

Without anything to hide behind and finding herself in the corner of the large entryway, Sophia searched the space. The hallway was punctuated with a grand staircase split in two at the landing, which went off in different directions, creating a balcony on the second floor overlooking the entryway. She could see a hint of the dining hall and living areas past the staircase.

It made the most sense to Sophia that her father's desk would be in a study, which should be on the first floor with the common areas. She pressed her back against the wall and sidestepped, looking for flying objects being launched at her head and still wondering what Lunis was trying to tell her. What was it she must not do in the presence of a ghost?

Maybe I shouldn't blink, she thought, her eyes adjusting to the dark. There was a strange bluish light radiating from an unknown source somewhere that allowed her to make out some details.

A sawing noise made Sophia tense as she neared the first archway.

Maybe I should breathe, she thought, realizing she was lightheaded from not taking in any air.

The sawing grew louder.

Maybe I shouldn't let the ghost see my fear, Sophia thought. She was visibly shaking.

At the entrance to the next room where the sawing sound was coming from, Sophia braced herself. Sucking in a breath, she peeked around the corner and saw something that filled her with rampant fear.

She bit her tongue. Nearly screamed. Froze.

So much for not feeling fear, she thought as she witnessed a pale blue ghost of a teenage boy sawing through his arm, which was chained to the wall.

His gaze jerked to Sophia, eyes full of fright. "No magic can open the lock. I've tried. The only way to free myself before the flood drowns me is to cut myself."

Sophia covered her mouth and watched as the boy continued to saw, pain covering his face. He wailed, filling her ears with a sound she'd never forget.

"Papa, why?" the boy screamed, continuing to saw through his arm. "Why, Papa?"

Sophia wanted to run to the boy. Make him stop. Tell him he didn't have to relive this nightmare over and over again. Then a vase soared at her head. Her dragon enhanced reflexes caught the image in her peripheral vision just in time, causing her to duck into the room with the tortured boy to avoid getting hit.

There was another exit on the adjacent wall. Sophia kept her eyes from the bluish figure of the boy, realizing he was giving off the light that allowed her to see.

Although her instinct told her she needed to save this ghost, she knew doing it directly wasn't the answer. She needed to find the source.

Loud footsteps overhead stole her attention.

For some reason, she knew they belonged to Luther Peters.

Sophia peeked around the corner to the next room.

There it was—her father's desk.

She wasn't sure how she knew it was Theodore Beaufont's desk, except something deep in her felt connected to it. Sophia had the urge to run to the desk, pull open the drawer, and grab his book.

As the footsteps echoed overhead, she knew she couldn't do it.

There was another mission here that deserved her attention.

You're a dragonrider, she told herself. *You fix the world. You solve problems. You free those who need help.*

Sophia allowed herself to turn back and peer at the boy who was desperately cutting his own arm off to escape the floodwaters.

Whoever he was, he deserved to be freed. All of the Peters did, she thought as she retreated the way she'd come, back toward where the stairs led to the second floor—which was no doubt full of more horrors.

CHAPTER TWENTY-FIVE

Sophia didn't know what she was going to do to fix the Peters. She knew she couldn't rush away from this place and allow the horrors to continue to play out day after day. What could be worse for souls than to relive the worst possible moments of their lives?

She thought she was prepared to climb the stairs. Prepared to find whatever was creating the stomping noise. As she ascended, a woman's body raced toward her, tumbling head over feet as if she'd been pushed. Sophia didn't dart out of the way in time, and when the ghost raced through her, she felt a chill unlike anything she'd ever experienced. It was as if her core had been frozen and would never be warm again.

She jumped to the side as the ghost tumbled to the landing at the bottom of the stairs. The woman's head rested at an unnatural angle, her arms and legs contorted as her eyes stood wide open.

Sophia forced herself to pull her gaze away from the horrific sight and to the top of the stairs. It was then she met Luther Peters and wished she hadn't. Wished she'd grabbed her father's book and run. Wished she'd never entered the Peters' house.

Luther was dressed in a starched suit, his hand resting on the railing as he peered down at her with a hollow expression in his dark eyes.

Sophia finally understood what it meant to have her blood run cold. She shivered as the figure of Luther Peters casually ambled off, as if he were leading her in a new direction.

Again she could have run. She could have gotten the book and abandoned this haunted house.

Instead, Sophia lifted her foot and forced herself to climb the stairs to follow the murderer who resided somewhere on the second floor.

CHAPTER TWENTY-SIX

A dozen books were launched at Sophia's head. They ricocheted off the shelves lining the wall when she made it to the top of the stairs. This time instead of ducking, she shot each one like she was holding a gun, knocking them to the ground one after the other.

When she'd shot down the last book, she studied the landing on the second floor. There was a doorway off to the left, illuminated by blue light. The others were dark.

That must be where Luther was, Sophia thought, drawing in a breath.

She took a step in that direction and the floor vibrated under her feet, followed by a thundering sound.

Sophia paused, held her breath, and listened.

She heard terse muttering. It echoed through her head like it was on surround sound. Pressing her hands to her ears, she thought she'd go deaf from the incessant babbling trying to take over her thoughts.

Soldiering on, Sophia pushed forward. It felt like she was moving through mud to get to the room where Luther Peters must be. It was as if the sound were a thick fog that was hard to cross.

Sophia forced herself to take each deliberate step, knowing she couldn't give up after coming this far. She didn't know what she'd find the murderous ghost doing. Worse, she still didn't know what Lunis was trying to tell her to do. All she knew was that she had her instinct.

And you have me, Love Bug, a voice said in her head.

Sophia halted. Tensed. Listened, waiting for the voice to come back.

She didn't recognize the voice, but she'd heard the name it used before. Reese had said it to her often, but only when referring to their father.

"Daddy used to say you'd be the one to save our family, Love Bug," her sister would say while teaching her spells she should have never learned.

"The day you were born," Reese recounted one sunny afternoon from the conservatory in the House of Fourteen, "Daddy rushed in and said, my little Lady Bug is beautiful. Come and meet the newest member of our family."

"Love Bug" was the name Theodore Beaufont had affectionately called his daughter Sophia. She didn't remember it, but others had told her. Maybe in the recesses of her memory, she had glimpses of the blond-haired, blue eyed Councilor for the House of Fourteen, holding her baby hands and saying, "It's a pleasure to meet you, Love Bug. I can't wait to take you on adventures."

Sophia sucked in a breath, grieving for the moments she never had with the man she never really met. She'd never pitied herself for not knowing her parents, but at that moment, hearing his voice, she understood the grief she'd always witnessed in her sibling's eyes.

Suddenly she knew why Liv often cried herself to sleep. Or why Clark awoke in the morning appearing vacant, seeming lost like he was looking for someone. Her siblings had intimately known Guinevere and Theodore Beaufont—their parents.

Sophia had always counted herself lucky she hadn't fallen in love with the people who haunted her siblings, but right then, more than anything, she wanted to have a memory of these people the ones she loved desperately.

"There were no better people in this world than our parents," Ian had once told her. "They did what no one had the courage to do and loved fiercely, without abandonment. If you were lucky enough to catch their eyes, then you felt their warmth, their acceptance, their unwavering affection.

Sophia choked suddenly on tears she hadn't even realized were surfacing. She searched for Luther Peters, worried he was about to launch more books at her. She searched for her father, sure he was there somewhere. Was he a ghost too, like the others? There were so many questions and no time to answer them as the thundering from the adjacent room vibrated the floor and wall.

The next convulsion nearly sent Sophia to the floor. She bumped into the nearby wall, bracing herself as screams echoed from the room where she knew Luther Peters had to be.

CHAPTER TWENTY-SEVEN

The ragged breaths running through Sophia's lungs were unfulfilling.

She didn't care. It was time to face the demented ghost of a monster.

Sophia knew in battle, it was important to have a plan. She didn't have one, and oddly, she was okay with that.

Throwing caution to all her teachings, she swung into the next room and stood squarely in the threshold of the room, wanting to have the element of surprise.

A dozen knives and swords soared in her direction at once. Sophia allowed her feet to drop out from under her and fell flat to the floor as the blades roared overhead, hitting the wall behind her and sticking in like darts.

She peeled her face up and looked up at the image of the ghost standing in the room in front of her.

Luther Peters stomped on a pile of paper as if he didn't see her. "I'm ruined! I've lost it all! We're done!"

He continued to dance angrily over the bits of paper, shredding them to pieces.

Sophia caught the sound of rushing water down below on the first floor. She dared to duck out of the room she'd just entered and spied the blades that had nearly killed her sticking out of the wall. A brief glimpse over the side of the balcony told her what the water was all about. The flood from the past was starting, the one that drowned the boy who didn't successfully cut off his arm. The one that covered Luther Peters' wife's body after he threw her down the stairs. The one that still covered most of the property and made it unusable.

Sophia shook her head, not knowing how to fix this problem, but knowing she had to. She quickly retreated back to where she found Luther Peters, her instinct leading the way.

At the entrance to his bedroom, she tensed as she found him holding a gun to his head.

"Stop!" Sophia yelled, not knowing why, but feeling it was the only thing right to say.

CHAPTER TWENTY-EIGHT

The ghost of Luther Peters halted. He turned his head and looked at Sophia.

She wondered if ghosts could see her and realized he could, at least. That might mean she was screwed.

He blinked at her, cold soberness in his eyes as he regarded her with confusion.

"Why?" His voice came out like a vibration from a stringed instrument.

Sophia looked around the bedroom, searching for clues. She didn't know why he shouldn't kill himself or why she should stop him from being the murderer he was. She felt she should try.

"I know how to fix your problems," she said. She didn't know where those words had come from. It was the strangest sensation. She'd literally opened her mouth and words had rushed out—and they felt right.

Luther Peters lowered the gun and continued blinking at her, a deranged expression in his eyes that should have sent her running. Instead, she stood straighter.

"Come down to the first floor," she continued. "I know how to save your family. I know how to save you."

Again, Sophia didn't know where those words came from. She had uttered them with her mouth, but she didn't remember speaking them. It was the weirdest magic she'd ever witnessed, yet it felt like something she should trust.

"Downstairs?" Luther Peters questioned. "But that's where—"

"Not anymore," Sophia interrupted, not totally knowing what they were talking about.

"David isn't down there?" he asked.

She found herself shaking her head.

"And Dora?" he asked again.

Again Sophia shook her head. "You can change all that. Just come downstairs."

She was just about to turn and lead him to the stairs when the ghost who shouldn't have been able to reached out and grabbed her wrist, holding Sophia with an intensity she knew she couldn't break free of.

"I can't change the past," he said bitterly.

Sophia shook her head. "No, but you can mend the wounds. That's what solutions do. That's what *I'll* do."

He peered into her eyes with an intensity that tried to burn her from the inside out. His grip on her felt like fire. Sophia couldn't pull away from it, but she also wasn't afraid, even as he held her, pinning his gaze to hers.

Slowly, he released her, and pushing her with a strange cosmic force, ushered her forward. "Show me."

Unsure what she'd do when she got this angry ghost downstairs, Sophia ambled forward and the murderous ghost followed her.

CHAPTER TWENTY-NINE

Sophia was grateful to find no dead bodies at the bottom of the stairs. Things had changed in the last few minutes. There also wasn't any floodwater pouring into the house. To her relief, the boy wasn't in the first room trying to saw off his arm.

She had no idea what the strange voice that had spoken through her wanted to show the ghost of Luther Peters, or how it would change everything. She was afraid she had nothing, and he'd just end up killing her when she came up empty-handed.

At the entrance to the study, Sophia stopped, stalling as she peered into the eyes of the ghost.

"Well?" Luther Peters asked, absolutely on edge.

"Well," she said, looking over her shoulder at her father's desk.

"I knew you were like all the rest!" Luther yelled and threw his hands in the air. The sawing, flooding water, and stomping overhead started to echo in Sophia's head. She thought it would make her go deaf. Strangely, over the rush of noises, she heard a faint whisper, and she focused, concentrating intently.

My desk, Love Bug, the voice of her father said in her head. *At the back of my book.*

Sophia knew running could get her killed, but that was what she did. Sure enough, objects were thrown at her head right away. Vases. Lamps. Figurines. Sophia ducked as she ran, swerving to avoid the shards of glass and clay.

She yanked open the middle drawer to her father's desk and felt around, finding papers and ink wells and other things but not a book. Meanwhile, objects continued to be hurled at her, and Sophia had to duck under the desk. She kept awkwardly feeling around in the drawer, trying to find the object she'd come for, which would be her salvation in this moment of desperation.

Sophia was just about to give up when the hard back of something hit her fingers. She changed the angle of her hand, nearly dislocating her arm as she yanked the book out of the top drawer.

Feeling a surge like she'd never had before, Sophia darted to her feet.

Luther Peters decided to throw everything he had at her. Knives, swords, China plates, fireplace pokers, muskets, and many other objects flew in Sophia's direction, all meant to end her.

She held up her father's book, nearly clenching her eyes shut as she held the small object up to shield herself.

The objects meant to be her demise all halted in midair, then spiraled in place. After a moment, they dropped to the ground, close to the feet of Luther Peters.

He glanced down, confused.

Sophia gave the same questioning expression to the book in her hands. Recognizing this was her opportunity, she withdrew the certificates from the back of the book, finding them just where her father said they'd be.

"Here," she said, handing them to Luther Peters after walking over to him.

"What are these?" he asked, studying the pieces of paper.

"They are how you can save your family," she explained.

He read the pages, which were apparently bonds worth a great deal. His eyes enlarged. "But the past is over and done."

"And yet, there's always time for salvation," Sophia countered, again not knowing where the words came from. "You can always rewrite your ending. Just don't do what you did. Take the bonds. Don't harm your family. Take charge. Leave. Change what happened. Stop repeating it."

The ghost seemed absolutely confused. The deranged expression crossed his gaze again, but just when Sophia thought she'd have to defend herself, he took the bonds and turned toward the door.

He looked over his shoulder and studied her. "If I leave with these, if I set my heart on a new path…"

She nodded. "Then you set them on one too. You free yourself from the choices you made by making new ones."

The words felt right. They felt good. She couldn't explain the bonds or how she knew they were in her father's book, and that was the most telling part of any of this. It told her something much larger than her life was in play.

"Okay," Luther Peters said, swallowing. "I'll try."

He ambled out of the study, seeming almost drunk, like the moment had filled him with total disorientation.

Sophia let him get all the way out of view before hurrying after him, compelled to know how this story ended.

To her relief, the floors weren't flooding. The boy wasn't sawing off his arm. The woman wasn't at the bottom of the stairs.

The front door to the Peters' residence was wide open. She couldn't understand how Luther had crossed the space so fast. She ran for the front door, her father's book clasped in her hands. She didn't stop until she was to the front porch and saw what lay before her.

It wasn't the wide-open sprawling yard of the great plantation that caught Sophia's breath. That was beautiful since she remembered an hour before when it was flooded. It wasn't the hills stretched out in all directions with fertile fields, which made her pause.

It was the man standing nobly in the center of the grassy lawn, a woman on one side of him and a young boy on the other, their ghost figures casting the strange blue light around them. They turned and looked at Sophia with grateful smiles.

"Thank you," Luther Peters said, waving the bonds. "You didn't save our lives, but you saved my soul."

Sophia didn't know what to say, so she just held her father's book to her heart, knowing he had done it all.

She understood then that those in the grave could impact the living and vice versa.

CHAPTER THIRTY

Returning to the Gullington filled Sophia with warmth even though the cold winds whipped through her when she entered the Barrier. Seeing Lunis mended her heart after the ordeal with the Peters family, and she felt a warmth that made it seem like she'd never be cold again.

She strode across the Expanse, her father's book in her hand and a smile on her face as her dragon flew down from the Cave. Gracefully he landed, shaking like a dog after a bath.

"You survived," he stated, pretending to be surprised.

"Or I'm a ghost," she teased, reaching out and stroking his face as he affectionately leaned down and sniffed her.

"You smell like mossy water and nail polish," Lunis observed.

She nodded. "That seems about right."

"I'm certain you're the only dragonrider to wear such a combination of scents."

"I have to know, what is it you were going to warn me not to do when I was at the Peters'," she said, holding up the book Lunis would have already known she'd successfully secured. "I must never what?"

He blinked at her, his blue eyes full of the ancient wisdom and confidence she loved. "In true Sophia fashion, you did exactly what

133

you weren't supposed to, but somehow it worked in your favor. A man would have gone in there and battled that ghost. You knew he could touch you, and using magic, you could have destroyed him, banishing him from this Earth."

"But then his soul—"

Lunis nodded. "Would have been lost forever. You saved him. You rewrote the past."

"I get that he was bad," Sophia reasoned. "He broke when he lost all his wealth. He should have never done that, but I wanted him and his family to have a second chance. A way to do things right."

"You're not supposed to change the past of a ghost," Lunis explained. "I was going to tell you that from the collective conscious-ness of the dragons. According to my ancestors, you must never try to save a ghost. They have to figure things out on their own or be condemned to repeat the past."

Sophia shrank back and shook her head. "So we're just supposed to allow others to suffer, even if there's a way to save them?"

"Are you asking my ancestors or me?" Lunis questioned.

"Both," she answered.

"I believe we have a social responsibility to help one another," he explained. "I like that you offered Luther Peters an option, somewhat rewriting history. It stopped the cycle he was perpetually locked in and would have been for all of time, I believe. He thought he was doomed and kept reliving the reality he thought couldn't be any other way."

"But…" Sophia began, sensing there was a flip side to this coin.

"The dragons would say he was meant to be locked in that reality," Lunis told her, tilting his head back and forth as he considered this idea. "They would have thought it was his punishment to be trapped in the doom he'd created."

"But so were his wife and child," Sophia argued.

Lunis nodded. "I agree, and that's why I'm glad you didn't hear my advice, and you did things your own way. Also, I believe in second chances. I believe in ridding this world of evil through forgiveness. You gave that to Luther, and now his property can be used once more.

His haunting has stopped. All because you did what most wouldn't have. Most would have gone by the book and got out of there, but Sophia never takes the easy way out. You truly want what's best even when it puts you in peril."

She shrugged and looked down at the book full of her father's wisdom. "I think I just inherited this tendency from amazing people."

Lunis' head glided down, affectionately rubbing against Sophia's. "I think you undervalue who you are at your core regardless of where you came from."

"Maybe," she offered, running her hands over the leather-bound book.

"It was him, Sophia," Lunis said, a knowing in his eyes when she looked up at him. "I know it's hard to understand and even harder to explain, but I believe your father found a way to communicate with you when you were in the Peters' house."

She let out a weighty breath. Of course, Lunis knew she'd been doubting that part of the experience. She wanted to believe her father had been there in some capacity, that he'd led her. Spoken through her. Saved her. Yet, it was like holding onto the person and how could she ever let him go if she believed he could help her from the grave?

"How…" she asked, a strange hope in her eyes.

He indicated the book in her hands. "Remnants of a soul attach themselves to many different objects. It wasn't him, but also it was. The essence of him. Life is mysterious like that. You can't rely on your father ever coming back, but you can count on his wisdom and guidance being forever a part of your life if you're open to hearing it."

Sophia smiled up at her dragon. "I'll always be open to it."

CHAPTER THIRTY-ONE

F lipping through the pages of Theodore Beaufont's book was like having a conversation with the man himself. All her life, Sophia's siblings had worked their father's phrases into lessons, sharing tidbits of the wisdom he'd offered to them. Those quotes had stuck with Sophia, but not like reading the actual handwritten words of the man himself.

She felt like she was sitting across from him at the dining table as her eyes ran over one of the quotes scribbled across the side of a page: "It's healthy to have a devil's advocate."

Sophia looked up, her eyes on the windows running the length of the dining hall. She didn't often take afternoon tea since she was usually out of the Castle during that time and never really had the opportunity for such things. After her last adventure, she really needed the break. And she was waiting on information from Mae Ling on where she'd find the monster guarding Papa Creola's token. That gave her the perfect opportunity to flip through her father's book, memorizing the pages before she gifted it to Liv and Clark.

She could only imagine how much they'd value the book, having a much more distinctive memory of Theodore Beaufont.

Sophia flipped a page, amazed by how she could see the way her father worked, based on his notes. He'd written horizontally all over the pages, filling up each line. Then it was wrapped around the sides vertically, crammed into the margins. His penmanship was always clear, as were his ideas, giving her something to think about.

She read one such phrase that gave her pause, "The way we do things is almost more important than the things we do."

"You look like you're time-traveling," Mahkah said, striding into the dining hall, his hair windswept and his clothes covered in mud.

Sophia glanced up, surprised to find another rider taking tea. "Oh, how astute of you. I guess I am." She closed the book. "I found a diary kept by my father. It has many of his words of wisdom in it and makes me feel like he's here."

Mahkah took the seat opposite Sophia as Ainsley entered, carrying a tray of sandwiches, chocolate-filled croissants, and scones.

"Looks like you have company after all," the housekeeper said, setting the tiered tray down beside the pair. She snapped her fingers and a teacup and saucer appeared in front of Mahkah. "Who wants brandy in their tea today?"

Mahkah offered her a polite smile. "I'm good, but thanks."

"S. Beaufont?" Ainsley asked with an expectant expression.

Sophia smiled too. "I'm also fine."

Ainsley sighed. "You all are a bunch of goodie-goods. I should have gone to work for that brood of vampires when they inquired about my services."

She hustled back to the kitchen before Sophia could inquire into these vampires. They were supposed to be extinct. One coven popped up recently, but Liv took them out. There was always a concern vampirism would surface again, seeking to take over the world, but hopefully not with the House of Fourteen properly policing magic once more.

"So this book…" Mahkah indicated the leather-bound volume. "Do you want to share any of your father's words of wisdom?"

Sophia smiled, absolutely wanting to share. She flipped it open randomly and found a passage that spoke to her. "Here, he talks about how magic is an endless artform."

Mahkah poured himself some tea and smiled appreciatively. "Yes, I could agree with that. You can spend a whole life studying it, a lifetime as long as a dragonrider's, and still not even completely understand it. Your father was obviously a wise man."

"He is...well, he was...or wherever he is, I guess still is in some regards," Sophia offered. For the first time in her life, she didn't feel like people were really gone when they died. Somehow, they could hold onto parts of this Earth, offering their wisdom or love or guidance when they wanted. Or they could haunt, spreading evil. There were options, Sophia had learned.

"He's gone," Mahkah stated, seeming to understand. "I'm sorry. I just thought since you are so young, your parents would still be on this Earth."

Sophia took a sip of her tea. "You'd think, but most of the Beaufonts have perished fighting for justice. I think we are bound to that mission, and in a way, it's cursed us, nearly erasing our name."

"I think anyone who upholds justice will face dangers, but that's a legacy that ensures you live longer in the hearts of those you saved," Mahkah thoughtfully offered.

"I want to believe that's true, but it's hard knowing so many who I've loved have been lost," Sophia said, finding herself surprised to be sharing this with Mahkah. He was such a stoic type. Quiet and reserved, but when he spoke, it got Sophia's attention. She inherently liked the man who was the current expert on dragon riding and care. He never said much, but when he did, it was strangely profound.

Glancing down at the book, Sophia smiled. She'd found another of her father's lines that spoke to her.

"What is it?" Mahkah asked, seeing the interest on her face.

"I think I like this one," she said, reading from the text. "'The best way to face fears is to prepare for them.'"

Mahkah nodded. "It's the opposite of the head-in-the-sand approach."

Sophia was about to reply when her phone rang in her pocket. Surprised anyone was calling her, she withdrew it and was equally surprised by who the call was from.

"Mae Ling?" Sophia asked, holding the phone to her ear.

"Yes, dear," her fairy godmother said on the other end of the line.

"Have you determined where the—" Sophia's eyes flicked to Mahkah, who wasn't hiding his curiosity as he eavesdropped. Deciding she didn't mind, Sophia cleared her throat. "Where the monster is guarding the thing?"

"I haven't, my child," Mae answered. "However, the answer lies in your hands."

Sophia's eyes darted from side to side, trying to understand what the mysterious woman meant. "Huh?"

"I mean that literally," Mae stated.

Pulling the phone away from her ear, Sophia looked at it, expecting a message to be scrolling across it. There was nothing new there, just the wallpaper of Sophia with Clark and Liv standing arm and arm.

"I meant the other hand," Mae said.

Sophia put the phone back to her ear and looked down at her other hand, which held her father's book. "You mean the answer to where to find Papa Creola's monster is in my father's book?"

"Yes, that's exactly what I mean, dear," Mae said, sounding satisfied. "I can tell you what page, but if you'd rather find it on your own..."

"No, tell me," Sophia encouraged. She wanted to read every word in the book, but time was important, and she'd already spent a lot of it on side missions. It would be best if she got to the next mission sooner rather than later.

"It's on page one-twenty-six," Mae Ling stated.

"But the pages aren't numbered," Sophia argued.

"And yet, I'm certain you know how to count," Mae said and then hung up.

Sophia placed the phone on the table and began flipping through the pages, counting.

"That sounded like an important call," Mahkah observed casually.

"It was," Sophia answered, paging through the book, nearing the one-twenty-six.

"And you're searching for a monster," Mahkah continued. "What is it guarding?"

She flipped up her head. "Why does it have to be guarding something?"

"Well, why else would you go after a monster that you don't know where it's located?" Mahkah questioned. "If it was creating havoc, then you'd know where it was and go after it to protect. But since you don't, then that means it's protecting something."

Sophia pursed her lips to the side, strangely impressed by the dragonrider's logic. "Yeah, it's guarding something. I can't really go into details."

"I figured that much," Mahkah stated, taking a sip of tea. "As long as it's not a dragon, I have no interest."

On page one-twenty-six, Sophia read her father's notes:

The beast who guards the save point is none other than Hydra—the dragon with seven heads and a spirit that would be hard for one magician alone to defeat.

CHAPTER THIRTY-TWO

Sophia nearly choked even though she wasn't even drinking tea right then. Mahkah noticed her attempts to gasp for breath and leaned forward, curiosity written on his usually placid face.

"Everything okay?" he asked.

She glanced up from her father's book, weighing her options. "Dragons, you say?"

He nodded, tilting his head to the side. "Is the creature you're going after a dragon?"

She checked the book again. "Well, sort of."

"What do you mean?" he asked.

"Well, it appears to be a mythical type of dragon," she explained. "Not the kind we're used to or anything."

Mahkah's eyebrows raised. "You've got my attention."

Sophia could go after Hydra with Lunis and maybe be successful. Getting the token was important, and she didn't want anyone else to know about her mission to find *The Complete History of Dragonriders*. She didn't know anyone who talked or inquired less than Mahkah, and she also didn't know anyone who had a better knowledge of dragons. If she was honest, trying to defeat Hydra, the dragon with seven heads that grew back after being severed, scared her worse than any other task she'd encountered thus far.

"What would you think about going with me to fight the legendary Hydra?" Sophia asked quietly. Her eyes darted around; she was afraid they might be overheard.

Mahkah stood at once, his hands pinned on the table. It was rare to see the enthusiasm in his eyes, almost making him bounce up and down. "I'll go. Let's do it."

Sophia drew in a breath and sat back in her seat. "First, we have to talk."

Mahkah got control of himself and took his chair once more. "Of course. What is it?"

He was still vibrating with excitement.

"I have to recover something from Hydra, and you can't ask about it," she said carefully, watching his micro-expressions for signs he might resist.

He didn't, though. Instead, Mahkah agreed at once, nodding. "I figured as much. You have a mission. Hydra is a part of it. I'll help. No questions as long as you can guarantee whatever this mission is about only helps the world at large."

Sophia thought for a moment. "I believe so. I mean, it should further our purpose as dragonriders."

"Okay, then there will be no questions from me," Mahkah promised. "I trust you, Sophia."

"The other part," Sophia began slowly, sensing this was going to be the rub. "Is that we have to kill Hydra."

And there it was, Sophia realized, watching as Mahkah's excitement faded immediately. "But it's…"

"An ancient and powerful mythical creature," she completed his sentence. "I get that. And I know you probably value it."

"I didn't even know it was still alive," he stated.

She nodded. "It's working for Papa Creola, but he wants me to relieve it of its duties. In doing so, I have to defeat it."

"So, regardless of whether I accompany you…"

Sophia drew in a breath. "I'm going to try to kill it whether you help me or not."

He nodded. "I thought so. Well, then I'd rather see this incredible creature, even if it's only in death."

Sophia leaned forward, a smile on her face. "Now, I don't suppose you have any ideas about how to actually kill the thing, do you?"

"I absolutely do," Mahkah affirmed, sharing a victorious smile.

"You do, what?" Hiker asked, standing squarely in the archway to the dining hall with a skeptical expression on his face.

CHAPTER THIRTY-THREE

S ophia tensed. Hiker was the last person she wanted to see right then. She stuffed a scone into her mouth and muttered through the crumbs, "Nofing, sir."

"Well, I'm glad to see you both at the Castle," Hiker said, coming into the room and eyeing the assortment of goodies on the tray. "If you're taking tea, it means you're ready for a mission."

Sophia grimaced. This was going to be harder than she'd expected. "Actually, sir, I just stopped off here to refuel and recharge."

He lowered his chin and regarded her with a long, cold stare. "You're not ready for an adjudicator mission, then?"

"I want to be," she said, grinning widely. "But I have to go and do a thing first."

"A thing for Papa Creola, right?" Hiker asked as Ainsley buzzed out of the kitchen, holding an empty tray.

"Oh, sir, are you taking tea too? This is like Christmas at the Castle," Ainsley babbled excitedly.

"We're not having Christmas at the Castle," Hiker grumbled. "And no, I'm not taking tea. I simply noticed two of my dragonriders slacking off in here when they don't have the time or inclination for missions."

"But I made scones," Ainsley said. "Actually, I didn't. The Castle did. But I chatted with it the entire time. Therefore, I feel like I made them."

"Would you leave us be?" Hiker asked the housekeeper.

"My name is Ainsley," the shapeshifter elf said, rolling her eyes and giving Sophia a look. "You'd think he'd know that by now, but I don't think he'd recognize me if I slapped him in the face. Maybe I should go and test the theory."

"You can try," Hiker said, a warning in his voice.

Ainsley sped off for the kitchen. "First time I have a few down for afternoon tea, and none of them are being fun about it. No pinkies in the air. No pleasant talk about the moor. No giggling with mouths covered. Just dirty dragonriders, smelling up the place."

Hiker blanched, discreetly lifting his arm and sniffing. "I'm not dirty."

"Nor am I, sir," Mahkah agreed.

Sophia shrugged, smelling her gardenia soap still fresh on her skin. "You both could be a bit cleaner, but whatever."

"You are off on another mission for Father Time, is that right?" Hiker asked, his hands on his hips and his light-colored eyes narrowed on Sophia.

She nodded. "It shouldn't be that big an ordeal. I promise when I return, I'll be ready to take on anything you want."

"It might be for you to pack your bags and find another place," Hiker threatened.

Sophia, used to his threats, picked up her tea and took a sip.

The leader of the Dragon Elite turned his attention to Mahkah. "Well, it is a good thing I can count on my most reliable dragonrider to take on missions for me, or this place would go to hell."

Mahkah stood at once, his hands clapping to his side as he bowed slightly to Hiker. "Sir, I regret to inform you, but I want to accompany Sophia on her mission."

The growl that escaped Hiker's mouth felt large enough to blow Sophia's hair off her shoulders.

"Is this a joke?" Hiker asked Mahkah.

"No, sir," he answered. "It's just, this is a great opportunity, and I'd really like to be part of it."

Hiker turned his seething gaze on Sophia. "You're taking one of my riders on one of your Papa Creola missions? Do you wish to tell me anything now?"

"I don't know the details, sir," Mahkah answered for Sophia. "Just that there are monsters that interest me very much. I hope it's okay."

Sophia gave Hiker an apologetic smile when he rotated to face her again.

"Sooner or later, Sophia," Hiker began, "you're going to have to tell me what you're up to."

"I'd be happy to," Sophia sang, taking a bite of her scone and thinking of holding *The Complete History of Dragonriders* and relishing in the look on Hiker's face.

"Okay," he said, drawing out the word. "You two, do what you must. It is in your favor that I'm still researching and don't have any real pressing matters at the moment."

He looked around the empty hall, undeniable regret in his eyes. "I do look forward to when...*if* we recover from this mess."

Sophia couldn't help but feel the sadness. The dragonriders were almost extinct. They had lost their way, and their leader's confidence was waning.

She wanted to believe this would pass, but she had no way to confirm that. All Sophia Beaufont had was an unwavering spirit and the desire to do everything possible to bring the Dragon Elite into a new era.

And for some strange, irresistible reason, she firmly believed it started with finding *The Complete History of Dragonriders*.

CHAPTER THIRTY-FOUR

The location in Sophia's father's book wasn't specific, but according to Mahkah, it didn't have to be.

"There is only one Mountain of Truth," he stated, standing next to Tala. The waning sunlight streaked across the Expanse, making her brown scales appear almost red.

"I don't understand," Sophia asked, brushing her hand over Lunis. "You know where this Mountain of Truth is?"

Mahkah nodded, mounting his dragon. "Yeah, but portaling there will be a little different."

"Why?" Sophia joked, laughing. "Is it on a different planet?"

With a serious expression, Mahkah nodded. "Actually, yes. Oriceran is absolutely a different planet."

"Wait." Sophia tensed. "Are you serious? I can't portal to a different planet."

"Think of it as a different realm," Mahkah amended. "Pretty much the same planet, just a different space and time. Father Time sent you on this mission, right?"

Sophia nodded. "Well, yeah."

"And he knew you'd have to find Hydra?" he questioned.

"Well, yeah," she repeated.

"Then you can get to the Mountain of Truth," he confirmed. "I doubt I could, but I'm thinking he's granted you that portal capability if he knew you'd need to find whatever Hydra is guarding."

"Yeah, but Papa Creola couldn't even tell me where the location was," Sophia argued.

Mahkah grabbed the reins on Tala. "Couldn't or wouldn't?"

Sophia thought for a moment. The way everything had lined up with her finding her father's book with the location of Hydra being recorded in there was a bit coincidental. "Yeah, he probably knew and was just leading me on this goose chase. Do you think I'll be able to open the portal to this Mountain of Truth?"

Mahkah held out a hand, almost like presenting. "Only one way to find out. I'll follow."

"Do you think we can breathe on this Oriceran?" Sophia asked, preparing to ride Lunis.

"I think so," Mahkah said, holding back a laugh.

"Anything else you can offer about this place that I should know?" Sophia asked.

"I've never been there, obviously," Mahkah offered. "I hear the queen who is in charge is very kind, her kingdom full of peace, and all the chaos she didn't want to deal with is hiding on the peaks of this mountain which is not at all what it seems, full of monsters, tricksters, and treasures."

Sophia grabbed her own reins, giving Lunis a look of uncertainty. "Sounds about like every other Tuesday. I say we make haste."

CHAPTER THIRTY-FIVE

The air always felt different outside the Barrier. Not like it was colder, but denser, like everything inside the Gullington was lighter.

Sophia knew what she had to do, but she also had a great deal of doubt surrounding it. How was it she could create a portal to another planet?

You're riding a dragon, and you doubt you can open a portal to another planet? Lunis asked in her head.

Well, you are *from Earth,* Sophia argued.

As far as you know, he countered.

Ha-ha, she said with no humor. *It's just strange I should be able to do this. I didn't even know this Oriceran place existed.*

Most don't, he said.

Wait, you know about it?

There is limited information in the collective consciousness about the planet, he explained. *Apparently, Earth and Oriceran are connected through magic.*

Awesome explanation, Sophia said with zero enthusiasm. *Just chalk it all up to magic, and no other details are needed.*

What do you want, science? Lunis snorted with laughter in her head. *Again, you're riding a dragon. Oh, and you're talking to one too...in your head.*

Because of this connection between Earth and Oriceran, I can open a portal there, you think, Sophia questioned.

Only one way to find out, but yes, it makes sense Papa Creola granted you this gift for your purposes, Lunis assured her.

He could have told me, she grumbled.

When have you ever known the man to be forthcoming with information?

She sighed. *I'm holding out hope that being an elf will change him.*

I don't think you can stick around on Oriceran long, Lunis mused. *I believe it would cause an imbalance of sorts. The same is true for going to other time dimensions, from my recollection.*

So when I get this token and visit the save point in the past, I shouldn't stick around in the past, Sophia asked.

I wouldn't, Lunis answered. *So you shouldn't. We are always meant for our own time and place of origin.*

What if Liv didn't help mortals to see magic and everything did have to be reset to before the Great War? Sophia questioned.

Then we would have all gone back to that point, Lunis explained. *It would have been a collective restart, and therefore it would be fine. When you find the token, then just you will be traveling into the past. You have to do what you need to do to find the book, but then you must leave. Otherwise, I think you could cause problems.*

I mean, Sophia said, thinking over the idea, *I should at least browse around and see how things were.*

I think in small doses, it will be fine, Lunis stated. *Nothing is going to happen until you open that portal to Oriceran.*

Sophia realized she'd been stalling long enough. They were well past the Barrier now. She gave Mahkah a tentative expression.

He nodded in confirmation, his look seeming to say, "You can do this."

Gulping, Sophia lifted her hand and focused on the Mountain of Truth. A hundred yards ahead of them, a portal opened, shimmering blue and green around the edges.

Sophia didn't know where it would take them, if it would work or what they would find on Oriceran. She was growing accustomed to trusting her instinct and embracing risks.

She held her breath as they slipped through the portal.

CHAPTER THIRTY-SIX

The air, wherever they were, was a stark contrast to Scotland. It smelled of smoke and ash and was thick with humidity.

The portal had stuck them in a cloud of pinks and greens. Sophia coughed, at first worried she couldn't breathe on this strange planet. After sucking in a sip of air, she realized she could breathe, but it did feel different than what she was used to.

The clouds obscured the terrain below them, but in the distance, Sophia noticed a peak edging out of the swirling pinks and greens. She glanced back, relieved to find Mahkah riding behind her, a cautious expression on his face.

She slowed Lunis to allow Mahkah to ride up beside her. Before they had left, he'd briefly told her how they would defeat Hydra. She knew from the legends Hydra had seven heads. When sliced off, the heads grew back. The way to defeat the monster was to cut off the head and seal it with dragon fire instantly before it could regrow. Mahkah had advised that Sophia be in charge of slicing off the heads, and he and Tala would seal them. It seemed like such a straightforward plan, Sophia felt confident they would defeat the beast in no time.

The wings of the dragons pushed the thick clouds away, making the mountain more visible. It was mostly covered in rocks and a strange bluish gaseous substance.

Mahkah pointed to the peak ahead, his intent obvious to Sophia. They needed to land.

The rocky top rose sharply, with a flat platform next to a huge opening. It seemed like the most obvious place for Hydra.

Ready for this, Lunis said, instantly responding to Sophia's intention to land on the other side of the flat land, opposite the cave.

She didn't have to respond. Lunis could feel both her hesitation and her confirmation. It was time to draw out the seven-headed dragon.

Without making a single noise or disrupting the gravel underfoot, Lunis landed on the edge of the flat land. Mahkah and Tala slipped down and took the spot next to Sophia.

She lifted her chin and surveyed the area. Even if they had a plan, this was going to be a deadly challenge. She guessed the token was in the cave somewhere. First, they'd need to lure Hydra out. Then slaughter it. Only after, would she be able to take what she needed to complete this challenge.

She glanced at Mahkah, grateful he was with her on this mission. Sophia could think of few as resilient and competent as the three-hundred-year-old dragonrider next to her.

That was why the strange expression that crossed his face made her pause.

"What is it?" she asked in a whisper, knowing he could hear her easily due to his enhanced senses.

A goofy giggle fell out of his mouth. "It smells like a fart."

CHAPTER THIRTY-SEVEN

"What?" Sophia asked, wondering if her enhanced senses were failing her and she had misheard Mahkah.

He slid down from the back of his dragon, nose pinched, and waved his hand in front of his face. "Seriously, what did Hydra eat?"

"What the hell is going on?" Sophia asked Lunis.

I'm not sure yet, he said as he studied Tala, who was blinking rapidly like there was something in her eyes.

"Mahkah, are you okay?" Sophia asked, sliding down Lunis' back and searching her friend's eyes. They were definitely different-looking, but she wasn't sure how.

"I think the seven-headed dragon had too much of that Taco Ring you talk about," he said, still waving and trying to clear the air.

"Do you mean Taco Bell?" she asked, wondering why this was even a conversation.

"Yeah, remember when you got us that from Uber Eats and Evan ate that burrito the size of his face, and then—"

"I don't need to relive that story," she interrupted. "You don't seem like yourself. Are you all right?"

He scrunched his nose. "I'd be a lot better if a wind would blow that smell out of here. Tala, make a fan." He turned to his dragon, who had her eyes closed like she had decided this was a good time to take an impromptu nap.

The air on top of the Mountain of Truth was pretty smelly, but never in a million years would Mahkah be the one to point this out. He would never mention it, just stare placidly at the cave with their assignment, preparing to complete the task. The person before Sophia didn't seem at all like the Mahkah she knew as he wiggled his finger into his ear and then pulled it out, eyeing the ear wax he'd unearthed.

He's regressed, Lunis stated in Sophia's head.

She turned to her dragon, her eyes wide. *Regressed? Like, he is a young child?*

Yes, it appears so, Lunis answered. *Tala is trying to find a way to remedy the situation. Something on the Mountain of Truth is causing him to have the maturity of a child.*

Why isn't it affecting me? Sophia questioned

He lowered his head and blinked into her eyes. *Because you, my love, are still young, and even when you were a child, you never had a moment of immaturity.*

That made sense to Sophia. Clark always said she was born forty years old, which was probably one of the reasons she was the youngest rider to magnetize to a dragon.

So how do we fix him, Sophia asked. *I can't have a ten-year-old boy helping me slaughter Hydra. He'll be giggling the whole time and making fart jokes.*

Tala thinks she's found a solution, Lunis offered.

Sophia perked up, grateful they had a way to fix Mahkah. *Okay, what is it?*

The look of remorse that crossed Lunis' face was unmistakable. *You need to punch him in the face.*

CHAPTER THIRTY-EIGHT

W*ait, what,* Sophia questioned, again wondering if she was mishearing things. Lunis was in her head, so that wasn't likely. She felt his thoughts as much as she heard them.

I need to punch him in the face, Sophia asked.

Or you can kick him in the head, Lunis offered. *It's really up to you.*

But why?

The end result is you need to knock him out, Lunis answered.

Sophia watched as Mahkah pulled out his sword and ran his eyes over it. *Are you serious? Isn't there another way,* she asked her dragon.

"Neat-o!" Mahkah exclaimed. He put the tip of the sword in the dirt, laid his head on the hilt, and began circling it over and over, trying to make himself dizzy.

Well, Lunis began, also watching the spectacle. *You can leave him like he is and try to defeat Hydra, but I'm not sure how successful we'll be if we've got to babysit at the same time.*

Sophia watched as Mahkah dropped his sword and staggered away, looking like a drunk. "Oh, man. That was a killer ride. Soph, you got to try that."

"You do remember why we're here, right?" she asked him.

He teetered back and forth, looking like he might fall over. "I don't remember, but hey, want to race me toward the cave? Last one there is a rotten dragon's egg."

Mahkah started for the cave, foolishly leaving his sword lying on the ground behind him.

Sophia didn't grant herself a moment to think. She shot her right hand forward as if she were throwing a baseball, and a cosmic ball of light sprang from her fingertips and headed in Mahkah's direction. He was weaving back and forth so much she worried her attack wasn't going to connect with him, but he darted back into its path just as it was about to pass him. The ball hit his shins, knocking his legs out from under him.

He rolled over, coughing up dirt with an offended expression on his face. "What did you do that for?"

Sophia shook her head as she walked over to him. "To save your ass, you toddler."

"I know you are, but what am I?" he spat back.

She shook her head again, realizing she was going to have to assault her friend. He couldn't stay in this immature form and be of any help to her. Unfortunately, she didn't think a spell would work to make him unconscious. He needed to be reset, and the best, most effective way to do that was a good old-fashioned blow.

Still sitting on his tailbone, he extended a hand to Sophia as she approached. "Help a brother up, would you?"

"Sure," she said, grabbing his hand and hauling him up. When he was on his feet, Sophia powered up her other fist, using a combat spell Wilder had taught her. "Sorry about this, brother." She brought her hand around and threw it straight into Mahkah's face, knocking him to the ground.

CHAPTER THIRTY-NINE

"Well, I feel horrible," Sophia muttered, shaking her hand, which was already throbbing.

Tala approached Sophia, shaking her large head. *You did what you had to do. Don't feel bad.*

"No, his face is hard as a rock," she corrected, still trying to dispel the pain in her fingers.

Good thinking combining the combat spell with the punch, Lunis said, having taken his place on the other side of Sophia.

She nodded appreciatively. "I only wanted to hit him once."

Lying face-down on the ground, Mahkah was mostly motionless except for the gentle movement of his back as he continued to breathe, to Sophia's relief.

Well, it appears to have worked, Tala stated, watching her rider.

"You mean, he'll be his usual mature self when he awakes?" Sophia asked.

The dragon shook her head. *I'm not sure. Our psychic link hasn't returned yet, but you knocked him out, and that was the goal. We just have to wait and hope that when he comes to, he's back to normal.*

"I wonder how long he'll be out?" Sophia mused.

It's hard to say, Tala replied in a speculative tone.

The ground under their feet rumbled. Rocks cascaded down from the wall around the cave. A roar filled the air and sent a blast of wind through Sophia's hair.

Her eyes widened in horror. "Wake up, Mahkah! Hydra is coming!"

CHAPTER FORTY

The ground continued to quake. If the opening to the cave was any indication, Hydra was huge. If that hadn't given it away, the beast was knocking her off-balance with each stomp of its feet. She wasn't certain but guessed the monster had just awoken from a nap and wasn't happy about it.

Rushing to her friend, Sophia turned Mahkah over and shook his shoulders as she frantically looked toward the cave opening, where rocks continued to rain down.

"Come on, Mahkah!" she urged. She wondered if a spell would work. It could backfire, though, and just keep him asleep. Anything to do with sleeping and waking was a mixed bag when it came to magic.

Desperate, she whipped her head up and glared at Tala. "Can you help?"

I can take him away if we need me to, she offered.

We need his help to defeat Hydra, Lunis argued. He came around to stand between Sophia and the cave with a protective glint in his eyes. He unfolded his wings, making him appear larger.

"Well, right now, he's useless," Sophia complained. She continued to shake the limp figure of Mahkah.

Try hitting him again, Lunis suggested.

"That's how I got in this position," Sophia argued.

The first dragon head materialized in the opening of the cave, nearly making Sophia faint in fright. The sheer size of the head was equal to Lunis' body. Hydra was huge.

The head opened its mouth, showing two rows of needle-sharp teeth and blood-red eyes. It let out a vicious roar that sent a wind across the plains, nearly knocking Sophia on her butt.

Not hesitating, she brought the palm of her hand across Mahkah's face and slapped him hard.

He shot upright, throwing an arm up to defend himself. Sophia backed away immediately and gave him a tentative expression as he shook his head, appearing disoriented. She still didn't know if he was back to normal yet.

Inclining forward, she looked for clues. "Mahkah, are you okay?"

He blinked to try to clear the confusion from his head and pressed his eyes shut before shaking his head. "Yeah, I think so," he said in his usual calm tone. Running his hand over his jaw, he worked it back and forth. "What hit me? I don't remember a thing."

"We will discuss that later," Sophia said, backing up for the sword Mahkah had dropped in the dirt. Not taking her eyes off the entrance to the cave, she reached back and grabbed the hilt and tossed it in Mahkah's direction. Using the reflexes she was used to seeing him display, he grabbed the sword at once. "Right now, we are going to have to act fast. A sleeping dragon has just been woken, and he's pissed."

Mahkah turned to follow Sophia's line of sight just as the other six heads swam into view, their eyes full of hatred and their mouths salivating with intense hunger.

CHAPTER FORTY-ONE

Hydra was absolutely massive as he stalked out of the cave, his seven heads swimming around his round body.

There was a brief moment where Sophia considered abandoning this whole token thing and letting *The Complete History of Dragonriders* book go. However, Beaufonts didn't back down from challenges. They didn't turn tail in the face of danger. If they did, the world would be a different place, and far worse off. Fear might be running rampant through Sophia's every muscle, but she was going to face Hydra, no matter what.

Mahkah's eyes were wide as he looked over his shoulder at Sophia with an expression on his face that seemed to say, "What the hell have you gotten me into?"

At least he was back to his old self. Sophia couldn't think of anyone she'd rather have by her side to take this giant creature down.

Maybe Hydra was always the angry type. Maybe the lack of visitors made it so he didn't know how to host very well. Or maybe it was because he sensed Sophia and Mahkah were there to end him and take his job, and he was offended. For whatever reason, all seven of his heads pointed in their direction, their necks stretching out as their eyes burned violently red. In unison, they all opened their mouths, and murderous roars ripped from them.

Sophia was certain she would never be able to hear properly again. Her hair whipped back from her face, and her boots inched back slightly from the ferocious wind that spilled from the seven mouths.

"I don't think he can breathe fire," Mahkah stated, backing up even with Sophia.

"Well, that's a plus," Sophia said as she studied the mostly black dragon and his rippling muscles in the waning Oriceran sunlight. What looked like lava streaks ran over his sides and underbelly.

"Yes, but it means his bite is venomous," Mahkah explained.

"It's always something," Sophia said with a sigh, looking at the sky. "Angels, you can't just let us have the upper hand, can you?"

As Hydra stomped forward, Sophia's teeth rattled in her head as if she were experiencing a major earthquake. The monster appeared more like a serpent than a dragon, with webbed spikes running the length of his back. Sophia hadn't spotted his tail yet but could only imagine it was another deadly device the beast could employ in his favor.

"I would say we have no upper hand whatsoever," Mahkah said, his voice vibrating. "But it's probably because of the angels we're still alive."

Are we going to kill that thing anytime soon? Lunis asked casually.

She whipped around and raced for her dragon. In a series of swift and efficient movements, Sophia grabbed the reins and threw herself into the saddle.

With a gradual rise of her hands and silent intention, Lunis rose, following Sophia's lead. Beside them, Mahkah had mounted Tala and taken her to the left as Sophia veered to the right.

"You know what to do!" Mahkah yelled loud enough that Sophia heard him over the falling rock and thundering of the ground.

"Don't die," she replied and pulled Inexorabilis from its sheath. Flying in and cutting off the heads of this monster had seemed a lot easier in theory. With so many heads swimming around and the potential of a deadly bite, she wasn't certain she could get in close enough for the job, although she had to try.

Cutting through the thick neck would take effort, too. It was easily the length of her sword, which meant the attacks would have to be precise. That wasn't something Sophia figured she'd have the luxury of, with chaos circling all around her.

As Lunis flew closer to Hydra, Sophia's pulse quickened. She was certain few people would willingly fly toward this beast when the option to escape was available. Mahkah flew in on the other side, darting around heads as they tried to snap at him. Tala flew like a leaf in the wind, graceful and light. She easily wove in and around the heads, negotiating them like she could anticipate their movements.

Lunis, on the other hand, wasn't as nimble, nearly running into one of the heads and having to duck at the last moment. That sent Sophia off him, and she fell to the ground.

She rolled over at once and jumped to her feet, her sword still in her hands as one of the heads lowered down, its nostrils breathing hot air onto her as its red eyes narrowed. There was pure hostility in its gaze, and she tensed as another head lowered at her back.

Sophia was trapped.

CHAPTER FORTY-TWO

The head in front of Sophia didn't grant her much room as it moved in closer, obviously not acquainted with personal space rules.

The glow of its red eyes was so bright up close, they made Sophia's own eyes ache and water. Its hot breath casting down on her made her sweat, and the head, which she named Terry, smelled like rotten meat.

Holding her breath, Sophia assessed her options.

There weren't any.

With Terry literally breathing down on her and Krysta up on her junk from behind, it was impossible to use magic. Her sword was in her hand, but swinging it was impossible.

Slimy green drool dripped from Terry's yellow teeth as she sneered at Sophia, sniffing her as if to decide what kind of condiments to put on her snack.

Without warning, the head shot up. Krysta, at Sophia's back, knocked into her, emptying her of breath. Sophia allowed the momentum to send her forward and threw herself into a front roll. She barely made out from between the heads, but Sophia didn't stop running until something blue caught her eyes.

As Lunis ran past her, Sophia dove and grabbed the saddle, pulling herself onto his back swiftly. He rose into the air, flying away from the beast, which was screaming like a spoiled toddler.

As Sophia tried to catch her breath and ready her sword, Lunis swerved around, taking them back toward Hydra.

Thanks for the save, she said in his head.

Thank Mahkah and Tala later, he replied and then added, *if we survive this.*

Oh, Sophia said, watching as Mahkah and Tala ran interference, shooting fire and arrows at the monster. Mahkah appeared to have exchanged his sword for a bow and was rapidly sending attacks at the various heads, some shots sticking into the sides and others whizzing past them but still serving as a distraction as Sophia and Lunis worked to recover their position.

Girl names, huh? Lunis asked, a laugh in his voice. *When did you decide Hydra's heads were female?*

Well, maybe not all of them are, Sophia reasoned, her shoulders down low as she searched the turmoil they were about to reenter. *Maybe three or four of them are female and the rest male. I'm not sure why they have to be all one gender.*

Maybe because they share the same body, Lunis posed.

She shook her head. *This is the twenty-first century. Be open minded, would you?*

Why was the first one who nearly ate you for lunch Terry? Lunis sounded amused.

Because she reminded me of this girl I took classes with who stalked me, always making up rumors about how I cheated and that was why I aced all the tests.

Oh. And Krysta? he asked.

Did you see Dogface all up on my business, not even granting me an inch of breathing space? Sophia explained. *Some people just have no manners.*

And who is that one bobbing around separate from the others, begging for our attention? Lunis questioned, indicating one of the heads dancing around like a cobra coming out of a wicker basket. Maybe it was trying to mesmerize them, although its position away from the rest had put it in a compromising situation.

Sophia stood in the saddle and raised Inexorabilis. *That is Susan,* she stated. *And she wants us to make an example out of her.*

Cool, Lunis said casually. *First, though, may I suggest you magically enhance your blade to be larger?*

Sophia slowed her dragon's progress, momentarily thrown off by his idea. *That's a genius idea,* she stated and cast a spell that transformed Inexorabilis so it was slightly larger, hopefully making what she had to do easier. Thankfully, the larger size didn't make the blade heavier, but she did need two hands to hold it.

Susan bobbed around, seeming to taunt them as they neared.

Sophia caught Mahkah's attention and signaled to him she was about to do her part. He darted under the snapping jaws of Terry or Krysta, or maybe it was Carol or Keith.

It was difficult to stay balanced as Lunis swerved, feinting one way and then the other, trying to lure Susan, the lone head, away from the pack. That wasn't going to last for long, though, as Mahkah changed position, going on the offensive.

Sophia hit the bobbing head with a stunning spell, which she immediately knew wasn't going to last on the mythical creature. Susan's eyes momentarily glazed over, and it froze. It was obvious the beast was fighting the spell, and Sophia knew she had seconds to act before it broke free and did something unpredictable.

The only reason she didn't act when she was nearly in place was Mahkah was still booking it around the other heads, not quite in position.

The twitching of Susan's eyes was the first clue it was breaking out of the spell. The forked tongue that slipped through is yellow teeth was another clue. The rippling of the lava lines running up its neck was the final hint.

Now, Lunis encouraged, veering to the side.

Sophia raised the sword over her head as Lunis rose higher and brought Inexorabilis down hard and fast. It hesitated on the top of Susan's head, making her certain she'd fail, but she remembered to combine the effort with a combat spell—the same one she'd recently used on Mahkah—and to her relief, the blade slipped all the way through the meaty neck, severing the head.

It fell to the ground, smashing like a giant pumpkin and sending blood everywhere. From the neck, hot lava spewed as it shot around like an uncontrollable fire hose. Sophia and Lunis flew out of the way as Mahkah and Tala took over. The brown dragon opened its mouth, expertly following the dancing neck as she spat a neat stream of fire at the severed portion, seeking to cauterize it before the head grew back.

Sophia would have stayed to watch and help, but two large shadows crossed overhead, casting her in darkness.

Looking up, Sophia saw the eyes of the heads she was pretty certain were Terry and Krysta.

"Hey, ladies," she said meekly and held the reins tighter, preparing for her next move.

CHAPTER FORTY-THREE

The blast of fire that radiated from the severed neck sent the two female heads in opposite directions, allowing Sophia and Lunis an opportunity to escape.

Hydra was even more pissed than before as the other heads spiraled around, chomping on the thick Oriceran air and letting out vicious roars.

Mahkah had successfully cauterized the wound, which meant no new head would grow back. They still had six more heads, and if legend were to be believed, the job would get harder with each head because the beast would grow more desperate.

That means we need to be strategic, Sophia said in her head to Lunis.

That is your *middle name, isn't it*, he replied.

It should be, she told him, considering her options.

What about that repeat spell you've been practicing? Lunis suggested.

Sophia nearly barked a complaint but realized Lunis was right. She hadn't mastered the spell, not even close. It would require a great deal of power to fuel it, but it did make the most sense. The spell, if done correctly, would use one action and repeat them on all enemies.

You can do it, Lunis encouraged, flying so haphazardly it was almost making Sophia sick.

Well, it's worth a shot, she agreed, looking over her shoulder at Mahkah. He was back to flying around the thrusting heads. There was no time to communicate to him what she was planning. He would figure it out as soon as she tried it, whether or not she was successful.

And then he'd have to act fast. Sophia wouldn't be able to help since she'd probably be too depleted from the spell. There were so many things that could go wrong with a spell of this sort. It wasn't just the hope the spell took out all the enemies at once. There was also the concern that it had to target the right enemies and didn't go after one of her compatriots. Sophia had to be very deliberate and focus on the heads of Hydra and not confuse the spell with one of the two dragons darting around in the sky, or their riders.

She pulled in a breath, knowing timing was important. Hydra was still recovering from losing one head. Soon the half female and half male multi-headed dragon would be raving mad and doing everything possible to take out those posing a huge risk.

Which head? Lunis asked as Sophia stood on his back, once more raising Inexorabilis.

Sophia spied the strange eyes of the head lifted highest. Maybe it was the extra spark of mischief in the beast's eyes or that she had a lot more green slime dripping from her mouth. For whatever reason, Sophia instinctively knew it was Terry.

Take me up there, she stated. *I'm taking her out, and hopefully her brothers and sisters will fall at the same time.*

CHAPTER FORTY-FOUR

The one thing most fighters don't prepare for when in battle is the unexpected. How can one? How does one know what they won't expect?

Sophia had been taught how to fly by the very best, and thankfully, Mahkah was not too far away. When she and Lunis took off toward Terry and were caught in an updraft, she was grateful for the words he screamed across the space.

"Go with it!" Mahkah yelled. His words were partially obscured by the screeching wind.

It sought to tear them in two. If Lunis resisted or if Sophia tried to steer him in another direction, it would have taken them in two different directions and sent Lunis to the ground and Sophia into the air.

It was like jumping into a tornado, something no one in their right mind would do. If they found themselves inside the spinning vortex, they'd look for the first way out. Sophia and Lunis knew to go with it and embrace the chaos. So Lunis folded his wings in to make himself as compact as possible and allowed the wind to send them upward in a mass of confusion and uncontrollable power.

Sophia wasn't sure how long it went on. She felt like she was plummeting through the Earth's ozone at an insane rate, about to blast into pieces when they halted suddenly, suspended in the air, a strange cosmic force around them.

For a few seconds, everything moved in slow motion. Most things stopped around them. Sophia looked sideways at Lunis. He blinked at her.

Spots of radiant light dotted all around them, making the tiniest details suddenly visible. That's when Sophia realized she wasn't on her dragon. The panic hit her mind at the same moment everything went back into hyperspeed. Sophia was suddenly falling fast back toward the Earth. The vortex was gone. Lunis was a strange mass of ungraceful movements as he freefell and tried to get himself in the right position for flight. The ground was quickly approaching, its hard surface promising death.

Just when Sophia was prepared to take the coward's way out and close her eyes, Lunis rotated so his wings were upright and his underbelly faced the ground. Then he shot forward, diving under Sophia and knocking her in the face, head, and stomach but managing to glide under her until she was back in the saddle once more.

Not missing a beat, he shot up to fly dangerously close to the neck of Terry, who was distracted by the strange vortex now spinning around her face. Her red eyes shot down at the last moment, but Sophia was already in place, her mouth quickly repeating the words of the most complex spell she'd ever used. Not only did it take a great deal of power, but Sophia had to quickly locate the other five heads. All of them were focused on Mahkah, who was running interference, knowing Sophia needed the distraction.

Sophia raised the giant sword and swung it, using solely her own muscle power since all her focus had to be on the repeating spell.

The expression of horror on Terry's face when the blade connected with its scales gave Sophia a pure moment of satisfaction. She brought the blade across while thinking of her contempt for bullies and wrongdoers and her desire to preside over justice. To her astonishment, the blade cut through cleaner than before, severing one of Hydra's heads and sending it tumbling nose over mouth to land with a splat.

Once more, everything slowed down. Sophia looked around at the other five heads, which had paused. She didn't know if the spell had worked or if she needed to come up with another strategy. Then she knew there couldn't be another approach because the spell, whether it had worked or not, had drained her magical reserves.

She slumped onto Lunis, finding it difficult to hold her head up. Her vision blurred. She desperately wanted to sleep right then. She would have fallen into a dreamless stupor if the screams around them hadn't woken her up.

There were murderous sounds as blood and lava shot out of the five necks after something invisible sliced through them and the heads tumbled to the ground.

Mahkah's astonishment at the sight was a beautiful thing, but he recovered quickly and started cauterizing the wounds before the necks could grow more heads. It had to be quick work, but he and Tala darted around, her shooting fire as the necks jerked around like a chicken with its head cut off. The reference nearly made Sophia laugh until she noticed one of the heads was still narrowly attached to the neck, hanging by a thin sliver of skin. She was about to race up to it and cut through it completely when the skin stretched just as Mahkah was flying next to it, his attention on cauterizing the other wounds. The dragon head broke free of the severed neck and fell toward the ground. It would have been fine, except the teeth of the hungry dragon scraped across Mahkah's back and down Tala's tail as it made its final descent.

Dragon and rider had been marked by Hydra, and when Sophia's gaze connected with Mahkah's, she knew from his expression that the results might be deadly.

CHAPTER FORTY-FIVE

The headless beast crashed to the ground with such force the cave behind it began to tremble. Rocks spilled off the sides and tumbled across the platform, knocking into the massive monster and covering it.

Veins of lava spiraled under the black skin of Hydra, making it inflate. The peak of the Mountain of Truth was about to come down. Worse, it appeared Hydra was going to explode lava everywhere.

Sophia steered Lunis toward the fallen rider and dragon. They had landed as ungracefully as she'd ever seen the expert rider do. Tala staggered, trying to get her feet under her, but fell on her face. Mahkah jumped from his dragon, concern evident in his every movement. He looked to be having just as much trouble controlling his limbs as his dragon and collapsed to the ground after only a few steps. He tried to push up and recover, but it didn't appear he could.

"We have to get them out of here!" Sophia yelled. She encouraged Lunis to fly after the pair. The blue dragon sped, flapping his wings faster than ever before.

Hydra was growing in size like a hot air balloon being inflated. The ground under it and the dragon and rider were vibrating so hard it would have been nearly impossible for them to stand even if they weren't injured. The cave behind Hydra was dangerously close to falling.

Sophia ignored everything and slid off Lunis before he had even lowered all the way down or slowed and landed in a crouched position. She hurried to Mahkah to help him up.

She knew better than to ask him if he was okay. The way his eyes rolled back in his head when he tried to focus on her told her all she needed to know. "We're getting you out of here. The Castle will fix you."

"B-b-but the reason you came here," he stuttered. His head wove back and forth.

Lunis had landed beside Tala and was trying to help, but there wasn't much he could do with the ground rumbling and rocks banging into them.

He's right, Lunis said to Sophia. *You know what you came here for.* His gaze darted to the crumbling cave.

Sophia opened a portal to the area just outside the Barrier. It shimmered faintly, a product of her magic reserves being low, but after a moment, it solidified. "Lunis, you have to take them through."

But Sophia, Lunis argued, conviction in his eyes.

"You have to help them," she ordered with a rueful expression on her face. She didn't want Lunis to leave her and entering a cave that was about to collapse was definitely not on the list of things she wanted to do, but they'd come this far. They'd defeated Hydra. Papa Creola had been adamant she be in charge of the token if she defeated its guard. That was what she'd done, and she had to take on the responsibility.

Sophia, Lunis said, real fear in his eyes.

"I demand you take them through," Sophia said. "You once told me I got to make three demands of you, remember?"

He nodded. *The first was to allow you to ride me.*

She managed a smile as she helped Mahkah up. He was sweating profusely. "And now I demand you take them through. Call the others. Get Mahkah to the Castle and Tala to the Cave. I'll return when I can."

Lunis pulled in a breath, regret heavy in his eyes. He knew she was right, both to demand this and also to not abandon their mission. *Okay, be fast.*

Sophia walked Mahkah over to Lunis, Tala on the other side. The rider held onto the blue dragon when Sophia released him.

She tried to look into Mahkah's eyes, but they were mostly closed. "Lunis will get you home. You'll be okay. Thank you for what you did."

Maybe Mahkah had no response, but it was more likely he simply couldn't manage one.

The ground quaked hard under them and nearly sent Sophia into the portal. Lunis extended his neck quickly to give Sophia something to grab onto. She reached out and held her arms around her dragon's head, hugging him to her. Briefly, they looked into each other's eyes.

"Come home as soon as you get the token," he said, his gaze intense.

"Nothing will keep me from you," she said and stepped back and to the side to make way for them. "Now hurry, get them home."

Without another word, the blue dragon led Mahkah and Tala through the portal, leaving Sophia alone on a crumbling mountaintop with a mythical creature that was going to explode soon.

CHAPTER FORTY-SIX

The veins of lava had continued to swell and protruded out of the black dragon. Sophia didn't know what would happen when the creature exploded, but she was certain that was how its story ended.

She weaved around the many heads of the monster, nearly falling on Terry or Susan or whoever it was as she made her way for the cave entrance. Rocks rained down from overhead, but she covered her head and sprinted forward, not hesitating to enter.

Sophia wasn't sure what she expected to find when she entered Hydra's cave, but what she found wasn't it. The cave, which she'd have expected to be large enough to house a seven-headed dragon, was tiny. Hydra's cave was the size of a closet. Sophia instantly backed up, wondering if she'd entered it the wrong way.

She worried killing Hydra had done something to the cave. When she entered again, she knew it had to be right because hanging high on the cave wall was a golden coin.

"The token," Sophia said and nearly fell as the largest tremor yet rocked the Mountain of Truth.

Rocks and dust rained down from overhead. She covered her head and wondered how she was going to get to the coin. It was much too high for her to reach, and she worried about using magic since she needed enough to portal home.

The cave grew furiously hot, as if Sophia had just stepped into a dry sauna. Her brow began to pour sweat, and she felt like she might start roasting.

When she stuck her head out of the cave, she saw what was causing the intense heat. Hydra was seconds away from exploding. If it was hot here before, Sophia could only imagine what it would be like when the dragon exploded.

A giant thundering sound filled the air. Sophia looked up as the peak crumbled and came sliding down the side of the mountain. She ducked into the cave as boulders rained down, sending dust and debris all over. The entrance was almost completely covered, making the heat even worse, like she was in a stone oven.

Sophia's eyes connected with the token. She was out of options. As she held out her hand, she simultaneously drew the token to her and made a silent prayer portaling was allowed inside the cave. If not, this would no doubt be her final resting place.

The gold token raced across the short distance and met the palm of her hand, hot to the touch. Sophia didn't flinch from the burn but instead sent all the rest of her energy into creating a portal home. To her relief, the cave did allow for portaling, but the tunnel that appeared flickered, not materializing fully.

Her magical reserves were too low. Sophia was out of energy, and without that, she'd never make it home.

Think, think, think, she chanted in her head, trying to come up with a solution as the rocks continued to rain down outside the cave entrance and the temperature grew so hot her head felt close to bursting.

Sophia remembered something she'd read in her father's book when reviewing it. "Very powerful magical objects can be used as energy sources in a pinch, but one must be careful because they can also burn out magic if they are extremely powerful."

Sophia turned the token over in her hand, seeing where it had burned her. This object was no doubt powerful. What did she have to lose? Either she used it and died or stayed there and died.

Drawing in a hot breath, Sophia leeched power from the token, directing it at the faint portal. The portal grew solid.

A large rock hit Sophia in the head, and she jumped through the portal just before she lost consciousness. The last thing Sophia remembered was the rush of welcome cold air on her cheeks and the sight of the green hills as she stumbled through the portal. Then she fell face-first, enjoying the cool grass on her burning face.

Everything faded.

CHAPTER FORTY-SEVEN

"Her pulse is strong," a familiar voice said over Sophia. She worked to open her eyes but felt held hostage by sleep. In the palm of her hand, she felt the token, still hot to the touch but no longer burning her palm.

"Well, then, I say we leave her here," Hiker grumbled. "Lunis is with Tala in the cave, Evan is with Mahkah, and Wilder is gone, so I can think of no other way for her to get to the Castle."

"I can think of someone who can carry her." Now that Sophia was coming to, she recognized the voice of Ainsley.

"If you want to carry her, be my guest," Hiker said with a laugh.

"I could use magic, but why should I do that when you've got those perfectly capable arms?" Ainsley argued.

"Me?" he asked, sounding offended. "You've got to be kidding!"

"Well, she has a head injury, which is pretty typical for the little dragonrider to show up at the Castle with," Ainsley stated matter-of-factly. She was referring to when Lunis had dropped her at the stairs of the Castle after she passed out at the facility north of the Gullington.

"It looks like a scratch," Hiker stated.

"Yeah, it's nothing the Castle can't fix," Ainsley agreed. "She does look to have been blasted by something hot, though."

He sighed. "She was probably at the beach, sunning herself."

"You know damn well that's not true," Ainsley said, fire in her tone.

"I wouldn't know where she's been since Sophia won't tell me," Hiker ranted, frustration in his tone. "And now Mahkah and Tala have shown up with bizarre injuries neither one of them can explain, and of course, Lunis isn't talking."

"Then may I suggest you pick up this girl and take her to the Castle?" Ainsley asked. "Maybe if you do something nice for Sophia, she'll do something nice for you and tell you what's going on."

Hiker muttered something under his breath.

"What was that, sir?" Ainsley asked.

"As the leader of the Dragon Elite, you wouldn't think I'd have to do favors for my riders to get them to cooperate and share information," he growled.

"And yet, your management style hasn't fostered such reciprocity, so whose fault is that?" Ainsley questioned.

Strong hands reached under Sophia, picking her up from the cold ground with ease. "It's obviously mine."

Ainsley harrumphed, sounding pleased. "Good. Admitting we have an issue is the first step toward fixing it."

CHAPTER FORTY-EIGHT

The sound of heavy boots thundering back and forth across the floor stirred Sophia from the sleep that tried to hold her hostage. She peeked open one eye, to find the source of the noise to be exactly who she'd guessed it to be.

In her hand, she still had the gold token. She clenched her fingers around it, grimacing at the burn on her palm.

To her surprise, when she lifted it up, her head didn't hurt at all, and she felt raring to go, energy flowing in her once more.

Hiker halted at the sight of Sophia sitting up in her four-poster bed.

"Oh, good. Thanks for keeping it down while I slept," she said, pushing her hair out of her face and yawning. She was still wearing her armor, which was covered in dirt and rocks.

He grimaced at her. "Oh, did I wake you with my pacing? Well, I wonder why I'm so restless? Maybe it's because one of my riders is currently out of commission, having been attacked by some venomous creature, and his dragon is suffering from a similar situation. And then I have another rider who is a secret-keeper, and her dragon is much like her."

"You should fire her," Sophia said, swinging her legs over the side of the bed and stretching. "Thank you, Castle, for the repair job. I feel ready to go."

"The question is, where are you going?" Hiker asked, his hands on his hips. "A mission for me?"

Sophia slipped the token into her pocket and nodded. "Sure thing, sir. I just have to go run a real quick errand first. I'll stop by your office when I'm done."

"When will that be?" he asked, narrowing his eyes at her.

She slid off the bed, testing her legs. It was amazing how much more refreshed she felt than before. "Hard to say. Maybe an hour, maybe a week."

Hiker stepped in front of Sophia as she tried to pass him, hoping to escape to the restroom where he wouldn't dare follow. "Sophia, tell me what happened to Mahkah."

"He'll be okay, right?" she asked, pretty certain he was based on Hiker's level of concern. If Mahkah was in mortal danger of not recovering from Hydra's bite, Hiker would have shown fear rather than irritation.

He nodded. "Yes, we believe he will be fine. He just needs rest. It would help to know what attacked him."

"I don't think the Castle needs to know that information," Sophia argued. "I think you do."

He nodded again. "Yes, would you mind sharing with me?"

"We killed Hydra," she stated.

The expression of shock that covered his face was one of the best reactions Sophia had ever caused in someone. The man's mouth hung open, and his eyes were wide as he stared at her.

"H-h-hydra? As in, the seven-headed dragon?" Hiker questioned.

She nodded and stepped around him while he was momentarily confused and disoriented. "Yeah, that's the one."

"That's a legend," he argued.

Sophia shook her head. "It's actually not. Just because it's on another planet, people think that."

"Wait, you took Mahkah to another planet to kill the legendary Hydra?"

"Well, he wanted to go, and I needed help," Sophia said, taking a seat on her pink bean bag and working to unlace her boots.

He shook his head, trying to dispel all the questions racing around in his mind. "What? Why? I'm mean…how?"

Sophia pulled her boot off and emptied it in the waste bin next to the table. "Papa Creola asked me to relieve Hydra of a job he assigned the creature long ago. To do that, I had to slaughter the beast, and Mahkah was in charge of cauterizing the wounds. He got attacked by one of the heads at the last moment and hence the venom."

"But why?" Hiker asked, scratching his head.

Sophia pursed her lips and gave him a regretful expression.

"Oh, for the love of the angels, you all are going to have to start sharing information with me," he complained.

"Have you told the others Thad Reinhart was a dragonrider yet?" Sophia asked.

He shook his head.

"Why is it I get the impression you're hiding a lot more from us?"

He crossed his arms, a scowl making his forehead crease with wrinkles. "Leaders are supposed to keep secrets."

She emptied her other boot, large rocks rolling out of it. "I get that you think so, but they are also supposed to garner trust."

He gave her an expression of offense. "Are you saying you don't trust me?"

Sophia simply gave him an expression that said, "What do you think?"

Hiker thundered for the door. When he was almost to the threshold, he pivoted. "I get I haven't always been the greatest leader in your eyes. We started off rough, and I'm trying to recover the Dragon Elite while Thad is out there secretly hoarding power. I don't know what I'm up against, and my riders don't seem to care for me."

"It's not that, sir. It's just—"

Hiker held up his hand, interrupting her. "I get it. Wilder works for Subner. You have missions for Papa Creola, and we all know Mama Jamba is the one really in charge, and she's all but ordered me to lay off you. However, that can't last forever." He drew in a breath, seeming to relax. "I'll admit I'm struggling with coming into the new era of dragonriders. We've had a series of blows I never anticipated. It's easy to feel defeated when I know we are all that's left. Sooner rather than later, my riders are going to answer to me and no one else, otherwise there will be no more Dragon Elite. I will see to it."

Sophia nodded, proud to see the fire begin to burn in Hiker. It was what needed to happen; he needed his courage back. He had to get angry enough before he took back the reins and steered the Dragon Elite into the future.

"Yes, sir," Sophia agreed, pushing up from the beanbag and wiggling her toes, happy to have them free of her boots.

He turned to leave but didn't reach the door before Sophia called to him, "And sir?"

He looked over his shoulder at her, impatience on his face.

"Thank you for carrying me to the Castle," she said, offering him a smile.

CHAPTER FORTY-NINE

After checking on Mahkah and touching base with Lunis, Sophia headed to the House of Fourteen. She was relieved to hear the injured rider and dragon would make a full recovery.

Ainsley had mentioned the Castle was feeling strangely giddy since they returned. She offered that usually the Castle went quiet when it had to work to repair a hurt dragonrider, but not in this instance.

Sophia simply nodded, not disclosing the Castle must have known she was much closer to completing the task it had assigned her. Who knew what this closet in the House of Fourteen was all about or why the Castle wanted her to find it. She had to admit she was curious. More than anything, she had worked to get *The Complete History of Dragonriders* and couldn't wait until the Castle delivered on its end of the bargain. Hopefully, it would be well worth all the effort and risk.

The burn on Sophia's palm was much better, which she was grateful for. It didn't hurt anymore, but there was still a faint outline from where she'd held the hot token.

When she stepped into the House of Fourteen, she was grateful to find the golden arched entrance hall deserted. Opening the palm of her hand, Sophia glanced at the token and wondered how it turned back time to send her to the "reset" point.

She studied the coin and read the inscription on one side, realizing there hadn't been any words there before. She was sure, having studied the coin a lot when at the Castle.

Now on one side, it read, Present day, and there was a picture of the House of Fourteen, the Castle, and another smaller building. Sophia pursed her lips, thinking before turning the coin over to read the other side.

She laid it flat on her palm and tried to make out the words. The images were the same, but on this side, it read, Reset Point.

Sophia tilted her head to the side, wondering how to flip the timeline, but just then, everything turned black. She felt like she'd gone blind.

Trying to blink or feel anything, Sophia began to panic. Thankfully, spots of lights appeared, and Sophia's vision began to take shape once more. She wasn't standing in the same entrance hall as before. Well, she was, but this one was different. For one, it wasn't covered in gold with the language of the founders dancing along the walls or with the statues of the founders of the House lining the long corridor.

Instead, the short hallway was black and white, as if Sophia had stepped into an old movie. The ceiling was still arched, but the statues were missing. Something she couldn't quite place her finger on was different about the House of Fourteen, but Sophia believed turning back the clock roughly several hundred years could have been the reason.

Lifting her hand, Sophia noticed how she contrasted starkly to her environment. Her arm and hand were in color, whereas everything around her was black and white. *Interesting,* she thought, wondering if that meant she was the ghost in this reality.

"Now I need to find this closet," she said. She ambled down the corridor toward the residential wing where all the closets were located. Sophia was about to move into the area when a figure she recognized walked right in front of her, heading into the Chamber of the Tree. Sophia recognized the man's large form and features. What made him appear like a completely different person than the one she knew was his demeanor.

Hiker Wallace appeared as a confident man, ready to lead a powerful army as he strode through the Door of Reflection and into the Chamber of the Tree. He wore the traditional clothes she was used to seeing him in, but there was something very different about the man. He seemed whole, unmarked by the years of being ignored when mortals couldn't see magic and the Dragon Elite became obsolete.

That was why even though Sophia had a mission to find the closet and knew hanging out in the reset point for long wasn't safe— according to Lunis—she had to at least take a peek and spy on the leader of the Dragon Elite.

CHAPTER FIFTY

The Chamber of the Tree was as different as the entrance hall, filled with black and white figures and no twinkling starry sky overhead. There was still the bench with the council members and a row of Warriors, all standing straight with their hands pressed behind their back.

The white tiger and black raven were also present, but Sophia knew they had pretty much been with the House of Fourteen since the beginning. The sky of lights was also a relatively new addition to the House, which was why it wasn't in the reset point. That had been how they symbolized magicians once they were registered using magitech.

To Sophia's relief, almost no one glanced at her when she entered the Chamber of the Tree. However, Jude, the white tiger who represented truth and honesty in the Chamber of the Tree, looked straight at Sophia with a speculative glare in his eyes.

She pulled her attention away from him as a scratchy voice began to talk. It was a man she'd never seen but had heard a great deal about —Talon Sinclair.

His long white hair and pale skin reminded her of Adler's, his relative who wouldn't have been born yet.

"What do you want?" Talon asked, his chin down low and light eyes scrutinizing.

When Hiker stepped forward, Sophia realized Talon was speaking to him. "I want the House to recognize the danger we're facing."

A great deal of muttering echoed around the room.

"If you will," Hiker said in a commanding voice. "Thad Reinhart is powerful, and I firmly believe he's working on something that could potentially harm us all."

Talon laughed and looked at the other Councilors, whom Sophia didn't recognize. The bench looked the way she was used to seeing it in the present time, with both magicians and mortals with chimeras.

Sophia knew one of the magicians was one of her relatives. There would also be one of the Takahashis' relatives on the council since they were also a founding family.

"Really?" Talon argued, His tone was filled with condescension, "I thought the Dragon Elite could handle everything on their own."

"We can," Hiker stated. "But why must we do so if there is a war brewing?"

"A war?" one of the Councilors said in shock. "Surely you are exaggerating."

"No," Hiker exclaimed. "Thad Reinhart is working on something. I have reason to believe he's in league with other powerful organizations."

Talon dismissed him with a shake of his head. "Really? Who would want to work with the Rogue Riders?"

"Someone who wants power!" Hiker declared. "If we use our collective resources, I believe that whatever is coming, we'll be prepared to handle it."

"You want our help?" Talon asked with a laugh in his voice. "Do you also want us to work with elves? How about the gnomes? Oh, and let's invite the fae and giants."

Almost all the councilors laughed, save for two.

"Yes, I think we should all work together," Hiker insisted adamantly.

Sophia couldn't help noticing the confidence he showed. He was the epitome of a leader. Yet what Hiker was up against, she knew from studying the Forgotten Archives, was much larger than the Dragon Elite or anything else. This was the reset point. This was the calm right before the Great War. After this, magitech would make it so mortals couldn't see magic anymore. Magicians and everyone else forgot the history. The whole world spiraled into a different era, and the Dragon Elite became ghosts. This was the moment before everything was nearly lost forever.

And Hiker Wallace had seen it. He knew.

No one had listened to him, and the world suffered for it for several hundred years.

"With all due respect," Talon said, his tone impatient, "the Dragon Elite have never wanted our help. You think you're so much better than us—"

"Our rule trumps yours," Hiker interrupted.

"As you constantly remind us," Talon fired back. "Now you're the one who needs our help. What are you worried about that's going to harm us all? Thad Reinhart is only one man. He only has a handful of rogue riders left, isn't that right?"

Hiker combed his hand over his chin. "Yes, we've nearly destroyed all the rest."

"Then what do you think this Thad Reinhart will do?" Talon asked.

Hiker shook his head. "I don't know, but I sense he's got something…a technology of some sort."

"You sense?" Talon questioned, a laugh in his voice. "You want us to band together to follow you based on a sense?"

"You have to believe me when I tell you my feelings on this should be trusted," Hiker argued.

This was such a strange way to hear Hiker talk, but it also endeared him to Sophia. She wanted to yell, "He's right! Listen to him."

Instead, she stayed quiet and watched history unfold.

"And technology, really?" Talon asked. "Whatever are you talking about?"

"Magitech," Hiker explained to Sophia's surprise. "I know Thad has been working on something called that."

"How do you know?" Talon questioned.

The leader of the Dragon Elite simply shook his head. "I can't say. If you don't listen to me, there will be a battle. That is inevitable. The Dragon Elite will be at the epicenter, and then it will ripple out and affect both the magical and mortal worlds."

Talon sighed as if he were growing bored with the conversation. "I really don't think you've given us enough evidence to do anything. We, the House of Fourteen, are strong. The magical economy is the most stable it has ever been. Our relations with the other races are in good standing. The mortal and magical worlds work together seamlessly. There is no reason to believe we are in any peril."

Hiker growled, balling up his fists. "You don't understand—"

"I'm not sure I do, but at this point, we have to move onto other business," Talon said dismissively.

Hiker turned. His eyes swept over the stoic warriors before he shook his head and charged past Sophia and out of the Chamber of the Tree.

She knew no one could see her in the reset point.

She also knew she'd just witnessed the moment before everything changed and sent the world into the dark ages.

CHAPTER FIFTY-ONE

Sophia couldn't believe it; Hiker had been right since the beginning. He had seen the catastrophic events before the storm. He knew the Great War was coming. Knew Thad Reinhart was a part of it. He apparently hadn't realized the Sinclairs were also central to it.

As she followed Hiker out of the Chamber of the Tree, Sophia considered her options. She needed to find the hidden closet, which was apparently visible in this time. Part of her wanted to follow Hiker Wallace out as he marched toward the entrance, but that wasn't what she was there for.

Instead, she went through the door to the residential wing, knowing the mission before her was more important than understanding the Viking. She already had more compassion and understanding for the man who just an hour ago had been trying to get her to see him as a leader. It was ironic to her that she saw him in this era as one of the most competent leaders.

She shook off the vision she'd seen and focused on the black and white reality before her. Before, when she was operating blind, finding this mysterious closet had been tough. Doing it now with the clue she needed to be in a different time period was still tough. There were still hundreds, maybe thousands of closets to check. Sophia didn't know how many it would take or how long, but she was prepared to do what needed to be done.

As she stood at the bottom of the stairs that seemed to go on forever, she hoped, silently prayed, to the angels it wouldn't take too long.

To her utter astonishment, when she opened her eyes, there was the same glowing, sparkling dust running up the stairs as when Quiet led her to Devon's bow. She blinked at it for a moment, wondering if she was really seeing what was before her. Gold dust sparkled on the stairs, snaking its way up and disappearing.

Sophia wished Lunis was in her head so she could consult him on these events. She knew all his energy was centered on Tala, as it should be. She was alone, yet she didn't feel that way. In this strange black and white world where she was the only color, it felt like someone was watching out for her and helping her when she would have otherwise been lost.

Sophia climbed the stairs, deciding to follow the strange gold dust that hadn't steered her wrong before. It had led Wilder to a sea monster that had almost killed him, but the end result was they recovered Devon's bow, which Subner quickly destroyed.

Sophia shook her head, not knowing if she was doing the wrong thing, but knowing she'd come this far and needed to continue forward. Even if it was for nothing, she had to know whatever she'd done was for something. She had to know how this ended.

CHAPTER FIFTY-TWO

The gold dust ended at the entrance to an unmarked door. Sophia found that strange since most of the doors were for family residents. She didn't even remember seeing this door on that level, and she'd been through the area thousands of times over the years.

And yet there was this strange unmarked door the gold dust disappeared into. Deciding to take a chance, she looked over her shoulder and checked to ensure she wasn't being followed in the black and white world before turning the doorknob.

It opened without incident, and Sophia pulled back the door, expecting to find a magical world.

To her surprise, all she found was a small closet. It was about like when she found the closet-like cave where Hydra had lived before they killed the ancient beast.

Sophia's eyes took a moment to adjust to the darkened space. She stepped into the small closet, finding brooms and dustpans and something she could have sworn was a magitech rocket. She decided not to touch it.

The gold dust ended when she was inside the closet, but she stepped outside immediately to check.

It led into the closet and went nowhere else. She decided this was her only plausible option, so she stepped back into the closet and shut the door.

It was only once she was shut in the dark with the cleaning tools and the rocket Sophia saw it.

She knew once she laid her eyes on the object, it had to be what she was looking for—exactly what the Castle wanted her to find.

CHAPTER FIFTY-THREE

A switch.

It was clear to Sophia as soon as she saw it. She had been looking for the switch on the wall before her in the dark closet.

She had no idea what the glowing blue switch did or why it was there, or why she'd never seen anything like it at the House of Fourteen before.

All Sophia knew was the switch needed to be flipped.

Her hand didn't hesitate as she lifted it even with the lever. The entire time, she'd felt like she'd been led, and something told her she had to follow through.

Strangely, she felt more fear right before she flipped the switch than she had before she helped to kill Hydra. A line from her father's book came back to her.

It's the things we think change nothing that create the most pivotal moments in our lives. They are game-changers. They are the irreversible we would never reverse.

The switch was stuck from disuse. Sophia had to really pull to get it to come down. When she finally wrestled the lever down, nothing happened.

She worried she'd been wrong or misjudged.

Then she felt something warm in her pocket. Sophia pushed her hand in and pulled out the gold token that controlled the reset point in the two histories. Spiraling around the coin was the sparkling dust.

Sophia didn't understand but was smart enough to follow the clues. She held the coin in her hands and opened the closet door, not sure what she should expect. When she glanced into the hallway, the area was still black and white.

I'm still in the past, Sophia thought.

She pulled the door shut, holding her breath as she held the coin, a speculative thought in her head.

Leading with her thumb, Sophia turned the coin over until it read, Present Day.

A flash of light punctuated the movement and the switch disappeared. A feeling of familiarity filled Sophia.

She tensed, having no idea what she'd done but sensing it was of momentous importance.

With a tentative hand, she pushed open the door of the closet to find something that was utterly impossible.

CHAPTER FIFTY-FOUR

Sophia was in the Castle.

Somehow, she'd been in a closet in the House of Fourteen several hundred years ago and ended up in the Castle in the present day, or at least, she thought it was present day.

She didn't allow herself a moment to figure out if it actually was the present day. Instead, Sophia stepped into the closet and shut the door and found the switch she thought had disappeared. She flipped the lever and stepped through the door.

To her amazement, she found herself back at the House of Fourteen. A few speculative steps told her it was the present day.

Sophia, or actually the Castle, had created a portal between the Castle and the House of Fourteen. Or someone had, and she'd just reactivated it using the token for the reset point. The implications were overwhelming and the consequences? The wrath of Hiker.

Maybe he wouldn't find out, she thought.

This should have been impossible because no one could enter the Castle directly, and no one but the Dragon Elite and those who served them could step through the Barrier into the Gullington. And yet, Sophia had found a direct path from the House of Fourteen into the

Castle. Actually, she now believed with the Castle's help, she had created the portal, and she expected to pay for it bitterly.

She put herself back into the closet, closed the door, and prayed she could fix this problem and get *The Complete History of Dragonriders* before Hiker figured out what she'd done.

Sophia stepped through the door of the portal she'd accidentally created to find the second person she really didn't want to know about what she'd done.

"What have you done, S. Beaufont?" the shapeshifter yelled, her face so red it matched her auburn hair.

CHAPTER FIFTY-FIVE

S ophia clenched the gold token in her hand, clenching her fingers around it as her pulse quickened. She was suddenly lightheaded.

"I-I-I can explain," Sophia stuttered.

"Can you?" Ainsley asked, her voice as tight as the expression on her face. She strode past Sophia and poked her head through the door Sophia had just come through. Looking around, Sophia realized she was in the corridor beside her room, and the door was brand new. Unlike the other doors in the Castle, which were arched and covered in crown molding, this one was rectangular and done in the design of those found in the House of Fourteen.

Ainsley stuck her head through the door briefly before disappearing. When she returned, she looked madder than hell, her eyes fuming.

"Can you explain?" she spat. "Because for the love of the angels, I'll never get the dust out of the Castle now!"

"Well, you see, I didn't actually know what I was doing," Sophia said in a rush.

"This seems like a great story," Ainsley said, cocking her hip and sticking her hand on it. "Spoiler alert: it ends with your death, I'm thinking."

"Because you're going to kill me?" There was a strange hope laced into her tone.

The housekeeper shook her head, seeming to enjoy this. "Oh, no. I mean, I'll probably go back to not washing your towels for a bit, but I can't stay mad at you for long, S. Beaufont."

Sophia blanched. "Wait, you weren't washing my towels?"

Ainsley waved her off dismissively. "That's old news, and you didn't even notice, so what's the point?"

"I did, actually," Sophia replied. She had wondered the other day why her towel was stiff and dirty in places.

"Okay, so out with it," Ainsley encouraged. "Tell me why Hiker is going to kill you."

Sophia looked at the new door. "Do you think he will? Maybe he won't notice."

The shapeshifter laughed before morphing into the form of Hiker Wallace, complete with kilt and sour expression. The only thing to give her away was the distinct scar over her right temple in the exact place it was when Ainsley was in her usual form.

She turned around and paced away several steps before casually turning back around and stomping through the corridor. In the form of Hiker, she halted in front of the new door, which stood out like a sore thumb in the Castle. "Something seems different here." She sniffed. "I'm sure it's just the immaculate care Ainsley is showing to the Castle since I've given her a pay increase, and by that, I mean I've actually started to pay the beautiful lassie." She then glanced around speculatively. "Well, I'll just stomp over to my office, passing through this corridor I've crossed every day for the last four-hundred some odd years and not notice anything that's out of the ordinary."

Sophia slouched with defeat. "Okay, so there's little chance Hiker won't notice I've created a portal to the House of Fourteen?"

Ainsley returned to her normal appearance, a proud smile on her face. "You can try creating a disguise on it."

Sophia's face brightened with a smile. "Oh, that's genius. Thanks, Ainsley." Pointing at the new door, Sophia conjured up a cloak she hoped would mask the door and make it blend into the rest of the stone wall around it.

To her relief, the door faded away completely, replaced with the brick and stone appearance it used to have. After only a few seconds, a crack appeared in the middle of the area and spread out like a spider's web before exploding with dust and smoke to reveal the portal door once more.

Sophia sunk again. "For fork's sake. Why won't that work?"

Ainsley's laughter was high-pitched and slightly evil. "Because you can't façade the Castle. It won't even allow me to change my wall color after four hundred and some odd years." She looked around, getting the distant expression she often wore when she was about to talk to the Castle directly. "I've never liked putrid green."

She paused, listening to the response. "Well, you changed S. Beaufont's room to pink. I don't get why you can't give me what I want."

Another pause.

"I think cheetah print is classy," Ainsley declared with a defiant expression on her face. "And I know you only redesigned S. Beaufont's room to be more in line with her taste to get her to do this, but she's going to wise up to your antics."

Sophia shook her head. "Wait! First off, you know the Castle got me to make this portal door?"

Ainsley rolled her eyes. "Haven't you been listening to this conversation?"

"Umm, just the one side," Sophia answered. "And what do you mean about 'wise up to the Castle's antics?'"

At this, Ainsley gave a cunning smile. "Go on then, S. Beaufont, and tell me how this portal door came to be in the Castle?"

"Well, it all began when I asked the Castle to pretty please with sugar on top lead me to *The Complete History of Dragonriders*," Sophia started.

Ainsley held up a hand, pausing her. "Hold up a second, dear. I want to get comfortable for this. I sense it's going to be good, although it will end in tragedy." She swiped her hand through the air, and the high-backed chair against the far wall slid out and across the corridor until it was just behind Ainsley. Without turning around, she took a seat, casually crossing her ankles and daintily laying her hands on her knees. "Now, please continue, S. Beaufont. I want to hear every detail of how you get swindled and die."

Sophia's eyes fluttered with annoyance. "Swindled? What? No, anyway, the Castle told me to go find a closet in the House of Fourteen—"

"Told you?" Ainsley asked.

"Well, so to speak," Sophia answered. "Then I couldn't find the closet, and a magical talking lynx informed me I needed to find the closet at another point in time."

"So far, this is all sounding very boring," Ainsley said with a yawn.

"I'll skip most of the details," Sophia replied. "I fought Hydra to get this token thingy—"

"Nearly getting the only dragonrider I actually like killed," Ainsley interrupted.

"Well, yeah, but…wait, you don't like me?"

Dismissively, Ainsley shook her head. "It always depends. I'm an extraordinarily fair-weather friend. There is no unconditional love in my heart for anyone." The housekeeper's face shifted suddenly to anger as she got that distant expression again.

"You watch your insinuations," Ainsley warned, obviously talking to the Castle once more.

"Okay." Sophia went on, "Anyway, I got the token, went back in time, found the closet, flipped a switch, changed the timeline again, and then voila." She held up a hand to the portal door. "It appears I've created or found or whatever a door that connects the House of Fourteen and the Castle in the present day."

Another yawn spilled from Ainsley's mouth. "May I suggest that when you tell that story again, you use hand puppets or something? It's all very boring and predictable."

"Yes, maybe Hiker won't kill me if I have visual effects to add to the story." Sophia groaned. "I know how much he loves technology."

"Oh, this is going to be worse than when Evan created a fire spell that caused the Expanse to burn continuously for a solid decade, making us all smell like barbeque and constantly have to fight the fire to keep the Castle from burning down," Ainsley said, still sounding bored.

"Wait, how is this worse than that?" Sophia questioned. "And that really happened?"

"It did indeed, S. Beaufont," Ainsley told her. "But that was during the blackout years, and we didn't have anything else to do, so I guess it was all right."

"Ainsley, do you really not get paid to work here?" Sophia asked, remembering what she'd said earlier. The question irked her suddenly, even though she had many other questions for the housekeeper.

She shrugged. "No, I just work here for the thrills and excitement."

"But why?" Sophia asked. "I mean, how did you even get this position, and why do you stay?"

Ainsley scratched her head as she thought about the question, her finger grazing the scar on the side of her head. "You know, Miss, I can't recall. I want to say it's because I love riders and dragons and wanted to serve the Dragon Elite, but that doesn't sound like me. Actually, reptiles used to gross me out in my old life. I'm not entirely sure how I got here. The whole memory has faded."

Sophia gave her a skeptical expression. "That's very strange."

"Is it?" Ainsley asked. "I guess. When you've been around as long as me, I think forgetting things is normal. I mean, I don't even remember how I got this here scar." She pointed to the mark on her temple.

"You don't?" Sophia questioned. "How could you forget that? It seems like it was likely a near-deadly blow."

She shrugged. "Probably. I don't recall anything about it. Used to bug me all the time. All the centuries of nothing to do around here helped me to forget."

Sophia thought about this for a moment and decided she should catalog this information for later investigation. "So, the portal door," she resumed, steering the conversation back to the more pressing matter. "Can you help me keep Hiker away from it for a bit? Just until I figure out how to explain it or get the Castle to cover it up?"

Ainsley's eyes sparkled with delight. "Oh, yes. I love any opportunity I get to deceive that man. I'll just tell him the Castle is doing monthly construction on this corridor and he has to take the long way around to his room. It will take him an extra five minutes to get there, and he'll grumble bitterly the entire time about it."

"Great," Sophia said with zero inflection. "Then he'll be extra mad when he finds out what I'm hiding."

"If," Ainsley corrected.

"Right," Sophia said. "I mean, maybe the Castle will delete the portal door."

"I doubt that," she sang.

"I wonder why it even had me create this passage between the House of Fourteen and here," Sophia mused. "Do you think it wants the members from there to be able to come here?"

Ainsley shook her head. "No, they won't be able to. Rules are pretty sparse around here, but one thing is certain: only the Dragon Elite and those who serve them can cross into the Gullington or enter the Castle."

"Oh, well, and a magical lynx," Sophia corrected, thinking of Plato.

Ainsley gave her a hesitant expression. "Is that why I found cat hair in the pantry? I thought the spell I used on Evan was finally starting to work." She shrugged. "Oh, well, I'll try a different spell. Maybe something that turns him into a toad."

"If no one can come here, what's the point of the portal?" Sophia asked.

Ainsley thought about that for a moment. "I'm guessing it has to do with magical energy sharing. I don't remember things all that well, as we've already discussed, but I remember the Castle was once connected to the House or something like that. I think it had to do with energy. I mean, it appears you've simply unlocked a door that was probably there all along."

"So there!" Sophia exclaimed. "Hiker can't be mad. It's not my fault."

The housekeeper cackled. "Oh, that's cute, S. That's real cute.

Hiker can be mad on a clear day when he's been served breakfast in bed with absolutely no problems in his life. I've seen him."

"Fine," Sophia grumbled. "I'll sort him out after I figure out what to do with the portal, and the Castle delivers on its end of the bargain. Maybe Hiker will be happy with me for recovering *The Complete History of Dragonriders.*"

Another laugh. "You are too much. Have you thought about going into stand-up comedy like those guys you show me on the YouTube?"

"It is just YouTube, no 'the,'" Sophia corrected. "And you're starting to make me think the Castle isn't going to make good on its promise."

"I warned you not to go making deals with this place," Ainsley stated with conviction.

"I know, which was why I worded the deal just right and made it promise," Sophia said.

"Oh, well, if you did a pinky promise, then never mind." Ainsley's head tilted back as she continued to laugh.

"I did what the Castle wanted," Sophia argued. "Why wouldn't it make good on its end?"

Ainsley's face turned quite serious. "The Castle has its reasons for hiding that particular book, and I'm guessing it isn't handing it over just because you risked yours and Mahkah's life and went on a wild goose chase for it. I hate to break it to you, S, but I believe you've been had."

Sophia grimaced. "Why would you say that?"

"Because if the Castle wants you to have something, then you do. If it doesn't, you won't. And when it wants someone to do something, well, it makes promises it doesn't intend to fulfill."

Sophia growled and clenched her fist by her side. She didn't want to believe a word of this, and yet this mysterious, sentient Castle was the strangest being she'd ever known, and it probably shouldn't be underestimated.

Ainsley stretched, yawning again. "I'm going to go put up construction blockades at the end of the corridor to keep Mr. Wallace from seeing what you've done. You see? When I promise, I make good on it."

"Thanks," Sophia grumbled. As the housekeeper strode away, her long brown skirt swayed with the movement.

"Oh, but on the bright side," Ainsley sang over her shoulder. "At least you got that really cool thing that sends you back in time. I'm sure you can do all sorts of fun stuff with it. I'd ask to borrow it, but I'll just steal it from your room when you're away on a mission."

"Right," Sophia said, drawing out the word. She realized the gold token could never leave her side. She was its protector now. She'd made a promise to Papa Creola and would keep that.

Ainsley was right. Although she couldn't spend a lot of time in the past, she didn't see the harm in doing a little snooping and seeing what things used to look like before the dark ages. Before everything changed for the Dragon Elite.

CHAPTER FIFTY-SIX

After the housekeeper had left, Sophia faced the portal door. "Castle, please tell me Ainsley isn't right, and you're not actually going to go back on your end of the deal?"

Silence greeted Sophia's ears.

"Right, and about this portal business you got me to do for you," Sophia began. "You are going to fix it so Hiker doesn't murder me, right?"

No answer.

Sophia crossed her arms and seethed. She tried to come up with a threat that could impact the Castle, but she couldn't think of one. The Castle was all-powerful. There didn't seem a way to make it deliver on the deal or get rid of the portal now that she had created it.

Then she remembered the switch. "Oh, what if I go back to the House of Fourteen and hit the switch in the other closet in the past? I bet that would—"

The candlelit chandelier creaked overhead. Sophia caught movement as the structure fell from the ceiling. She dove to the side, rolling out of the way just before the chandelier connected with her head.

The fixture hit the ground with a great crash. Sophia covered her head as she continued to run, putting as much distance between her and the flying debris as possible. Bits of wood and candles were scattered everywhere, creating quite the mess. Now this part of the corridor really would be under construction.

Sophia stuck her hands on her hips and narrowed her eyes at a wall. "That's how you're going to play, is it? You'll just take me out?"

A suit of armor at her back tipped forward and hovered above her, suspended in the air like it was about to crash down on her. Sophia didn't flinch.

"You'll kill me to keep the portal open?" Sophia asked the Castle. "Is that right?"

The suit of armor rocked back on its heels, and as if it had a real person inside, the knight lifted its large sword, brandishing it at Sophia.

She simply narrowed her eyes, holding the gold token in her hands. Her gaze drifted to the portal door. She knew the Castle could read her thoughts and had no illusions. It realized what she was going to do next.

Holding her breath, Sophia sprinted for the door, intending to go through it. She heard the armored suit charging after her, but she was much faster. However, as she leapt over the broken bits of chandelier, the portal door disappeared.

Sophia felt around on the wall, looking for the handle, but there was nothing there. She heard the armored suit continuing to lumber in her direction. Thoroughly fed up with the Castle, Sophia lifted the gold token.

"Fine, you can block me that way, but I've got other options," Sophia said and flipped the coin from present day to the other side, sending her back to the reset point.

Everything went black.

CHAPTER FIFTY-SEVEN

As before, light started to sprinkle into Sophia's vision, illuminating the space around her and allowing her surroundings to take shape. Also like before, when everything was clear, her environment was purely black and white. She was in the past again, at the reset point. However, this time she was in the Castle.

Thinking she'd outsmarted the Castle, Sophia spun and looked at the portal door. It was there just like before.

"Ha-ha," she exclaimed, stepping forward.

As before, the door vanished just as she was about to grab the handle.

Narrowing her eyes, Sophia considered kicking the wall. "You're being really rotten, I hope you realize!"

There were other options, but Sophia didn't want to even think about them since the Castle would learn what she was considering and try to stop her. More likely, try to kill her. She worked to block her thoughts with a technique Clark had taught her.

The gold token in her hand, she readied to turn the timeline back to the present day, when a voice she recognized echoed down the corridor.

"He's adamant a war is brewing that will affect even the House of Fourteen," Ainsley said, hustling through the hall in Sophia's direction. She looked almost the same as she did in the present time, except maybe younger in small ways. Fewer wrinkles. And the scar! It was gone.

"I fear he is right," a man striding beside her said. Sophia had never met this man, but she felt like she had. He was none other than Adam Rivalry. She recognized him from the painting of the dragonrider that still graced the top of the first landing of the stairs in the entry.

Just like in the painting, Adam's long white hair hung around his narrow face. He was tall and thin, unlike Hiker, who was built like a line-backer. The older dragonrider also had a long white beard, which he was currently tugging.

"Well, I'm not sure what we can do if the House of Fourteen refuses to listen to us," Ainsley said, hurrying past Sophia. No one seemed able to see her in this reality either. Curious to hear their conversation and learn more about the Dragon Elite before the reset point, Sophia sped after them, the gold token in her hand.

Ainsley wasn't dressed in her usual plain brown clothes. Most days, Sophia found her in a long burlap-type dress, wearing clunky boots. At this point in history, she looked less like a housekeeper and more like royalty in a beautiful dress made of velvet that cascaded on the floor behind her as she moved down the corridor. Her long red hair was elegantly braided down her back, Normally Sophia saw her with it loose and frizzy, hardly looking brushed and lacking any style. Around her neck and on her fingers she wore huge gems that looked very expensive and heavy.

"I know we will have to battle Thad and his army of rogue riders soon, but I fear the biggest danger will affect the mortals," Adam said in a conspiratorial whisper.

Ainsley cast him a worried expression. "Why is that?"

"Recently, I snuck away to spy on Thad," Adam said in a hushed voice. Sophia had to close the distance to hear him properly.

"You know Hiker told you not to do that," she admonished.

He shook his head. "And you know I do what I damn well please, regardless of what that man says."

She smiled at him despite the disapproving glint in her green eyes. "Good thing you're his best friend, or I fear he'd have kicked you out of the Castle long ago."

Adam chuckled good-naturedly. "He could damn well try. Can you imagine if he ever got to be like that, simply throwing riders out of the Castle for not behaving? We'd have no one left."

The pair stopped at the first landing of the staircase, looking out at the entrance hall. Sophia had been so engrossed in their conversation that she hardly noticed they'd walked the distance.

The painting of Adam and his dragon Kay-Rye didn't hang at the top of the landing like it did in the present day. Instead, there was a rather long painting of the Dragon Elite riders, two rows of men in armor. The first row consisted of a dozen men on one knee. At their back was another dozen men, their chins held high and bravery radiating from their regal stares. Behind them was the Castle, with a rare blue sky in the distance.

Sophia knew the Dragon Elite used to have healthy numbers, but she didn't realize just how many riders there used to be or that they gave off such authority. They were the world's adjudicators, Sophia reasoned.

Ainsley and Adam looked out over the entrance hall as many of the men depicted in the painting hustled back and forth, running toward the dining hall or in the direction of the weapons room on the far side.

They made cheerful comments to each other, their camaraderie evident as they prepared for something. Sophia could only guess it was the Great War that preceded the dark ages when mortals were disallowed from seeing magic for several hundred years. This was the Dragon Elite's last day before their numbers were slashed and their roles as adjudicators were erased.

"What is it you learned on this secret spy mission?" Ainsley asked Adam in a whisper.

He leaned closer to her. "I saw Thad Reinhart meeting with Talon Sinclair."

Ainsley's head whipped around so fast her braid nearly whacked Adam in the face. "Are you certain? He's a Councilor for the House of Fourteen."

Adam nodded. "I realize that. What has me more worried is it appeared Thad was selling Talon something he called 'magitech.'"

Ainsley's eyes widened. "What's that?"

Adam shrugged. "I don't know, but I've heard Hiker mention it in reference to Thad. He said he had a hunch Thad was doing something with magitech but couldn't say why."

"You know why," Ainsley stated ominously.

Adam nodded. "Of course, I do."

"Why?" Sophia heard herself say as she stepped closer to the pair.

They didn't answer her question, though. Adam continued, "I was too far away to make out everything they said, but I know I heard something about mortals being cut off from magic."

Ainsley's mouth fell open. "How could that happen? I mean, that's one of the worst possibilities. Can you even imagine?"

Adam shook his head. "I don't even want to fathom the possibility. It would hurt the whole world. It could destroy magic since they are the ones who keep the balance for it."

"Are you certain of what you witnessed?" Ainsley asked.

Adam toggled his head back and forth. "I'm not entirely. I do believe Thad has given something to Talon."

"This magitech you speak of," Ainsley stated.

Adam nodded. "But the true implications aren't clear."

"Then you can't say anything," Ainsley said with conviction.

"I agree," Adam affirmed. "I reasoned Talon could be trying to trick Thad. Maybe he's setting him up."

A look of hope flickered on Ainsley's face. "Maybe the House of Fourteen is going to join us after all."

Sophia wanted to run forward and tell them they weren't. Warn them that drastic action had to be taken right away.

"That was my thought," Adam said.

"And if you go to Hiker right now with this information, he won't have enough details to do anything about it," Ainsley reasoned.

"I realize that," Adam stated. "I think it's better to wait and see what happens after today."

"Yes. Hiker is still confident he can negotiate with Thad," Ainsley said, her eyes searching the men below as they sped through the entrance hall, excitement and tension brewing around them.

"I hope he can," Adam said, his voice grave. "After what I did to Ember, I'm not sure Thad will be as reasonable as we expected. I think this only ends with destroying that man."

"You know Hiker will have trouble doing that," Ainsley warned.

"Then I'll do it." Adam drew in a breath. "I owe him that much. I owe Hiker my very life."

"Thad didn't lose it because you killed his dragon," Ainsley reasoned. "Remember, he's always been the bad one. He should never have lived. We know that now. We know when there are two, one must always be killed."

Adam took this in before agreeing with a nod. "I know. And he isn't as powerful as he once was, so maybe he can be reasoned with. Maybe this will be swift."

"My only concern now is how the House of Fourteen will play into things," Ainsley said. "That bit about Talon is curious."

"Keep it between us, please," Adam encouraged. "There's no reason to worry until after today if things don't go well. If everything fails today, then we will investigate this magitech more fully and determine what it is and how to stop it."

Ainsley agreed with a nod as Adam offered her his arm. She was so different than her usually kooky self as she took his arm and allowed him to lead her down the stairs where the men all halted at the sight of her, bowing respectfully and muttering, "Good day, Ms. Carter."

She nodded to them and smiled pleasantly like she was a queen being led through a crowd of her people.

Sophia wanted to run after them and warn them. Tell Adam and Ainsley that after today they wouldn't have another opportunity. This was the reset point. It was the last possible moment before everything shifted. This was the day when Thad Reinhart and his forces battled the Dragon Elite. The leader of the Rogue Riders had appeared to have lost, but he didn't. Thad faked his death and went into hiding, building an empire he'd later use to try to crush the Dragon Elite, the Earth, and anything precious left in the world.

It dawned on Sophia what the magitech Thad Reinhart had sold to Talon Sinclair was.

"Of course!" she exclaimed, clapping a hand to her mouth. Talon Sinclair had bought very powerful magitech he'd placed on the top of the Matterhorn to broadcast a signal to all mortals. It was this signal that after this day in history made it so mortals could no longer see magic, and combined with serious spells, changed the world forever, putting it into the dark ages.

Everything suddenly came together for Sophia, weaving a picture of history she could not change that made perfect sense. Of course, Thad Reinhart was behind mortals not being able to see magic. He knew it was the best way to make the Dragon Elite obsolete.

And who better to instigate the whole thing than Talon Sinclair, who later would be discovered to loathe mortals, thinking they undermined the House's mission? It was he who'd shoved them out of the House and turned it from Fourteen to the House of Seven, which was how it would be known until the true history was unearthed.

It was hard for Sophia to stand there and watch the old Dragon Elite line up, exuberance in their every movement. They thought they were going to waltz into battle that day and swiftly win. They probably returned later and celebrated a momentous victory, believing they'd ended the reign of Thad Reinhart and the Rogue Riders.

Tomorrow they'd awake to the reality mortals couldn't see dragons. They couldn't see anything connected to magic. The Dragon Elite would be useless overnight.

Sophia's heart sank.

She was about to rush down the stairs to continue to watch more of the history unfold when a figure appeared beside her. It was the groundskeeper. She had to look down to take in the gnome.

Quiet, like the others in this reality, was black and white. Unlike the others, he was looking straight at her, as if he knew Sophia was there.

As if that wasn't enough, he pointed at her hand, a determined expression in his narrowed eyes. When he spoke, she couldn't hear his words, but she could read his lips.

Very clearly, she saw him mouth, "Go home."

CHAPTER FIFTY-EIGHT

Sophia held the gold token in her hand. She had a whole host of questions when she returned to the present day at the Castle. She blinked, feeling like it had been an eternity since she'd seen color.

She was standing in the same place—on the first landing of the stairs overlooking the entrance hall. She searched around, thinking she'd see Quiet or Ainsley or any of the Dragon Elite. When she turned around and saw the large painting of Adam and Kay-Rye, her heart leapt. Then she realized they were just an image, and they didn't exist in this time.

Her mind was racing with so many questions she nearly forgot the Castle hadn't delivered on its end of the bargain to give her *The Complete History of Dragonriders*.

Quiet could see her at the reset point, but why?

Then there was Ainsley, who didn't appear to have been a house-keeper several hundred years ago.

Even stranger were the hushed words Ainsley had shared with Adam. They seemed to know something about Hiker no one else did. They were reserved when they should have been aggressively going into battle. The Dragon Elite had all but celebrated a decisive victory.

It pained Sophia's heart to think about it. Seeing the past hadn't been as illuminating as she thought. It was like watching a sad movie, knowing how it all ended and unable to do anything about it.

"The answers to all these new questions…" Sophia mused to herself as she climbed the stairs, something building in her.

When she was back in the hall where the portal door had been, Sophia halted, looking around. The door was still gone, but she knew that wasn't entirely true. It was there, but the Castle just had it hidden because otherwise she'd go through and undo everything.

She still had her plan of how she could ultimately deal with the Castle if brute force and ranting didn't work. Sophia felt betrayed.

She was enraged.

Maybe it was because she'd just watched the happy Dragon Elite before they were erased. Maybe it was because her heart ached for Hiker, who'd known something horrible was coming and had tried to warn the House of Fourteen and been dismissed. For whatever reason, Sophia wanted someone to take her anger and frustration out on, and the Castle seemed like the perfect entity.

"The answers I want are in that damn book!" Sophia yelled. She turned around and threw her hands down at her side. "Give me what you promised me! Give me *The Complete History of Dragonriders.*"

The Castle could have answered her, she realized. It sometimes spoke to Ainsley. The shapeshifter had often told her it spoke in mysterious ways. It had communicated to her with the drawings in the condensation on the window. However, the Castle remained quiet.

"I'm warning you, you're not going to like me when I'm mad!" Sophia bellowed. "We've gotten along in the past. You've been good to me, but you're not going to like me if you don't give me what you promised."

She waited, listening to her heaving breath and not hearing any reply from the Castle.

Vibrating with anger, Sophia tried one last time. "You can try to kill me. You can send chandeliers down on me and suits of armor, but I won't back down. Are you going to give me what I want?"

Again, silence followed.

Sophia nodded, pursing her lips. "Very well, you stubborn old Castle. You've asked for it."

CHAPTER FIFTY-NINE

Sophia felt a lot like Hiker as she stomped through the Castle, her eyes teeming with anger and hostility bounding in her chest. She rarely allowed her emotions to overwhelm her. Right then, she felt ready to explode.

She took the stairs two at a time and hurried for the weapon's room she had passed on occasion. This was Wilder's domain, but she needed to borrow something.

To her surprise, Wilder was sitting on the bench in the center of the room when she entered. He glanced up at her, maybe as surprised as her to find Sophia staring around the room, having just bombarded into the space.

"Hey, Soph." Wilder slipped the object in his hands down beside him, trying to hide it.

She turned her attention to surveying the many weapons that lined the wall. There were large and small swords. Knives and many other blades were secured on the wall. Sophia knew Wilder could feel the experiences of the weapons in the room. It didn't surprise her that he spent most of his time here. He knew his gift was a curse and also his very strength. She believed that since Subner had taken him under his wing, telling him the truth about having given him this ability, that Wilder was now more embracing of it.

"Hey, I need an axe," she said, looking around for one that wasn't too big or small.

"Like for throwing?" he asked.

She shook her head, striding over to a pair of axes that might work. "For destroying."

"Destroying what?" he asked, his voice careful and his blue eyes sparkling with curiosity.

"Treachery," she said through clenched teeth.

"That sounds interesting. Can I watch?" he asked.

She shrugged. "If you want." Pointing at the wall, she said, "I'll take that one."

Wilder's eyes shifted between her and the axe which glistened in the firelight. "Are you sure? That's Grim the Destroyer. It's seen some—"

"Yes," Sophia interrupted. "Give it here. Grim the Destroyer sounds perfect."

Hesitating, Wilder took the axe off the wall and carefully handed it to Sophia. All his actions were slow, which her movements contrasted greatly with as she turned with the axe and sped out of the weapon's room, heading for the corridor where the portal door was located.

Sophia thought it might be possible to expose the portal door, but that wasn't her end goal. She just wanted to cause pain. She wanted to win. She wanted to make those who didn't live up to their bargains feel remorse.

At its heart of hearts, which she wasn't sure it actually had, Sophia believed the Castle felt. It had to be possible to reason with it. There must be a way to get the Castle to cooperate. She just had to find it.

CHAPTER SIXTY

When Sophia veered up the stairs to the second story, it got Wilder's attention. Before, he'd been casually following her like he wanted to see her cut down a tree on the Expanse.

"What are you doing?" Wilder asked, sprinting to catch up with her.

"Making someone pay for breaking their word," she said through clenched teeth.

"Soph, you can't do that!" he yelled, his eyes bulging.

"Watch me," she stated, stomping through the corridor until she neared the place where the portal door should be. It was still missing.

The pieces of the broken chandelier still littered the floor. Ainsley had found it and was cleaning it up. The housekeeper glanced up when she heard Sophia and Wilder and rose from her stooped position, her lips pursed.

"You made it mad, didn't you?" Ainsley asked, sticking her hands on her hips. It was strange for a moment to see her in her brown burlap dress and her hair a mess. After the recent vision of her as some sort of royalty, the current image didn't compute.

Sophia shook it off. "It started it," she fired back, holding the axe in both hands. "It's refusing to deliver. We made a bargain."

Ainsley shook her head and clicked her tongue, her hands still on her hips. "I told you…" she warned.

"After everything I went through, it tried to kill me," Sophia stated, throwing her hand at the debris covering the floor.

"Who?" Wilder asked, looking at Sophia and Ainsley.

"The Castle!" both women yelled in unison.

He stepped backward, shaking his head. "What. Is. Happening?"

"General deceit and total manipulation," Sophia seethed.

Ainsley looked impressed as she surveyed the axe. "What are you going to do with that?"

"Remodel," Sophia answered simply.

"W-w-wait," Wilder stuttered. He came to stand between Sophia and Ainsley as if she planned to use the axe on the housekeeper. "What are you going to do?"

Sophia stepped around him. "You'll find out, Wild. And Ains, why is it you don't remember how you became the housekeeper for the Castle?"

Ainsley blinked at her, obviously confused by the random question. "I'm not sure, S. Like I told you, it's been a long time since then. I get flashes, though. Sometimes it comes back to me suddenly, and then I forget again."

"Do you remember not being a housekeeper and living here?" Sophia asked.

Ainsley answered, "No, but that sounds lovely. I don't have to dust the shelves and try to pass old meat off as fresh?"

"What?" Wilder asked in shock. "You don't really do that?"

She waved him off. "Of course, I don't."

"And that scar." Sophia pointed to her temple. "When did you get it? Do you remember that much?"

Ainsley's hand reflexively went for the scar on her temple. "I don't, S."

Sophia might not have been on this Earth for very long, but she knew without a doubt that Ainsley Carter was under a memory spell. "Do you remember the day before mortals weren't allowed to see magic?"

Ainsley appeared as serious as Sophia had ever seen her. The housekeeper's eyes were lost in thought for a moment. "No, I don't. Should I?"

Sophia stepped around the elf and centered herself in front of the wall where the portal door should have been located. "Yeah, you absolutely should."

"Why don't I?" Ainsley asked speculatively.

Sophia pulled the axe back and gritted her teeth. She looked over her shoulder at Ainsley, who she realized was a victim to circumstances blanketed in mystery. "That's exactly what I want to know." She turned her attention back to the stone wall. "Give me the book or you are going to pay. Last chance, Castle."

The silence that greeted her words was all the answer Sophia needed. Wilder interrupted, "What book? What are you talking about?"

She gave him an unyielding expression. "The book that tells the history Ainsley has forgotten. The one that explains why so much of our history as the Dragon Elite is unexplainable. The one that exposes all of Hiker Wallace's secrets. The one that fills in the missing gaps, telling *The Complete History of Dragonriders*."

Wilder's eyes grew large. To Sophia's relief, he didn't try to stop her.

Neither did Ainsley. She put her hand out in Wilder's direction like she was looking for comfort, not something she'd ever needed before. "I have forgotten...quite a lot, actually, and every time I wonder about it, I forget again. I get distracted by something, and then another decade rolls by before I question why I don't remember the past." Just like that, it dawned on the housekeeper. Her gaze was tragic when she looked at Sophia, wide-eyed. "You've figured it out, haven't you? I'm under a memory spell, aren't I, S. Beaufont?"

Sophia nodded. "Yes, I think so, and I'm going to figure out why."

Wilder reached out and took Ainsley's hand, comforting her. She already looked to have recovered, her attention darting back to the broken chandelier on the floor.

"Oh, I'd better clean that up, right?" Ainsley said, pulling away from Wilder, the hurt evaporating from her eyes. She had already forgotten what they had been talking about, the very topic of a memory spell making her overlook that she couldn't remember a thing.

"No, you should wait," Sophia answered. "There's about to be a lot more to clean up." She pulled back Grim the Destroyer and swung it at the wall of the Castle, breaking through the stone and treachery. She hoped she broke its resolve, too.

CHAPTER SIXTY-ONE

The stone wall crumbled at the point of impact. Sophia unwedged Grim the Destroyer from the wall and pulled it back again, combining her next attack with a combat spell.

The axe sunk into the wall, sending a spray of rock dust through the air. When Sophia pulled it out this time, several loose rocks fell to the floor at her feet.

The third time she pulled back the axe, she yelled, "Give. Me. What. You. Promised."

The axe sank into the wall like it was a butter knife cutting through bread. She yanked it out and watched a great deal of the wall come down.

The Castle made no attempt to answer her or reply to the demolition. Knowing Ainsley and Wilder were still watching curiously at her back, she swung around and gauged their musing expressions.

"I will win this," Sophia said, her breath ragged.

"Yes, and I see you're about there." Ainsley pointed at the wall that had been the source of Sophia's attention.

She turned to find the wall completely repaired, not even a speck of dust on the floor by her feet. Clenching her teeth together, Sophia launched Grim the Destroyer through the air and made the blade of the axe stick deep into the wall.

Yanking hard, she tried to take the axe back, but this time it was really stuck. "Give it to me," Sophia said through gritted teeth, referring to both the book and Grim the Destroyer.

The axe wasn't budging, so Sophia stuck her foot on the wall and tried to create leverage as she pulled.

"Really put your back into it," Ainsley encouraged behind her, sounding amused.

"I can help if you'd like," Wilder offered thoughtfully.

"I've got it," Sophia spat, sweat pouring down her brow.

The Castle had made a claim to the axe, Sophia realized as she tried to take it back, continuing to pull.

"Okay, well then, I've got a thing I've got to do," Wilder said discreetly.

Sophia watched as he retreated back toward the staircase. He cast a speculative look at her over his shoulders, his hands in his pockets, and a strange way about him. He was up to something, but come to think of it, she realized everyone in the Castle was. She'd deal with him later. Or she wouldn't, and he'd keep his secrets buried like all the rest.

Scrunching up her face, she gave the axe the biggest tug yet. It released from the wall, making her stumble backward from the momentum.

Sophia ran at the wall, vibrating with anger, and threw the axe into it, but this time it didn't even make a dent. It was like she was beating a wall made of diamonds. The blade of Grim the Destroyer just bounced off.

"You are revolting!" Sophia yelled, pulling back her foot and kicking the wall, realizing she was running out of options.

"What is going on here?" Hiker Wallace asked at Sophia's back.

She tensed. Gripped the handle of the axe. Let out a long breath.

"Oh, S. Beaufont, Hiker is coming," Ainsley said in a loud conspiratorial whisper.

Shaking off the strange desire to laugh, Sophia turned around to find the leader of the Dragon Elite standing squarely in front of her, gazing down with a demanding expression on his face.

"Thanks, Ains," Sophia said with zero inflection.

"What is the meaning of the blockades at the end of the hallway?" Hiker asked Ainsley.

She pointed down at the broken bits of the wooden chandelier. "There's construction going on here. You'll have to go around."

Sophia was less worried about Hiker coming down this corridor now the portal door had disappeared. What did it matter anyway? So what if he knew? What would he do, fire her? Withhold secrets? The Castle not delivering on its end of the deal had stripped her of her resolve. She really didn't care if Hiker was pissed. Either way, she still didn't have any answers, and she'd risked a great deal for nothing.

"I'm not going around," Hiker grumbled. "And how did the chandelier come down?"

"The Castle tried to kill me," Sophia muttered, turning her attention back to the wall and attempting another swing. Again, the wall was unrelenting, the blade simply bouncing right off.

"And that's why you're trying very poorly to harm it?" Hiker asked, actually sounding amused.

"Oh, this is going to be good," Ainsley said, snapping her fingers and summoning the high back chair from before. She took a seat, looking to try to get extra cozy before she waved her hand and summoned a bowl of dried dates from the kitchen downstairs.

With Hiker and Sophia both giving her impatient expressions, she waved them on. "Alright. I'm ready. You can continue."

"What are you doing?" Hiker asked her, irritation heavy in his voice.

"I have a front-row seat to the greatest show this Castle has seen in quite some time," Ainsley stated, popping a date into her mouth.

"Why are you eating dates?" Sophia had to ask.

"They are the perfect show snack." Ainsley took another bite.

"No, you're thinking of popcorn," Sophia corrected.

"Oh, I probably am, but I don't have any of that," Ainsley replied regretfully. "Can you Uber Eats me some? Wait, no, I almost forgot—show. You guys continue. Go on, then."

Sophia turned her attention to Hiker. "Why is it she can't remember how she got that scar or why she started working here for the Dragon Elite or really pretty much anything that happened around when mortals couldn't see magic?"

He rolled his eyes. "Because she's a daft elf who probably dips into the cooking sherry a bit too much and spends her days having conversations with a stubborn old castle."

"Yeah, about this ornery old castle," Sophia said, turning her attention back to the wall. Her adrenaline to assault it with the axe had all but evaporated. Instead, she pulled back her foot and kicked the wall again, not hurting her foot or making any impression on the stone.

"Why is it you're mad at the Castle?" Hiker asked curiously.

"Because it's a deceitful creature who runs our lives, taking what it wants and not giving us what we ask for," Sophia seethed.

Hiker nodded appreciatively. "Now you get where I'm coming from."

"Yeah, I guess I do," Sophia muttered, trying to figure out her next course of action.

"It took my books, remodeled my office, stole my clothes, and has pretty much confined me to living in a closet," Hiker offered, strangely sympathetic.

"Oh, closets," Ainsley gasped. "Spoiler alert…"

Sophia shot her a punishing look. Hiker gave Ainsley a curious one.

"What's that about a closet?" Hiker asked the housekeeper.

"Nothing," Sophia said at once. "She's obviously munching on dates that have gone bad."

Ainsley eyed the small dried fruit in her hand. "Oh, that seems about right. I think all my dates have gone bad, which is why I'm here."

"What is this about closets?" Hiker asked, not giving up on the question.

Sophia shook her head. "Since we both loathe the Castle, can we have Christmas?"

"I'm not following this line of reasoning, but no, no, we can't," Hiker replied.

Sophia slumped, thinking she could ask the Castle for *The Complete History of Dragonriders* for Christmas. What did it matter? Like Ainsley had said, if the Castle wanted her to have something, then she would. If it didn't, then she wouldn't. It was as plain and simple as that. For whatever reason, the Castle didn't want her to have the book. Or maybe it didn't want her to have it *yet*.

Sophia turned the new idea over in her head, trying to think of all the little clues the Castle had given her. She knew about *The Complete History of Dragonriders* because the Castle had given her a copy of *The InComplete History of Dragonriders*, taking it from Hiker's collection and not allowing him access to it.

The Castle had sent her on a mission that had not only connected her new home to her old home, but had also made her the protector of the gold token. It held the reset point, giving her a way to glimpse incredibly pivotal moments in history. From there, she'd learned so much about Hiker, Ainsley, Adam, the Dragon Elite, Thad Reinhart, and the House of Fourteen. She knew Hiker used to be a courageous leader.

She knew he saw what no one else did. He'd warned them, and there were so many other things the brief glimpse of history had provided.

With Hiker Wallace staring down at her skeptically and Ainsley chewing nonstop on dates, something crucial occurred to Sophia. The Castle, as deceptive and plotting as it was, might have rhyme to its reason.

CHAPTER SIXTY-TWO

aybe, she thought, *the Castle is waiting for the right moment to give me the book.*

The flames of the candles in the sconces lining the corridor grew brighter. It was one of the ways the Castle communicated, often meaning yes.

Sophia directed her attention to Hiker and studied him. *Was it possible the Castle wanted him to be a part of her finding* The Complete History of Dragonriders, she wondered?

Again, the flames grew, sending more light around the hallway.

Hiker noticed, his eyes sliding to the side. "What's going on, Sophia?"

"I think I need to tell you the truth," she said carefully, waiting for a reply from the Castle.

For a third time, and more intensely than the rest, the flames shimmered brighter.

"The truth about what?" Hiker asked, lowering his chin and regarding her with hooded eyes.

"Oh, yes," Ainsley said, scooting back on her chair. "This is going to be good."

"Would you get out of here, woman?" Hiker bellowed over his

shoulder to her. "Don't you have some vegan dish you're going to try to pass off to me as having real meat?"

"No, not today, sir." Ainsley popped a date into her mouth and chewed. "You're not going to be at all hungry after this since you'll have S. Beaufont's blood all over your hands. I seem to remember you don't like to eat after killing, but the memory is fuzzy." She pointed at the bits of chandelier like she was seeing them for the first time. "Oh, someone should really clean that mess up."

"Yes, someone should," Hiker seethed. He turned back to Sophia. "What is this thing you need to be honest with me about?"

Before Sophia could answer, the portal door appeared again as if the Castle was trying to help out with the conversation.

"What. Is. That?" Hiker asked, articulating each of the words and spiking them with hostility.

"It's a door, sir," Ainsley replied with a snicker in her voice.

"I see that," he stated. "Why does it appear out of place in the Castle, like...like..."

Sophia knew it would only take him another few seconds to figure it out, and she didn't think it polite to interrupt. Better if he came by all this on his own.

On cue, Hiker's eyes widened as the realization dawned on him. "Why does that look like a door from the House of Fourteen?"

"Do you have life insurance, S. Beaufont?" Ainsley asked. "I don't know what that is, but I read an article about it in one of those magazines you keep in your room."

"You mean, my diary?" Sophia questioned, remembering she'd said something in passing about the subject, referring to her parents.

"Oh, is that what that is?" Ainsley asked. "I thought it was just really strange stories about a silly girl who makes questionable life decisions."

"Thanks, Ains," Sophia said.

Hiker pointed. "The door. Tell me now."

Sophia sighed. "Okay, so I wanted *The Complete History of Dragonriders* and knew the Castle had it, so I made a deal with it. I'd do something if it would in return give me the book."

Hiker's face gradually shifted to a nice shade of pink as she spoke.

"Anyway," Sophia continued, trying not to be flustered by his growing anger, "I had to fight Hydra to get this gold token, which gave me access to the reset point, where I found a portal door between the House of Fourteen and the Castle."

"You *what?*" Hiker yelled.

"And there it is," Ainsley said with a delighted giggle. "I told you he wasn't going to like the idea well before you attempted the task."

Sophia shot her an angry look. "You didn't either."

"Oh, well then, S. Beaufont, Hiker won't like it if you open a portal between here and the House, just in case you're wondering."

"Thanks, Ains," Sophia muttered.

"You reopened the portal between the Castle and House of Fourteen?" he asked, his voice simmering with frustration.

"'Reopened,'" Sophia mused. "Yeah, that makes sense. So you knew about it?"

"Of course, I know about it," he spat. "I closed the bloody thing ages ago."

"Why?" Sophia questioned.

"It's not important," he said dismissively. "There's no reason for the two to be connected anymore. The way I see it, there never was."

"Well, the Castle disagrees." Sophia pointed over her shoulder at the portal door. "And after all my efforts, the Castle now refuses to pony up and give me *The Complete History.*"

At this, Hiker smiled. "As much as I despise this bloody castle sometimes, I agree with it this time. For once, I'm glad the Castle is a wanker who doesn't deliver on its promises."

"Why is that?" Sophia asked, still holding onto the axe.

"Because the book doesn't belong to you, and there's zero reason you need to have it," he fired back.

"Is it because it's hiding secrets you want to stay buried?"

"It shouldn't matter," he replied. It was a standoff.

"Well, it does matter because we as the Dragon Elite can't do our job if we don't know what's going on or the history," Sophia reasoned.

"You as the Dragon Elite aren't doing anything to help our mission because you're off searching for things that don't concern you," Hiker argued.

"I wouldn't be doing that if you would just be honest," Sophia stated. "I know you're hiding something. The Castle knows it."

Hiker laughed. "You think the Castle wants you to know the history? If it did, you would. There's a reason it isn't giving you the book. And—"

"Sorry to interrupt your lovely chat," Ainsley cut in. "But I think you all need to see something."

The pair of them swung around, following the direction the housekeeper was pointing. On the opposite wall from the portal door appeared another one. This door was arched like most of the rest in the Castle.

It shimmered for a moment before becoming solid.

"I'm not going through that door," Ainsley joked. "The last time I went through a magical door that appeared out of nowhere, I found myself in this damn castle with a never-ending contract."

"What?" Sophia asked the housekeeper.

She shrugged. "I mean, that's how I remember it, but the details are murky at best."

Sophia shook this off and refocused on the door. She knew she'd done it. Whatever the Castle wanted her to do, she had. It had just given her the path to *The Complete History of Dragonriders*.

The problem was, it had also given it to Hiker Wallace, who she knew wanted the book just as badly as she did—to keep for himself. The glint of mischief that flashed in his eyes when he looked at her told Sophia he would do just about anything to beat her to the book.

CHAPTER SIXTY-THREE

Moving faster than Sophia had ever seen him, Hiker darted forward as he held his arm out to block her path. He pushed her back, not hard, but enough to slow her progress as he took the lead to the newly illuminated door.

In one stride he was at the door and pulling on the handle, which appeared to be locked. Sophia tried to get around him, but he kept shoving her back.

"Use the axe!" Ainsley suggested.

Sophia hadn't realized she was still carrying Grim the Destroyer and dropped the axe. She jumped to the side and watched as Hiker pulled the door handle, trying to get it to turn.

"Come on, you blasted Castle," he growled, shaking his head. "Don't you play with me now."

"I don't think it wants you in there," Ainsley sang, utterly entertained by the whole thing.

Finally, Hiker took a step back and released the door handle. "That's fine. As long as no one else can get in there, where I suppose it's keeping *The Complete History of Dragonriders.*"

"It is indeed," Ainsley affirmed, crossing her legs and leaning back.

Hiker flashed her a murderous expression. "What else do you know, woman?"

Ainsley covered her mouth and giggled like a little girl. "Oh, now, you know I can't tell you anything that would remotely be of help to you."

He nodded. "Yeah, I do know that about you."

With Hiker's attention still on Ainsley, Sophia stole her chance and darted forward to grab the door handle before he could push her back again. He reached for her when her fingers wrapped around the handle.

He gave her a threatening expression but then shook his head. "It's locked, Sophia. Get over it and move on. This isn't worth your time or attention."

She pretended to consider his words for a moment. Feigned resignation. Took a step away from the door, taking her hands off the handle.

"Good, I'm glad you're listening to rea—"

Sophia interrupted Hiker as she leapt forward again and grabbed the handle with a defiant expression on her face. She held the handle in her fingers and Hiker's determined gaze with her eyes.

Worry crossed his face before he shrugged it off and took a step away, apparently tired of this game.

With her gaze still on the leader of the Dragon Elite, Sophia turned her fingers, and the door handle rotated in her grasp.

"Oh, talk about a twist I didn't see coming," Ainsley commented, leaning forward. "The door opened for Sophia!"

Hiker's eyes widened. "Don't do it, Sophia!"

She froze, realizing she was seconds away from being tossed to the side by the Viking-sized man only a few feet away. Lowering her chin, Sophia kept her hand on the handle.

She drew a breath and wordlessly put a shield between her and Hiker, then prayed silently.

As the large man dove for her, Sophia yanked the door open.

From the corner of her eye, she saw Hiker hit an invisible wall as she darted into the darkened room.

She knew the shield wouldn't stand up to Hiker long, and he got through it just as she yanked the door closed.

Sophia stepped back, less concerned about what was lurking in the darkness of the cramped room than if the leader for the Dragon Elite could get through the door and murder her.

The door handle jerked but didn't rotate.

Letting out the breath she'd been holding, Sophia relaxed. Hiker couldn't get through the door.

CHAPTER SIXTY-FOUR

B anging erupted immediately.
"Get back out here, Sophia Beaufont!" Hiker yelled, his voice making the door shake. "That's an order!"

Sophia turned to take in the small space. The ceilings were low and covered in cobwebs. The paint was peeling on the walls, and there were no windows to illuminate the room. The only light came from a single lantern sitting in the middle of the floor, and beside it was a large leather-bound book covered in a thick layer of dust.

"Can you hear me?" Hiker exclaimed, continuing to beat on the door.

"I think the dead can hear you," Ainsley joked. She was probably doubled over laughing from witnessing all the antics.

"Open up this door right now and give me that book!" Hiker bellowed.

Sophia glanced around the room, looking for options. She guessed she'd have to sit down right there and read the book, which might take her a fortnight based on the size. Hopefully, the Castle would feed her and maybe renovate the space with a bathroom.

"DON'T YOU READ THAT BOOK!" Hiker yelled.

Sighing, Sophia shook her head. It was going to be really difficult to concentrate with Hiker going on.

"I'm warning you, Sophia," he continued. "If you don't get out here, you're done with Dragon Elite. I've never been so serious. You'll be out for good!"

Sophia didn't always take Hiker seriously, but right then, she did. Whatever was in this book, he didn't want her to find out, and although she wanted to know the information, she didn't want it more than her position with the Dragon Elite. She knew Hiker was hiding something. He had already hidden the fact that Thad Reinhart had been a dragonrider. That secret wasn't the worst, so she reasoned whatever else he was hiding wasn't either. She didn't need to know at the expense of losing her home.

Surrendering, Sophia knelt and reached for *The Complete History of Dragonriders*.

"Okay, I'm coming out," she called. Her hands hesitated right before she closed her grasp around the book.

"Good," Hiker said with a relieved sigh. "And I want the book."

"What?" Ainsley asked in mock surprise. "You want that book? I had no idea."

"You shush it, woman," he grumbled. "Come on, then, get back out here."

"I'm coming," Sophia called. "I just have to get the book."

When her hands wrapped around *The Complete History of Dragonriders*, three things happened simultaneously.

An electric shock pulsed through her hands, nearly making her drop the book.

The lantern extinguished.

Another door appeared on the opposite side of the room, illuminating the space as it glowed brightly.

CHAPTER SIXTY-FIVE

"*S*OPHIA!*" Hiker yelled. "What are you doing?"

Waking from her daze, Sophia shook her head and focused on the new door that had appeared. She glanced over her shoulder at the one she'd come through, where an angry Viking was waiting to take her book and probably still punish her for her insubordination.

"Maybe she fell asleep," Ainsley offered.

Hiker's growl echoed through the door. He was madder than hell and probably needed an opportunity to calm down. Sophia reasoned she'd followed the Castle this far, and it had illuminated this new door.

Without hesitating, she strode over to the mysterious door, the large book pressed to her chest.

When her fingers wrapped around the handle, she held her breath and wondered if this one would be locked for her.

She rotated the knob, and to her relief, it turned. Pulling the door back an inch, Sophia hesitated and looked over her shoulder at where she'd come from again.

"Sophia, get out here!" Hiker boomed.

"About that," she said, her voice much lower. "There's another doorway that's just appeared and—"

"Don't you do it!" Hiker yelled.

"The thing is…" Sophia's voice trailed away since she was unsure of what to say.

"I told you you'd scare her," Ainsley offered.

"You did not!" Hiker snarled.

"Oh. Well, if you keep yelling like that, you'll scare S. Beaufont."

He beat on the door, making it rattle. "Don't go through that door! Come here this instant."

Sophia didn't want to lose her position with the Dragon Elite, but she wanted answers. And the Castle had provided her with a solution. She couldn't ignore it.

Letting out a weighty breath, Sophia shook her head. "I have to, Hiker. Please understand."

"No!" he yelled as she darted through the door, entering a completely different world.

CHAPTER SIXTY-SIX

The Great Library was as breathtaking as Sophia remembered it. Although she had been in the incredible library in the House of Fourteen, she knew this wasn't it. There was something about the Great Library in Zanzibar that made it different from any other place she'd visited. It had a unique feel, unmatched by any other.

Sophia turned back to the door she'd just come through and found it had shut behind her. She guessed that somehow the Castle had opened a portal to the Great Library. If this stayed, it would make it much easier to get to the library, meaning the dragonriders wouldn't have to find the Fierce to lead the way and also take them through a dangerous obstacle course.

The tall ceilings of the Great Library rose so high it was hard to follow them all the way. The bright light streaming in through the many windows made Sophia squint. The smell of pages cloaked in dust was the most welcoming scent.

Sophia couldn't think of a more perfect place to crack open *The Complete History of Dragonriders* and read all the secrets of Hiker Wallace. She pressed the large volume to her chest, relishing in how well everything had worked out so far.

Coming around a set of shelves, Sophia found the perfect reading corner, complete with large, furry pillows and a cozy bench.

Finally able to let go of the stress of the last several hours, Sophia laid the book on the bench and decided to get comfortable before a long study session.

She was folding herself into place when the large, ancient book flew from its spot and landed in the bony fingers of the librarian of the Great Library.

Sophia's mouth popped open as she jumped to her feet. "Trinity!"

The skeleton clanked his teeth together, his eye sockets seeming to smile. "Hello, Sophia Beaufont! I see you delivered on your end of the deal and brought me the only copy in existence of *The Complete History of Dragonriders.*"

"I did, but I was hoping to read it first," Sophia replied, remembering she'd promised to bring the book straight to Trinity if she should find it, based on a deal they'd made. She had sort of forgotten that part.

"You can totally have the chance to read it," Trinity said, holding the large book to his chest as he swayed with excitement, his bones making clattering noises. "But first me. Remember our deal."

"Can't you simply make a copy of it and give it to me?" Sophia asked.

He shook his skull. "I wish I could, but this is the only book I've ever encountered that can't be copied. That's why I want a chance to read it cover to cover, and then it will go back to its rightful owners, the Dragon Elite."

"But—"

"Oh, the rich history," Trinity interrupted, running his bony fingers over the cover affectionately. "I pride myself on knowing everything, and I do, except about the dragonriders. Thanks to you, I'm about to fill that gap."

"I see, but maybe we can read it at the same time?" Sophia suggested.

He considered that and then shook his head. "I'm afraid I've waited too long for this to share the experience, but I do promise to give the book straight to you when I'm done with it."

"Which will be?" Sophia asked. "You speed-read, right?"

He shook his head. "I'm not certain how long it will be, but I will want to relish every single word. I know that much."

She grimaced. "I don't think that's necessary. I mean, most of the words are just 'the,' 'and,' and unimportant pronouns."

"Oh, but those are my favorites," he argued.

"And you've probably read most of what's in there when you perused *The InComplete History of Dragonriders*," she continued, trying to convince him to give her back the book.

"Regardless, I want to start at the beginning and read all the way to the end so I get the complete experience."

Sophia slumped in defeat. "Is that so?"

"Yes, and I'd like to have complete quiet, so unfortunately for you, the Great Library is closed." Trinity pointed in the direction of the door she'd come through. "Isn't it nice you opened up a nifty portal between the Castle and here? I can't go through it, but it will make it easier for the dragonriders. I wonder how that portal even came to be. I guess the only way to find out is to read this book."

Sophia kept trying to find a way to get Trinity to share the book as he ushered her toward the door, his demeanor growing more demanding by the moment.

"Now, you'll get your book back," he began when she was pretty much pressed against the portal door. "Keep in mind, the sooner you leave, the sooner you will get it back."

Regretfully, Sophia nodded and went back through the portal.

She was going to have to face Hiker's wrath, which would be all the more based on the bad news she had to share with him.

CHAPTER SIXTY-SEVEN

As Sophia had expected, Hiker was waiting for her when she exited the small room. He halted his pacing and ran his eyes over her, confusion springing to his face when he realized she didn't have the book.

"Where is it?" he demanded.

Ainsley had apparently gone back to cleaning or found someone else to harass since the chair was back in its place and she was gone.

Sophia pointed over her shoulder and muttered something inaudible, feeling like the groundskeeper, Quiet.

"What was that?" Hiker asked, striding over to her.

She slumped, defeat enveloping her. "I don't have it."

"Wasn't it in there?" he asked, appearing both confused and relieved.

She nodded. "Yes, but I went through the other door, which led—"

"To the Great Library," he guessed.

"Yeah, how did you know?"

His gaze rose to the ceiling. "Remember, I closed the portals."

"Oh, right." She cringed. "Yeah, so I went through and found Trinity. He and I might have made a deal that if I found the book, he got to read it first."

Hiker actually smiled, relief in his blue eyes. "You didn't even get to crack it open, did you?"

She shook her head and stuck her hands in her pockets.

"And when he returns it, I'll ensure it comes straight to me," Hiker said with confidence.

"That's your right as the leader of the Dragon Elite," she replied in a tight voice.

"Oh, you remember I'm still the leader around here, then?"

"Am I fired?" Sophia asked, ready to face the consequences for her action.

Hiker studied her, the smile fading from his face. "No, I guess not since you didn't actually read the book, but I won't stand for any more of your rebellious behavior. I might have a long way to go to recover my role as leader, but I am still that."

"I realize that, sir," Sophia stated. "I'm sorry."

"Are you?" Hiker asked.

"Yes. It's just, the Castle and Papa Creola keep leading me in different directions," Sophia admitted.

"I get that." Hiker sounded sympathetic. "I know they have agendas that aren't congruent with mine. You might consider you are a pawn in all this."

"Do you think so? Or is it maybe whatever you're hiding, it's time to uncover?" Sophia dared to ask. She had little to lose at this point. It would take Hiker a century to get over her behavior.

"I get you think knowing all the history is important, but it isn't," Hiker argued. "Not for you or Ainsley or any of the other riders. I made that decision a long time ago, and you'd do well to respect it."

"I can, sir," Sophia said. "I will quit asking you about it or searching for answers. I won't even read *The Complete History* even if Trinity gives me the book directly. I'll turn it over to you."

Hiker nodded proudly. "Good. That's how it should be. Now, I want you out on the Expanse. You'll train for the rest of the day, and tomorrow you'll report to my office for an adjudicator mission. Is that clear?"

Sophia nodded. "Yes, sir. Very much so."

"Very well, off with you, then," he said, waving her toward the stairs.

She hustled off before pausing and turning back to the leader of the Dragon Elite. "One last thing, sir?"

He lowered his chin and scowled at her. "What?"

"I get that you have your reasons for keeping secrets," she began, her confidence building as she spoke. "I just wonder if you're hiding things to protect the Dragon Elite and the world at large, or…"

"Or what?" he growled.

She shrugged. "Or are you hiding them to protect yourself?"

CHAPTER SIXTY-EIGHT

Hiker didn't answer Sophia's question. When he stormed off in the other direction, she knew she'd been formally dismissed from his presence.

Head down, she dragged herself out to the Expanse for training, feeling demoralized.

She was surprised to find the grounds buzzing with activity. Lunis, Bell, and Simi were training by the Cave. Evan was riding Coral through the cloudy sky, and Wilder was practicing his combat skills. Mama Jamba sat on a bale of hay, her nose in a book called *Death Becomes Her*.

"So, what happened?" Wilder asked as she approached. "Did you get the Castle to cooperate?"

She pulled her mouth to the side, watching as Mama Jamba glanced up briefly from her book, obviously eavesdropping. "Yeah, sort of, and then I got outplayed."

"It's better this way, sweetheart," Mama Jamba called from the other side of the combat area.

Sophia nodded, finding it hard to see any silver lining just yet. "Yeah, I'm sure you're right."

Wilder laughed. "She is Mother Nature. I don't think she's ever been wrong."

"There was the time I made dodo birds," Mama Jamba said, raising her book again and reading. She dropped it suddenly, a thought occurring to her. "Oh, and Florida."

Sophia wanted to laugh, but her heart just wasn't in it. "What are you working on right now?" she asked the other dragonrider.

Wilder's eyes slipped to the side. "I wish I could tell you, but Subner swore me to secrecy."

"That's right, more secrets. Oh, how I love them," Sophia said. "Well, maybe you'll at least spar with me. Hiker sent me out to train, and I really shouldn't have put it off this long." Her expectant gaze drifted to Mama Jamba. "Unless you think…"

The woman with huge silver hair and pink lips smiled. She pointed to something behind Sophia. "Well, actually, Quiet can tell us right now if you should commence training."

"Right, and why is he in charge of such things?" Sophia asked.

"Well, naturally because he's in charge of the grounds," Mama Jamba stated.

"Naturally, Sophia," Wilder said, elbowing her in the side. "Don't you know anything about how these things work?"

"Obviously, I don't," Sophia grumbled as the gnome approached from the Castle.

"Quiet, my love, do you think we're ready for Sophia to continue her training?" Mama Jamba asked when he got near.

He replied, his message inaudible to most. Mama Jamba understood it.

"Well, there you go," she said, pursing her lips and raising her book back up to her nose.

"There you go, Sophia," Wilder said, continuing to laugh.

"Actually, can you interpret, Mama Jamba?" Sophia asked. "I didn't catch all that. Well, none of it, really."

"You didn't?" she questioned, acting surprised. "Oh, well, he said you should definitely throw yourself into training after the first of the year. We are ready for it. First, you're to go to Hiker's office. He wants to see you pronto."

"He said all that?" Sophia questioned, thinking the few seconds the gnome had talked couldn't have been long enough for him to say all that.

"Yes, and he also told me it's time to name the new sheep," Mama Jamba said.

"You name the sheep?" Sophia questioned. "All of them?"

Wilder laughed. "How heartless are you. Of course, Mama Jamba names the sheep. They have feelings, you know."

She gave him an angry scowl. "Would you shush it?"

"I name all my creatures, dear," Mama Jamba stated, "but only after I've had a chance to get to know them. Some I know before they are born, like you, my children. But the sheep, well, I wait until they've chosen a religious affiliation so their name fits them."

Sophia wanted to laugh; she thought Mama Jamba was pulling her leg. When the old woman's expression didn't change, she had to chalk it up to another absurdity of the Gullington. She leaned over and whispered to Wilder, "Did you know the sheep chose a religious affiliation?"

He gave her a mock expression of offense. "Of course! Simi will only eat the atheists."

She narrowed her eyes, instinctively knowing he was lying. "You're so full of it."

He leaned over, giggling in her ear. "I didn't even know the sheep were named. For some reason, all the secrets of this place seem to come out when you're around."

"Speaking of secrets," Mama Jamba said, not taking her eyes off her book, able to hear them perfectly even though they were whispering, "Hiker's office, Sophia."

She blinked, looking at the gnome and the old woman. "I was just with him. What could he possibly want? Maybe to berate me some more?"

Quiet muttered, again something inaudible.

Mama Jamba nodded. "I agree completely."

"Me too," Wilder said, puffing out his chest and pretending he understood what they were talking about.

Sophia slapped him on the arm. "Oh, would you stop it?"

"Never," he said with a wink.

Sophia's gaze darted back to Quiet, and suddenly she remembered him from the reset point at the Castle. She recalled him looking directly at her and telling her to "Go home." There was something very strange about the groundskeeper, and if anyone was keeping secrets, it was him. Right now, she had to go talk to the Viking and hope whatever he had to say to her didn't involve the phrase, "Get out."

CHAPTER SIXTY-NINE

"Come in," Hiker said when Sophia neared the threshold to his office. She stopped in the doorway, noticing the office was even smaller than before. The sofa had disappeared as well as the desk since there was absolutely no room for them. The tiny window that had been on the opposite wall was gone. The most surprising thing was, the Dragon Elite Globe was missing.

There were only the shelves and a few other items on the floor where Hiker stood. The space resembled the small room where Sophia had found the book.

"You'll forgive me if I don't come in. I don't know where to stand," she said, leaning in the doorway, not knowing where she'd fit if she did enter.

He nodded.

"So, the Castle…" Sophia looked at the small area.

"Yeah, it remodeled again," he muttered.

"Because?" she questioned.

"I've been thinking…" Hiker began, his eyes intense. "Really thinking about things I don't usually allow myself to contemplate."

He seemed different from a little while ago when she left him, like he'd jumped into a time warp and gone through an evolution.

"That sounds serious," she suggested, sort of wishing there was a place to stand in his office. She felt awkward hanging out in the doorway.

Hiker took a step like he was about to start pacing and then halted. There was no space for it. Resigned, he turned to face her. "I have something to tell you. I mean, I realize I don't have to tell you anything. You are entitled to none of it, but I think the Castle wants me to. I think this is what it's all been about."

"I do love a good riddle, sir," Sophia began, "but can you be more specific?"

"Sophia, the other riders have been here for hundreds of years," Hiker started. "The Castle never led them on these missions to find my book. It didn't show them Adam's room. Every rider is unique in their own way, but you? Well, I think your mission is...more important in some ways."

"Sir?" Sophia asked, confusion in her voice. "Please excuse me, but I have no idea what you're talking about."

He ran his hands through his beard, seeming to wrestle internally with something. "There is something about you, Sophia, that is changing everything. Things that have stayed buried for a long time aren't anymore. You brought back Mama, and although I love that woman, along with her came problems I can't hide from anymore."

"You mean, Thad Reinhart?" Sophia guessed.

He nodded. "He's gotten too powerful, and it's all my fault."

"Because you thought you killed him and didn't?" she asked.

Hiker shook his head. "No, because I was supposed to kill him and didn't. I failed on purpose."

"You *what?*" Sophia exclaimed.

He hung his head. "Well, I think it was more subconscious than anything, but looking back, I didn't really try, not like I should have."

"Didn't you say the Dragon Elite leveled his castle with Thad in it? That sounds like trying," Sophia offered.

"It does," he replied. "I also knew Thad was in the basement where he would probably be safe. It gets worse."

Sophia didn't know how it could. Hiker had allowed a bad man to live, but for what reason.

"Even when we bombed his Castle," he continued, "I knew he wasn't dead. I thought he'd wither and fade without his dragon, but deep down inside, I've known for quite some time Thad wasn't dead, that he was out there and alive."

"How could you know, sir?" Sophia asked, her attention piqued.

Hiker faced her directly, his sober gaze hanging on her. "Sophia, I'm going to tell you something that has far-reaching implications. Only Quiet and Mama know it, but I realize now, everyone needs to, and it starts with you."

"Why, sir?" Sophia asked.

"Because if it wasn't for you, none of this would change," he reasoned. "And also, you and I are a lot more alike than we are different."

"What?" she questioned.

"Sophia, Thad Reinhart is forever connected to me. I often knew in the past where he was or what he was doing, or even now, I know he's alive and growing more powerful," Hiker admitted slowly. "He is my twin brother."

Sophia blinked at the leader of the Dragon Elite. She didn't understand the implications of this confession, although it seemed very important.

"Mama said she wasn't making anymore twin dragonriders after us, but then you came along," Hiker stated.

"Oh, yeah," Sophia said. She usually forgot she was a twin. "But Jamison died at birth."

"Yes, which explains why you are so powerful," Hiker said almost dismissively.

"What?" Sophia asked.

He sighed. "When there are two, they both are as powerful as normal magicians. However, when one dies, the power they own transfers to the other, making the other more powerful. This used to be common knowledge, but then twins began to learn this and would murder each other."

Sophia gasped in shock. "That's horrible."

Hiker nodded. Gulped. "I agree. It was a really dark part of the magician's history, and that's why many don't know the information anymore."

"I inherited Jamison's power," Sophia said, computing the implications of what she'd learned.

"Yes," Hiker affirmed.

"Why wouldn't you want Mama to have twin dragonriders anymore?"

"Because twins as dragonriders go a step further, but I'm not entirely sure why," Hiker began. "Only the angels above do. When a twin is chosen as a dragonrider, the other is automatically chosen by a different dragon. If one magnetizes, the other will too. Maybe to model the light and dark of the world, or to mirror yin and yang, one is always inherently good and the other one bad."

The laugh that spilled out of Sophia's mouth seemed abrupt and then rude. She covered her mouth. "Wait, do you think I'm bad?"

He shook his head. "It's obvious you aren't. If your twin had survived, he would have been, though. I'm certain of that."

A cold chill ran down Sophia's back. She couldn't fathom that the twin she'd never known and always thought of so fondly would have been evil. So many fantasies about having Jamison to play with had always taken up her childhood. She'd been sure if she'd only had him, then her childhood wouldn't have been so lonely, but now she wasn't so sure.

Jamison would have been bad.

Then it hit Sophia hard. Her mouth popped open. "Thad is the bad twin."

Hiker nodded, his eyes red and full of regret. "I'm afraid so, and I knew he wasn't dead all these years because I can feel him. Worse yet, I knew he was growing powerful and taking over, or at least I knew on a subconscious level."

"Your connection to him is how you knew he was up to something horrible just before the dark ages," Sophia said mostly to herself as she remembered the memory from the reset point.

"What?" Hiker asked.

"You warned the House of Fourteen about the magitech," she explained. "It wasn't because you had intel like Adam, it was because you could sense something about Thad. You two have a connection like all twins do, and therefore you share information."

"I don't know where you get your information, but yes, that's correct."

Sophia explained about the gold token and the reset point and everything she'd seen.

"Then you probably want to know what happened to change everything that night," Hiker began, regret in his voice. "The battle was supposed to be swift. Thad's numbers were low. We were strong. He had one advantage over me, and he knew it."

Sophia sucked in a breath. She knew not to interrupt, but the silence between them was almost too much.

Finally, Hiker said, "I knew long ago I needed to kill my brother, but I couldn't do it. And he knew that better than anyone."

And there it was. Hiker had hesitated when his greatest enemy had opposed him. He'd allowed evil to survive when his job was to fight it.

"This was why Adam took out Ember, Thad's dragon, when it should have been me," Hiker continued. "Adam was trying to stop Thad, but instead, he killed the dragon. None of it would have happened if I had been willing to stop my twin. Adam knew I couldn't harm my brother, no matter what he did. Later, when the final battle was almost over, it was up to me to take down the leader of the Rogue Riders. I hesitated, and Thad did what he did best and took the advantage. He came in to take me out, delivering an evil blow."

"He was going to kill you," Sophia guessed.

"Yes, but I didn't fight him. I couldn't. Only one person was willing to do that for me." Hiker sucked in a breath and gave Sophia the most pained expression she'd ever seen on anyone's face.

"Who was it, sir?" Sophia asked, although she felt she already knew. "Who fought Thad for you?"

"It was Ainsley," Hiker admitted. "She saved my life."

CHAPTER SEVENTY

"Ainsley jumped in front of the attack meant to kill me," Hiker continued, "and it nearly destroyed her. It is because of her I stand before you now. She paid the ultimate price for her bravery. The attack didn't kill her; the Castle saw to that. However, it wiped her memory, and nothing I've ever done has ever been enough to recover it."

Now she knew.

Sophia understood so much. Hiker's regret. His inability to take proper action against Thad Reinhart. Why Ainsley had the scar, and why she couldn't remember so much. It also told her something only those looking between the lines would know.

"She must have loved you very much," Sophia said softly.

Hiker's head jerked up. "No. We were associates. Maybe friends, but that's it. Why would you say that? She was an advisor for the Dragon Elite."

Sophia smirked. "Sir, if I may, one only risks their life like that for someone they love deeply. Maybe you didn't know about her heart, but it is the only reasonable explanation for her actions."

He shook his head adamantly. "It wasn't like that. We were on the battlefield. Negotiations were going to commence. I knew I needed to kill Thad. I knew he'd never face his punishment as he hadn't when he tried to flee the first time when Adam tried to stop him and accidentally killed Ember. It all happened so fast. He threw a curse meant for me. Ainsley jumped in front of it. I tried to deflect. It worked, but not well enough. Thad fled, and Ainsley paid the price for my cowardice."

"Not being able to kill your twin isn't such a bad thing," Sophia reasoned.

"It is when he's the worst human being, capable of so much corruption," Hiker said, stomping. "And now he's back, and I know what needs to be done, but doing it, well…"

"You have your demons to face first," Sophia said. "Are you going to tell Ainsley the truth?"

His eyes cut to her. "I can't."

"But sir, you said you'd tell the others the truth," she argued.

"I meant about Thad," Hiker stated. "I didn't know you'd seen the past—the portion about Ainsley."

"She deserves to know."

Hiker pulled his beard. "I can't. Even if I did, I'm certain she'd just forget again. Anything connected to that part of the past, she won't remember. It was the only way, I'm guessing, the Castle was able to save her from a curse which would have otherwise killed her. She had to forget it all."

"Ainsley hasn't always been the housekeeper for the Castle," Sophia mused.

"No," Hiker answered. "She was once a powerful strategist for the elves and one of the most trusted advisors of the Dragon Elite. After the incident, it was clear she couldn't leave the Castle on a long-term basis. If she does, she grows confused and gets sick. She must always live within these walls or she'll perish."

"But she's a housekeeper," Sophia argued. "That can't be the life she wanted."

"And it's not the one I wanted for her!" Hiker boomed. "What choice did I have in any of this?"

Sophia didn't answer, but she hoped her defiant expression said enough.

"I get this is all my fault," he said in a hushed voice a moment later. "If I'd stopped Thad, this never would have happened. Now he's back, and another war is brewing. I feel it. I know he's got many plans for corruptions which have already been set in motion." He thrust his hands into his hair on either side of his head. "I-I-I lost my confidence that day, Sophia. And all these years since, I've been…"

"Holding it together," Sophia said, finishing his sentence. She suddenly saw Hiker Wallace so clearly. She was grateful for the opportunity to see him at the reset point in the House of Fourteen. It gave her a glimpse of the leader that brought all this together. He had once been a competent leader, leading the Dragon Elite, the most powerful magical group on Earth, to greater heights. Being pitted against his twin had nearly ruined him. Sophia couldn't imagine having to fight one of her siblings. It would probably break her too.

"Sir," Sophia continued, realizing Hiker was still processing his confession, "I know you failed in the past to stop Thad, but I believe the experience has taught you something valuable. And you have us. We will help you. Together, I think we can win this; stop Thad once and for all and preserve this Earth for future generations."

"Thank you," he said quietly. "This is when I remind you our numbers are small and Thad has built an empire and an army."

"We have strategy," she argued. "We have each other. And I want to believe being good makes us more powerful."

A small smile rose to his eyes. "I want to believe you're right."

"What now?" she asked.

"I tell the others what we're up against," Hiker promised. "Once you all know, I will be back into a position of accountability. And we prepare. We build our reputation as adjudicators. We rise up. I suspect Thad will come at us with everything he has. All he's ever wanted was my demise."

"So he could have the power you share as twins," Sophia guessed.

Hiker nodded. "And we are the dichotomy. Good versus evil. He represents everything I oppose. He'd rather this Earth perish than be at peace."

"Then we will stop him," Sophia said with conviction.

"No," Hiker argued. "This time, I have to do things right. When it gets to that point, it needs to be me. I have to be the one to stop my brother, and I can't hesitate. Otherwise, I'm certain everything will be lost for good this time. You don't get a third chance to do things right."

Sophia sucked in a breath. "Okay, then we will help you prepare."

"Thank you." He smiled faintly.

"Thank you for telling me this."

He glanced at her. "It was what you said about hiding secrets to protect myself. I'd been telling myself for the longest time I needed to hide the truth to protect the Dragon Elite. To protect my men...I mean, you all. To protect the world from an evil I didn't know how to fight."

He worked his lips, wrestling internally. "When you said that, I realized I didn't want to face the truth. I didn't want you to know my secrets and weaknesses because then I'd have to deal with them, which is how it should be. So there it is. Those are the things I've kept from you. If you had the book, you'd find out on your own."

Sophia was about to say something, but the explosion of events that happened right then cut her off. Before their eyes, Hiker's office shifted suddenly, expanding, furniture materializing, a row of windows taking shape across the far wall and books filling the shelves on the walls.

The leader of the Dragon Elite rotated and watched as the transformation happened. When he completed a circle, he blinked at the space in awe. His gaze finally centered on Sophia, astonishment heavy in his eyes.

"I knew it," he whispered.

"The Castle..." Her voice trailed away.

"It was punishing me for keeping secrets," Hiker admitted. "When you and I argued about the book, I had an inkling of what it wanted me to do. It wanted me to confess, and now that I have, it has given me back that which I held dear."

Hiker reached out and ran his fingers over the Elite globe. "Every leader of the Dragon Elite has led from this office with the tools I once had." He brought his gaze up and ran it affectionately over the hundreds of books lining the shelves, an array of muted colors. "The Castle was trying to tell me I wasn't being the leader you all deserved."

"You are now because you know what you have to do," Sophia confirmed. "And you know you can't run from it anymore."

Hiker's blue eyes shone across the space as he nodded. "Yes, Thad Reinhart, my twin brother, must die, and only by my hands."

CHAPTER SEVENTY-ONE

E verything lately had been about books for Sophia. She figured it made sense, though, since they had always been her most steady friend—her companion when she couldn't show the world who she was.

She and Hiker weren't so different. They were both twins. They both had secrets. Sophia was powerful from a young age, having magic before children should. Still, she knew what it was like to hide, as Hiker had done.

And now, she understood exactly why she'd come into her magic so early on in life. It was because of Jamison. Having lost her twin at birth transferred his power to Sophia. It confounded her how different her life would have been if he had lived.

They would have both gone on to become dragonriders. One of the five shimmering eggs in the Cave would probably have magnetized to Jamison. He wouldn't have joined the Dragon Elite, as she had. If what Hiker had said was true, he would have gone away on his own and pursued plans of a selfish nature like Thad and Logan and other dragonriders who hadn't been cut out for the Elite.

It was strange to be relieved for the first time in her life her twin was dead. She couldn't imagine having to kill him, as Hiker would

281

have to do with Thad. All of this suddenly begged the question of why twins who were dragonriders were divided as good and evil.

It must have to do with the dragons, Lunis offered, talking in Sophia's head.

There is nothing in the collective consciousness of the dragons that explains it, she questioned.

Not that I'm aware of, he stated.

I feel like we're on the precipice of learning a lot of why things work the way they do for the dragons and their riders, Sophia said, pausing outside Liv's apartment and holding the small wrapped package to her chest.

I think you're right, he offered. *Something opened up with Hiker's confession.*

Just imagine when he tells the others, she stated.

I have a feeling it will change very little, he said. *I think you and I completing training will change everything, though.*

Why do you think that?

Because of something Mama Jamba said to me the other day, he replied.

Oh? she questioned curiously. *What is that?*

Well, when you were having your conversation with Hiker, he began, *Mama Jamba told me to put everything into our training.*

Well, that doesn't mean much, Sophia contemplated.

Yeah, but then she said, "Completing your training will change everything." Lunis snickered.

Sophia rolled her eyes. *You're so clever with your remarks and how you time them.*

Aren't I, though, he said, sounding proud of himself. *You know what the key to good comedy is?*

Wha—

Timing, he interrupted.

Sophia giggled. *You should go into standup comedy,* she joked.

Can you just imagine? he asked. *A dragon up on a stage, telling jokes about things like how we're depicted so poorly in films. The stereotype of angry dragons is giving us a bad rap.* Lunis' voice took on the tone of a comedian leading into a joke. *Why do the dragons in Game of Thrones have to be so hostile? Sure, we roast those we don't like and have claws for days, but so does every diva in LA.*

Ba-dum-DUM, Sophia said, shaking her head. *You will have to work on your jokes.*

Yeah, I'm not quitting my day job just yet.

Good, she said, stopping by the door, her excitement building. *Okay, I'm ringing off. I have to see a Warrior about a thing.*

Tell her I said to brush her hair, Lunis joked.

Liv loves it when people tell her that, Sophia said.

And by love, you mean, she loathes it.

Exactly, Sophia said, grabbing the handle and pushing the door open. She was looking forward to what she got to do next.

CHAPTER SEVENTY-TWO

Sophia loved the House of Fourteen. The Castle was her home—hopefully, her forever home if it was up to her. Yet there was something about Liv's apartment that held an inexplicable comfort for her.

Just entering the once tiny studio apartment filled Sophia's heart with nostalgia. Liv and Clark had renovated the space to be quite expansive with multiple bedrooms, a large balcony, and multiple places for entertaining, which Liv said she didn't like to do. Sophia knew better. There was nothing her sister liked better than to have her friends all around her and the opportunity to make them smile.

The smell of vanilla and lavender hit Sophia's nose, instantly reminding her of her sister.

"Soph, is that you?" Liv called from the living room. "Get in here and tell Clark he needs a new hairstyle."

Sophia giggled as she came around the corner to find her siblings cuddled up next to one another on the sofa.

"Don't you think he'd look good with a mohawk?" Liv asked tousling Clark's short blond hair.

He yanked back, grimacing at her. "No, I've already told you I'm not changing styles."

"You've been wearing that same hairstyle since you were born," Liv argued. "I think you're overdue for a change."

"I'm not a person who does change," he said, trying to fix his hair as he looked at his reflection in the glass of a picture on the wall beside him.

"That reminds me," Sophia began. "Lunis says 'hi' and that you should brush your hair, Liv."

She smirked. "Tell Burn-a-dette he needs to mind his own business and get his own jokes. That's Bermuda Lauren's line."

"Actually, I think Lunis is working on new material right now." Sophia shook her head. "I'm afraid it's probably going to get a bunch of tomatoes thrown at him."

Liv patted the sofa beside her. "Come sit. Tell me why you're here, not that I'm complaining. I thought we were doing Christmas festivities tomorrow. I don't have your gift yet."

"That's okay." Sophia took the spot next to Liv, cuddling close.

"No, it's not," Liv argued. "I mean, how hard is it to fix up a 3D printer that can create another 3D printer?"

"You just told her what her gift is," Clark admonished.

"No, I didn't," Liv stated. "I told her I needed a 3D printer that could create a 3D printer, which is how Alicia is going to get me her gift."

"Which is?" Clark demanded.

"A 3D printer," Liv admitted. "It's all very complicated, but there you go, Soph. You did ask for one. It's just, making one from scratch would take time, so I suggested Alicia tweak her fancy-dancy 3D printer so it can make us another one. It's working on it, but it is no Santa's elf. You might not have it until Valentine's Day."

Sophia smiled. "I'm good with that. It's the thought that counts."

"Well, speaking of thoughts," Liv began, "I was thinking that for Christmas—"

"I actually can't come tomorrow," Sophia interrupted, suddenly feeling small.

"You can't?" Liv and Clark asked in unison.

"No," Sophia admitted. "Hiker, after much berating, has agreed to let us have Christmas at the Castle. It's the first time ever." She sighed fondly. "You should see the decorations. I've never seen anything so beautiful."

"I'd love to see the decorations," Liv grumbled. "But you live at a place that is called the Elite and doesn't allow outsiders into it."

Sophia laughed. "I know. I'd take pictures, but every time I do, the Castle deletes them from my phone. According to Ainsley, it's not photogenic."

"You won't be here for Christmas," Liv said, disappointment evident in her tone.

"No, but I'm here now." Sophia extended the package she was holding. "And if the thought is what counts, all the credit goes to Clark. This was his idea."

Her brother bolted forward, his eyes wide. "You didn't, Soph?"

She nodded proudly, trying to hold in her excitement. "I did."

"Didn't what?" Liv asked, looking at her sister and brother.

"Open it," Sophia encouraged, pushing the package into her hands. "The thought was Clark's."

"What you had to go through to get it..." He shook his head in astonishment.

"I'll admit it was an ordeal, but I survived, and I'd say there are some souls who are better off for the field trip," Sophia stated.

Liv took the package and gave her sister a tentative expression. "What is this?"

"There's only one way to find out," Clark said, his voice vibrating with excitement.

"Okay," Liv said, drawing out the word. Carefully, she peeled back the paper, not tearing it as she revealed the book inside.

Her hands began to shake as she turned over their father's book. "My God! Soph... Clarky... You all..."

Tears filled Liv's eyes as she opened the cover and read the first line on the first page:

Familia Est Sempiternum.

With a great fondness and wet cheeks, Liv ran her fingers over the words. "I can't believe you found Daddy's book." She looked up, shaking her head in amazement. "What did you have to go through to get this?"

Sophia shrugged. "No worse than what I've done to recover other books."

Liv began to flip through the pages, the tears falling faster now. "His words make it feel like he's here. This is by far the best present you two could have ever given me."

Clark leaned over her shoulder and snuggled close to her as he read the pages with her. "He was the wisest man I've ever known."

"I didn't know him," Sophia admitted. "Not like you two, but after reading this book, I have to agree. There is magic in those words."

Liv smiled at her sister. "That's because his words were full of love, and that is the greatest magic in the world. Never forget that, Soph."

"I won't," Sophia said, wanting to freeze this moment in time forever. The Beaufonts had been through so much. Lost so much. But they loved with such abandonment, refusing to let their traumas harden them; it was like they'd been spelled. Maybe in another life, when magicians were being created, someone did spell them always to be happy, no matter what.

And so, the Beaufonts were created to protect justice and love each other for all of time.

Liv wrapped one arm around her brother and the other around Sophia and pulled them close. "I love you both with all my heart."

Liv's affection was contagious, and Sophia found her own cheeks wet with happy tears. "I love you both, no matter what, forever."

"*Familia Est Sempiternum,*" Clark said, hugging his sisters with a fierceness that promised never to let them go and always protect them.

That was what the Beaufont children did for each other. The three siblings would never turn on one another, no matter what.

Sophia wanted that for all families, but she knew that wasn't how the world worked. Without a doubt, she'd die for her siblings. Unfortunately, some would do anything to kill their sisters and brothers because the world was made of good, and with that came the inevitable evil.

CHAPTER SEVENTY-THREE

The Christmas cracker wasn't a tradition Sophia was familiar with. Apparently, the guys at the Castle weren't either since Hiker hadn't allowed such festivities for the Dragon Elite.

She held her side of the cracker and gave Evan a challenging expression.

"I'm going to win this, Smalls," he threatened.

"You get it's more about the experience and less about winning, right?" she asked him.

He shook his head. "You have so much to learn, young'un."

They yanked in unison, the cracker making a loud popping sound as it split apart.

Sophia was left holding the shorter side.

Evan held up the container that held his prize. "Winner!" He pointed in her face. "Loser."

"So mature," she said. She shook her head at him as he unfolded the paper hat he found inside the cracker and placed it on his head.

Holiday carols filled the living area, which was exquisitely decorated. The Castle had outdone itself after Hiker had allowed Christmas, filling up every space with flocked garlands and raising a tree covered in red and silver ornaments.

The House of Fourteen was usually incredibly decorated for the holidays, but it paled in comparison to this. Lights twinkled down the banisters of the stairs, and the smell of cinnamon and orange zest greeted Sophia's nose at every turn.

"Well, how about a consolation present?" Wilder asked, handing Sophia a horribly wrapped medium-sized package.

"Thank you," she said, blushing. She noticed his brown hair appeared windswept, although Lunis had said Simi hadn't been out of the Cave all day. She didn't know what Wilder was up to, but she couldn't say she wasn't desperately curious. "I didn't know we were exchanging presents. I..." She looked around suddenly and grabbed a fork off a tray on a table. "I only got you this fork."

He grabbed it, pretending to be in awe. "Fork? What's a fork?"

She smiled at him. "I'll teach you how to use it."

He held it to his chest. "My first fork. I'll treasure it forever. Now open your present, and I'll teach you how to use it."

Sophia laughed at the wrapping. "Did you do this yourself?"

"Hey," he barked. "I can ride a dragon and fight a dozen men at once. I don't need to be able to gift-wrap."

She waved him off. "It's good to be well-rounded."

Sophia pulled off the paper and immediately knew why he'd had such a challenge wrapping her gift. Most people would have trouble wrapping a grappling hook. "How did you know I wanted this?" she asked, thinking immediately of Liv. Her sister had been the one to give her the idea for the gift.

"Because when you were trying to convince Hiker to let us have Christmas at the Castle, you kept saying, 'If we don't celebrate here, how am I going to get a grappling hook?'"

Sophia laughed. "Well, I was hoping he wanted me to have a grappling hook for missions and would give us Christmas for practical reasons." She held the present to her chest. "I love it, though. Thanks so much. And I'd love lessons on how to use it."

He held up his fork. "And I love my first eating utensil. Soon you'll be able to take me to fancy restaurants, not that I'm asking you on a date or anything."

Sophia shook her head. "You aren't even ready for a run-down pub yet, so don't worry. You teach me how to use the grappling hook, and I'll help you be less of a Neanderthal."

"It's a good partnership," he agreed.

Sophia looked around as Evan played with his prizes from the Christmas cracker and Mahkah and Quiet played a calm game of chess by the fire. It was good to see Mahkah up and around. She hoped this was the last time he was injured for a while. He had a record going at this point.

Everyone looked up from the presents and the festive foods Ainsley had served when Hiker Wallace strode down the stairs into the main area. He was dressed the same, but there was something different about the leader of the Dragon Elite. He appeared lighter. Less troubled.

The riders knew his secret. Everyone had understood, and their allegiance to Hiker was all the stronger for it. Ironically, the thing he thought would make him appear weak to his dragonriders had endeared him to them.

"What, no Father Christmas outfit?" Ainsley asked, carrying a tray of hot cocoa.

Hiker rolled his eyes and shook his head at the housekeeper. There was sympathy in his eyes Sophia realized had always been there, but she'd missed it before. There was more to Ainsley's and Hiker's story; she knew it. And like she'd uncovered the other secrets, she planned on figuring out theirs.

Sophia had already decided one of her upcoming missions was to help Ainsley recover her lost memory. She wasn't sure why, but she wanted that for the shapeshifter. Maybe it would hurt at first, but she hoped in time it healed her and brought her some peace.

"But first, your training," Mama Jamba said at her shoulder as if she'd been in her thoughts, listening.

"Excuse me?" Sophia asked.

"I agree she needs her memories back," Mama Jamba said, also wearing one of the paper crowns from the Christmas crackers. She also appeared to have had a few hot-toddies, the whisky making her cheeks flush pink. "But I was right about what I said to Lunis."

"Completing our training will change everything," Sophia recited, remembering what her dragon had told her.

"It will save the Dragon Elite, or it will destroy it," Mama Jamba continued, hiccupping.

"So, no pressure then, right?" Sophia joked.

Mama Jamba placed a comforting arm around Sophia and pulled her in tight. For a girl who couldn't remember her mother and who'd had few nurturing experiences in her lifetime, she suddenly felt an unconditional love like no other. It was the affection of a mother—unwavering and with an irresistible favor for their child.

"I'm sorry if you feel a lot of weight on your shoulders, my lovely dear," Mama Jamba said, her Southern accent stronger thanks to the whisky. "And yet, get used to it, because if you survive what comes, the world will rest on your shoulders off and on for a long, long time. The angels and I have put certain balls into motion, and we were hoping you'd kick them around for a few thousand years."

Sophia gulped, the implications of what Mother Nature was saying staggering.

A few thousand years was a long time to watch over the Earth. And yet, Sophia Beaufont wouldn't have it any other way.

Whereas some wanted a quiet life, with peace and cuddles, Sophia wanted the opportunity to secure that life for mortals, magicians, elves, gnomes, giants, and all creatures great and small.

She also wasn't opposed to a few cuddles here and there when the time presented itself. Peace was a nice idea, too.

Feeling grateful as she watched the Christmas festivities around the Castle, Sophia smiled, believing the Dragon Elite were headed in the right direction. They had challenges to face. Enemies who were truly evil. They also had a second chance, a leader who was renewed, and a spirit literally fueled by the essence that created life itself.

To Sophia, those were good odds. She felt she'd chosen the winning team, but only time would tell.

CHAPTER SEVENTY-FOUR

Over four hundred and fifty years ago

Having ripped the fabric of his cloak into pieces, Hiker Wallace worked fast, knowing he was losing blood quickly. Without the warmth of his cape, the chill of the Highland air made his teeth chatter, but it was more important to stop the bleeding from the knife wound in his leg than stay warm.

The blade had hit an artery, based on how much it was bleeding. The magician was too light-headed to use magic to seal the wound. Even if Hiker could use magic, he wasn't competent enough with healing spells to ensure it wouldn't backfire. His quiet life, traveling across the highlands and looking for meaning, hadn't offered Hiker many opportunities to learn different branches of magic.

In his forty years on Earth, Hiker had run across few people during his travels. It had been a surprise to him to find the one person he'd been trying to avoid most of his life in the middle of nowhere.

"Hiker!" Thad Reinhart yelled. His voice echoed over the green hills and carried across the loch in the distance. "Come out, come out, wherever you are!"

Hiker tensed behind the boulder where he was hiding. His twin brother sounded close, and why wouldn't he be? Of course, Thad had gained on him. Thad could run much faster than Hiker, always the more agile one, and with the leg wound, he had a considerable advantage.

"You know, I've been trying to find you for over two decades!" Thad yelled, his Scottish accent thicker than Hiker's due to his lack of education. His voice sounded almost giddy with excitement. "You do know that, don't you? You bloody coward. You've been running for way too long."

Ever since Thad found out if one twin died, the other would inherit their magical power he'd been trying to murder Hiker. It had simply been an extra motivation. Thad had been trying to kill Hiker since the beginning. His nature was to take out anyone who had more than him—anyone he considered had wronged him, even if inadvertently.

Hiker's mistake had been in just existing. No matter what he tried to do, his twin brother would never accept him. And magic made it all the worse.

Hiker tied another bit of his torn cloak around his wound and tried to breathe through his mouth as the searing pain nearly made him pass out. He pulled the shredded cloak back over his shoulders, careful to stay low.

It was only a matter of time before Thad found him in his hiding spot. Hiker should have realized it was only a matter of time before his twin found him in general. He knew their connection gave them hints about the other. Often he saw flashes of Thad's life—the people he swindled, the treasures he'd stolen, the ones he abused...killed.

Living in the highlands had made it easier for Hiker to shield his thoughts from his brother. Time had helped too. But it hadn't lasted, and now Thad had found him and would finish him for good.

"You gave it all up for this!" Thad yelled, his voice closer. Hiker pictured him sweeping his arms wide at the vast rolling hills all around them. "You had the riches I deserved. The parents I should have had. The life meant for me. And you gave it all up because you were scared, knowing if you stuck around, I'd kill you, you bloody coward."

Hiker heard his brother spit and assumed Thad was wearing a look of disgust.

He couldn't argue with a word he said because Thad was right. Hiker had run, had given up his family's legacy, his inheritance, and a prosperous life. But what had he been supposed to do? It was kill Thad or be killed by him. There was no other way.

He'd even offered to split the inheritance, but his twin wouldn't go for it. Thad had contended he should have had it all from the beginning.

The twin's parents had both died when they were infants, forcing the children to be separated shortly after birth. Hiker had been sent to live with his father's parents, an affluent family who owned a lucrative business and were considered very respectable. The Wallace's were loving people who gave Hiker many opportunities to learn and succeed. They sent him to the best schools and gave him the very best of everything. They even made efforts for Hiker to spend time with his twin, who lived on the far side of town.

Thad went to live with their mother's family—the Reinharts. They lived in squalor and were considered criminals by most. Thad was often abused or neglected, but any time the Wallace family tried to get him away, they were fought. The patriarch of the Reinhart family, an angry drunk, argued Thad was the last he had of his daughter, and he wouldn't let him go. He didn't really want the boy. Mostly he just wanted another thief in his charge. He wanted someone he could abuse and control. Someone who could help run his scams and do his bidding.

The boys grew up living very different lives. Thad had never forgiven Hiker for the life he considered so much better than his.

One might contend it was circumstances which made Hiker the good-hearted man and Thad rotten to the core, but like attracts like. When the boys were divided up shortly after birth, the good twin was magnetized to the healthy home, and the bad one sent with people more like him.

Thad's heart had been blackened from the beginning. Hiker later learned that much when he researched connections between twins, trying to shield his brother from finding him. That had been shortly after it came to light that when one twin died, the other inherited their magical power.

What neither twin knew was, destiny had dictated their path from the beginning. Thad had been born bad, and Hiker, good. It was set up that way for a reason. The angels had seen to it. Balance in the world was important, and these two men were a part of that. Soon, they'd meet their matches.

All twins destined to ride dragons fulfilled a certain destiny. One was always good. The other was purely bad. There was no escaping it. Only the angels and Mother Nature knew the true reason for this.

These two men knew they were twins but no more because their true destiny hadn't found them—but it was about to.

"You know," Thad said, his voice no longer booming. He was dangerously close. "I should have killed you when I had the chance. When we were in the womb. All I would have had to do was wrap my umbilical cord around your neck, and none of this would have been an issue. Alas, I did not and now…"

The cold wind stroked Hiker's face; almost a comforting thing, he thought. It was followed by the opposite as his twin rose over him, standing on the boulder where he was shielding himself.

Hiker stiffened.

It had all come down to this.

There was no escaping. He knew that much. The expansive hills offered many paths for escape, but none were available to Hiker in his current condition. He wouldn't get ten yards before his brother struck him down and killed him for good.

He wanted to close his eyes and not watch as Thad pulled a sword from his belt, a greedy look on his face, but he wouldn't allow himself to look away. Although Hiker had run all these years, it hadn't been to avoid his own death. It had been to avoid his brother's. There was no reality where he could fight Thad and kill him, and that was the only option as far as his twin was concerned. Ironically he'd now die by Thad's hands because he was unwilling to fight him.

Hiker Wallace was anything but a coward. He simply didn't have what it took to keep fighting someone he wanted to love. His heart, time and time again, failed to understand why Thad wanted power when love was the better option. Why Thad hurt others when peace could heal him. There was so much Hiker didn't understand about his twin.

When Thad stood on the boulder above Hiker, he forgot it all and tried to make amends with the man who had haunted him all his life.

"I'm sorry," Hiker said, looking straight up into his brother's eyes as he stood above him, making him crane his neck. "I'm sorry you don't want me alive. I'm sorry you had to live with the Reinharts. But more than anything, I'm sorry you'd rather have my power than the life we could have had together."

A cold chuckle lacking all humor spilled from Thad's mouth. He was poised, ready to jump down in front of his brother and deliver the blow he'd dreamed of for so long—the one that finished Hiker. But, as was Thad's style, he was going to relish the moment.

"I never wanted you as my twin or my brother," Thad said through clenched teeth. "Why share this world with the inept when I can rule it alone!"

Hiker saw the telegraphed moves that signaled what his brother would do next. It was the flexing of his muscles. The arching of his back. The glint in his eyes. Hiker knew he wouldn't be able to escape the next series of actions.

When Thad jumped off the boulder, sword in hand, Hiker was astounded by what happened next.

A large shimmering red *something* shot across his vision. It happened so fast he only caught a glimpse as it knocked Thad off the rock and launched him several dozen yards, where he landed in the grass and rolled down the hill, far away.

Hiker had never seen a beast like the one that landed right after Thad was thrown. His brother continued to roll head over feet as

Hiker tried to stand, one hand on his injured leg and one hand on his weapon.

Upon getting to his feet, he surprised himself by dropping his sword and letting it fall to the grass. He only caught a brief glimpse of Thad as he recovered. He looked up with shock as the great magical creature unfurled her wings before tucking them into her massive body, covered in sparkling scales.

The good twin had never seen a dragon. He thought they were just lore. As he looked into the ancient eyes of the dragon whose name he knew by heart, for no apparent reason, he knew dragons were real—and this one, somehow, someway, belonged to him.

With his remaining strength, before the pain in his heart and his leg made him sleep, Hiker sunk into a low bow and showed his respect to the dragon.

"It is a pleasure to meet you, Bell," he said when he rose, not at all understanding what was happening, but embracing it at once. He had no clue how he knew the dragon's name or knew her at all, but like magnets, he felt the draw.

The dragon lowered her massive head, her eyes shimmering with acceptance for the magician before her.

We've always known each other, Hiker Wallace, she replied. *But only now can our lives together commence as they were always meant to.*

Thad Reinhart watched from the bottom of the hill, his eyes burning with hatred. Not only had he failed to kill the one man he'd wanted dead for so long, but now Hiker had something else he wanted.

He turned and sped for the mountains, intent on finding another way to end his brother.

Little did he know, waiting for him by the stream where he'd seek refreshment, was his own dragon.

And like him, Ember's heart was black.

Like Thad, she'd been born that way.

CHAPTER SEVENTY-FIVE

"Whose balls are freezing right now?" Evan asked, his teeth chattering.

"This shouldn't come as a surprise to you, but not mine," Sophia answered as she pressed her hands deeper into her wool-lined pockets.

"My balls aren't freezing either," Ainsley said, striding out of the Castle carrying a tray with glasses of whisky.

"Why do we have to do this?" Evan complained and squinted in Hiker's direction.

All of the riders, Ainsley, and Quiet, were gathered in front of the Castle, the only light came from the stars in the darkened sky and the flames burning in the windows. All of the electrical lights, which the Castle had started to include in different areas, especially for the Christmas decorations, had been extinguished for the countdown. Hiker wasn't a fan of the growing trend of electric items being included in the Castle, but Sophia was confident he'd come around in time.

"First-footing is a tradition," Hiker explained. "And since Sophia is making us celebrate holidays—"

"Making?" she interrupted. "I refuse to apologize for bringing a bit of cheer to this place."

"Yes, but you should apologize for the five pounds I've put on eating holiday sweets," Ainsley said, handing a glass to each person.

"You're a shapeshifter," Wilder said, taking the whisky. "Can't you just shift to a form where you are five pounds lighter?"

"I can, but then I'm not my authentic self," Ainsley said self-righteously, lifting her nose.

"You once spent an entire year in the form of a giant," Evan pointed out.

"It was only because I was mad at the Castle and wanted to wear out the furnishings faster with my larger form," Ainsley explained.

"If you all are quite done, it's almost time for Hogmanay," Hiker said, holding up his glass of whisky and queuing the others to join him in a toast.

Hogmanay was the Scottish word for New Year's eve and came with its own traditions. They were all new to Sophia, except for the idea of toasting with a nice drink after the countdown.

For this occasion, Hiker had broken out a very old bottle of whisky but grumbled about it. Sophia knew better, though. He was coming around, and it had all started with his confession to her about being Thad Reinhart's twin.

His office was back to normal, but she suspected the Castle was still finding ways to annoy him. Not because he was keeping a secret but rather just because the sentient building liked to be entertained.

Eyeing his watch, Hiker began, "The New Year starts in five, four, three, two, one."

When the countdown was over, everyone cheered, "Happy New Year."

Sophia clinked her glass with the others before taking a sip. Her insides were instantly warmed from the whisky, which could make her start sweating if she drank enough of it, although it was bitterly cold on the Expanse.

"You're not making us link arms and sing Auld Lang Syne, are you?" Ainsley asked the leader of the Dragon Elite.

"I don't think anyone wants to hear you sing," Evan said, finishing his drink and holding it out to the shapeshifter. "I'd like more."

"And I'd like you to have manners, alas that reality is not happening, just like your refill," Ainsley stated and poked her tongue out at the dragonrider.

"Fine, I'll get it myself." Evan stalked for the Castle door.

"No, you won't." Hiker reached out and held Evan back by the shoulder. "First footing."

Evan cast him a backward glance. "Yes, and you said that means a tall, dark, and handsome man has to be the first one to enter the 'house' at the start of the New Year. That's me."

"Why can't it be a female?" Sophia asked.

Hiker regarded her with mild irritation. "Because that's considered unlucky."

She rolled her eyes. "I swear, if the Dragon Elite had a human resource department, I'd lodge a complaint."

He blinked at her and returned her challenging expression. "But we don't, so get over it."

"I think it should be Mahkah who does the first footing because he's nicer than the lot of you," Ainsley said, smiling at the quiet dragonrider still nursing his drink.

"Thank you," he said and blushed.

Quiet muttered something as he strode out to the grounds, his drink in hand as he sauntered away.

"Oh, Quiet, I would have picked you, but you aren't what we'd call tall," Ainsley called after the gnome, who was still muttering and obviously agitated.

"It's going to be Wilder," Hiker declared. He pointed at the door, his eyes on the dragonrider standing next to Sophia.

"Why does he get to do it?" Evan complained.

"Because I drew straws, and his was the one I picked," Hiker said definitively.

Ainsley elbowed Mahkah in the side and whispered loudly, "I think it's because he's got a man-crush on him."

Wilder tilted his head to the side as he ran his fingers through his brown hair and smiled. "Why, thank you. I'd be happy to do the first footing. I am tall, dark and—"

"Full of yourself," Evan interrupted.

"You're one to talk," Sophia said.

"What are you all doing out here?" Mama Jamba called at their back as she hurried across the icy grounds toward the Castle.

Hiker blinked at her in confusion. "What are you doing out here? Where have you been?"

She smiled up at the large man. She looked small in comparison. "Papa Creola and I have a long-standing tradition on the New Year. He winds the clock, and then we—"

"Kiss!" Evan exclaimed, laughing.

"Show some respect," Hiker scolded.

"Oh, no, he's absolutely right," Mama Jamba said with a giggle. "We smooch at the start of the New Year."

"You do?" Sophia asked, trying to picture the hippie elf kissing Mama Jamba.

She nodded. "Yes. We missed one year, and the consequences were far-reaching." She leaned forward and in a conspiratorial whisper said, "That was the year Pepsi Cola was invented. We're still trying to fix the ramifications to come out of that."

"Like childhood obesity?" Sophia asked.

"Like there are certain venues which only carry Pepsi products," Mama Jamba answered. "What are you all doing out here freezing your tails off?"

"Balls," Evan corrected.

"You watch your mouth in front of Mama," Hiker admonished before turning his attention back to Mother Nature. "We were just about to do the first-footing."

"Oh!" she cheered. "I love that you're being so festive this year." With a smile, Mama Jamba pointed to the front door of the Castle. "Go on then, Wilder. Go on through."

"What?" Evan threw his hands up. "Why Wilder?"

Mama Jamba leveled her gaze on him. "Because his straw got pulled, obviously."

"Yeah, obviously," Wilder said and headed for the front door.

Sophia shuffled forward, following the group as Wilder stepped over the threshold. "Thanks for allowing this," she said to Hiker in a low voice.

His gaze shifted to her, his face expressionless. "Well, I guess it was overdue."

"And thanks for the cookie bouquet you got me for Christmas," she said.

His brow wrinkled. "What are you talking about? I didn't get you a cookie bouquet."

She nodded. "No, no, you didn't. But since you asked, my birthday is in the summer, and I'd totally love a cookie bouquet."

"What's a cookie bouquet?" Hiker asked.

"Pretty much exactly what it sounds like," she answered, enjoying the warmth of the Castle as she entered.

"And where do I get these cookie bouquets?" he questioned.

Sophia's face transformed with shock. "Are you really going to get me one for my birthday? I can get you some names of companies who make them."

Hiker shook his head. "No, one of my next projects as a world adjudicator will be to dismantle all companies who make cookie bouquets."

She scowled at him. "Ha-ha."

"Sophia," Mama Jamba called from the staircase, pointing at the second floor. "I want you in bed right away. You have training early tomorrow morning."

"But there's more whisky," Ainsley said, holding up a bottle of amber-colored liquid.

"Mama says Sophia is going to bed, so that's what she's doing," Hiker ordered. He also held up a hand and pointed to the second floor.

Sophia couldn't help but smile as she trudged for the stairs. "Yes, Mom and Dad."

At the base of the stairs, Mama Jamba leaned forward and planted a kiss on Sophia's cheek. "Happy New Year, dear. Please rest up since this will be your biggest year yet. Well, until the next one, if we make it past this one."

"On that somber note," Wilder said, "sleep tight, Soph. Dream good dreams, and don't worry about the Earth ending."

Sophia smirked. "Yeah, I'm sure I'll drift right off to sleep after this."

CHAPTER SEVENTY-SIX

A peaceful wind rolled across the Expanse as Sophia and Mahkah strode out toward the Cave the next morning. Everyone in the Castle was still sleeping after the late night of celebrating. It had been difficult for Sophia to fall asleep, but not because she was worried about her training or the future. There was that, but mostly it was because Evan kept yelling things from the first-floor like, "I'm tall!" "I'm handsome!" "I'm the darkest one here!"

The icy grass crunched under their boots as they moved in the direction of the dragons lounging in the morning sun on the Expanse.

"Do you have everything you need?" Mahkah asked her.

She patted her sides. "The clothes on my back, my sword, and a whole lot of hope. I have everything I'm allowed, but not sure about need. I could use a bag of Doritos for the trip."

He released a small smile. "I get you're not allowed a lot for such a long and arduous task, but it's the only way."

When Mahkah told Sophia her next training with Lunis was to venture out into the middle of nowhere with no supplies and survive for a week on their own, she wasn't excited. They couldn't use magic to survive in the Australian Outback. Instead, they had to rely on each other to find water, food, and shelter.

Similar to a walkabout, this training exercise was supposed to be reflective for the pair, to help them to know their inner selves. It was also apparently going to bring them closer or drive them apart. The way they came out of the experience was crucial to whether they passed or not.

Not only did Sophia not want to sleep in a place with some of the most dangerous animals in the world without magic, but she was sad to leave the Castle. It felt like a strange thing to do on the first day of the New Year. However, Mama Jamba had been adamant Sophia throw herself into training, and this was apparently one of the hardest tasks to complete. If she got through the walkabout with Lunis, hopefully the rest of their training would be considerably easier.

Lunis was rolling around in the grass like a dog after a bath when they approached. The other dragons were eyeing him with obvious speculation. It seemed to Sophia, the stranger the other dragons found Lunis the more it encouraged his odd behavior. At first, he'd worried about being so different from the others, having been raised at a different time with different influences, but now he seemed to embrace it.

The blue dragon rolled onto his feet and ran over when Sophia was near. Affectionately she glanced up at the majestic dragon. She sensed he was extra playful this morning, trying to put her fears at ease with his light nature.

For someone who hadn't gone a day without magic since she was a toddler, it was bizarre to Sophia to consider not using it for a week. Even weirder was the idea of feeding herself when she'd always had such things provided for her. But that was the point in the training exercise, and although Lunis wasn't going to allow her to starve, Sophia knew she had to learn how to fend for herself. A dragon's job wasn't to support their rider. It was to be a part of an equal partnership.

Are you ready for this? Lunis asked her, his tone enthusiastic.

"Of course," she said, trying to inject excitement into her voice.

While Lunis is gone, Coral remarked, *who is going to make an exorbi-*

tant amount of noise in the Cave and go on for hours about who is winning on the Disguise?

The show is called the Mask, Lunis corrected. *And you will just have to survive without me. I'm certain you'll be bored to death within a day or two.*

The purple dragon scowled at him, impassively batting her eyes. *And yet somehow, we've survived for hundreds of years without your nonsense.*

Hundreds of long, boring years, Lunis stated. *You're going to miss me. Just you wait.*

Coral shook her head and took off, rising high in the sky and circling around before heading for the flock of sheep on the Eastern hills.

"Don't eat the agnostic ones," Sophia called after the dragon. "Their indecision will give you a stomachache."

Lunis cringed. *Oh no, you didn't.*

"What?" Sophia complained. "Mama Jamba said the sheep have religious affiliations. You're talking to ancient dragons about reality television, but I make a joke about agnostics, and that's too much?"

I think Mama Jamba was pulling your leg, Lunis offered. *I don't think sheep are religious.*

"Why, because they aren't educated on such things?" Sophia asked.

He shook his head. *Because they tend to be more scientifically-minded.*

Sophia laughed. "You're so ridiculous. I can't believe I'm even having this conversation with you."

"To be honest," Mahkah cut in, stepping up beside Sophia. "I can't believe I'm listening to this discussion between a dragon and a rider."

Sophia offered him a wink. "We are a unique pair."

"Indeed, you are," he agreed, bowing respectfully. "And I look forward to you both returning. Things won't be the same here without you. You might have noticed I tend to be of a more serious nature."

Get out of town, Lunis said with mock surprise.

Mahkah flashed a subtle smile. "Having you two around is good for us. I've often thought the older dragonriders took themselves too seriously, and you help to liven things up."

"I will admit my impression has been the same," Sophia stated. "Dragonriders do seem serious."

That's because crusty old men, set in their ways, get crotchety, Lunis stated.

"I won't argue with that," Mahkah said, not at all offended by this observation. "Your perspective is refreshing."

"Thank you," Sophia said, returning the slight bow.

"Now, just one more thing before you leave." Mahkah held out his hand.

Without missing a beat, Sophia slapped his palm like he was offering her a high-five.

He shook his head. "No, I think you know what I want."

She sighed and rolled her eyes as she fished into her pocket. Of course, Mahkah knew she'd been trying to smuggle her phone on the trip. She withdrew the iPhone and handed it over. "I was just going to take it so I could chronicle our experiences and later blog about it."

"I don't know what blog is, but you know the rules," Mahkah instructed.

She nodded. "Yes, no electronics, magic, or contact with any outsiders."

"That's right," he affirmed. "Any of those things will end your training, and you'll have to restart it from the beginning."

"One week," Sophia stated, chewing on her lip. It seemed like a long time to go without her phone or magic, but more than anything, her friends. She could hardly believe how much she'd grown accustomed to having the other dragonriders, Ainsley, and Quiet around.

She was grateful she'd have her best friend. That would get her through. Even if she didn't know how to purify water or hunt or anything else, she had Lunis, and that was what mattered most.

CHAPTER SEVENTY-SEVEN

The last bit of magic Sophia and Lunis could use for a whole week was to create and close the portal into the Australian Outback. Technically, dragons flew by way of magic, but that was apparently permissible.

"Seems like there are some loopholes to this magic using business," Sophia mused as they flew toward the mostly flat red earth sprinkled with vegetation. Mountains framed the area, and a stream ran through the hills.

I wouldn't advise pushing any boundaries on this, Lunis said as he landed. *If you break a rule and we end up here longer, we're going to have words.*

Sophia laughed. "You just don't want to miss the Super Bowl."

Don't be ridiculous, he replied. *That's in February. There's no way we'll be out here that long. But going longer than I have to without Netflix and frozen yogurt isn't advisable for my overall morale.*

"It's a good thing you were born in the twenty-first century," she offered. "Could you imagine being born when Bell was?"

He sighed and shook out his wings before folding them elegantly beside his body. *No. Did you know she has never had frozen yogurt?*

Unsurprisingly, it was hot in the Australian Outback. Sophia peeled off her cloak and tied it around her waist. "I'm certain you're the only dragon ever to have frozen yogurt."

The Outback was what Sophia had expected. Miles and miles of trees, bush, mountains, and, she suspected, creepy, crawly creatures waiting to attack her in the night.

"So, first things first," she said, surveying the area.

Where's the Starbucks? Lunis asked.

Sophia pointed. "I think it's on the other side of the ridge."

Cool, I'll race you.

"Lun, I'll never win that race, so no."

He nodded and ran his long claws through the dirt. Observing how it moved told him something about this place. *I think our first order of business should be to find shelter.*

Shielding her eyes, Sophia looked out at the desert before them. "Maybe we should set up camp beside that bush, or that one." She indicated the two areas. "I don't know, which bush do you think has the fewest scorpions who will want to crawl into my pants?"

Hard to say, he muttered, considering the question. *I think we'll want to be close to a water source and have the shade of the mountains.*

Sophia gazed at where the closest water source was, according to her earlier dragon's-eye view. It was at least a five-mile trek. She wished they had planned better and landed by the river rather than in their current location. Mahkah had instructed her to land right after going through the portal. He was very serious about them not using magic, and although Lunis could fly, she wasn't supposed to ride him until the week was up.

Sophia wasn't sure how Mahkah or Hiker would know if she broke the rules, but something told her they had their methods.

"Okay, let's hoof it," Sophia said, starting toward the river.

Cool, Lunis chirped. He unfurled his wings and instantly received a punishing glare from Sophia. *Oh, so now you don't want me flying because you have to walk?*

"It doesn't seem fair," she retorted. "Aren't we supposed to be together anyway? Bonding."

Fine, he surrendered. *I'll walk with you, but if we see a snake, I'm airbound.*

"You've got to be kidding me!" Sophia exclaimed. "You're a freaking dragon."

Have you seen snakes? Lunis argued. *I'm still human...I mean, vulnerable. I have feelings, you know. I'm allowed to have fears.*

"Is this when we start bonding, discussing all our memories and whatnot?" Sophia asked.

Sure, Lunis began, ambling beside her, moving slower than he had to keep pace. *Why don't you share some of your fears with me?*

"Well..." Sophia thought for a moment. "I used to be afraid of the dark but—"

But now you love it because you know there's more to fear in the light than otherwise, Lunis interrupted.

She nodded. "Yeah, I guess you have access to my thoughts."

Are there other fears I don't know about? Lunis asked.

"Well, I worry about you and I being successful. A lot is resting on our shoulders, and—"

Of course, you always worry about Liv in her role as Warrior for the House of Fourteen and Clark finding happiness since he's prone to being overly anxious, Lunis cut in again.

Sophia slumped. "Is there anything you don't know about me?"

He shook his head. *Sometimes you say something I know you're going to say, but you say it in a way I wasn't expecting.*

She sighed. "Well, how about you? Tell me something about you I didn't know, like that you're afraid of snakes."

I'm really not, he confessed. *I just said that to make you laugh.*

"It worked," she affirmed.

Okay, about me... Lunis thought for a moment. *Well, when I hatched—*

"I was there," Sophia interrupted.

Right, he growled. *Well, let's see, my favorite flavor of fro-yo is—*

"Cookies and cream," she cut in. "You think you're allergic to honey, but you have no scientific evidence to back that up."

Because you won't take me to a doctor! the dragon complained.

Sophia shook her head, ignoring his outburst. "You can read but not phonetically, which is why you mispronounce words so often. You're a Virgo, which means you think you know everything. You say your favorite show is *Nailed it* on Netflix, but it's actually *Doctor Who* on BBC. You wish you were all Hollywood, but you're really all nerdy. And Taylor Swift is your spirit animal."

Lunis halted and gave her a perturbed expression. *First off, reading is hard.*

"You were born with the skill," Sophia pointed out. "Try having to learn on your own without the collective chi of the dragon to be able to do things."

Sounds hard, Lunis said unsympathetically. *No, thanks. And I like* Nailed It, *but how can I not be a fan of David Tennant? He's so dreamy.*

"You're so weird," Sophia laughed.

And I'm not apologizing for Tay-Tay, Lunis stated. *She's a real American diva. I think we should get tickets for the next show.*

"Why not just fly in and sit on the top of the amphitheater?" Sophia suggested.

Because I want access to the concessions, Lunis argued. *Maybe we get a private box?*

"Maybe…" Sophia's voice trailed away as she tried to think of something Lunis didn't know about her or something she didn't know about him and could ask.

"I don't think there's anything we don't know about each other," she finally said.

"I was going to mention that," he offered. *So a week together? This won't get boring.*

Sophia shrugged. "It's like we're alone with ourselves because you are, in essence, me and I'm you. It would make sense there would be a little less conversation and a lot more introspection."

This is when we start contemplating our navels, he said.

"You don't have a navel," she corrected.

I know, but you do, so I can live vicariously through you.

"I hope that's not going to work in all situations," Sophia muttered.

Well, I feel like I know what it's like to have a uterus, he shared.

"Gross," Sophia shot back at him.

Do you feel like you know what it's like to breathe fire? he asked.

"No, not at all," she answered.

Oh, well, then, you might want to work on your connection to me, he suggested. *Maybe if you connect to me during this walkabout, you'll feel the chi of the dragon more.*

"First, we have to walk about five miles." She pointed to the mountains in the distance.

Lunis shook his head. *Can I request no more puns for the week?*

"You can, but I can't guarantee it," Sophia replied.

After a long silence of kicking up red dirt and nothing else, Lunis huffed. *Soooooo…*

"Yeah, sooooo," Sophia replied.

Do you sort of feel like an old married couple? he asked.

"Yeah, and it didn't take us that long to get there," she replied.

Do you miss the guys?

"Maybe. Actually, strangely, yes," she admitted.

I miss the other dragons.

"Well, I don't miss Evan yet, so that's a good sign."

I'm sure we'll figure it out, Lunis said. *This week is supposed to bond us.*

"Or make us hate each other," Sophia offered.

Yeah, I'm sure seven days in extreme heat and horrible living conditions with zero chance of frozen yogurt won't do that for us.

Sophia looked meaningfully at her dragon. "Please, and I ask this from the bottom of my heart. Please don't eat me this week."

He nodded. *I will try. You try not to use bad puns, and hopefully, we will meet in the middle.*

CHAPTER SEVENTY-EIGHT

By the time Sophia made it to the river, she was starving. She'd been too nervous about the walkabout that morning to eat breakfast, which was now backfiring on her.

"So, we have to feed ourselves." Sophia looked around at the dry vegetation.

"That's going to be harder for some of us than others," Lunis said, his gaze drifting to a mob of kangaroos traveling across the bush in the distance. They were quite a distance away, but the chi of the dragon made it so the pair could easily spot them. Lunis gave the mob a hungry glare before giving Sophia a questioning expression.

"Oh, fine." She waved him off. "Go on then. Go get a kangaroo. I'll gather some berries or something."

"Don't eat anything blue," he suggested. "That's age-old wisdom."

"What about blueberries?" she asked.

"That's the exception," he stated.

"How about a blue dragon?" she continued to ask.

He shook his head. "Whatever you do, don't eat a blue dragon. Bad stomach aches will result in serious cramps."

She shrugged. "Doesn't sound worse than when I eat nachos from Taco Bell."

"May I suggest," he began, "not eating nachos from Taco Bell."

"You can," she offered. "But I reserve the right to ignore such bad advice."

"Okay, so I'm going to go hunt a kangaroo," Lunis said, his eyes hungry as he regarded the mob in the distance.

"And I'm going to find a platter of nachos somewhere in the near vicinity," Sophia said, looking around speculatively.

Lunis glanced at the area, a skeptical glare in his eyes. "Yeah, good luck with that. If you don't find any, I'll share my kangaroo with you."

Sophia shook her head. "No, but thank you. I'm catching my own dinner, and then we will set up camp."

"And collect water," Lunis reminded her.

Sophia sighed. "This whole thing is a lot of work."

He nodded. "It's a full-time job. Just wait. You'll see."

It seemed more like a threat rather than a promise, Sophia mused as her dragon flew off into the clear blue sky, leaving her to fend for herself.

CHAPTER SEVENTY-NINE

S ophia kicked around the dirt by the tree she was stationed by and considered her options.

"This is not such a big deal," she said to herself, realizing she had already started to lose her mind if she was talking to herself in the Outback. *Sooner rather than later,* she thought. "All I need to do is find dinner. No biggie. People have been doing it since the beginning of time."

The sun was still high in the sky, and Lunis looked close to selecting his entrée for dinner. She had a sword and could go and slaughter a beast, but that would mean traveling. She'd already crossed many miles across the Outback and felt as hot as a furnace, the heat really starting to register for her.

"It would be better if dinner came to me," she mused, thinking of Uber Eats, but knowing it wasn't an option.

A scratching noise from under the base of the tree where she was stationed caught her attention.

Sophia turned to the sound. "That seems like dinner is calling."

She crouched down low and stuck her face into the hole next to the tree. It was deep and dark, and she really didn't like the idea of digging in there to draw out prey. What she really wanted was whatever was in there to come out and say "hi" to her. Then she could use Inexorabilis to slice it in half and cook it over a fire.

"Fire," she said, looking around speculatively. "That's right, I need to be able to make fire without magic."

It shouldn't be hard since she'd prepared for this part of the adventure, studying up on ways to make fire. The tree with her dinner under it provided not only the perfect source for fire but also the ideal way to draw her food out.

It was a eucalyptus tree, and its oil was considered extremely flammable. Not only would the flaking bark make great kindling, but the oil would make a great fire starter. Sophia smiled triumphantly. As a bonus, the eucalyptus oil would also make a great bomb—one she'd throw into the burrow to draw out her corned beef and hash, or rodent, or whatever it ended up being.

She hoped it would be corned beef but had serious doubts.

CHAPTER EIGHTY

*D*o you really think that's going to work? Lunis asked.
    She pushed the sweat pouring into her eyes away with the back of her hand. *No, I'm just making homemade bombs because I don't think they will work.*

Sarcasm is the scared man's way of keeping others at a distance, Lunis intoned. He was trying to sound sage-like, but a hint of mischief in his voice rang through.

Where did you get that proverb from? Sophia asked.

I made it up, Lunis said. *Dragons are considered very wise, so I was thinking of coming up with a bunch of dragon proverbs. Maybe publish a book of them.*

You need t-shirts, Sophia said, wrapping the soaked eucalyptus leaves in dry twigs like a bird making a strange nest. She'd been playing with figuring out the best design for her homemade bombs. It needed to have a fuse of sorts, and of course, an explosive element, but not so explosive it killed whatever was hiding in the burrow under the tree. She just wanted to scare it out, and then she'd sword it up and serve it on... Sophia looked around. She'd have to serve it on a leaf or something since the Outback was fresh out of plates, it seemed.

I like the way you think, Lunis approved. *T-shirts are a good idea, and we can make a board on Pinterest.*

You're not allowed to use my Pinterest account anymore.

Because I keep filling your boards up with baking recipes, he replied.

Yes, that's exactly right, she answered. *And you don't even bake. I don't get the logistics of how a dragon would bake. Like, can you work a hand mixer?*

He snorted with laughter in her head. *I think you're missing the hint. I don't bake, but I do enjoy baked treats. I was thinking one of us should take up the hobby.*

Sophia returned the laugh. *You think I need a hobby?* You have *heard I'm a dragonrider in training with a mysterious mission resting on my shoulders, according to Mother Nature.*

I'd heard rumors of that, Lunis agreed coyly.

Just because you've taken up this hobby to create dragon proverbs with an author slash T-shirt business doesn't mean I need side projects, Sophia replied.

I'm just trying to help you live your best life, he bragged.

Then I need you to work on your proverbs because that one about sarcasm didn't have a ring to it at all, Sophia complained. *Maybe say something about how sarcasm is the result of talking to stupid people.*

I don't think you get the point of these dragon proverbs, Lunis argued. *They are supposed to lift people up, not insult them.*

Are you sure that by pointing out their stupidness it won't help? Sophia challenged.

I don't think "stupidness" is a word, Lunis stated.

And yet, you've just used it, Sophia fired back.

I think you misunderstood the context in which I used it.

Sophia held up the homemade eucalyptus bomb she'd made and admired her handy work. *I have no idea if this will work, but it sure is pretty. I should make stuff with my hands.*

Like jewelry, Lunis remarked.

Sophia rolled her eyes. *I was thinking like weapons or explosives or spyware or something cool.*

Bracelets are cool, Lunis disagreed.

You are so strange, Sophia said, going to work building a fire.

I'm going to go be strange while I eat a kangaroo, Lunis offered. *You good down there?*

Yeah, I'm about to be eating corned beef hash, she said, creating a spark and watching the kindling catch.

I think the heat is already starting to get to you, Lunis said dryly. *If you think corned beef is hiding out under that tree, you might be a bit disappointed.*

I can pretend wombat tastes like corned beef, she reasoned.

Aw, you're going to eat a cute little wombat. Lunis sounded offended.

Says the dragon, she fired back. *Who incidentally eats sheep.*

Just the cult ones that want a way out so they can return to the mother ship, Lunis sniffed.

Sophia shook her head and fanned the flames, proud of the fire she'd built. *I don't know what's under the tree, but I'm eating it.*

We shall see, Lunis said, sounding skeptical. *I'll bring you a roo if all else fails.*

Keep your kangaroo, Sophia told him. *I'm having wombat tacos.*

She turned and faced the burrow, her homemade bomb in her hands.

Now let's hope this works, she thought, her stomach starting to growl from hunger.

CHAPTER EIGHTY-ONE

"Magic," Sophia remarked. She held the handmade bomb close to the flames to get the outer portion to spark. "I don't need no stinking magic. I've got this."

When the casing caught on fire, Sophia threw the eucalyptus bomb into the burrow. She heard it hit the dirt and roll a few feet.

Now was the moment of truth. If this didn't work, Sophia had to figure out another way to catch food. She had to figure out something since she couldn't just bomb holes in the Outback to get lunch.

The bomb exploded just as she had planned—like a firecracker, and made the ground and tree rumble.

Sophia withdrew Inexorabilis from her sheath and stood at the ready, waiting for the wombat or whatever to scurry out from its burrow. Maybe it would be a family of rodents and she could make lunches for the week.

A scratching noise followed a small plume of smoke that shot out of the hole. Sophia narrowed her eyes and listened as the noise grew louder and closer.

Something black and furry popped out of the burrow. It was hard to make out with the smoke surrounding it, but it didn't move like a furry creature.

The mysterious animal made a series of scratching noises as it scurried from the hole. It stayed in the path of the smoke, keeping it partially obscured.

As far as Sophia could tell, it was about the size of a bowling ball, but its limbs were strange and moved at odd angles.

Sophia stepped forward and tried to get a closer look just as a breeze knocked the smoke away and revealed the bizarre creature.

"Oh, hell," Sophia said, backing up a step.

CHAPTER EIGHTY-TWO

The creature before Sophia represented a common phobia for most people. Not for Sophia, though. Living with her eccentric sister Reese had broken her of being fearful of spiders. The kooky magician had forbidden anyone in the family to kill any spiders who entered their residence, saying they were good luck.

Reese probably just wanted them for potions, but many did believe having spiders around was good luck. Reese had often said the spiders thought they were roommates and killing or kicking them out was just plain rude.

However, even Reese would have tensed at the sight of the large spider before Sophia. Its beady red eyes were intently focused on the source of what had stirred it from its home.

It regarded her with menace as it ground its pincers angrily, the threat obvious in its actions.

Sophia tightened her grip on her sword and wondered how spider soup would taste.

Soup? Really? Lunis questioned. *In this heat?*

It was more of a joke than a plan, Sophia retorted.

Can you handle that large arachnid, or do you need my help? Lunis asked.

Sophia scoffed. *Go get your roo. I've got the itsy-bitsy spider.*

All right, then, Lunis replied.

Sensing the spider was about to charge and pounce, Sophia prepared her defense.

A cacophony of scratching echoed from under the tree, making the base vibrate more than when she'd bombed it.

The spider froze. Sophia did as well. She held her breath and waited.

When a mound of black spilled out of the burrow, she bit her tongue and cursed under her breath.

CHAPTER EIGHTY-THREE

One giant spider wasn't a big deal to Sophia, although it was inevitable she'd break a sweat fighting the thing since she was sweating profusely just standing there.

The hundreds of spiders that had hurried out of the burrow would be much more of a challenge to fight. Based on their angry red eyes and threatening pincers moving back and forth, a battle was imminent.

What about now? Lunis called, having seen the force facing off against Sophia. She backed up, making room for the spiders, which moved in unison like an army getting ready to charge.

I'm good, she lied, watching the sidelines as the spiders forced her back, nearly making her trip.

Her hands were shaking on her sword's hilt, but she kept her breathing steady as she watched for the first attack.

Okay, well, my dinner is hopping away, Lunis began. *Let me know if you have trouble wrestling yours.*

Sophia wasn't worried about wrestling her next meal. For the first time ever, as she looked at a hundred hairy, angry spiders, she was worried about her dinner eating her.

The first spider, maybe the original one that had scurried from the burrow, sprang at her, hopping like a kangaroo and making considerable progress. She brought her sword around like a baseball bat and swung it as the spider screamed like it was sending a volley of insults at its attacker.

The sword connected with the large spider and knocked it several dozen yards.

Home run! Lunis exclaimed.

Sophia rejoiced, feeling the victory run through her. Celebrations were short-lived as three spiders simultaneously jumped at her from three different directions. The scream that shot out of Sophia's mouth was purely reflexive. The attacks that followed absolutely weren't.

Sophia brought Inexorabilis around, bringing it low to hit the first spider on the right, then up to get the one in the middle and low again to get the creature on the far side. This time, the side of the blade didn't hit the monsters, but rather the edge. It sliced through them and the pieces fell to the red earth.

This only seemed to enrage the creepy beasts, which obviously didn't like watching their mates slaughtered. Not taking the hint that Sophia was a force not to be messed with, they all inched forward, making her take another step back.

You sure you don't want some fire? Lunis asked.

You get to fly, Sophia replied. *Who said anything about fire, though? That seems a lot like magic.*

Hey, can I help it if I cough and fire comes out? Lunis argued.

Sophia shrugged and guessed the dragon had found another loophole for using magic, but she wasn't going to chance it and have to start over. *Keep your fire to yourself,* Sophia stated as an idea occurred to her.

The spiders were inching in closer to her, and she sensed they were about to attack, probably all at once. Before that happened, she had to reduce their numbers drastically.

Sidestepping, Sophia was careful to keep the pack of spiders in her sights. They moved in concert with her, scampering to make up for the distance she tried to put between them. They were planning something. Sophia wasn't sure how she knew, but the way they moved in formation told her they were working together—a strange, silent communication obviously happening among them.

Sophia's eyes darted to the fire she'd made when it was to the side of them.

The arachnids' gazes shifted to the fire as if they were figuring it out.

These were smart, magical spiders, she guessed.

I don't see why I don't get to use magic when I'm fighting a bunch of magical creatures, Sophia complained. She was going to have to make her move soon.

Because life isn't fair, Lunis said. *On a side note, kangaroo tastes pretty good. Could use some barbeque sauce, though.*

What does it taste like? Sophia asked, careful not to give the spiders any hint of what she was planning.

Kind of like venison and buffalo, Lunis described.

You've had buffalo? she questioned.

No, but an ancestor did, he replied.

Sophia nodded, and to her surprise, all the spiders nodded too, copying her movement. "That's odd," she muttered.

They are mirroring you in an effort to understand what you're going to do next, Lunis offered.

Oh, so if I do this... Sophia said, sidestepping three feet to the right.

All the spiders followed her action, hurrying in the same direction.

She jumped and the spiders all hopped.

I don't get it, Sophia mused to her dragon.

I don't think they do either, Lunis said. *Try doing something defensive.*

Okay, Sophia said, taking a step backward.

All the spiders took one step in her direction.

Okay, Lunis said, intrigued. *Now try doing something offensive.*

Sophia lifted Inexorabilis.

The spiders all posed, rising up on the tips of their legs and growing taller.

What does this mean? she asked Lunis.

It means that with what you're planning, Lunis answered, *you better be ready for retaliation. They will respond to you in kind. Retreat, and they will follow. Try to get away, and they will match your movements. Attack, and they will, too.*

What if I smile at them and give compliments? Sophia questioned.

You can try it, Lunis answered.

"Hey, guys," Sophia began with a smile. "You all sure are interesting."

All the spiders crouched like they were part of the same beast. Their red eyes bulged as they hugged the ground, and they appeared like they were about to spring.

No compliments, Lunis exclaimed. *They don't like to be softened up.*

"You guys sure are ugly," Sophia spat, grimacing at the angry spiders.

To Sophia's surprise, a dozen of the giant spiders hopped into the air and fell back down, landing on their backs with their legs flicking like they had just kicked the bucket.

Can this be possible? she asked the dragon.

Interesting, he mused. *It appears that like the old adage, words do break their bones.*

That's so odd, Sophia mused, edging farther to the side. The remaining spiders copied her movement. *So if I run, they'll follow. If I attack, they'll retaliate. And if I criticize them, they'll kick the bucket.*

Yes, but I'd warn you against throwing out a bunch of insults, Lunis said. *There are a lot more of them than you, and I don't think you can kill them all with words.*

What makes you think that? she asked.

Well, try it, he suggested.

Sophia focused on the family of angry spiders. "Hey, guys, you sure are pretty dumb."

Again, a dozen spiders jumped and then landed on their backs, their legs kicking. However, three of the largest flew straight at her face. She screamed, ducking as the first passed over her head. One went by her arm, scratching her with its long pincers. The other attached itself to her leg, holding on furiously with its legs.

"What?" she exclaimed. "Get off!"

Sophia threw a punch at the spider's head as it sank its teeth into her leg. She screamed from the pain, her voice echoing over the Outback.

Hey, you scared the kangaroo away, Lunis complained.

Sophia raised her sword and thrust it down like a toothpick, spearing the spider attached to her and making it release her. Instantly, her leg throbbed from the bite.

Sorry, not sorry, she said to Lunis. *What's the deal with these things.*

Some appear to be copycats, Lunis stated. *Some are young enough that they are hurt by words.*

And the rest? Sophia said, backing up and watching as the two other spiders who had attacked her rejoined the group.

They are murderous and out for blood, Lunis told her. *It's pretty interesting because just one approach won't work on these guys. If you attack, some will retaliate. If you insult, some will die.*

And if I retreat? Sophia suggested, favoring her leg as she sidestepped.

Then they are going to come after you and most likely attack, stripping the flesh off your bones, Lunis explained.

Sophia gulped. *Okay, then it's time for a two-pronged approach.*

I like it, Lunis said, already privy to her idea by spying her thoughts. *Fight the aggressive ones with force and the sensitive ones with words, but you better be fast because one false move and you're spider food.*

Thanks, Sophia said, grateful to be in position. All of the spiders' eyes were locked on her, even though the small campfire she built stood between her and them. They didn't seem to notice, or maybe they didn't realize she had positioned herself there for a specific reason.

She was absolutely certain they knew what she was planning when her eyes skipped to the homemade eucalyptus bombs lying a few feet away. She'd made extra, not knowing if the first would be enough. Now she was glad she had.

They all tensed, about to spring in her direction in a collective attack.

Sophia moved fast, using the speed of the chi of the dragon to drop her sword and grab a bomb in each hand. She hurled them at the spiders, ensuring they passed through the fire on their way.

"You hairy little beasts need a total makeover," Sophia spat as the bombs exploded in the pack, sending up spider parts. The guts rained down from the sky, landing all around the survivors. Several sprang up like popcorn kernels and landed on their backs.

That's *your insult?* Lunis asked with a laugh. *"You need a makeover?" Why don't you tell them they are only of average intelligence?*

Sophia had four more bombs. She launched two of them as the creatures broke out in total chaos.

I'm a bit preoccupied here, Sophia retorted as another dozen spiders exploded. *Why don't you be in charge of the insults?*

I can do that. Lunis chuckled. *Say something about their mom. They probably all have the same one.*

I don't think spiders care what you say about their mom, Sophia argued.

It's worth a shot, Lunis offered as she darted for the last of the bombs. The closest spider tried to cut her off, leaping in her direction and shooting a strand of silk at her. She ducked and kicked the creature like a football, knocking it into the trunk of the tree that was its home.

It squeaked as it landed on the ground next to the two dozen spiders who remained, their red eyes all on Sophia. She bounced the last remaining bombs in her hand, knowing she needed to make the last attack spot on or risk being eaten alive.

"Hey, where's your momma?" Sophia asked, which made all the spiders tense. They tilted their heads in unison, their eyes enlarging like they wanted to hear what she was going to say next. "Yo momma is so fat, she can't even jump to conclusions."

Oh, no. Lunis growled in disappointment.

What? Sophia questioned as the spiders scampered forward, none of them dying.

Try again, the dragon encouraged.

"Fine," Sophia began, pulling her arm back and launching one of the bombs. It landed in the middle of the horde, exploding a dozen spiders and sending guts all over her boots. She sneered. "Yo momma's so stupid, she stared at a cup of orange juice for twelve hours because it said, 'concentrate.'"

Wow, that was bad, Lunis said.

I'm sort of busy right now, she argued, firing her last bomb through the fire and exploding another dozen spiders. There were only about ten left, but Sophia was out of bombs, and her insults didn't seem to be working.

She backed over to her sword and they all copied her movement.

"Yo momma..." Sophia began, kneeling, her arm outstretched.

Before she could think of her next insult, something bigger than all the rest of the spiders surfaced from the burrow. It seemed to have trouble pushing itself through the hole, its legs long, and its body the size of a beach ball. The thing was hairier than the others, its face elongated, and its red eyes large and menacing.

"Whoa!" Sophia said, nearly tripping over her feet as she backed up. She looked the large spider over. "Yo momma is so ugly, she makes you all look adorable."

CHAPTER EIGHTY-FOUR

The ground shook under Sophia when the ginormous spider took a step forward, its pincers working.

That is one ugly spider, Lunis declared.

Tell me about it, Sophia said, landing in bug guts with her next step. This seemed to add insult to injury, and the momma spider scuttled forward, moving fast across the dirt.

Sophia barely had enough time to bring up Inexorabilis before the spider was on her. Its pincers were inches from her throat when she threw up her blade.

She held her sword like a shield, trying to push the beast back by kicking its large body. Its legs reached for her on either side of the blade, but it didn't try to come any closer.

There's something about the sword that repels it, Lunis stated.

Sophia waved the blade like a torch, and sure enough, the spider retreated a few inches.

"Hey, Momma, you're so ugly that if you threw a boomerang, it would refuse to come back," Sophia said, swinging Inexorabilis and making the monster jump back to avoid getting cut.

I don't think insults work on Momma, Lunis suggested. *Or maybe your jokes are just not good enough to be offensive.*

Sophia spied the spider sending a shot of silk in her direction just in time to dive out of the way. It hit the fire, putting it out completely. She rolled over and sprang to her feet.

So she doesn't like Inexorabilis, Sophia mused, trying to figure out her options. She didn't have any more bombs or fire.

You can call your trusty dragon, Lunis hinted.

He's busy eating a steak dinner, she replied. *And he's way over there on the other side of the Outback.*

He could come back in a few seconds, he promised.

And what, take all the fun? Sophia said, feigning to one side and trying to throw Momma off. The spider didn't fall for the trick and instead thrust one of her many long legs into Sophia's side with surprising force and making her hit the side of the tree with a thud. That was the source of her current dilemma.

That's going to leave a mark, Lunis said.

Sophia shook her head and tried to push up but found Momma bearing down on her, literally breathing down her neck.

"Hey," Sophia said nervously, smelling the rancid breath of the beast that was about to slit her neck. The impact with the tree had been more than disorienting, and Sophia realized she'd dropped her sword.

Her fingers scrabbled through the dirt, finding only bug guts. She whimpered as the spider bore closer to her, its pincers making promises she couldn't understand but got the gist of.

Soph, Lunis said, a question in his voice, *you still got this?*

She shook her head erratically.

"No!" she exclaimed, abandoning all attempts to be a lone badass. "Help, Lunis!"

She expected it would take him a bit to rescue her. Momma would sink her teeth into her and that would be the end of it, but before she even had a chance to suck in a breath, the giant spider was hurled off her.

Sophia caught a glimpse of her blue dragon, the body of the spider in his mouth, before he jerked his head up and to the side, releasing

Momma. She landed fifty feet away on the red earth in a cloud of dust and exploded, green goo spraying around her, sending a rancid smell through the hot air.

CHAPTER EIGHTY-FIVE

Ragged breath spilled over Sophia's cracked lips, making her chest rise and fall rapidly as she tried to process what had just happened.

Lunis glanced over his shoulder as the mound of spider melted into the earth, steam rising up from the carcass. Casually he turned back to Sophia, a sly grin on his face.

"How long had you been there, waiting for me to ask for help?" she asked.

"Since pretty much the beginning, lurking in the shadows," he replied.

Pushing up, she tried to dust herself off, to no effect. "There aren't any shadows to lurk in around here."

He nodded. "Yeah, it's probably the middle of the day," he observed. The sun was high in the blue sky, not a cloud in sight.

"You didn't think I could do it?" Sophia asked, covering her nose against the putrid smell that filled the air. The dead spider bodies were starting to cook, between the hot ground under them and the scorching rays of the Australian Outback sun above. "You didn't think I could take out the colony of spiders?" She couldn't keep the offense out of her voice.

"Of course, I did," he argued, looking around. "And you obviously did just fine on your own, judging by this aftermath. Do you think we can eat spider? Because if so, we've got food for days. Maybe we jelly them. How do you think spider jam tastes on toast?"

Sophia grimaced. "Ew, that sounds horrible. I refuse to eat spiders, and besides, we don't have any toast."

Sensing she was still upset, Lunis centered his attention on her. *I knew you'd be okay on your own—*

"Okay?" she questioned. "Like I'd get by until I needed you to rescue me?"

Sophia couldn't help it. She knew she was being unreasonable, but it felt right to her. Maybe it was the heat or the hunger or the thirst or the fact her leg was throbbing. She suddenly remembered being bitten and jerked her attention down. Her pants were torn where the teeth of the spider had sunk into her flesh. Green goo swam around the bloody wound in her leg. It didn't look good. Maybe it was the sight of her injury or the poison from the spider, but something made her head swim suddenly with dizziness.

Sophia, I knew you could handle the spiders, Lunis said, his voice comforting, his attention on her wound. *But we are supposed to be able to rely on each other. That's what I'm there for—to help.*

Sophia took a step and instantly regretted it. The lack of adrenaline made the pain in her leg fully apparent. "You never need me to save you, Lunis!"

I haven't yet, he reasoned. *But we have many years for that to change. We're a partnership. I can't do things you can and vice versa. So what that I stepped in at the last moment and saved you? You cleared a hundred spiders on your own using your ingenious bomb-making skills and quick thinking.*

Sophia gave him an annoyed expression. "I insulted them with yo momma jokes."

But you figured out one of their weaknesses, Lunis said.

"Yeah, I guess," Sophia said with a sigh, not at all feeling better.

What do you want me to say? Lunis asked, his expression hard. She knew he was exhausted too, but for different reasons. His belly was full, and his body was used to extreme heat. Because she was connected to the dragon, she knew he was taxed from worry about her, having to watch her battle the spiders and stay back until she asked for help. This just made her angrier.

"I want you to tell me the truth," she argued. "You didn't think I could handle the momma spider by myself."

Lunis shook his head. *You know what's in my head. Do you really hear me saying that?*

Sophia studied him, realizing that his mind was completely open for her to explore. She had tiptoed through his mind many a time, but usually only went as far as to read the thoughts he supplied her. When they scried, she saw what he saw. But in this rare instance, she had full access to his mind. And there it was, sitting neatly on top.

Sophia bit her lip and tasted blood. Her skin was already painfully cracked from the heat. "You thought I would need your help to defeat her."

I thought you could handle her, Lunis argued. *But to defeat her, yes. I thought after battling her children, you'd need some help. It doesn't mean you couldn't do it, but you might have gotten seriously injured.*

She threw her hand at her injured leg. "What do you call this? I'm trapped in the Outback with a poisonous bite and a dragon who doesn't think I can fight on my own! And it smells horrible!"

That's because someone got bug guts everywhere, Lunis said with a laugh in his mental voice.

His attempt at humor wasn't going to work on Sophia right then. She swung around and charged off for the lake, needing some space.

Soph! Lunis called after her.

She didn't turn around. Right then, she needed to be alone. She needed to figure out why she was so angry. And she needed to fix her leg…without magic.

CHAPTER EIGHTY-SIX

I t didn't matter that Sophia knew she was being unreasonable. Her
ego was instigating this fight, the first one she'd ever had with her
dragon. And yet, there was nothing she could tell herself to just get
over it.

She dragged herself to the lake without turning around even
though she could feel Lunis staring at her retreating back.

They needed each other in the Australian Outback. They needed
to bond to pass the training—more so than ever before. They needed
one another to survive the week.

The issue was that she firmly believed Lunis would survive fine
without her. Sophia felt like the weak link. She was the one who
needed her dragon in order to survive, and it made her feel entirely
worthless.

She settled down on a rock next to a clear shore of fresh water and
hesitated before submerging her leg. Sophia was aware there could be
all sorts of flesh-eating bacteria in the water. Or as was more in line
with her luck, piranhas were probably swimming around, waiting to
chew off her leg once she stuck it into the lake.

It was throbbing with so much pain she really couldn't handle it
any longer. Ripping her pant leg all the way up to the knee, Sophia

nearly passed out at the sight of the bite. It was oozing with green slime and quickly swelling.

She refused to look back over to the tree where she knew Lunis was stationed, regarding her like a lost puppy. Sophia didn't want her puppy. She wanted not to need her puppy. She wanted her puppy to need her a tiny bit.

Sophia was the vulnerable human, who might have extra magical powers thanks to those she'd inherited from her twin, but they did her no good out in the Australian Outback when she wasn't allowed to use magic. She sighed with defeat.

She was just a girl here. Nothing special. No unique talents. Just a plain, old girl.

"Without magic, I'm just a loser," she said, sinking her leg into the water and finding it strangely cool even though the heat outside was so high. The water wrapped around her wound and instantly provided relief.

"Without water, I'm a total loser," a voice said in front of Sophia.

Her eyes snapped open. She hadn't even realized they were closed or that she was close to dozing off, the sun making her lightheaded.

She searched around, thinking maybe it was Lunis talking, although the voice was higher pitched than his.

He was still by the tree and currently kicking around in the dirt and launching bits of spider carcasses across the Outback—apparently letting off steam, which ironically was spiraling through the air, coming from the body parts littering the ground.

Yanking her focus back in the direction of the voice, Sophia looked around until she found a pair of eyes resting above the water, a long tail swooshing back and forth a little behind it.

She pulled up her legs, worried she was about to be eaten by the crocodile swimming in the water before her. To her shock, it smiled at her, its eyes not at all appearing hungry like she would have thought.

I'm not going to eat you, the crocodile sent to her mind as if it had read her thoughts. *I don't want to die.*

Sophia's leg hurt outside the water, and since she was hallucinating, she sank it back down into the cool lake. "Who are you?" she asked. Talking to a crocodile was not the strangest thing to happen to her that day, one in which she made homemade bombs from a eucalyptus tree and fought a hundred large spiders. Oh, and had an argument with a dragon. Her life was so bizarre.

I'm Smeg, the crocodile replied. *I mean, I go by many different names, but that's the one the Beaufonts know me by.*

Sophia knew she was hallucinating badly, but she decided to embrace it. *Why not,* she thought. She was going to die in the Australian Outback from a spider bite, talking to a croc.

"Beaufonts?" she asked, thinking it would be fun and take her mind off her pain to indulge the croc. This hallucination, fueled by her imagination, was probably going to be pretty entertaining. "You've met others in my family?"

Well, most recently, Warrior Liv Beaufont in the swamps of Louisiana, Smeg answered.

Sophia shook her head. How dumb her subconscious was that it hadn't figured out this horrible logistic issue with its hallucination. "If you recently met Liv in Louisiana, how are you here in the Australian Outback? Did you fly?"

He chuckled. *Don't be ridiculous. I'm a crocodile. Of course, I can't fly.*

"Right, what was I thinking," she said, shaking her head. "So, how did you get here?"

Magic, he answered. *I go wherever I think I'll find the most entertaining conversations. You see, that's usually what I'm after. Have you heard any fun facts lately? I really like learning things. Oh, and I like words. My new favorite one is "conundrum." Just say it. It feels funny on your tongue.*

Sophia gave him a questioning expression. "You're a very strange croc."

He nodded, water splashing up around his head. *It's true. I'm the strangest. Not like the other crocodiles. None of them talk to me, but they are boring anyway. Most of them never travel.*

Sophia shook her head, her mouth parched. "You're a magical crocodile who talks and travels, is that right?"

Yes, and you're a dying magician on a walkabout in the Australian Outback, right? he asked.

Sophia laughed morbidly. "You've figured me out."

I love playing these kinds of guessing games, Smeg said, circling around in the water and obviously excited to have made a new friend.

"Yeah, it's a delightful game," Sophia said, looking longingly at the water.

I wouldn't drink the lake water, Smeg offered like he knew what she was thinking. He was a figment of her imagination, so what did it matter.

"Why?" Sophia questioned. "Because it's going to kill me?"

Exactly, he answered.

"As you previously mentioned, that's not so much a problem for me since I've been bitten by a poisonous spider and will probably die from it," Sophia stated dully, swaying slightly.

Oh, that's not why I thought you were going to die. Smeg's eyes darted to Sophia's leg and he grimaced. *Tough luck on the bite. Yeah, you'll probably die from that, but not before you are eaten by the hungry dragon over there. That was why I wasn't going to try to eat you. I didn't want the dragon to get mad at me for taking his meal. Oh, well, and you're more use to me as a conversationalist than as food.*

Sophia followed his gaze and saw Lunis still stalking her from a distance. "Oh, that's my dragon. I don't think he's going to kill me. Maybe, though. I did yell at him."

Oh, I didn't realize it was a domestic dispute, Smeg said. *Yeah, he's probably going to kill you. Domestic stuff gets the most out of control. Believe me, I know.*

Sophia couldn't help but laugh. "How do you know?"

I'm a good listener, Smeg offered. *Anyway, yeah, you'll probably die from the bite first. Within the day. I can tell your sister Warrior Beaufont if you want, if she visits a large body of water soon. Do you know what her travel plans are?*

Sophia gripped her leg, the pain starting to shoot upward. "Sorry, I'm not aware of her upcoming plans. Right now, I'm more concerned about funeral arrangements."

Well, you don't have to die, Smeg offered. *I have a solution.*

That got Sophia's attention. "I don't want to die. What can I do?"

Use magic, Smeg said with satisfaction.

Sophia laid back on the rock and looked up at the blue sky. "Yeah, well, I guess I'll die."

She knew they could start over with the training. Maybe that was what needed to happen. She already felt like such a failure. She really didn't want to die as one too. The Australian Outback was supposed to be hard. If it wasn't, it wouldn't be such an important part of the training.

To cure yourself, you just have to go over there and collect one of those dead spider bodies, mix it with some of the plants over there. He indicated a brightly colored bush in the distance. *And then it's a simple spell. So easy.*

"Cool," Sophia agreed. "I'll get right on that as soon as the world stops spinning."

So you and your dragon are mad at each other, Smeg stated, rather than asking.

"Really, I'm just mad at him."

Oh, what did he do? Smeg asked. *Did he steal your boyfriend? Talk about you behind your back? Put you off for another dragon?*

Sophia shook her head and wondered what the hell was wrong with this strange magical crocodile. "No, he saved my life."

No. He. Didn't, Smeg said, punctuating each of the words.

Sophia sighed. "I know it sounds dumb, but we are supposed to be a partnership, and I ride him because I'm little and can't fly. He has the fire powers, and when everything is dire, he swoops in and saves the day. All I do is act sassy and navigate. I'm pretty worthless in this partnership."

Smeg nodded, seeming to understand her plight. *Yeah, you don't seem to be carrying your own weight.*

"Thanks," she said dryly, biting on the word.

Have you considered letting him ride you? he asked.

Sophia gave the magical creature a long, annoyed stare. "You do get that there is a size difference, right?"

Oh, sure, I guess if those are your limitations, he answered. *I'm just trying to help you troubleshoot this problem.*

"There's no troubleshooting it," Sophia said melodramatically, her head feeling full of hot lava. "I'm the invalid human, and he's the awesome dragon. He can fly. I can sit. He can hunt. I can get bitten. He can withstand the elements and know everything from the dragon's consciousness. I can school him in a game of *Mario Kart*."

Sophia knew riders and dragons had been working together in a mutual partnership for hundreds of years. She'd never read anything in the *Incomplete History of Dragonriders* about ego problems and riders feeling marginalized. Yet, Sophia was the first female rider, and she had feelings. *Maybe that was the problem, though,* she reasoned. Maybe something would be in *The Complete History of Dragonriders,* although she was still waiting to get the book back from Trinity.

When you put it that way, Smeg began, *I totally get your point.*

Sophia nodded, wishing more than anything she had a glass of water. "Yeah, I'm the worst. He's the best. I'm lame. He's awesome, and—"

Before the poison totally takes you out, you mind if I share something with you? Smeg asked.

"Well, when you put it that way, yeah, whatever."

Dragons are much stronger and more powerful than magicians, Smeg explained. *They are the strongest magical creatures on this planet. In comparison, magicians are extremely vulnerable.*

"Your speech isn't helping as much as you might think," Sophia remarked.

I apologize. I dropped out of college because of a class I had to take for public speaking, the croc admitted. *Anyway, regardless, why do you think dragons chose to be partnered with humans, knowing humans were the much weaker species?*

The poison in her body made it difficult to think, so Sophia simply shrugged. "I don't know."

You have your own advantages, Smeg explained. *He might be able to fly or withstand high temperatures or tear things apart with his claws. But humans, I think if you really meditate on this, you'll find you offer some-thing crucial for you two. Without it, not only would your dragon not live as long, but more importantly, his life wouldn't be as fulfilling. It's important when considering the value of a partnership that we do not get stuck on the strength one provides and overshadow the traits another gives. Reason can often be considered just as important as power. Strategic thinking, I'd contend, is a superior skill to prowess. Knowing how to combine the skills of a magician with a dragon, well, I think that's something only a human can truly do because they know how to compromise, which is not something the dragon readily understands. If they do, it's only because of the influence of said human.*

Smeg swam in a circle, flicking his tail playfully upon the surface of the water. *Anyway, just my two cents for what they are worth. Really, what do I know? I've just been around for a few hundred centuries, having random conversations with tons of beings through time.*

Sophia swayed, the scenery in front of her blurring as her vision dimmed. "Yeah, what do you know, O strange figment of my imagination?"

Sophia, Smeg insisted, *I'm real. Everything I've said is true. If it weren't, then how would I know every dragon and rider has gone through similar internal conflicts?*

She pointed at him, feeling drunk. "Because that's what I want you to tell me, so I don't feel like such a failure."

But you aren't, Smeg argued. *You, just like Hiker Wallace and Bell, are going through the first feud of many.*

Sophia laughed. "Oh, good job, subconscious. You had the imaginary talking croc bring up Hiker and Bell to legitimize the strange message from my made-up hallucinations. Good one."

Okay, I can see you've already figured this all out, Smeg said, churning something under the water and making the lake swirl.

"Yeah, that's right," Sophia said triumphantly. "I can't fool myself."

No, you can't. A large clump of something like seaweed shot out of the water beside Smeg and landed with a splat next to Sophia.

She was so out of it she hardly budged when the pile of wet weeds landed just behind her on the rock. "What's that for?"

For when you pass out, so you don't bust your head open on the rock, Smeg said thoughtfully.

She smiled. "Thanks. But I'm okay. I'm going to hang out with you, my alter ego, and talk for a bit longer."

Sounds good, Smeg said. *I like talking.*

Sophia swayed and thought how nice it was her hallucination had created a pillow for her, although she wouldn't need it. Then her hand slipped out from under her, and her eyes closed as she fell into blackness.

CHAPTER EIGHTY-SEVEN

The sopping mossy thing under Sophia's head smelled like fish. She was lying flat on the rock, sort of.

"Hold still, would you?" a familiar woman's voice said just in front of Sophia.

The bright sunlight made it incredibly hard for Sophia to open her eyes. The searing pain on her leg made it a lot easier when she sprang up to a sitting position, clutching her calf.

"Now, now," the woman said. "Leave me to it, would you?"

Sophia blinked. She really was hallucinating to find Bermuda Laurens, the giantess author of *Mysterious Creatures*, hovering and casting a shadow down on her.

"Oh, first a talking croc and now this," Sophia said, throwing herself back, the seaweed cushion softening her fall.

Bermuda, who was wearing a brown safari outfit and hat, turned for the lake. "Smeg was here? Of course, he was! That chatty Kathy. I bet he talked your ear off."

Sophia pushed up to a sitting position. "When I die, will the hallucinations stop?"

Bermuda shrugged. "I don't know. It will be a while before you have an answer since today isn't the day you die. Nor anytime soon, I believe." The giantess was still tending to Sophia's leg, although it progressively hurt less with every passing moment.

"What do you mean?" Sophia asked. "I've been bitten by a magical Outback spider. I'm going to die from this unless I can gather that plant over there and mix it with the dead spiders and a bit of magic."

"Right," Bermuda chirped, shaking off her hands after bandaging Sophia's leg. "Which is what I've done."

Sophia's vision cleared all at once, and she realized what she was seeing was actually real. "You're here! You are actually here with me in the Outback!"

Bermuda looked around, shaken by Sophia's sudden outburst. "Do you mean me?"

Sophia nodded profusely. Her vison was clear, although her mouth still felt like chalk.

"Of course, I'm here," Bermuda confirmed. "And a good thing. I found you passed out, minutes away from a coma. Strangely, I don't remember the path which took me to you or how I got here entirely." Her gaze redirected as she looked to where Lunis was still hiding by the tree. "Oh, but of course, dragons can do all sorts of things when they want to save their rider, like call to those who can help them by using the chi of the dragon..."

"What?" Sophia asked, looking around. "Lunis called you here? But you can't be here. I'm on a walkabout. He is too. Did you use magic on me? Oh no, it's all over!"

Bermuda watched as Sophia threw her fist down on the rock and then grimaced from the act.

The giantess said, "When you're done, I have something to say."

Sophia squirmed for several moments before making her face straighten. "What is that? And are you certain you're not a figment of my imagination?"

"Quite," Bermuda answered. "And you didn't use magic. Neither did Lunis, although he is magic, so it's hard for him not to use it. Just feeling things, like what he did that drew me to you, is magic. That's the way of dragons. But you shouldn't have to worry about it ruining your training. You didn't perform magic to heal yourself. I found you passed out and fixed you without your consent. You can't be blamed for that."

Sophia nodded and wiggled her toes, noticing the feeling coming back in her leg. "What are you doing in the Outback?"

"I can't tell you that," Bermuda said flatly, holding out a cup to Sophia. "You can have this because I've given it to you, and if you don't drink it, I'll knock you out, and you won't survive the Outback."

Sophia didn't need many reasons for water when she was parched, but she was grateful Bermuda was making her feel less like a loser for having help on her walkabout.

"You really found me, and your help is okay?" Sophia asked, draining the cup.

Bermuda took it back when it was empty. "Yes, and in the future, you'll want to boil the water in this lake for your supply, especially if Smeg was in it."

"Thanks," Sophia said, feeling more herself, although her stomach growled almost on cue to remind her its needs hadn't been met yet. "I don't suppose you can feed me without breaking the rules too?"

Bermuda shook her head, surveying the area. "No, I'm sorry, I can't do any more in good conscience. You were moments away from passing out just now from dehydration, hence the water. The injury, well consider that coincidence. I've done this all for you so far, and therefore you can't be blamed. But if this is a real walkabout, the challenges you face and overcoming them are part of your journey. I can't short you of that."

"Well, I did slaughter a hundred spiders," Sophia confessed.

"Yes, the rarest Spindle spider," Bermuda said bitterly. "I'd be angrier about this except after decades of searching for the creature I have some samples I can study. At least I've made progress, although I'm certain you've just moved them from endangered to extinct."

"Oops," Sophia said. "Blame Lunis. He killed the momma."

"That's why he's over there sulking," Bermuda observed. "Dragons are so very sensitive."

"They are?" Sophia asked and then shook her head. "No, he's over there sulking because I'm a jerk who got mad at him for saving my life."

For all Bermuda Lauren's calloused behavior, she nodded quite sympathetically. "It's hard being the more vulnerable one in a relationship which is supposed to be a partnership. But the shortcoming is yours, my dear. Once you realize your unique gift, your importance, then all those problems will disappear. For now, you're wrestling with your demons, not his."

Sophia mulled that over, recognizing how much sense it made the more she thought about it. The advice was very similar to what Smeg had told her.

She was grateful Bermuda was there and had found her. She wanted to talk to the wise giantess more and have her explain this new realization to Lunis and share other insights. "Will you stay for dinner? I don't know what we're having, but I'm obviously cooking."

Bermuda backed away and shook her head. "Oh, no. I have an expedition awaiting me, and you have a walkabout to continue. You're entitled to a guest here and there on your travels, but at the end of the day, it needs to be just you and Lunis. But I'll see you again soon, Sophia Beaufont. There is little that can keep our paths from intertwining."

"So, it's okay that we spoke?" Sophia asked, still worried she'd done something wrong to end her training.

"It's impossible for a person such as yourself to go anywhere, even a place as remote as the Outback, and not meet someone," Bermuda explained.

"But I was told I couldn't speak to anyone," Sophia argued.

"Yes, meaning you couldn't seek out anyone, but so far, it seems as though I've been the one talking to you." She shrugged. "Besides, a walkabout is not about being away from others. It's about learning how to be with yourself, which it sounds like you're getting a new course on."

"Yes, my demons have come out on this trip."

"Embrace them," Bermuda offered. "Invite them in and talk with them. It's only then you can send them on their way."

"That's lovely advice," Sophia said.

"And it's all you get until the next time, my dear." Bermuda looked out at the seemingly endless terrain and sighed. "Do try to not die or get maimed. The world needs you, Sophia Beaufont."

She offered a tentative smile. "I'll try."

"Well, goodbye for now." The giantess gave her a rare smile and strode away, the Australian Outback swallowing up her large form as she disappeared into the unforgiving landscape.

CHAPTER EIGHTY-EIGHT

S ophia was hesitant to slide off the rock and onto her injured leg but knew she couldn't hang out by the lake forever, like a lost mermaid.

Lunis was waiting for her. She needed water. And there was a lot more they needed to do if they were going to survive the Australian Outback together. But first, Sophia had to eat crow and say some things to her dragon.

She felt like the proverbial mermaid taking her first step onto the ground. To her surprise, her leg wasn't throbbing. A bandage covered the wound, which would hopefully keep it clean from infection. It also kept it away from Sophia's eyes, which was probably a good thing.

Her first step was a bit wobbly, but when she resigned to trusting her leg and whatever Bermuda had done to heal her, the next several steps were much smoother.

With a tentative glance back at the lake, Sophia said in a hush, "Thank you."

If it hadn't been for Smeg and Bermuda...well, she'd be heart-broken and close to dead. She really didn't think Lunis would let her die there on the rock, but with the anger boiling inside of her, there was little he could do to get her cooperation.

Sophia understood then how resentment and bitter feelings spoil relationships. They wall off the heart so little good can come through. Without heart, a person simply grows cold inside, losing track of what matters most—love.

Being cold right then in the actual sense would have been good. Instead, it was the peak of the day, and with the sun barreling down on her, she thought her boots might melt right off.

The tender expression full of hurt and longing Lunis flashed Sophia as she approached nearly made her crumble like her leg was giving out. She knew what he was feeling because she was feeling it too, not just because of their connection but because she'd caused it.

"I'm sorry," she began when closer. "I—"

We only say sorry when we've done something wrong, Lunis interrupted.

The smell of the rotting spider carcasses was disgusting. Sophia waved away flies and the smell. "I did do something wrong," Sophia admitted. "I lost sight of what's important."

I don't know how frozen yogurt came into this, he teased, instantly lightening the mood.

Sophia flashed him an amused expression. "Lun, what is with you and fro-yo, lately?"

It's the heat making me think of cooler things, he answered.

"I thought you liked things hot, like lava."

He thought for a moment. *I like both. I can withstand the heat, but that doesn't mean I prefer it. I was built to withstand many extremes, but when all is said and done, I prefer our comfortable life together, not because of the posh couches and amenities, simply because of you.*

"Thank you," Sophia began again, hoping Lunis let her get out her rehearsed speech before she forgot it. "I realize my ego—"

It's a good speech, he cut in again, a sneaky expression in his eyes. *But I've already heard it.*

She sighed, knowing keeping things from him was nearly impossible. Lunis knew her thoughts almost at the same time she thought them. Only in conversation when they were bantering back and forth did she give him any surprises.

"Fine, well, I'd know what you were thinking in response to my excellent speech, but I was passed out, and my head is still swimming from the poison," Sophia admitted.

I wasn't going to let you die, he insisted.

"No, you magically called Bermuda Laurens over to save me."

He swished his tail back and forth, creating a welcomed breeze. *She wasn't too far away, and I knew she'd want to see the Spindle spiders.*

"Yeah, she's not as mad as I figured about taking them out." Sophia gazed around at the disgusting mess of dead spiders and wondered why they were hanging out there when they could be just about anywhere else in the Australian Outback.

The other dragons are still of the old mind, Lunis began, his voice careful and very intentional with every word. *They prefer the Cave cold and hard because they believe dragons can't have luxuries, or it makes us soft. They prefer the harsh cold or extreme heat. They crave battle. They think our suffering makes us better, but I think they're wrong.*

Sophia, I've never believed, even with the knowledge I have of my ancestors, that I need to suffer to be a better dragon. Maybe I'm naïve or young or inexperienced, but I've known since the beginning the only thing that makes me better is you.

Sophia tensed inside and held in tears, knowing she couldn't cry—mostly because she needed all her fluids, but also because she didn't want to interrupt.

No, you can't always save me due to our obvious size and magical differences, Lunis continued. *What you do for me is better than swooping into a battle and rescuing me. Every day since I hatched, you've reminded me what is most important in this world. The dragons have almost forgotten, so consumed with experiencing constant suffering. They have their riders but think the humans are to provide perspective and partnership. In all honesty, without you all, we'd lose sight of why we fight, why we started fighting. Dragons have a long history of killing each other and other creatures because of our constant desire for war. We are given our history through the collective consciousness, but it's so long we forget how it started. It is humans—our riders—who remind us why we started fighting. It was for love.*

Sophia's feet brought her forward as Lunis' head lowered. She caught it in her hands and looked deep into his eyes, seeing more than just his pure intention and deep affection for her. Sophia, at that moment, saw the very soul of her dragon—intertwined with hers for all time.

CHAPTER EIGHTY-NINE

Never again did Sophia want to be mad at Lunis. It felt exactly the same as being mad at herself. Warring with one's self was impossible to win.

She knew there would be other conflicts between her and her dragon. They had to remember they were connected but weren't the same. It was their unique abilities that made them so good for one another.

"Okay, so I vote we move away from the graveyard of gross spider carcasses," Sophia said, still feeling tender and raw inside.

Oh, I thought this was our forever home, Lunis joked. *We'd plant a bed of tulips over there and use the dead bodies of our enemies as fertilizer.*

She laughed. "I don't think tulips or anything that isn't strong and hearty as hell can grow in this place."

We should probably think about food for you before the sun goes down. Lunis' gaze drifted off to the area around the lake where the mountains provided some shelter.

"And we need to set up a camp and start another fire," Sophia offered.

Leave the fire to me, Lunis said proudly.

"No fair," Sophia complained. "You get to fly and use fire and call helpers to you, and it's not considered magic."

And you get to benefit from my loophole, Lunis retorted. *Also, you get to use all your skills and charm because they also aren't considered magic, but we both know better. It's all relative.*

Sophia winked at him. "Good point. Okay, you make a fire over there, and I'll catch something for dinner." She pointed to an area of the rock wall with a series of corners that would be ideal for shelter.

What are you planning for food? Lunis asked, obviously trying to keep his skepticism out of the question.

She pulled her sword from its sheath. "How hard can it be to fish?"

The answer was very hard. It was extremely difficult to fish with a sword. Sophia had remained frozen, standing in the shallow and patiently waiting for a fish to swim by. Then she'd spear her sword at the creature, but it invariably hurried away before being impaled.

You're using force, Lunis said.

Am I supposed to persuade them to jump onto the end of my sword? Sophia joked.

No, but if you soften your mind, you might find attack is more proactive and less reactionary, Lunis offered, gathering wood for the shelter. *The abruptness of your movements frightens the fish. If you strike with more precision and fluidness, they will be speared before they even know what hit them.*

Haha, Sophia replied, laughing at his pun. *Is this like that Bruce Lee, "Become the water" thing?*

Yeah, that works, Lunis replied, starting to arrange his shelter.

Sophia pulled in a long, meditative breath and tried to calm herself. Lunis was right. She had been tensing while waiting for the fish to approach. As soon as she saw one, she threw the sword at it, a very reactionary movement.

Trying not to rush and edging the constant hunger from her mind, Sophia waited for the next fish to swim into her area. It became apparent that when one was hungry, the screaming desire for food made one reckless and drove away that which one wanted. The desperation was a loud siren sending everything nearby into chaos and making it scatter, which wasn't the way dreams were realized.

She breathed when she felt anxious and impatient. She embraced the uncertainty. She invited in the waiting and got comfortable with it. This felt like what she was supposed to do with her demons per Bermuda and Smeg's advice.

Running from one's problems usually only brought them closer. This brought a poem to Sophia's mouth. The words echoed in her mind, although she didn't remember memorizing the words of the great poet Rumi:

"This being human is a guest house.
Every morning a new arrival.
A joy, a depression, a meanness,
some momentary awareness comes
as an unexpected visitor.
Welcome and entertain them all!
Even if they are a crowd of sorrows,
who violently sweep your house
empty of its furniture,
still, treat each guest honorably.
He may be clearing you out
for some new delight.
The dark thought, the shame, the malice.
Meet them at the door laughing and invite them in.
Be grateful for whatever comes.
because each has been sent
as a guide from beyond."

When she'd finished whispering the poem, Sophia found herself close to tears again, amazement dancing in her being. She didn't know how she knew the poem or where it had come from, but its words were perfect and reflected her current evolution.

The chi of the dragon, Lunis offered. *It is connecting you with all.*

Sophia nodded and felt a delightful chill running over her arms even though it was still hotter than hell in the Outback.

"Invite them in," she said mostly to herself, holding her sword and welcoming the impatience. Welcoming her imperfections. Welcoming more failure if that was what it took to get where she needed to go.

She didn't startle like before when a large shiny fish swam into the waters by her feet. Also, unlike before, she didn't plunge her sword into the water, missing the fish and scaring it away.

Sophia didn't move at all. She simply watched the fish peck around at the rocks. She studied it as it curled and moved through the water, managing its path with the current pushing it one way and then another.

To her amazement, Sophia felt no quick impulse to kill the creature she desperately needed for replenishment. Yes, she wanted the fish, but something inside of her had changed. She didn't feel the need to chase it. To trap it before it got away. Deep within her being, she knew the fish was hers, and it would come to her if she simply relaxed.

It was that thought that led to another: All things which were truly hers couldn't be scared away. They were all there for the taking as long as she remained keenly focused on them, knowing they belonged to her.

A man who desperately desires gold pushes it away when he races for it. But the man who knows the gold is already his simply has to shut off the light at night and wait for it to be delivered to his door in the morning.

Sophia had the strange desire to close her eyes as she kneeled soundlessly, not disturbing the water where she stood with a single ripple. With her free hand, she reached blindly into the water, not in a rushed movement, but definitely a stealthy one and grabbed the fish, pulling it out of the water and holding it victoriously above her head.

She learned what she wanted was merely a thought away, no more, no less.

CHAPTER NINETY

The water was boiling over the fire in a large rock Lunis had thrown against the ground and broken to hollow out. The many fish Sophia had caught were roasting over the flickering flames. Rider and dragon were hard at work creating their individual shelters.

Sophia hadn't played with building blocks much growing up, but she was pretty happy with what she'd constructed when she stepped back to admire it. She'd taken a series of sticks and created a rooftop to provide shelter from the unrelenting sun. It was built between the corners of two rock walls to give her protection from multiple directions. It wasn't a resort with central air and plumbing, but it would do until she found more supplies and maybe added another wall and a door.

Lunis stepped even with her, similarly admiring what he'd done. Sophia couldn't help herself. She burst out laughing at the sight of his shelter, nestled adjacent to hers.

What? he asked, sounding offended.

"Let's see how you did," Sophia began, using the voice of the host from Lunis' favorite Netflix show, *Nailed It* where amateur bakers were expected to replicate seriously difficult cakes and follow the complicated design. "This is what you were trying to make." She held her hand out at the shelter she had made, which had a clean design and was practical in every way. "And here's what you made."

The structure Lunis had crafted looked like a bonfire with long logs that poked up in different directions in the corner of his rock wall.

Nailed it, he sang with no enthusiasm.

"Where exactly were you planning on sleeping in there?" Sophia asked, craning her head to check out the awful structure.

"Over there to the left...or right." He shook his head. "I was just going to wedge in there and have the sticks cover me.

"Good idea." Sophia laughed. "But how about you share my structure? It should be large enough for the two of us."

He nodded appreciatively. "It's nice that what I suck at, you do competently."

Sophia admired their camping area as the cooking fish filled the air with a smoky, savory smell. "I agree. Good job to us for surviving the first day."

Only six more to go, Lunis said, settling down close to the flames as Sophia went to work pulling the fish and water off the fire.

She was desperately hungry and thirsty, but it didn't bother her as much because she felt fulfilled from within.

CHAPTER NINETY-ONE

F or not having any seasoning, the fish wasn't bad, although Sophia wished she'd eaten fewer bones.

She'd drunk as much water as she could, feeling as though she'd never feel properly hydrated.

You're going to be peeing all night, Lunis said, settling down into the shelter when the sun began to set, sending an array of oranges and pinks across the sky.

The thought of having to venture off into the Australian Outback at night by herself without magic made Sophia set down the bowl of water. She ran her hand across her mouth and realized how dirty she was. Half of her pant leg was missing and there was dirt in every crevice she had, even some she didn't remember having. They had survived the first day, and Sophia was grateful.

She crawled in beside Lunis. He opened one of his wings to create a spot for her just as a chill hit the air, cued by the sun going down.

Sophia could hardly believe how fast it went from hot to cold in the Outback. She nestled into the warmth of her dragon, grateful when he laid his wing over her like a blanket and tucking her into him.

She found her eyes closing as the sounds of the Outback began to hum them to sleep. It was a strangely peaceful arrangement even though they were sleeping in the middle of nowhere after one of the hardest days either had ever experienced.

Sophia listened to Lunis' heartbeat under her ear and found herself smiling about the simple sound that meant the world to her. She cracked her eyes open and spied the stars peeking out in the vast sky. As they said their hellos to the world, Sophia decided it was her time to say goodnight to the Outback.

"Good night, Lun."

Good night, Soph, he said, holding her tightly, sweet need expressed in the small movement.

The growling awoke Sophia, making her stir out of Lunis' embrace. She knew at once he was already awake.

We're surrounded, he told her in her head.

How? Sophia asked, attempting to make no noise as she sat up.

Lunis adjusted to make room for her to move. *I'm guessing because we were both so exhausted that whatever it is got in without waking us. I'm sorry.*

Don't be, she reassured at once, knowing she'd slept through it all too.

Pushing the grogginess from her head, she willed her eyes to adjust to the dark. The fire had burned out, and the Outback was mostly blackness, save for the stars twinkling in the sky.

The growls came from different directions, meaning Lunis was correct. They were surrounded.

What are they? Sophia asked, spying pairs of reflective eyes here and there in the darkness before they jerked away, the animals scampering to the side.

My first guess was dingoes, Lunis responded.

Sophia caught the outline of one of the beasts as they moved closer. It indeed had the hunched back of a dingo, its sharp teeth shining in the darkness. However, when it growled, its eyes glowed red.

Oh, hell, Sophia said, grabbing for Inexorabilis beside her. *Those aren't normal dingoes.*

CHAPTER NINETY-TWO

The growling was almost deafening as Sophia and Lunis rose to their feet, the rock wall at their backs and an unknown number of enemies spreading out in front of them.

She could hear the strange dingoes charge around them, creating what she thought was an arch from wall to wall. They were, in fact, surrounded.

Sophia wasn't worried. She had Lunis. And Inexorabilis. What she wished, was that she could see something besides the strange flash of red eyes every now and then as the monsters ran past each other, their energy building as they got more excited, feeding off one another's eagerness.

Don't be overly confident, Lunis warned. *Even a regular dingo shouldn't be underestimated when in a pack. They know how to work together to bring down a water buffalo.*

Sophia nodded, knowing he was right. Too much confidence was the curse of any warrior. Sophia's sister, Liv, had told her once, urging her to always remain humble.

We need light, Sophia said.

Well, I could blast them with fire, and then we can go back to sleep, Lunis

371

offered. *I was having this great dream about gorging on nachos and binge-watching the new season of* Lost in Space. *I'd like to get back to that.*

I'd like to get back to that dream too, Sophia related. *However, I don't think blasting fire at these creatures blindly is a good idea. Can you relight the fire?*

You know I can, Lunis said and spat a neat stream of fire in the direction of the campfire, relighting the kindling. It wouldn't last long since it was almost burned out, but it stayed lit long enough for Sophia to make out the details that told her more of the story.

She shook her head and reflexively stepped in closer to Lunis. "Well, of course," she complained, speaking out loud. "They would have to be zombie dingoes."

CHAPTER NINETY-THREE

The fire illuminated a pack of dingoes who were uglier than most, which was saying a lot. Many of their red eyes were hanging loosely in the sockets of their rotting heads. The sides of many of them were missing, their flesh hanging and bones exposed. They were bits of blood and fur, hissing and growling at the pair backed up to the rock wall.

Of course, they are zombies, Lunis echoed. *Why would we expect anything normal at this point?*

Sophia brandished her sword and revolved in a half-circle, doing her best to intimidate each of the dingoes she faced off with. "Right. Well, after magical, giant spiders and talking crocodiles, I really should have expected this. Are there no normal animals out there anymore?"

I don't think the normal ones want anything to do with us, Lunis offered as the howling grew louder.

"Well, any bright ideas on how to deal with these guys?" Sophia asked.

Since they are zombies, I would speculate that killing them won't work, Lunis mused.

Sophia nodded and watched as one of them limped closer, drool flooding his mouth. "Yeah, they appear to have been killed a few times already."

I guess there's only one way to find out, Lunis remarked. *Shall I?*

Sophia knowing what he was asking, simply nodded.

He opened his mouth and pointed it to the north of their camp area where the pack started and spread out to the other side. After drawing a breath, the dragon sent a roaring blast of fire at the closest zombie dingo. The creature didn't retreat as one would expect.

Sophia watched as it dared to come in closer, jumping straight into their campfire as the flames licked at its body. It growled furiously, crouching low, and preparing to jump in their direction.

Lunis focused on the pack and started to revolve his head to the right to blast the rest of the creatures.

"Stop!" Sophia yelled, her hands vibrating with her sword. "The fire doesn't bother them."

This was abundantly clear when the fire halted, and two dingoes ran around their camp area, flames rising off them as they seemed to get more excited like the party had just started.

The closest one ran straight at them, his red eyes locked on the pair. When he was only a few yards away, he jumped, mouth wide and teeth bared. Flames engulfed him like he was a fireball. Sophia stepped in front of Lunis, trying her best pose of intimidation. She didn't waver as the beast soared straight at her. When it was about to clobber her, she stepped to the side and knocked her blade against the dingo's side. The beast dropped to the dirt, where it rolled, extinguishing some of the flames.

Lunis had come out from the wall and was knocking down dingo after dingo as they tried to attack him from the side. The ones who were on fire had run through the bushes, setting many of them on fire and making the dark night ablaze with orange.

Sophia swung Inexorabilis around, catching a monster in her peripheral as she spun. She stabbed the zombie in the midsection and kicked it off her sword, but that did little to stop it from coming at her again.

It lunged, its teeth nearly grazing her unscathed pant leg. She brought her other foot around and kicked the monster in the head, which seemed only to insult it and make it run back at her faster.

Meanwhile, Lunis was throwing the dingoes two at a time, launching them like softballs. This only seemed to encourage the monsters. As soon as they hit the ground, they were back on their feet and sprinting for Lunis.

Sophia had little time to check on her dragon, as she had two dingoes who were trying to make her into dinner, or a zombie. She knew magic could help her, although she wasn't sure how. There had to be a spell to stop the undead, but she knew magic wasn't an option. She could have turned to magic before, but the point of this exercise was to find other choices.

Giving up now would only make her job harder the next time. It was better to do this right the first time, even if it meant she might get bitten by a zombie. She hoped Bermuda hadn't gotten off too far if that happened, because she would probably need the giantess's help to heal herself, yet again.

CHAPTER NINETY-FOUR

For hours, Sophia and Lunis defended their camp, staying close to each other. Lunis only used fire when it grew too dark to make out their enemies. Lighting them up only seemed to excite the zombies. Still, they both needed the light.

Sophia sliced through the dingoes, but it did little to get rid of them. It seemed to slow a few, but only because it made it harder for them to spring off the ground and attack with their many lacerations or missing body parts. Lunis batted at the dingoes who tried to attack him, but even that became a challenge as his energy waned and theirs didn't.

There were a few desperate moments where Sophia almost resorted to magic when she thought they were about to be ambushed. She watched as a zombie's jaws nearly connected with Lunis' side. If it wasn't for his thick hide, the animal would have bitten him, infecting him with whatever had made it the way it was. In the end, Lunis was able to knock the beast away with a swipe of his tail, sending it into the rock wall, where it slid to the ground before popping back up, ready to keep playing.

Sophia could hardly breathe from the constant fighting and was close to making a costly mistake when the dingo she was fighting backed away, its red eyes narrowed on her like she'd finally done something to offend it.

She glanced at her sword and wondered if Inexorabilis had projected some new power that worked on these strange zombies. That's when she noticed the fires had burned out, but there was an orange light glowing on the horizon.

The sun was rising in the Australian Outback, and with it, the zombie dingoes were retreating, one by one.

The pack hurried away as the bright orange ball that promised to bring sweltering temperatures rose in the distance.

Sophia couldn't believe she was happy to see the sun that would make the day completely intolerable. However, it appeared the zombie creatures didn't do daylight, which meant Lunis and Sophia had some respite until nightfall.

She slumped next to her dragon, lowering her sword for the first time in hours. Her breath was ragged, and the cold chill of the retreating night air grazed over her sweat covered back made her shiver.

Sophia sank against Lunis, who staggered on his feet, exhaustion heavy in his body too. They had survived the night, but now they had another day that would bring its own challenges.

CHAPTER NINETY-FIVE

Sophia yawned, making her dragon copy her.

"How is that gesture even contagious for dragons?" she asked, laughing and wishing she could magic some coffee. She searched the scorched area, her brain looking for some coffee plants she could harvest.

Yawning is universally contagious no matter who you are, but especially if you spent half the night fighting zombie dingoes, he replied.

"If I had a nickel for every time you ever said that…"

You would have a nickel, he retorted.

"Coffee…" Sophia pulled her mouth to the side, thinking. "How do we make coffee from dirt, dry kindling, and a bunch of strange bugs?"

You didn't bring any magic beans with you, did you? Lunis joked.

Sophia shook her head. "If I did, Mahkah would have confiscated them."

She considered convincing Lunis they should duck back into the modest shelter and take a nap, but the temperature was already rising. Sophia knew it would be next to impossible for her to sleep in this heat, especially with Lunis radiating warmth.

There was also the fact they needed to hunt, eat, hydrate, and take care of their other personal needs.

Surviving was exhausting, she thought, pushing her dirty hair out of her face.

Okay, Lunis said, his voice slow and words slurred. *Do you want to be in charge of water, and I'll go and get us a kangaroo to roast?*

Sophia nodded, not even daring to argue she needed to hunt her own food. She'd come so far since the day before when she thought she had to do everything herself, to prove she could survive on her own. The walkabout wasn't about being strong enough on her own. It was about the two of them relying on one another and being strong enough together. Divide and conquer.

Lunis lit a fire before taking off, slumping at first before he recovered. He was fatigued from the long fight, but they would pull through together.

Sophia went to work to collect water to be boiled. It was slow work since she only had so many rock containers. Her pants were drenched within minutes, which reminded her she'd need a bath at some point.

After breakfast, she decided, wondering what her face looked like. She was pretty certain it was covered in dirt, and her hair was matted to her head in different places.

While she was trying to find more rocks to drop on the ground and crack open, to reveal a hollow center that made a nice bowl, Sophia found some pretty gemstones which, if polished, could be really nice. She collected a few and stuck them in her pocket, thinking they might make good jewelry.

She planned on spending the day surviving the Outback, but if the opportunity presented itself, she thought she might take some time to be creative. A nap might not be in her future, but some creative exploits could be her saving grace.

A short time later, Lunis returned, carrying a sizable kangaroo that was thankfully dead. He set it a safe distance away from the camp and went to work cleaning the thing with his claws. Sophia was grateful he was an expert butcher because she didn't want that job. She had collected enough kindling to keep them supplied through the next few days.

The next task was to determine how to protect the camp from the zombie dingoes. It wasn't certain they would be back come nightfall, but it was a safe assumption.

"Can we construct a border fence?" Sophia asked, biting into the meat, its grease dripping down her chin. Without a napkin to sop it up, she was forced to use the back of her hand to wipe it away. Suddenly she felt like one of the guys at the Castle, being all uncivilized.

Lunis thought for a moment as he ate his meat raw, not because he didn't like it roasted or seasoned. He was a cultured dragon, after all. Mostly it was because he didn't want to go to the extra work and said the kangaroo was fine as it was.

We could set some traps for them, he suggested.

"Yeah, that's a good idea," Sophia said. "Like some spikes under the ground and netting, maybe?"

He nodded. *I think it will slow them down, but honestly, it won't stop them. They are unrelenting.*

"Should we consider moving the camp somewhere else?" Sophia pointed up to the top of the mountain. "How about there?"

I think they can climb, Lunis stated. *And I think we're better off being close to our water supply and having the shelter of the mountain at our back. I hate to admit it, but if they could have surrounded us fully we may not have survived.*

Sophia agreed with a nod. She thought the same thing. It had been the only relief they'd had last night when they could put their back to the wall and know they only had to focus on three fronts.

"I wonder what they are all about?" she wondered. "Like, where did they come from, and what do they want?"

Besides to eat us and turn us into zombies? Lunis asked.

Sophia finished her food and washed it down with water. "Yeah, besides that."

I'm not sure, but hopefully they won't be back tonight.

Sophia rose and tried to shake off the dirt, which was sort of a ridiculous notion at this point. "I hope so, too, but if they are, we are going to be prepared."

CHAPTER NINETY-SIX

L unis and Sophia spent the rest of the day tirelessly setting traps for the zombie dingoes. She used her sword to sharpen stakes he'd then buried under the sand. Later they worked together to create some netting from bushes that had really tangled branches.

Using a rudimentary pulley system, they were able to set the traps up so a single action would activate them and scoop up the trespassing creature.

Sophia was pleasantly surprised by the end of the day that she had gone so long and done so many complex tasks without magic. Their traps were still full of faults, and she and Lunis worried the dingoes were smart enough to get around them.

One of us is going to have to keep watch, Lunis suggested.

"I'll take the first shift," she offered, having never seen him as tired as he was that day.

He didn't argue, probably knowing she wouldn't back down regardless. *Okay, but wake me up in a few hours and I'll take over. And of course, wake me up at the first sign of the dingoes.*

"Hopefully, they will find someone else to torture tonight," she said and settled next to her dragon as the sun set. She patted him affectionately as his heavy eyes closed and sent him straight into dreams.

Sophia knew that last night he could have taken off at any point and escaped the zombies. However, he couldn't take her, and so he'd fought by her side. She hugged into him, feeling more bonded to her dragon than ever before. Sophia hardly thought it possible since she'd known him since birth, and yet, turmoil had brought them closer.

Sophia could have opened a portal and escaped the carnage, but that would have been cheating. They were going to pass this training without breaking any rules. The other dragonriders had, and so would she.

It boggled Sophia's brain that Evan had survived the Outback for seven days when he complained if his toast was room temperature, but she guessed he could weather many different storms when he wanted.

The first watch went without any trespassing by the zombies, at which point Sophia gently woke Lunis and told him it was his turn to take over.

He did so without a word, thoughtfully squeezing her into him with his wing folded around her. Sophia had closed her eyes for less than a minute and was already deep in dreams when Lunis jumped to his feet, blasting fire up to the sky to briefly illuminate their surroundings.

They are back, he said, his words full of anger.

Sophia sluggishly got to her feet, nearly falling on her face. "Of course, they are. I think they are after my beauty sleep."

The dragon flashed her a smile, rejuvenated by his few hours of rest. *You look beautiful. But look alive. Something tells me the beasts are more rambunctious than last night.*

"What tells you that?" she asked over the chorus of growls in the distance, red flashing eyes sparking up the darkness.

Something dropped onto the roof over their heads, nearly making the structure buckle under them.

Sophia was instantly glad they hadn't taken to higher ground with the zombie dingoes jumping into their camp from above. She pulled out her sword, ready for whatever came next.

The dog peeked his head down below the roof as if to say hello, but Sophia wasn't in the mood for unexpected visitors. She brought Inexorabilis up and around, her tiredness making her break through the roof as she sent the mutt tumbling to the ground and rolling toward the perimeter of their camp where he fell onto one of the buried spikes, making him retreat as he howled.

The traps kept the zombies back but didn't deter them entirely. Again, Lunis and Sophia spent the entire night keeping the monsters away. It wasn't until sunrise the strange dogs retreated, leaving the pair more exhausted than the night before. Sophia actually slumped against Lunis, almost asleep on tired feet.

CHAPTER NINETY-SEVEN

*Y*ou need a nap, he said when all was clear.
She wanted to argue but had no energy to do so. Sophia allowed Lunis to lower her onto the dirt floor of the broken shelter where the sun was already streaming through, threatening any ounce of sleep. She had no idea how she'd rest with the temperature rising and her stomach starting to growl.

Before long, she forgot her troubles and fell into a dreamless sleep.

When Sophia awoke, she was in comfortable darkness. None of it made sense based on what she remembered. Turning over in the dirt, she tried to make sense of her world.

The darkness lifted, and Sophia found she'd been under Lunis' wing, which was nice and cool in contrast to the assaulting heat and brightness of the Australian Outback. It came shooting into her as soon as he pulled his wing away.

Good evening, Sunshine, he said, smiling down at her as she rose.

"Did you say evening?" she asked, stretching and noticing the sun was close to the horizon.

Yes, you missed most of the day, he answered. *But I saved you some roo.* He indicated the fire.

Her stomach lurched with desire at the sight of the roasted meat over the waning fire. "I can't believe I slept the day."

You needed it, he said.

"And you hunted and kept your wing over me?" she asked, going to work on the meat.

Well, not at the same time, he admitted. *I'm sorry. I had to leave you here in the scorching heat while I hunted, but you weren't alone for long.*

"Thank you," she said between bites.

Always, he said at once and then gave their broken structure a regretful glance. *I'm sorry I didn't have a chance to repair our shelter, but even if I had, I'm not sure I could have done much good.*

Sophia laughed. "Yeah, you probably wouldn't have nailed it, but the thought is what counts." She chewed and listened to the strange noises of the Outback for a moment before asking the question on both their minds. "So, tonight…"

Yeah, they will probably return, Lunis replied.

"And you spent all day watching after me and not able to set traps."

No, Lunis argued. *You spent half the night watching out for me. I simply returned the favor, not that there should be any of those between us. I do things for you because I want to, not out of return or obligation.*

"Well, still," Sophia stated. "Night is quickly approaching, and we have no traps, no structure, and I sense the dogs are getting smarter."

Lunis gave her a commiserating expression. *I was thinking the same thing. They seem to learn more each night and come back with better attacks.*

Sophia let out a breath, feeling heavy and lost.

They were exhausted, wrecked from the obstacles of the Outback. And yet, she wasn't even close to quitting. She allowed her mind to trail back to when they started this journey, a long and strangely short three days ago. She'd already learned so much since then and grown so much. She and Lunis had bonded in new ways. She remembered the poem by Rumi, and it washed over her like spring rain, which would have been wonderful, but it was only in the metaphorical sense.

"…an unexpected visitor.

Welcome and entertain them all!

Even if they are a crowd...who violently sweep your house...treat each guest honorably.

He may be clearing you out
for some new delight.

The dark thought, the shame, the malice.

Meet them at the door laughing and invite them in.

Be grateful for whatever comes.

because each has been sent

as a guide from beyond."

Sophia sucked in a breath, not believing what she was about to suggest. Before she could, Lunis rose, casting her in his shadow.

You aren't proposing... he began, sensing her thoughts.

She swallowed. Straightened. Nodded.

"I think we have to allow them into our camp," she stated with confidence. "We can't fight them. We have to welcome our demons."

CHAPTER NINETY-EIGHT

With the broken shelter littering the wall behind them, Sophia and Lunis lay together, both vibrating with anxiety.

It was strange to have options to get out of bad situations and not use them. Lunis could fly. Sophia could portal away. They both had magic. And yet, they were going to lie together and rest while furious beasts they'd battled for hours on end invaded their camp.

The sun's final rays spread across the Outback, making the land glow. Sophia was still exhausted even after sleeping all day. She was certain she'd stay up most of the night since she was too curious to shut her eyes properly.

"You need to sleep, though," she said to Lunis, knowing he was listening to her thoughts.

Just until they arrive, he promised and closed his eyes, obviously tired from the partial night's sleep and the demands of the day.

He was snoring within a minute, a comforting sound that joined the others of the Outback nicely.

When the rabid hounds showed up, Sophia didn't bolt into position like she had the nights prior. She started to wake Lunis but stopped herself. They weren't fighting the beasts. At least that was the plan, so she didn't see any reason to rouse Lunis from what seemed like pleasant dreams.

She'd heard him mumble polite phrases throughout the night like, "Thank you" and "Yes, please," making her believe he was dreaming of nachos and binge-watching television.

If things got dire, she'd definitely wake her dragon and happily fly off on him, admitting she was wrong. For the time being, he might as well sleep while she decided if her convoluted plan, centered mostly on faith, was correct.

The dingoes did as they had the first night and prowled around the perimeter, their red eyes flashing as they growled and made their presence known.

Sophia watched, her arms around her dragon. For a long while she watched them drawing nearer, taking their chances by inching in closer and closer. Her instinct was to fight. To rise to her feet and swing her sword and tell her dragon to defend.

She resisted and simply lay still, doing her best to ignore the zombie creatures. When they were close enough that she could smell them it was hard not to move, especially when they drew in so close their fur whisked her skin as they passed.

Lunis jumped to his feet and threw Sophia off him when they brushed him.

Sophia tightened her grasp around his neck and held him close. *Don't move*, she encouraged, speaking in his head.

You didn't wake me, he scolded, hurt obvious in his tone.

I'm sorry, she apologized and then shook her head. *No, I'm not sorry. You needed to rest, and there was nothing to see but the creatures stalking us.*

I wanted to see that, he demanded.

You've missed nothing, she stated as one of the monsters sniffed her boot, drool dripping from his mouth.

Lunis eyed the monster, and Sophia knew he was resisting his every instinct by not attacking.

Just allow them, Sophia encouraged.

One of the dingoes ran by, nipping the dragon's tail and darting away. It wasn't enough to draw blood, but it was enough that Lunis' head swung in the direction of the retreating mutt.

Just let it go, Sophia said, observing that since he awoke and started paying attention to them, they had become more rambunctious, just like on the other nights. When they'd fought the beasts, the dingoes got more enlivened. When Sophia was the only one awake, they had been pretty subdued.

Maybe she had been wrong not to wake Lunis, she reasoned, but she'd wanted to give him a chance to sleep. He was on guard now, and that seemed to have an effect on the dogs.

Lun, I think you need to close your eyes and relax.

How can I even consider that, he asked, stress coating his voice.

I know it seems counterproductive, Sophia said. *But that's what my instinct says.*

A pair of rather large zombie dingoes were approaching on either side of them, their fangs bared and their eyes glaring red.

But Sophia, Lunis argued vehemently in her head.

I know, she replied. *But trust me. Close your eyes. Relax. Invite them in.*

She felt Lunis rumble internally with unease. She knew this was against his nature, which always told him to fight. She also knew he trusted her more than anything else. The more she held onto him and encouraged him to relax, the more she knew he was closer to accepting that reality.

The two hounds were dangerously close, the sight of their internal organs hanging out of their body too close for comfort. Sophia took her own advice and closed her eyes.

She knew there were dangers in the world. There always would be, but she was safe and secure with the creature she was holding onto. She was safe as long as she quit running from danger and faced it head-on. Sometimes that meant fighting, and sometimes it meant simply facing what she feared.

When she was close to falling asleep, Sophia opened her eyes to find the dingoes almost nose to nose with her. She should have jumped to her feet and defended herself. Instead, she hugged her dragon, opened her mouth, and said, "Welcome to our humble abode. Enjoy your stay."

And with that, the rider and her dragon fell asleep, hoping the strangest magic they'd ever used worked.

CHAPTER NINETY-NINE

The dreams Sophia had that night were strange, yet they made her feel invigorated when she woke. Maybe it was simply the fact she woke up at all, which made her feel inspired.

Lunis stirred at the same time as her, just before sunrise, to find their camp empty. They were still in one piece, not a single mark on them from the zombie dingoes.

Sophia pushed up as the reality started to dawn on her. It was hard to believe it had worked.

We didn't fight, and we survived, Lunis declared, his voice clouded with disbelief.

"I think there's a beautiful lesson here," she stated, surveying their camp, which needed a lot of attention.

It's a beautiful Sophism, Lunis said, affectionately.

"Sophism?" she questioned.

Yes, things Sophia says and does that should be in a book.

"Or on a t-shirt?" she teased.

He batted his eyes at her, looking much more energized than the days prior. *My dragon proverbs go on t-shirts. Your stuff needs to be in libraries. Maybe even put on GIFs.*

Sophia laughed. "Oh, wow, I've gotten big enough for GIFs. What's next? Memes?"

Don't go crazy just yet, he joked. *But in all seriousness, you're the queen at knowing when to fight and when to stand down. The dingoes, we could have fought to the death. We could have defended ourselves every single night. But you pieced it all together and realized we didn't have to fight. That fighting only encouraged them. When we stayed still and gave them no reaction, they moved on, bored without any attention. I feel like the same thing happens in life all the time. You react to someone and it incites them. You ignore them and they go away.*

Sophia smiled, realizing how accurate his words were. "Yes, most people are zombie dingoes, aren't they?"

Yes, he affirmed. *And most try to fight them. Few have the good sense to close their eyes when a drooling monster is in their face threatening them. You knew to invite in your demons, and that was what saved us.*

Sophia let out a heavy breath, wondering if they had come full circle yet. She wasn't sure. They still had a few more days in the Australian Outback, which shouldn't be underestimated. "Well, you did catch our dinner for the last few days, which I think saved us."

Lunis gave her a meaningful expression. *Sophia, we saved each other. That's the way. The way it is now and for all time. You and I are nothing without one another.*

Sophia was skinnier than she ever remembered. She was dirty in every place possible. There were smells about her she wasn't sure would ever go away, yet she felt stronger and better than ever before.

Somehow by being broken down, she had found a part of her she absolutely adored. A part that complemented her dragon in ways neither had realized.

Sophia and Lunis still had much to learn about the world and each other. There was so much to discover. So many things to do and be. But right then, the pair felt completely bonded to one another and to the world they were trying to understand. One day they would save it, although neither knew that was going to be their destiny.

CHAPTER ONE HUNDRED

I t only took a day for Sophia and Lunis to find a routine that suited them. She spent the morning caring for the shelter, which didn't take long to repair.

The dragon hunted for them while she collected water. Later they ate, listening to the Outback and discussing things that were unique for them. They talked about ideas and philosophies, rambling on for hours about things neither had ever considered. Sophia found that whereas before she missed Wilder, Mahkah, Ainsley, Quiet, and maybe even Hiker and Evan, she didn't feel that way anymore. She felt fulfilled within in a new way.

When night began to fall, they both tensed briefly before remembering they weren't there to fight the Outback.

"We are here to be one with it," Sophia reminded. "We are here to be one with ourselves."

Lunis nodded. Doing as he had the nights prior, he curled up and made a space for Sophia.

The zombie dingoes returned every night and made their presence known. The pair got better at ignoring them. Not really ignoring. If one ignores their demons, they slowly take over. Instead, the two just quit giving their power away to the monsters.

They rested at night. They thought sweet thoughts. They prepared for the day ahead instead of giving everything away to the demons who would inevitably slay them with exhaustion if given the opportunity.

On the final day in the Australian Outback, Sophia rose, feeling more energized than when she had plumbing and the Castle provided everything for her. She wasn't sure why, since she hadn't had a proper shower or meal in a week. But somehow in the Outback, she'd found her own brand of magic and mixed it with Lunis' they'd managed just fine. She ventured to say they were thriving.

She didn't look much like before. Her pants had been altered to be shorts since she'd lost the one pant leg on the first day. Her shirt had been torn so many times she had pulled off the sleeves and repurposed parts of the fabric into bits she'd wrapped around her arms and wrists. She personified the look of a strange tribal warrior.

Her hair was a gigantic mess, as Lunis liked to remind her. However, she'd found a way to corral it back into a strange assortment of dread-like braids. Her face was covered in dirt most of the time, although she tried to take a proper bath in the lake most mornings.

Often, she hoped to see Smeg again, but the croc didn't surface. She suspected he'd moved on to a different body of water somewhere on the Earth and hoped to find him again in the future. He was helpful in his own crazy way.

Since they hadn't had to spend their time battling any more rabid dogs or giant spiders, the two had taken up hobbies. Sophia had started to make jewelry out of the stones she'd collected. Around her wrists and neck, she wore several bracelets and necklaces fashioned from homemade rope.

More surprisingly, Lunis had started painting, although Sophia had hoped he'd take up baking. Alas, he said that would be impossible since he didn't know how to come by any leavening ingredients in the Outback.

He had created beautiful paintings on the wall by their shelter using the clay from the lake and coloring it with dyes from wildflowers. The paintings were masterpieces Sophia had never seen in real life, complete with pictures of Scotland and Los Angeles and her travels. It was at nightfall on their last day she realized why she couldn't pull her eyes from the paintings.

"You created our life," she whispered to her dragon.

I immortalized it, he said. *But yes. It only seemed fitting since we were on this soul journey.*

"I like our life," Sophia said.

I think that was the point to all this, Lunis said. *If you came out of this not liking where you came from, you'd probably be stuck here until you figured out how to change it. But you like where we came from, and I daresay you want to go back, don't you?*

She turned, smiling wide at Lunis. "With all my heart. But what I realized more than anything is that no matter where I call home, which presently and hopefully forever is the Castle, I only ever want to be somewhere if you are too. I really thought growing up in the House of Fourteen was my home. And then my place with Liv. And later, the Castle. But now…after the Outback, I know the truth." Sophia reached out and stroked her dragon's face. "You are my home. Where you are, no matter if the conditions are pleasant or hellish, I want to be there. No matter what."

One hundred percent, Lunis said.

And as if prompted by their words, a portal opened beside them, sent by the Castle to bring them back to the real world, where there were real problems that needed their help now that they were aligned.

CHAPTER ONE HUNDRED ONE

The cold of the Expanse was such a contrast to the Australian Outback that Sophia slipped on her cloak first thing after stepping through the portal.

She drank in the fresh, clean air, enjoying how it instantly seemed to refresh her. The green of the hills was such a contrast to the red dirt and muted colors of the Outback it almost hurt Sophia's eyes.

The sight of the three dragonriders waiting for her just outside the Barrier was definitely welcomed. Sophia found herself rushing in their direction, realizing how much she'd missed them—even Evan.

Evan offered her a repulsed expression as she approached and reeled backward. Mahkah stood stoically, his hands pinned behind his back. Wilder had his arms extended, welcoming Sophia with a hug, relief evident in his blue eyes.

When she was close enough, he dropped his arms and leaned back, squinting at her with disbelief. "Wow, that's a new look for you."

Sophia glanced down at her ripped clothes, covered in dirt and grime. The armored shirt, once light-colored, was almost black. Sophia's nails were caked in mud. It would take Mae Ling...well, no time at all to clean them up, but Sophia would need to stop by and see her fairy godmother soon. She knew her hair looked like it belonged on a hippie, arranged into thick dreadlocks down her back.

Evan covered his nose. "Dude, which one of you smells?" he asked Sophia and Lunis.

"I took a bath this morning," Sophia replied. "Lun hasn't had one all week."

It's her, Lunis argued. *She took a bath in swamp water.* He glanced affectionately at Sophia. *There was a reason I didn't bathe.*

"I thought it was because you were pretending to be one of these guys," she joked.

"Welcome back," Mahkah said, bowing respectfully.

Wilder held out a single hand and went to slap Sophia on the shoulder but pulled it back just before connecting with her. "Yeah, welcome back."

"So, you didn't die?" Evan asked, his nose still covered.

"You're still here so wishing on those Outback stars didn't work," she teased, winking at him.

"You will have to tell us all about it," Wilder said, looking Lunis over.

"Yeah, let's start with what did you do to your dragon?" Evan asked, also inspecting him.

"I adorned him with jewelry," Sophia said proudly. Her dragon had her handmade necklaces arranged on his head like a crown. There were a few wrapped around his neck and legs, the shiny gems winking in the light.

She pulled a few bracelets from the pocket of her cloak and handed them out. "I made ones for each of you, too."

Evan gave his bracelet back and shook his head. "I'm good. I don't wear anything that reminds me of the Outback."

Wilder, however, slipped his on and tightened it on his wrist. "That's just because you were nearly eaten by a talking crocodile."

Sophia gave Evan a surprised expression. "Smeg tried to eat you? Oh, he was super helpful to me."

Evan sighed. "Of course, he was. Please tell me the zombie dingoes did try to eat you."

Sophia laughed. "You're so thoughtful. Who needs enemies when I've got you? And yes, the dingoes tried to eat us."

Evan punched the air. "Yes!"

Lunis lowered his head and looked at the giddy rider. *Well, until Sophia realized not to fight them, and they left us alone.*

Sophia stretched. "Then we got some proper rest."

The wide smile on Evan's face disappeared. "You what?"

"You didn't fight the dingoes?" Mahkah asked, intrigued.

"Yeah, would it have been cheating to tell us we'd encounter rabid zombie dogs?" Sophia asked, her hands on her hips.

"I'm afraid it would have been," Mahkah answered. "But again, you didn't fight them?"

No, we invited them into our house, so to speak, Lunis said, seeming much lighter as his head floated around, the necklaces making him look like a hippie too.

"W-wh-what?" Wilder asked. "You had a house?"

Sophia shrugged. "No, not really. Just a roof, but metaphorically speaking, we invited our houseguests in and welcomed them."

"They didn't chew off your faces?" Evan asked, his mouth wide and his eyes bulging.

"They totally did. This is my new face." Sophia shook her head.

"Well, it's dirty," Evan replied. "Have you looked in a mirror? And I think you have a bush in your hair. Oh, and have I mentioned you smell bad?"

"She smells rugged," Wilder corrected. "Like a cowboy or a girl who has spent a week in the Australian Outback."

"The zombie dingoes," Mahkah said, bringing the conversation back to the topic. "You really didn't fight them?"

"Well, we did for a couple of nights," Sophia explained. "However, it was going to be exhausting if we kept it up. It was a losing battle—"

"Which is the charm of the trip," Evan stated, crossing his arms and looking bitter about the whole thing.

Sophia shook her head. "Then I had the idea that we wouldn't defend ourselves. It seemed the more we fought, the more excited they got. When we started to ignore them, they became less interested and eventually left us alone."

Mahkah combed his fingers over his chin. "Interesting. A risk but a strategic one."

Wilder shook his head, astonished. "Simi and I fought those dingoes for seven days, sleeping during the day, and you simply closed your eyes and ignored them?"

She nodded proudly.

"I lived in a tree," Evan said, disgusted.

"I killed all the spiders under that tree," Sophia said.

"Well, you two obviously bonded," Mahkah said, looking at her and Lunis. "You completed all the objectives of the training exercise."

The group turned for the Castle, crossing the boundary to the Gullington and striding in time with one another. Lunis set off for the Cave when they crossed the Barrier. The Castle was a welcome sight in the distance. Sophia could already smell scones and couldn't wait to slip into clean clothes after a long hot shower.

"But the question is, did you have fun?" Wilder asked, a crooked smile on his face.

A week ago, Sophia would have scowled at the question. Now, she found herself nodding. "I wouldn't have called any of it fun, but rewarding, absolutely."

Evan's eyes were directed at the grass under their feet as he shook his head. "She didn't fight the dingoes. Dude, that's not fair."

Wilder slapped him on the back with a laugh. "It's a good lesson for us."

"Yes," Mahkah said, meditating on an idea. "Sometimes, we fight. Sometimes we ignore evil. It's knowing when to act and when not to."

The guys halted in front of the Castle, their cool demeanors suddenly fading and serious expressions taking over their faces. Sensing a new tension, Sophia looked at them.

"What is it?" she asked.

"Someone evil has surfaced since you two left," Wilder explained. "Thad Reinhart."

"Oh," Sophia said with relief. "We know about him."

"Yeah, but he's accelerated his agenda," Mahkah explained. "Hiker will want to see you."

"As soon as you wash that nappy hair," Evan added.

Sophia nodded. "Okay. I'll go straight to his office once I'm clean."

All the excitement from returning faded as worry took over. The expressions on the guys' faces told her that whatever had happened while they were gone wasn't just mildly bad. She got the impression it was catastrophic.

"And remember to wash behind…well, your everything," Evan called as she hurried up the stairs and into the Castle. "Wash twice."

CHAPTER ONE HUNDRED TWO

I t took more like five washings to feel clean. The brush nearly broke when Sophia tried to pull it through her locks. She considered keeping the dreadlocks, which Evan had had before he got electrocuted and all his hair was fried off. The thought that Evan had once sported the same hairdo was enough to make her work through the tangles, returning her hair to its usual sleek appearance.

When Sophia exited the bathroom, she was pleasantly surprised to find Ainsley tending the fire in her room. She'd also set down tea and scones for Sophia as if she'd read her mind about what she was craving.

"The Castle told me while you were showering you *needed* scones," Ainsley explained, rising from the fireplace and brushing off her hands on her apron. "Need seemed a bit of an exaggeration, but that's typical of the Castle."

Sophia realized how happy she was to see the housekeeper when she threw her arms around her and hugged her.

Ainsley tensed, her arms stick straight by her side. "S. Beaufont?"

"Yes?" Sophia asked, hugging Ainsley tightly.

"What are you doing?"

Sophia pulled away. "I was hugging you."

"Yes, but we're not hugging types around here," she said, taking a sudden step backward. "And you and I aren't really on those terms."

Sophia waved her off and took a seat away from the fire, having had enough warmth for ages. She picked up a scone, looking forward to her first refreshments since returning.

"Did you have a good time on holiday?" Ainsley asked, pouring her a cup of tea.

Sophia shook her head. "I was on a walkabout in the Australian Outback."

"Same thing," Ainsley said, standing back and looking Sophia over. "You lost weight. And you're sunburned. What are all those scratches on your arms from?"

Sophia glanced at the various marks on her skin. "Revolting spiders. If I never see one again, it will be too soon."

"Do you want me to clear out the family who lives under your bed then?" Ainsley asked.

She'd made that joke before, but Sophia was starting to wonder if it was a joke. Taking a bite of the scone, she relished its sweetness, perfectly crumbly and dense, as it melted in her mouth.

"I'd sure like to take a holiday like you all get regularly," Ainsley said, plopping down on the seat next to Sophia and putting her boots up on the coffee table. "I haven't left the Castle to do anything but go to town for supplies in ages."

Sophia nearly choked on her bite. She was one of the few who knew Ainsley couldn't leave the Castle for long or she'd fall victim to the curse Thad Reinhart had put on her, the one meant to kill Hiker. It had stolen her memory, changed her life, and given her the scar on the side of her head.

Sophia believed there had to be a way to change things, but right then wasn't the time to investigate. She wanted to take her time sipping tea and chewing on scones, but instead, she gulped down her tea and hardly chewed. Something was going on with Thad and his evil plans, and Sophia knew she needed to report to Hiker right away.

"The Castle missed you," Ainsley said, grabbing a scone and spreading clotted cream and jam on it.

"It did?" Sophia asked, perking up. "How do you know?"

"Because it told me," Ainsley answered. "It made portraits of you and Looney."

Sophia giggled. "That's a good nickname for him. I'm sure he'll hate it."

"Good," Ainsley chirped. "I'll be sure to use it and never call him anything else."

"The Castle and you," Sophia began, carefully. "You seem to understand it better these days, is that right?"

Ainsley tilted her head back and forth undecidedly. "I understand it when it wants me to. Sometimes the messages are clear, and other times they are just hints. It really depends on its mood. It was quite sour while you were gone. I had to do most of the chores twice since it seemed it wanted to be dirty in your absence."

Sophia laughed and took a bite of a cream cheese and cucumber sandwich. Somehow it was the best thing she'd ever put in her mouth. "It must have wanted to be just like me when I was in the Outback."

"The boys missed you too, although they wouldn't admit it," Ainsley offered. "Meals were incredibly boring. They kept looking around like they were expecting you to pop in late, wearing something colorful and humming one of your pop songs."

"That's nice to hear," Sophia said, smiling at the idea.

"You've changed a lot around the Castle since you showed up," Ainsley said. "Quiet says the biggest change is yet to come. Once you complete your training, he says."

"What?" Sophia lowered the sandwich and blinked at the housekeeper. "What does he mean?"

She shrugged. "Who knows, but he's never been wrong."

"And you understand him too," Sophia stated. "How is that?"

"I don't know why you people can't understand him," Ainsley said. "He's as plain as day to me."

There was weird magic surrounding the groundskeeper. Sophia

had understood him a time or two, the first occasion being when he helped her. Then he'd promised her, if she stuck around, he'd tell her his real name. She was still hoping he made good on the promise because it was of great curiosity to her.

"Ains?" Sophia asked after a brief moment of silence. It had never been a big deal for her, but now she was much more comfortable when it got quiet. "If you could go anywhere in the world, where would you like to go?"

The housekeeper chewed, thinking. "I'm not sure. Honestly, I don't even know why I don't just leave here and go on a walkabout. It's just that every time I consider traveling, I quickly lose interest."

Sophia nodded, knowing the Castle was behind the brainwashing, trying to keep Ainsley safe and alive, although the inevitable result was, she was sheltered.

"I guess I'd like to see a beach," Ainsley said after a moment of consideration. "It's been ages since I've seen the ocean and a cabana boy serving me drinks while I wiggle my toes in the sand seems just about like the best thing ever. Then I can say something really awful like, 'Life's a beach and then you dive.'"

Smiling, Sophia stretched to a standing position. "Well, I hope you get your beach vacation. Maybe Quiet will even join you."

"Oh, S. Beaufont," Ainsley scolded, sitting forward. "I don't leave the Gullington often because…well, I don't know why. There isn't any real need, I guess. But Quiet? He can't for hardly more than a few minutes."

"He can't?" Sophia asked. "Why not?"

Ainsley's expression changed. "You don't know? Of course, you don't know. Anyway, I've said too much."

"No, Ains," Sophia argued as the housekeeper busied herself picking up the tray and hurrying for the door. "Why can't Quiet leave the Gullington for long? I won't tell anyone."

"Pretend I didn't say anything," Ainsley said, the door automatically opening for her since her hands were full of the tray. "Now, you better be off. Hiker will be disappointed you survived, and I'm looking forward to hearing his grumbling on the matter. So off you go."

Sophia simply nodded and watched as the housekeeper sped out of the room. There were always more mysteries to the Gullington, waiting to be unraveled.

CHAPTER ONE HUNDRED THREE

The portrait of Sophia and Lunis was quite nice, she observed on her way to Hiker's office. It was a sizable painting, about two by four feet. The pair were standing in front of the Pond, the sunlight shimmering over the water as Sophia stood next to her dragon, one of her arms resting on his back.

"I missed you too," Sophia said aloud to the Castle.

The flames in the sconces lengthened in response.

"Are you going to tell me why Quiet can't leave the Gullington?"

There was no visible response from the Castle.

"Okay. Are you going to lead me on a scavenger hunt so I can discover the secret on my own?" she asked.

Again, the Castle didn't seem interested in providing any answers.

Sophia sighed as she headed for Hiker's office.

It was strange to see Hiker's study the way it was the first time she saw it. All of his books lined the shelves, and the Elite Globe was back in its place next to the bank of windows. The furniture looked great in the space and had plenty of room around it, unlike when the Castle had shrunk the area to a fraction of the size to punish Hiker for his secret-keeping.

The one thing different from before were newspapers from all over the world, written in different languages, lying all over the place. Even stranger were several television screens stationed around the office, all broadcasting news reports.

"I saw you were back," Hiker said, indicating the Elite Globe when Sophia ducked her head into the room.

Mama Jamba had a bunch of wadded-up tissues littering the sofa around her. The woman's nose was red, and her eyes were swollen from crying.

"Mama Jamba, are you okay?" Sophia asked, rushing over and taking the old woman's hand at once. She worried whatever Thad Reinhart had done was too far gone to stop. Was the Earth in total peril? Was it too late? Was this the end?

Mama Jamba sniffed and squeezed Sophia's hand. "Yeah, I'm fine. I just got finished watching *The Notebook*, and it still has me all emotional."

"What?" Sophia asked, not expecting that answer. "You mean, Nicholas Sparks' movie?"

Mama Jamba nodded and grabbed another tissue to dry her eyes.

"I told you these screens were for monitoring world events, not for watching that sappy stuff," Hiker said with authority.

Mama Jamba pointed to one of the televisions broadcasting a female reporter holding a microphone, standing in front of a picketing crowd. The screen changed to show the beginning of the *City of Angels* movie. "I'm in the mood to watch sad and depressing movies. Sue me. My Earth is in danger, and this is how I'm going to deal with it."

Sophia glanced at Hiker, a questioning expression on her face. He simply shrugged in reply.

"What's going on?" Sophia asked, looking at the two.

"Well," Mama Jamba began, wiping her nose. "There's this doctor, and she tries to save lives. That's Meg Ryan's character. And Nicholas Cage is an angel. Not like the ones who created the dragonriders. Fictional angels."

"Mama," Hiker interrupted, "I believe Sophia meant, what's going on in the world, not the synopsis for that drivel you're watching."

"Oh, well, then I won't spoil it for you, but you all talk quietly," Mama Jamba urged. "I'm going to watch this film and cry."

Sophia rose from the couch and shot the strange woman a questioning expression. "Hiker, is everything okay?"

He shook his head. "We'll get to that. Anyway, you returned from the Outback. Good on you. Not so hard, was it?"

Sophia eyed her fingernails, which were still not as clean as she would have liked. "I survived."

"And the dingoes?" he asked. "Did they take a toe?"

"She didn't fight the dingoes because she's smarter than the lot of you," Mama Jamba said, taking a bite out of a chocolate truffle. Sophia didn't remember seeing those there a moment ago.

"She what?" Hiker questioned. "Of course, she did."

"For two days she did, but then she figured it out," Mama Jamba said, her focus on the television screen in front of her. Briefly, she pulled her gaze away and looked at Sophia. "You're a smart one. That's how I know you'll finish training in record time. If you don't, well, we're all going to hell anyway at this rate."

Sophia had many questions, but before she could voice them, Hiker interrupted her thoughts. He apparently had his own questions.

"What does she mean?" he asked, pointing at Mama Jamba. "You didn't fight the dingoes?"

"They just wanted to fight," Sophia explained and gave him the full story.

When she was done, he stroked his beard, a skeptical glint in his blue eyes. "That's an interesting approach. It could have backfired completely."

"It's called faith, my dear. If more had it, I wouldn't be perishing," Mama Jamba chimed in, her attention still on the television as she finished another truffle. It was like she wasn't listening, yet she responded in time.

Hiker rolled his eyes. "Would you stop being so melodramatic, Mama? You aren't going anywhere, and neither is your Earth. I'll see to that, especially now that Sophia is back."

"Her training, Hiker," Mama Jamba sang. Her Southern accent

made the words sound soft, even though they were filled with demand.

"Thad has taken a serious advantage," Hiker argued, leaning across his desk and staring at the woman who was staring at the television as Meg Ryan delivered a speech.

"Which is why she's going to progress with her training," Mama Jamba said, holding out her hand, an Old-Fashioned materializing in her fingers. She smiled at it, although the gesture was marked by a tender hurt in her eyes. The old woman took a sip and then wiped her mouth. "Oh, that hits the spot. No one makes an Old-Fashioned quite like you, Castle."

"If we could focus for a moment, it would be wise," Hiker said, irritation in his voice.

Mama Jamba waved him on. "Go on then. I'll cut in when I see fit. But right now, it's getting to the good part, so y'all keep it down."

Hiker sighed and returned his attention to Sophia. "While you were gone, Thad accelerated his plans. I believe he's been working on them for quite some time. Maybe he wasn't planning on moving ahead like this quite yet—"

"He wasn't," Mama Jamba cut in, sipping her drink.

Hiker nodded, obviously annoyed at being interrupted. "Anyway, I'm guessing our presence has worried him, so he's taking action. I didn't realize how much control and power he has. His hands are in every part of the international government. He has corporations all over the world that contribute to widespread problems. He's instigating discord all over the globe." Hiker threw his hand at the many newspapers littering his desk. "I should have seen it coming. I should have known how powerful he was."

"Why didn't you?" Sophia asked, and instantly regretted it based on the scolding look he shot her.

"It's a good question," Mama Jamba said, coming to her defense. "You need to explain yourself, Hiker."

He obviously wasn't used to being ordered around by two women, one who questioned him and the other who made demands. After a moment, he said, "Thad and I used to be connected. I told you I worked to block him. Well, since I admitted he wasn't gone from this Earth, I've tried to find him." He pointed to the Elite Globe. "I tried to track him down, but he isn't one of us anymore, and he doesn't have a dragon, so my methods haven't worked. And I believe he's used magitech to block me now."

"Okay, that makes sense," Sophia said.

"Anyway, Thad is much more powerful and far-reaching than I envisioned," Hiker continued. "He's on the brink of instigating a war among strong countries who have devastating capabilities. They can't see they're going to destroy each other to settle their disputes, so I have to assume he's using magic to brainwash them."

"And money," Mama Jamba added. "Money is magic on the mind. It will make perfectly good humans do imperfect things."

Hiker nodded. "However he's done it, the ball is in motion, and it will result in a war."

"So that's what you're doing?" Sophia asked, pointing at the various televisions. "You're monitoring what's happening around the world based on Thad's plans?"

Hiker nodded and growled at the same time. "I didn't like bringing technology into the Castle, but you'd already done it, and I guess it was overdue. Anyway, I defaulted to the most practical solution. I need information, and I need it fast to deal with things."

Sophia wanted to congratulate him on the big step into the twenty-first century, but it seemed ill-timed. She'd wait until he was more used to having technology around since he was presently scowling at the closest television screen. That also might have been because it was showing a report about how neighboring countries were hours from a seemingly unstoppable war.

"Now that you're back," Hiker continued, "I want you and the other men—"

"Riders," Mama Jamba corrected, now chomping on popcorn.

Sophia had no idea where that had come from either, much like the chocolate and drink.

"The other riders are men," Hiker spat. "I think I can get away with saying it that way."

"I just think it would be better if you adopted more inclusive speech when referring to your riders," Mama Jamba chimed.

"Anyway, as I was saying, now that you're back—"

"She's got training to attend to," Mama Jamba interrupted.

Hiker sighed. "It will have to wait."

"It really can't," Mama Jamba argued.

"Well, we need all the riders intervening on these issues," Hiker declared. "Chaos is breaking out everywhere. If we aren't adjudicating, then Thad is going to—"

"Oh, he's going to regardless," Mama Jamba cut in. "He's too far ahead."

Hiker threw up his hands in frustration. "Thanks for the vote of confidence."

She waved him off, still watching the television. "This is your own fault for putting your head in the sand all those years. But it's not all lost. You just have to ensure you show up at the right time with the ammo. More importantly, you have to ensure you show up to the final battle as the right person. That's more crucial than the time and the place and everything that's happened before."

Hiker shook his head. "I don't know what you're talking about, Mama."

"I get that," Mama Jamba agreed, shoveling popcorn into her mouth. "Anyway, send the other riders on these adjudicator missions, but Sophia has to finish training. They can keep things at bay until we're ready for the war."

Hiker stood, his actions abrupt. He was vibrating with tension. "I don't want a war."

Mama Jamba glanced up at him. "I get that, son. But it's too late for that. You've let this go on too long. War is inevitable. Now it's just a matter of when and what you and your riders will bring when it happens."

"Mama," he began.

"Hiker, the war of the brothers was forecast by Papa Creola long ago," she said, her voice hoarse from crying. "I've known that. Now it's time you do too. And there's something else."

"What?" Hiker gave her a long cold stare.

"A good part is coming up," Mama Jamba answered, returning her focus to the screen and shushing Hiker.

He shook his head, frustrated by the woman. "Anyway, go finish your training, Sophia. When the time comes for war, you'll need to be ready. When I have to take Thad down, I'll need you prepared."

"Thing about that, Hiker," Mama Jamba cut in again, throwing a piece of popcorn into the air and catching it expertly in her mouth.

He turned his head to the side and gave her an impatient glare. "What?"

"Well, if we're being candid with one another—"

"We aren't," he cut in.

"Of course, we are," she disagreed. "Anyway, the thing is you're not in a position to face your brother right now, and I think we all know that."

"What are you talking about, Mama?" he asked, shaking his head at her.

"Oh, come on, dear. You know you lost your confidence," Mama Jamba said, pointing her finger at the screen and making her movie pause. "It's a good part. Can't miss this for you all."

"No, you wouldn't want to miss some Hollywood movie for the war efforts brewing on your planet," Hiker said, his voice dripping with condescension.

"No, I wouldn't," Mama Jamba agreed with a nod, not catching his sarcasm. "Anyway, it shouldn't be news to you that Thad has gotten fresh skills while you've been chronicling the monotonous events at the Gullington." She indicated the logbook on the corner of Hiker's desk.

He grimaced at the book and shook his head. "I have skills."

"He is aware of the modern world where you have refused even to acknowledge much has changed in the last few centuries," Mama Jamba continued.

"I have televisions in here, don't I?" he claimed.

"At my behest," she stated. "The final battle will inevitably be you and your brother, Hiker. Your riders have to get you there, but once they do, you'll be on your own, as you've often sent them on their own with only their training and their dragon for assistance."

"What's your point, Mama?" he asked, sounding weary.

"My point is, if you're going to face your twin, you have to bone up on your training," she declared.

He scoffed. "I'm as strong as I was four centuries ago when I magnetized to Bell."

She shook her head. "You're missing the point. I know you've been out on the Expanse practicing combat and lifting weights for centuries. You're strong. There's no doubt about it. And you know how to ride your dragon better than anyone. However, what you've lost over the years was the most crucial part of training for any in the Dragon Elite."

She was quiet for a moment.

Sophia glanced between Hiker and Mama Jamba, wondering which person would speak next. They seemed to be facing off, a staring contest between the two.

After a long pause, Hiker said, "What do you mean?"

"I mean, you need a refresher in training," she stated.

"I don't either!" he revolted.

"You also need an attitude adjustment," she fired back.

"A week in the Australian Outback might fix that," Sophia offered.

Hiker rolled his eyes.

Mama Jamba smiled and winked at her. "Good call, darling, but I think I have a better idea."

"What are you cooking up, Mama?" Hiker asked in a low voice.

"You've lost the connection with yourself," she stated.

"I have not!" he protested.

"Don't argue with me," she said, sounding tired all of a sudden. "Of course, you have. When have you needed to feel the intuition in your spirit? Not when you had no missions because the Dragon Elite were effectively useless for a few centuries. When have you needed to connect to the Earth? Not while you were hiding in the Gullington pretending you were useless."

"Mama," he began.

She held up her hand, pausing him. "Hiker, I love you more than anyone, but it's time I wake you up from this dream you're in. Thad is back."

"I know that!" he boomed.

"And you think you're enough to face him when the time comes," she fired back.

"I'm the only one who can face him," Hiker argued.

"I agree, dear," she said in a much quieter voice. "Nevertheless, you aren't even remotely in the right place for such things."

"What are you proposing?" he asked.

She lowered her chin, a mischievous expression in her eyes. "You know what the next part of Sophia's training includes."

"No," he said with a growl, his chin low to his chest and his eyes full of heat.

"Oh, yes, my dear," Mama Jamba answered.

"You don't mean…" Hiker trailed away, sounding almost as mad as Sophia had ever heard him.

"I absolutely do," Mama Jamba answered.

"But…"

"Oh yes," she answered in reply to the question he left hanging.

"I need to be here," Hiker reasoned.

"You need to do everything possible to win this war," she said.

"But the news reports." Hiker lifted his hand to indicate the closest television screen.

"You need to be ready for what's coming that only you can fight," Mama Jamba stated.

"And the men?" Hiker asked. Receiving a scolding expression from Mama Jamba, he shook his head. "I mean, the other riders? Who will give them their orders?"

Mama Jamba waved him off. "This isn't forever, Hiker. This is just a training exercise. Assign your riders and then go off on your own. You'll be back before you know it and better than ever. That's the hope anyway."

Hiker let out a long furious breath before starting for the door. "Come on, Sophia."

She gave Mama Jamba a questioning expression.

"Go on, my dear," Mother Nature encouraged, urging Sophia to follow the leader of the Dragon Elite.

"But…"

"But nothing," Hiker ordered. "Follow me. We have training to get to."

"I don't understand," Sophia said, taking tentative steps.

He turned at the threshold to the door and gave Mama Jamba a frustrated expression. "Nor do I. But the person I take orders from is never wrong. And she seems to think the next part of your training needs to commence, and I need to join you for it."

CHAPTER ONE HUNDRED FOUR

Sophia had to run to keep up with Hiker as he strode down the stairs to the first floor.

"Sir, what do you mean?" Sophia asked Hiker's retreating back.

He turned, letting out an impatient sigh. "I mean, I've been sent back to school by the one person I'm not allowed to refuse."

"You mean Mama?" she asked, pointing over her shoulder. Putting it all together, she sighed with a sudden realization. "Oh, so you have to take the training with me. Oh, wow, that's got to be..."

Sophia's voice trailed off based on the murderous expression on Hiker's face.

"Right," he growled angrily. "We need to journey off to the far side of the Expanse, past where you've been before to reach the far side of the Barrier on the edge of the Pond. Once we're there, we're outside of the conscious protection of the Castle and we can hear our internal voices, so—"

"Excuse me, sir," Sophia interrupted. "I'm sorry to stop you, but I have zero idea what you're talking about."

He nodded and let out another audible sigh. "I need you to go stock up supplies for a training exercise that will start first thing at sunrise tomorrow morning."

"With you, sir?" she questioned.

He nodded.

"And I get to bring things?" she asked. "Unlike in the Outback?"

"You get to bring food and water," he answered. "No electronics."

"We'll be gone for how long?" she asked.

"For as long as it takes," he replied.

"Well, since you've done this before, I was hoping you could fill me in."

"Why?" he asked, totally put off by the questions. "Do you have an engagement to attend?"

"Well, there are some babies being born I promised—" The impatient expression on Hiker's face cut her off. "You know what? I have all the time in the world. Well, until your twin brother ends it and then I'm busy shoveling coal in hell for the rest of eternity."

He glanced at the ceiling. "If nothing else, angels, please use this training to stifle her attempts at humor."

"So, I should meet you where and when for this lovely excursion?" Sophia asked.

He pointed to where they stood at the entrance to the Castle. "Be here first thing tomorrow morning. We leave then, and we won't be back until we're done."

Sophia nodded, recognizing asking for more information would only incite the man more. She was about to set off on a training excursion for an unknown amount of time with someone she followed and respected but couldn't stand. Worst of all, she was certain that too much time with her might drive Hiker Wallace to the brink of insanity. She wasn't sure he'd be safe to be around at that point.

Sophia wondered if this was the point of the training exercise.

Only one way to find out.

CHAPTER ONE HUNDRED FIVE

S ophia met Hiker at the front of the Castle at sunrise, as she was
told. She'd brought a bag of food and a canteen of water. Holding
it up, she shook it at his face. "I'm ready."

He grabbed the bag, pulled it out of her grasp, and threw it across
the entrance hall. "And now you're not."

Sophia didn't tense. Instead, she glanced over her shoulder to
where her food and water had exploded against the wall. "Did I
mishear the whole 'bring whatever you like' stuff?"

He shook his head. "But this is life, Sophia. Sometimes you're told
you get reparation, and then the world goes back on it."

"Are we still talking about our training and you and me?" she asked
tentatively.

"Mostly...not really," he said with a new bitterness in his eyes.

She pointed over her shoulder to where her supplies were. "So I
can't get that?"

He shook his head. "I've changed my mind. No supplies. We won't
be gone long. You just have to concentrate and make this the shortest
possible long part of the training."

Hiker turned and walked out of the Castle, his chin high. Sophia hurried after him, the cold air of the Expanse making her suck in a sudden breath.

"Did you just insinuate that this is the longest part of the training, sir?" Sophia asked, running to catch up with the Viking, whose strides were three times the length of hers.

He kept moving forward as he spoke. "It depends. Some riders take several months to finish this phase."

"Oh, hell…" Sophia said, halting and looking back to the Castle, considering going back for her food and water.

"And others have passed in only a short period of time," Hiker continued.

"Short period of time?" she questioned, not having moved even though Hiker continued to move in the direction of the Pond.

"It all depends on you, Sophia."

"Like seven days in the Australian Outback?" she asked. "Or like three days in the Sahara? Or like a month in Texas? Can you give me an idea here?"

"Follow me," he urged. "You don't need supplies."

She hesitated, really wanting to go back for her supplies. She didn't like the idea of once again being unprepared. When Hiker disappeared around the other side of the Castle, she sped after him, not wanting him to get out of sight. Yes, it was intimidating to go on an excursion with Hiker Wallace, but it was also a great honor. He might not think of her as his favorite rider, but that didn't mean Sophia didn't relish the time with him. For as many conflicts as the two had, she respected him greatly. She wanted him to like her. She wanted to like him. Maybe this was that opportunity.

"Are you sure I won't need supplies?" Sophia asked, sprinting to catch up with him. "Is it because I can use magic? I mean—"

"I'm certain of it," he answered, continuing to make for the Pond.

"Oh, well, can you explain, sir?" she asked, finally catching up properly. "You think we won't be out here long? Is it because you've already passed this training once?"

"That's part of it," he said, halting when they reached the water's edge and looking around as if searching for something.

"What's the other part?" she asked, wondering what he was looking for.

He gazed down at her with pure annoyance. "It's you, Sophia."

She felt like he'd just pointed an accusatory finger at her. "Me? What about me?"

"We won't be out here long because of you," he stated bitterly.

"Did I do something wrong, sir?" she asked.

He shook his head. "No, that's just the thing. It took Evan twelve weeks to pass this portion of the training. Wilder was out here for a blistering week. Mahkah, well, he's him, so only a few days. And Adam, well..." He chuckled at a long-ago memory. "The bloke never told me honestly how long this part of the training took him, but he hinted it was only a few hours, and you are more like Adam than anyone I've yet to meet...but I also don't get out much."

Sophia fumbled for words. "I don't understand what you're trying to tell me, sir."

Hiker licked his fingertips and held them out to the blistering wind that rolled across the Expanse.

He turned, not at all appearing to be a fun travel partner. "I'm saying I expect you, Sophia Beaufont, to do what you usually do."

Sophia blinked at him blankly. "Be a total pain in your ass and oppose everything you ask or demand?"

He shook his head. "No. Well, yes, I do expect that from you. I was just saying that similar to your excursion in the Outback, I expect you to pass through this one with exemplary marks, faster than most. You are Sophia-freaking-Beaufont. You do things the way you like, you challenge whenever you want, and you pass challenges by going to sleep instead of wearing yourself out for days. I suspect you'll be done with this one before the Castle is even rousing the others for breakfast."

"Oh. Well, thank you, sir," Sophia said, watching as Hiker muttered a series of incantations. She'd never seen him do magic quite like this, and it was thoroughly impressive. It was like a dancer doing ballet, captivating and original at the same time. She'd been around magicians all her life, and yet she'd never seen anyone do magic like Hiker Wallace.

A small boat that could only fit two people, or maybe one large one, or maybe one very large one and one tiny one, materialized in the water before them, sailing in their direction.

"Oh, bloody good. I call for a ship and I get a dinghy," Hiker complained, slapping his hands to his sides.

"We're sailing, sir?" she asked, remembering there was a sea creature that lived in the Pond who had tried to eat Wilder once when he went to retrieve the first bow ever made.

"Yes, but don't worry," Hiker said, pulling the boat onto the shore when it was close enough.

"Because you aren't going to rock the boat?" she asked.

"No, I will definitely do that," he said when she was in properly. He stepped in as he shoved off, looking out toward the coast on the other side. "But if you go overboard, I'll go too."

"Why is that, sir?" she asked.

"For one," he began, "if I return without you, Mama will have my ass."

"And the second part?" she dared to ask.

"If you tell anyone this, Sophia, I'll deny it vehemently," Hiker warned.

She nodded. "Go on, then."

"You, Sophia Beaufont, might be the person who saves us all."

She blinked at him in confusion. "Because I'm a woman and the Dragon Elite have never had one of those?"

He shook his head. "Because somehow, someway, you woke up the world. You woke me up, and here I am, sailing across the body of water that's been nestled outside my window for ages. I'm not thanking you, but I *am* blaming you. Thanks might come later."

Sophia smiled up at the leader of the Dragon Elite, enjoying sailing across the placid waters. "And cursed blame might also."

He nodded. "Yeah, it will be one or the other, but nothing in between."

Sophia held her chin up as they sailed to a part of the Gullington she'd never seen, enjoying the cold air and the excitement of a new challenge as the sun edged over the horizon.

CHAPTER ONE HUNDRED SIX

When the small boat came to the opposite shore, it wasn't what Sophia had expected. She wasn't sure what she'd been expecting. Maybe a hotel and casino and some sort of challenge to her credibility or nobility or some other bility. What they came to was another shore like the one where they'd boarded the boat, but no castle rose out of the green hills, only a lot of rock structures and more hills.

Sophia jumped out of the boat and helped Hiker haul it onto the shore, to his obvious surprise. He arched an eyebrow at her. She gave him an expression of astonishment when he regarded her like she was a three-headed sheep.

"What?" she challenged. "What did I do *this* time?"

"I just expected you'd stay in the boat," he answered.

"And have you chariot me up to dry land?" she retorted. "You really have a thing or two to learn about modern women."

"Do they do everything for themselves these days?" he asked. "They don't expect us to throw our cloaks over a puddle, so they don't get their shoes wet?"

Sophia glanced back at Hiker. "Was that really a thing they did? That sounds awful. Why couldn't they just walk around?"

He actually laughed. "They could have. Ainsley used to, yelling at the other women that they were..." His voice trailed off, disappointing Sophia, who was wearing a curious expression.

"Anyway, I'm just surprised by you sometimes," Hiker remarked.

"And you, sir," Sophia said, her hands on her hips as she surveyed the green hills. "So what now? Where's the Starbucks?"

"The what?" he asked.

"The place where we get an overpriced coffee and a scone the size of our face," she answered.

He shook his head. "Scones should never be... Oh wait, that's one of those jokes you like to tell."

"It's a truthitude," Sophia told him. "But it's modern-world truth, so it's a joke wrapped in the real world, which is what makes it funny. Get it?"

He shook his head. "Like most of your jokes, no, not really."

"Well, this is going well," she said dryly, looking off across the Pond at the Castle in the distance.

"We are going to hike toward the caves," Hiker said, pointing up the hill.

"Cool," Sophia said, starting in that direction. "The ones up here? Or the ones towards the top?"

"Neither," Hiker answered. "The ones ten miles away."

Sophia halted, her face finally taking on an angry expression. "Ten miles? Really? And you threw away my supplies because allowing me water or refreshment was totally against the rules when the others had them?"

He shook his head at her, granting her no sympathy. "You're Sophia-freaking-Beaufont."

Hiker Wallace, without another word, ambled in the direction he'd indicated.

Sophia hurried to get in front of the large man. "What does that mean—'You're Sophia-freaking-Beaufont.' Is that an insult?"

Hiker regarded her for a long moment before shaking his head. "Just the opposite. I just leveled the playing field. You're Sophia-freaking-Beaufont. Everything is easy for you. I send you to the Outback, and you don't fight. Now I'm going with you on the hardest part of the training. The hike isn't the worst part, but it's supposed to tire you out. Let's see how you do."

He edged around her and continued the trek.

Sophia didn't move. Instead, she put her hands on her hips and raised her chin. "Do you *want* me to fail, sir?"

He shook his head as he turned around to face her. "No, that's just the thing, Sophia. I've come to the point where I expect you to succeed, no matter the odds."

"I don't have it easy," she argued, sensing where he was going with this whole thing.

"I know," he replied almost on the heels of her words.

"I don't get all this given to me," she continued.

"I know that too."

"I've come by this through hard work," she insisted, unsure of what she was trying to prove.

"Sophia, do you know how many riders I've trained?"

She shook her head.

"More than you would expect. I've lost track at this point," Hiker answered. "They never make it this far in their training so fast with so many accolades. Many have died battling those zombie dogs in the Outback. I almost did. I didn't give you any provisions on this hike because you don't need them. I suspect we won't be out here long because I know what I have to do, and I think you'll figure it out faster than any of the others. Don't think this is favoritism, but you, Sophia freaking Beaufont, aren't like any other rider I've ever trained or known."

Sophia nearly choked after those words but recovered. "Thank you, sir."

"Don't thank me," he replied. "That might be a good thing or the death of us all. We will find out."

CHAPTER ONE HUNDRED SEVEN

In a perfect world, Sophia would have had a week or so to rest up after the Australian Outback before taking a ten-mile hike. However, she didn't live in a perfect world, even though she hoped to make it a better place. If she didn't kill Hiker on this arduous trek.

"So if you're hiking right now," Sophia began after they'd been silent for over an hour with only the sounds of their boots shuffling through the grass and the birds calling over the Pond. "Then it's Hiker hiking through the hikable hills, right?"

He sighed, obviously unimpressed by the little rhyme it had taken her over an hour to construct.

"We don't have to talk," he offered, stopping to rest at the top of a hill and pressing his hands into his lower back.

"What were you like as a child?" Sophia asked, unsure why she wanted to get under his skin so badly. It just seemed like the thing to do at this point. Yes, he'd been complimentary to her, but she thought it was him just being matter-of-fact. Hiker thought she was more than competent, but he also seemed really surprised by the idea like he was waiting for her to fail at some point and prove his initial judgment had been right all along.

"I was little," he answered, moving faster as they descended the hill.

"Were you playful or curious or mischievous?" she asked.

"We didn't play," he answered. "That was invented in the eighteenth century."

She nodded like this made perfect sense. "That explains it."

"And no, Thad was the mischievous one, as we've previously discussed," he went on.

"Right, and this is when you elaborate so we can have a meaningful conversation," Sophia suggested, still unsure why she was forcing conversation on Hiker. Something about these hills was encouraging her to talk, to want to learn, maybe even to tell her own story.

"I've always had rules," he began slowly, the words seeming difficult at first, like he was remembering something from long ago. "I crave order. Always have. If something is against the rules, I have a hard time even fathoming it. Thad, on the other hand, is exactly the opposite. He breaks the rules just for the fun of it. No respect for order or organization."

"So more like the 'ask for forgiveness rather than permission' type?" she inquired.

He shook his head. "I don't think he'd ever cared for forgiveness. And definitely not permission."

"Is it possible people are really born bad?" she mused, not wanting to believe such a notion. The far-reaching implications were too much. That meant prisons were necessary, and rehabilitation was less important. Sophia wanted to believe in a world where people were merely confused when they did wrong and could be taught to be better.

"I don't know," he said, considering the idea. "In Thad's case, I absolutely think so. I've met other dragonriders who were just like him, albeit not as evil. No one is quite like Thad in that regard."

"Other riders," Sophia contemplated. "Why do they seem so black and white? Are they all either good or bad? Or are there a lot of gray ones too?"

"Not that I'm aware of," Hiker said. "Most I've encountered fall on one end of the spectrum or the other. There isn't much in between."

"That's weird," Sophia stated. "I grew up with many different magician families, and they were all over the place. Most were good, being associated with the House of Fourteen, but there was always some bad to the people. Even I have been known to steal a donut from the kitchen on occasion."

"Get out!" Hiker yelled, turning abruptly to face Sophia, his face serious.

She halted, looking at him with mild annoyance. "Oh, shush it." Sophia hiked around him and took the lead.

"What were *you* like as a child?" Hiker asked after a moment.

She glanced at him, surprised by the question. "Little," Sophia answered, sticking her tongue out at him.

He rolled his eyes. "I mean, I get it's the sort of question that answers itself since you're still a child in many regards."

"I'm eighteen," she fired back.

"You're a child until you celebrate your hundredth birthday in my eyes."

"Is that when I get my cookie bouquet?" she asked.

He shook his head. "You get one on your five-hundredth birthday, just like I did."

"What did you do for your five-hundredth birthday?" she asked.

"You first," he insisted. "I asked you a question, and you haven't answered it. What were you like as a child? More of a child than you are now."

She thought for a moment, trying to figure out how to describe herself. "I was lonely."

The expression that crossed his face made her rush into an explanation.

"I'm not saying that for sympathy," she explained. "That's a fact. My older siblings had full-time responsibilities as Warrior and Councilor for the House of Fourteen, as well as taking care of our parent's business. Clark was always studying. Liv…well, she left before I can remember. For years, it was just me and my magic. No one could know I had it, though; Reese and Ian were clear on that point. So most of my education was private tutoring or just on my own. I didn't really want to play with the other kids anyway because they always found me strange, although I don't know why."

"Because you were born as an authority," Hiker said matter-of-factly.

"What?" she asked.

"All dragonriders are, according to *The Complete History of Dragonriders*. You remember, my book that you lost," he teased with a serious expression on his face.

"I didn't lose it," she protested. "Trinity took it and is keeping it in the Great Library."

"Which we currently have a portal open to in the Castle, thanks to you."

"You're welcome," she chirped.

"Anyway, I haven't read all of the book, and I don't remember a great deal of it," Hiker continued. "What I do recall states that dragonriders, since they are intended to be adjudicators, are born with a natural authority. When you were young, if you told a playmate to do something, did they?"

Sophia thought for a moment, trailing back in her mind to a distant memory. "Yeah, I guess they did. I always thought that was because I'm bossy."

"You are that," Hiker said. "But it's a bit more than just because you're a rider. We have a natural capacity as judges. Our rule strikes an accord in many."

"But this doesn't work on other riders, does it?" Sophia asked. "That's why you could never make Thad behave?"

Hiker nodded. "It's the ironic part of all of this. We bring order and justice, and our history has shown those we fight most often are ourselves. Other riders have usually been the instigators—the ones who threatened the peace we worked so hard for."

"Wow," Sophia mused. "Maybe it would be better if there were no more dragonriders."

Again, Hiker halted and faced her. "Don't say something like that."

"But sir," Sophia began, "we serve an important role, but if most of our efforts are in trying to make other riders behave, maybe it's just better if there aren't riders."

Hiker swallowed, a sober expression in his eyes. "I get your logic, but I have to believe the good riders bring more peace than the bad ones bring evil. And besides, there is only one bad dragonrider left. Once Thad is gone, then we can reign."

"Have you considered how you're going to take him down?" Sophia dared to ask.

A small stress line formed around Hiker's jaw. "I believe that's why I'm on this trek with you. So no, but hopefully on the way back, the answer will be different."

"Do we have to hike back, or can we grab an Uber?" Sophia joked.

"A what?" Hiker asked.

She waved him off. "It was one of those jokes you love so much and rarely get."

The pair hiked on for another hour in silence. Sophia was good with it, grateful they had a bit of conversation.

When they came to a cave opening surrounded by rectangular columns, Hiker paused.

"That's far out," Sophia said, admiring the stone structures which lined the sides of the cave. The blocks were so orderly they appeared man made, although it seemed unlikely.

"There's another more well-known cave on the other side of Scotland like this called Fingal's Cave," Hiker explained. "Mortals know about that one, but not Falconer Cave."

"Falconer?" Sophia asked. "Like the people who tame birds and wear eye patches?"

"I wasn't aware of the eye patch part, but yes," he answered.

"Well, I don't think they start off with it," Sophia joked. "Maybe just the really bad ones get their eyes poked out by the bird of prey."

"You're very strange," he observed.

"So, what's with this cave?" Sophia asked, studying the strange hexagonal columns which marked the entrance. "Does it have strange magical significance?"

Hiker shook his head. "The acoustics are good."

Sophia rolled her eyes. "Did you bring me out here to sing?"

"There will definitely not be any singing," Hiker answered. "The cave's acoustics are important for this part of the training."

"Because?" Sophia asked.

"You'll find out." Hiker strode onward a few paces before turning back to Sophia. "For my five-hundredth birthday, I had a glass of whisky and a quiet evening to myself."

"So it was pretty much like every day before," Sophia stated.

He nodded. "When you get to be as old as I am, the birthdays roll together."

"Well, maybe for your next birthday, someone will throw you a party with streamers and cake."

He scowled at her. "That person wouldn't see another of *their* birthdays."

Sophia laughed. "You and your threats are so cute."

CHAPTER ONE HUNDRED EIGHT

"Why didn't you tell me I needed to dress up?" Sophia joked when they entered Falconer Cave.

"Ha-ha," Hiker said with no humor, his voice echoing. The cavernous space was dark and cold, like most caves. However, there was something unique about the stillness in here, but Sophia couldn't put her finger on what it was.

"What are we supposed to do?" Sophia asked, looking around as her eyes adjusted to the dark.

"Sit and be quiet," he answered.

"You made me hike ten miles to a cave with fantastic acoustics so I could sit and be quiet?" she challenged. "You get why this might be the site of a murder, right?"

"First of all, I was your gillie, making your task of finding Falconer Cave easier," Hiker stated.

"'Gillie?'" she questioned. "Are you making up words again?"

He shook his head. "'Gillie' is a Scottish term for a guide who attends men while exploring the Highlands or hunting or fishing. They know the land better than anyone."

Sophia cleared her throat and gave him a pointed look.

Hiker rolled his eyes. "Sophia, I can't change history. In the past,

SARAH NOFFKE & MICHAEL ANDERLE

gillies accompanied men. Women didn't hunt, so that's the reason for the definition I gave you."

"Okay, fine," she acquiesced. "You were my gillie and helped me find Falconer Cave."

He nodded. "It took Evan a week because usually I just point to the general vicinity and tell people what to look for."

Sophia recalled the unique outward appearance of the cave. "Yeah, it would be easy to spot."

"Second of all," he continued, "the point of this training exercise is to get quiet."

"Which is why you do it in a place with great acoustics?" Sophia questioned.

"The acoustics help by magnifying the quiet," Hiker explained.

"Isn't that like multiplying something by zero?"

He simply shook his head before settling down on the rocky ground and crossing his legs.

"Oh, you are serious about this being quiet business, aren't you?"

"It is through meditation we come to understand ourselves, receive insights on problems, and become one with the universe," Hiker explained in a rehearsed manner.

Sophia settled on the ground. "Mama Jamba sent you out here because you've got to face Thad and don't know how?"

"Correct," he agreed. "I've never known how, but we always have an opportunity to become better than we were. To figure out the things that eluded us. But we have to do the work for it. Usually, that involves going within and finding our connection to the universe. It is there the answers are born."

"So, it's kind of like the whole idea that we're not in the universe, the universe is within us," Sophia stated.

He nodded, his hands casually resting on his knees, back straight and face calm. "Your experience meditating will be unique to you and what you need to know. I will offer this bit of advice: to connect with yourself, you must first connect with the world around you. Falconer Cave is ideal because it is isolated from everything around it, it is an anomaly unique on the outside and bare on the inside."

"Okay," Sophia said, drawing out the word. "When do I know I've achieved the training goal?"

"You will know," he said simply.

"Will you stop inundating me with information," she joked.

Hiker closed his eyes. "Do you hear that?"

Sophia paused. Listened. "What? I don't hear anything."

"Exactly," he said. "When you hear the voices of the angels and all their messages, that's when you're done. When you no longer have questions and intuitively know answers to things yet to be asked, you're done. When you can hear the spirit of the universe within you, you can go."

CHAPTER ONE HUNDRED NINE

Sophia didn't think she could simply pretend she'd heard the voices of the angels and pop out of the cave early. She'd meditated a time or two, but she'd never gotten much out of it besides a nap.

This was the strangest training exercise. How was she supposed to connect with herself or the universe? And how would she know when she'd achieved it? Would the messages from the angels sound different from the ramblings in her head?

Hiker seemed to think Sophia would have an easy time with this, which was why he had thrown her supplies out. After the long hike, she wished she had some water. Or a protein bar. Or a bed.

Her mind began to wander, combing over what she needed to do later. Then it drifted to all the chaos going on all over the world as a result of Thad Reinhart's planning. She hadn't been on any adjudicator missions in a while. That worried her. But she'd been busy with training and before that finding *The Complete History of Dragonriders*.

There was nothing like seeing the gold dust over an agreement struck between two parties who were once opposed, she thought, her mind quickly jumping around. After a long while of this, Sophia realized how loud her thoughts were, as if the cave was amplifying them.

They were inundating and seemingly unending, one thought leading to another and then another.

Taking a breath, she tried to stop her thoughts, which were like a contagious disease, spreading fast. It seemed strange to stop thinking. That seemed as easy as stopping breathing.

It was breathing that helped the most. When she focused on her breath, the thoughts slowed down and became less intense. After a bit, Sophia noticed her breath had elongated and her thoughts had followed suit, passing through her brain slowly and then drifting away. Whereas before she had judged every thought as good or bad, soon she found she was simply an observer, taking notice of the ideas without coloring them one way or another.

Soon her focus shifted to the area around her in the cave. She felt outside of herself in a very distinctive way. The temperature, she knew without knowing how, was exactly fifty degrees. There were sixteen different species that called Falconer Cave home. Of those, three were magical and unclassified, one of which was presently crawling on Sophia's boot.

She didn't feel the little creature but instinctively knew it was there. Usually, she would have jumped up and brushed the bug off. However, Sophia didn't even think of it as something else on her. She was the bug, and the bug was her. They were the cave, and the cave was them. They were the Gullington, and the Gullington was them. They were Scotland, and Scotland was them. They were the universe, and the universe was them.

These observations were followed by a strange silence that seemed to stretch on for eternity. It was this silence that had preceded Mother Nature and spawned a creature so powerful she could construct a world that was strong and also vulnerable. It was this silence that had filled the void before time was created. Before Papa Creola constructed how events moved on a continuum. The silence was the beginning, and it was everywhere still.

Sophia didn't know how long she sat in the cave, witnessing the birth of the universe in her mind. It could have been a minute or a hundred years. If it had been more than a day, she didn't feel hungry or tired or thirsty. She had hooked into the nourishment of the universe, and she realized as long as she was connected, all her needs were fulfilled.

From that place, Sophia knew she could heal the world's problem. She could erase the pain. She could become whatever she wanted. The idea of never leaving Falconer Cave was very tempting. She could fix everything just by maintaining her connection to the all-powerful source.

There were things she'd miss. Her friends growing old. Her family loving her. The opportunity to see tragedy and heroically risk everything for justice.

Yes, there were problems in the world she could mend in Falconer Cave with her mind, but it didn't mean she should. Being out in the world as a player on the chessboard was more important. Interacting with other players was part of a valuable experience for Sophia and for them.

Being a part of the world is more important than fixing it, she realized. *A perfect world was never the point.*

Sophia's eyes sprang open, and she knew instinctively she'd arrived where she needed to be. Her training in Falconer Cave was done. The angels had spoken to her, and they'd said, "You in an imperfect world is better than a perfect world without you. Wake up, our love. Go out and spawn a new age, Sophia Beaufont the Great."

CHAPTER ONE HUNDRED TEN

H iker wasn't in Falconer Cave when Sophia opened her eyes. The sun was streaming through the opening when she rose, but she didn't know how much time had passed. It could have been years for all she knew.

Upon exiting the cave, she found Hiker leaning against the outside wall with his foot up behind him. Bell and Lunis were in the distance, resting in the grass.

He eyed his watch when he saw her and nodded. "As I suspected. That's a new record."

"How long was I in there?" Sophia asked. "Did I exceed Evan's twelve weeks, or however long it took him to phone the angels?"

He shook his head. "No, you just made the record for the shortest amount of time."

"What?" she asked, surprised.

"It took you just a wee bit over an hour," Hiker explained, glancing at the Expanse where the dragons lay. Lunis was gesturing in playful ways, and Bell was doing her best to ignore him.

"Why do you think that is?" Sophia asked, sincerely wanting an answer to why she excelled. It all felt like a trick. Like false confidence she didn't want to fall for.

"I think a lot of it has to do with the fact you're a twin and he's dead," Hiker began. "I know that doesn't make you feel better because losing a twin, even if you didn't know him, is still tragic in its own way. The angels say twins are forever connected and share a unique power. But his death did grant you benefits to your magic."

Sophia nodded. She didn't mind that as an explanation so much. It wasn't something she controlled, though. In a way, she'd prefer to be as successful as she was because she worked hard for it and not because she inherited Jamison's power.

"But also," Hiker continued. "I think your gender grants you a unique perspective. As dragonriders and men, we do things a certain way. We always have. We rush into battle. Our instinct is to fight. Often the chi of the dragon takes us over, bringing out our aggression and ruling over us if we're not careful. But women are quite different. Your nature is to nurture, to create, to mend and gather. I think that's why you consider solutions to your problems that never occur to us."

Sophia nodded again, chewing her lip. Once more, this made sense, but it also attributed her success to a factor she didn't control. Her success being tied to her gender didn't make her feel any better.

"Then there's the fact that you're the first female dragonrider," Hiker went on. "I mistakenly believed you were elected to this position because you inherited your twin's power early, making you an exceptional magician. However, the angels have shown me something different."

"In your meditation just now?" she asked.

He nodded. "You're not the first magician to have their twin die at birth and receive their powers from the beginning. There are many records of this since it's a point of interest. The incredible, from an early age, have notoriously done one thing."

He paused, almost like he was begging her to urge him to continue.

After a moment, Hiker cleared his throat. "There's a reason children don't have magic. There's a reason education usually precedes the onset of magical abilities after the start of puberty. Magic held by children turns into instant gratification. In essence, it corrupts." He shook his head. "But we always have a choice, even as children. It's like when the universe presents different signs to you. Many think the signs are directing their path, but they're wrong. It's the ones you endorse, the ones you want to come true, that creates the path. You might be powerful because of something you don't control. You might be unique as a dragonrider because of your gender. But you're inevitably successful because of who you are and the choices you make. Sophia, you are good through and through, and the only one the angels have met who wasn't ruined by magic given at an early age."

Sophia blinked at him, utterly confused. "Your meditation was about me?"

He pursed his lips, seeming to share her confusion. "Yes, I was seeking solutions to how to deal with my own twin, and I received information about you. Who knows why, but I can't question the methods of the angels. They are never wrong."

"Okay," she said, continuing to chew her lip as she tried to absorb everything Hiker had shared. Sophia remembered being young and knowing she could have anything she wanted because of her magic— and she remembered knowing that if something didn't belong to her or it was wrong, it wasn't worth having. From the beginning, Sophia hadn't refrained from doing things out of fear of punishment. She'd refrained because being good felt good, and feeling good was what it was about for everyone at the end of the day.

"Oh, and Sophia?" Hiker resumed, pulling her out of her thoughts.

"Yes, sir?" she answered.

"The angels also told me you're exceptional because you are the first female rider," Hiker explained. "Just as Alexander Conerly, the very first dragonrider, was exceptional. That's how the angels intended it because we are the adjudicators for this world. We serve Mother Nature. We are supposed to be a force. The first of something must always be great, so others follow them. They make history and a name for themselves and that which they represent. So there you go— you're successful because you're a twin, you're a female, and you're the first. But also, and most importantly, remember you are successful because of what you choose."

He sighed and looked at the dragons. "My only regret at this point is the age of the dragons and their riders are dying. I would have liked to have seen a world with more female dragonriders. Maybe a year ago, I wouldn't have, but you've changed that. I think you provide a balance we desperately need, but alas, we are nearing our end."

Sophia found it hard to swallow. "Don't give up, sir. We never know how the universe will provide solutions." She glanced back at Falconer Cave, warmth spreading through her abdomen. "And although the angels didn't tell you how to defeat Thad, maybe they gave you a new motivation to do so."

CHAPTER ONE HUNDRED ELEVEN

When they returned to the Castle, Mama Jamba was curled up on the couch in Hiker's office, watching the movie *Beaches*, tears flowing down her face.

"Mama, why are you torturing yourself like this?" Hiker asked, shaking his head as he stomped into his study.

She sniffed. "Because if I'm going to be sad, then at least I'll be entertained. I could watch the news you have broadcasting and be sad about what's happening to my planet, but that's not what I want to do."

Hiker picked up the top newspaper from the stack on his desk that had just been delivered to his office via Ainsley. He shook his head. "It's getting worse. Countries are battling, threatening one another with deadly force and weapons of mass destruction."

"Oh, and the Golden Globes are coming up according to one of the articles in the *LA Times*," Ainsley said as she cleaned up all the used tissues scattered around Mama Jamba. She looked up at Sophia. "What are the Golden Globes?"

Sophia waved her off. "Nothing of interest."

Ainsley nodded dutifully and continued to pick up.

"How is it that one man could cause such global discord?" Sophia asked.

Hiker shook his head. "Thad has a lot of power and skill. If he ever committed to using it for good, he could have done great things. But that was never his way."

"Hiker, you look a hundred years younger," Ainsley observed. "Have you been using that face cream in S. Beaufont's room too?"

Sophia glanced abruptly at the housekeeper. "Is that where my lotion keeps going?"

The shapeshifter nodded, no guilt on her face. "Oh, yes. Quiet likes it too. Although he uses it mostly on his feet."

Sophia grimaced, hoping the gnome washed his hands before dipping into her lotion. "Is there no privacy in this place?"

"Of course, there is," Ainsley commented. "Oh, and by the way, you've been talking in your sleep a lot S. Apparently, you have a crush on a Scotsman, but I can't figure out any more than that. Can you talk a bit clearer in the future?"

Sophia's eyes fluttered with annoyance. "I do not have a crush. I have a bunch of dirty Scotsmen around me who burp at the dining table and chew with their mouths open, which is why they invade my dreams. My subconscious is obviously trying to work through the frustration the only way it knows how. And would you kindly not watch me when I sleep?"

Ainsley held up her hands as if in surrender. "Don't watch you when you sleep. Don't drug your food. Stop using your clothes to dust the rafters. You always have so many rules, S. Beaufont. But fine, I'll try and mind your privacy. No promises, though."

Mama Jamba wailed as she focused on the television. "Oh, Bette Midler is just brilliant in this movie. What is she doing these days, I wonder?"

"Mama, don't you think there's anything else you could direct your attention to?" Hiker asked, irritation in his tone. "You do remember war is brewing all over your planet, right?"

The old woman looked up briefly, seemingly stuck in a daze. "That's a great idea. I should pay Papa Creola a visit."

"Do you think he can help us?" Hiker asked, hope in his voice.

She shrugged. "Who knows, but I'm thinking of asking him to extend Bette's timeline. That way, she has more time to do great things."

Hiker threw the newspaper on his desk. "Am I the only sane one here?"

"If you are, then we're all in trouble because you lost your marbles a long time ago," Ainsley said. "And again, why do you look good enough to snog?"

Hiker gave her a repulsed expression. "Would you mind your tongue?"

She giggled. "Not by me. Maybe by Bell or Quiet. Or Evan. He's been wanting to lay a sloppy one on you for ages. I've heard him say it in his sleep."

"Evan is simply trying to suck up to authority," Mama Jamba supplied. "He will outgrow it in a few hundred years. Hiker is looking refreshed because I sent him to Falconer Cave."

"Oh, a good meditation is really great for the complexion," Ainsley said, looking at Sophia. "You went too? You look simply radiant. But you all weren't gone for a fortnight."

"No, Sophia is a quick study," Mama Jamba offered. "And Hiker knew what he was looking for, so his job should have been quick. Tell me, son, where is Thad, and how are you planning on taking him down?"

Hiker shook his head. "I don't know. The angels didn't tell me. Why don't you tell me?"

Mama Jamba returned her attention to the television. "You know I can't do that, Hiker. You have to fight your battles on your own. Tough love, you get it."

"You want me to protect your Earth. Save it. But you're unwilling to offer me anything?" he asked.

She nodded. "That's right, dear. I trust you'll get it done with the resources at your disposal…or you won't, and we'll all die from some nuclear explosions." She shrugged. "Can't wait to find out how this story ends."

"Resources," Hiker muttered, looking around his office. "I've got a globe that doesn't work on my brother, a bunch of newspapers that tell me war is imminent, television screens with anxious reporters who offer more opinion than fact, and not much else."

"Actually, sir, I might have a way of helping us to find Thad," Sophia offered.

Mama Jamba pulled a Twizzler from a package she hadn't had a few seconds earlier and took a bite. She pointed at Sophia. "Resources, Hiker. They are everywhere. They are people. Remember that."

He turned his attention to Sophia. "What do you mean?"

"Well, since I know Thad uses magitech heavily," Sophia began, "I took the gun Logan used on Lunis and me to my scientist friend. She's our foremost expert on magitech. Anyway, she's been working on a way to track the epicenter of where the magitech is originating. The source, if you will. She says hiding that kind of power is difficult. I can check with her and find out where she is with the process."

"You did this without my permission, going off on your own and taking initiative?" Hiker asked with a threat in his voice.

Sophia bowed her head, sighing. "I'm sorry, sir. I just thought—"

"No apologies," he interrupted. "Good work. And yes, you should check in with her."

"She also thinks she might be able to find other ways to fight Thad, circumventing security measures and whatnot," Sophia said, feeling proud.

"You mean, technology?" Hiker asked.

"You will have to embrace it if you're going to fight him," Mama Jamba said, chewing on the end of a red Twizzler.

"You have already allowed televisions into the Castle," Ainsley pointed out.

"That's different," he argued. "I need information and fast, and that seemed like the best way."

Ainsley smirked at him. "It's only a matter of time before you're sporting a phone and dragging around a shiny lapbottom."

"Laptop," Sophia corrected.

Hiker let out a weighty breath. "Yeah, I don't think so. This is ultimately my fight with my brother, and I'll do it the way I see fit. I don't believe it will involve technology. However, getting to Thad might involve magitech, I'll give you that much."

"You think by taking down Thad, you'll stop all the wars that are brewing?" Ainsley asked, reading one of the newspapers upside-down. "Don't you think the wars he's started will just continue? He's set the balls in motion."

For a brief moment, Sophia saw a shimmer of the person Ainsley used to be. She had been a diplomat for the elves, offering strategic advice to the Dragon Elite. It shone through for a moment, making the usually silly housekeeper appear refined and serious. Sophia wasn't sure which version of Ainsley she preferred. Maybe a mix of both.

"But he's the kindling, dear," Mama Jamba explained. "Take out that which causes the fire, and the adjudicators can do what they do best. I fear if they tried to intervene now, it would be a losing battle. Hate fuels hate. It has to be erased, and then love can grow."

Hiker nodded and gave the old woman a proud smile. "That's the helpful advice I've been looking for."

"Oh, before I forget," Ainsley said, looking at Hiker, "you got a message from the House of Fourteen saying they are freaking out about this war business and ready to take over, since, and I quote, 'the Dragon Elite can't do their job.'"

He lowered his chin and regarded her with hooded eyes. "When did this message come in?"

"A few days ago," she replied.

"Why are you just telling me now?" he questioned.

"Because you were all holed up in your office, fretting that something had happened to S. Beaufont in the Australian Outback," she answered. "I didn't want to add more stress."

"I wasn't fretting," he argued, cutting his eyes to Sophia briefly. "As your leader, it is my job to be concerned about your wellbeing and focused on your success."

"Right," Ainsley chirped. "That's why he kept pacing in his office and overworking his hair while he muttered, 'Stay vigilant, Soph. Fight the dogs. Come back in one piece.'"

Hiker gave Sophia a sympathetic look. "I echo what you said about us having more privacy in this place."

CHAPTER ONE HUNDRED TWELVE

The portal Sophia had opened up between the Castle and House of Fourteen might have irritated Hiker, but it made her commute a lot easier.

She found the closet door exactly where it had been in the corridor outside her room. She didn't need the gold token to go back and forth anymore, but she always kept it on her since she was the new keeper of the reset point.

Holding the coin in her hand, Sophia considered Hiker's last request before she'd exited his office moments prior.

"Meet with this scientist friend of yours," he had requested with authority. "Hopefully, she can help us find Thad. But before that, go tell the House of Fourteen they don't need to intervene in this matter. We are in charge of world affairs. We are the adjudicators for this planet. The Dragon Elite has this."

Sophia had been impressed by the leader of the Dragon Elite's confidence. It had changed since Falconer Cave. Hiker appeared more like the person he had been when she saw him during the reset point at the House of Fourteen.

Then he had urged the council to take action, explaining a war was brewing, and they'd dismissed him. This made her worry that her statement to the House of Fourteen would be ignored too. If they didn't take the leader of the Dragon Elite seriously, would they accept her word? A lot had changed since then, and the council was made up of new members. She hoped they'd be reasonable.

Sophia stepped into the closet like she had done before and closed the door. She was instantly cloaked in blackness. After a quick three count, Sophia opened the door to find the rush of old smells and sights greeting her eyes.

The House of Fourteen's dark wooden walls and intricate crown molding was such a contrast to the Castle with its cold stone and high ceilings. Similar to the Castle, the walls of the House were decorated with paintings of its members, and there were various artifacts on display in different areas.

Ignoring all this, Sophia made her way straight to the Chamber of the Tree, wanting to catch the Council before they were dismissed.

She was surprised to find her brother Clark pacing outside the entrance to the Chamber in front of the Door of Reflection.

He glanced up as she approached, relief on his face. "There you are. You're late."

She halted, confused. "I didn't realize we had a planned meeting."

"Well, we didn't," he explained, leaning forward and whispering, "Hester told me Trudy saw a vision of you visiting the House of Fourteen today and that it would be my best opportunity to catch you. I figured you were coming to explain why the Dragon Elite are failing in their mission."

Sophia let out a frustrated breath. "I have no intention of explaining anything to the council." She'd been struggling to find the right thing to say to the House of Fourteen based on what Hiker had said, but now, she knew exactly how to play things.

"Regardless," Clark continued in a hushed voice, "I suspect Bianca and Lorenzo are going to suggest a Dragon Elite take a place on the council."

Sophia nodded. She remembered overhearing their conversation when she was hiding in the Mantovanis' residence. "Yes, they think if they give us enough rope, we'll hang ourselves, mortals will hate us, and tension will break out on the council."

"Exactly," he affirmed. "That's why when they offer you a position, which I firmly believe they will, you should decline."

"Why?" Sophia questioned. "Do you think we will screw things up and cause a revolt?"

Uncertainty crossed Clark's face as he hesitated to answer.

"Are you serious?" Sophia nearly yelled. "You doubt us?"

He sighed. "It's not that, Soph. Of course, I believe in *you*, but the Dragon Elite aren't giving us much confidence. From our perspective, Hiker Wallace has been sticking his head in the sand, allowing Thad Reinhart to become more powerful."

"It's all by design," she fibbed.

Clark pursed his lips. "But really, I think you should decline the position because then you can't be held accountable."

"I will decline the position, but not for that reason," Sophia stated.

"What is the reason?" he asked.

She couldn't help but be angry at her brother, although she knew he was just looking at things the way he always did—logically. Sophia couldn't totally disagree with his perspective or the opinion the House of Fourteen had of the current situation. Hiker had made mistakes, but that put him in a perfect position to make better choices. She firmly believed he was the only one who could end Thad Reinhart.

What scared her, when she allowed herself to admit it, was that Thad was probably the only one who could end Hiker. If that happened, she feared the Dragon Elite were done for good.

If something happened to Hiker, it would be the end of an era.

CHAPTER ONE HUNDRED
THIRTEEN

The Chamber of the Tree was buzzing when Sophia stepped through the Door of Reflection a few minutes after Clark, so as to not make it obvious they had been talking.

Jude, the white tiger, stood on one side of the bench, his discerning eyes watching Sophia. Conversely, Diabolos, the black crow, took flight at the sight of her and perched close to the ceiling, which shimmered with twinkling lights.

Many of the Warriors were absent from the proceedings, off on missions. Thankfully, Liv wasn't. It gave Sophia confidence to know her sister was there standing stoically at her back.

She strode straight into the round room, taking the position in the center between the arc of Warriors and Councilors.

"Sophia Beaufont," Haro Takahashi began when she paused. "Have you come to update us on how the Dragon Elite is going to deal with Thad Reinhart?"

Shaking her head, Sophia put her hands behind her back. "No, I have not."

"You haven't?" Lorenzo Rosario asked, stroking his black goatee. "Then why are you here?"

"To tell you the situation is under control," Sophia answered.

Bianca Mantovani laughed, a cold, high-pitched sound. "Oh, that's too much. Even to those who don't follow world affairs, it's obvious you all don't have anything under control. Mayhem is breaking out everywhere, perpetuated by—"

"We are fully aware of the global events," Sophia interrupted.

"Then how does the Dragon Elite plan to deal with the situation that's building?" Lorenzo asked.

"We do not answer to the Council for the House of Fourteen," Sophia declared. "We supersede your authority, and therefore, I'm not at liberty to say."

"With all due respect," Lorenzo countered, his tone dripping with condescension, "we haven't seen anything like this since—"

"Right before the Great War broke out, which made it so mortals couldn't see magic and our history was forgotten," Sophia cut in. "Hiker warned you it would happen, and the Council ignored him. With all due respect, the Dragon Elite aren't in a position where we feel the need to explain our plans to you. We are back. We are prepared to handle Thad Reinhart. We plan to restore our reputation and status as world adjudicators. That is all you need to know."

Lorenzo lowered his chin, giving her a petulant expression, suddenly making Sophia feel small. She reminded herself she wasn't. She was a dragonrider and not the littlest Beaufont, as many from the House of Fourteen were used to seeing her. "Why can't Hiker Wallace report to us himself?"

"That's a good question," Bianca agreed, looking down the bench at Lorenzo. "If the leader of the Dragon Elite wants us to have confidence in his ability to handle this situation, he should at least meet with us, especially after we sent a message to him directly."

"He is just a tad bit busy," Liv said at Sophia's back.

"Warrior Beaufont," Lorenzo scolded, "I don't believe this matter involves you."

"Yes, just because your little sister is here, it doesn't mean you have to step in and save her," Bianca added snootily.

"No one needs to save me," Sophia said boldly. "I'm a rider for the

Dragon Elite, and I'm here by order of Hiker Wallace, who is concerned with more pressing matters. He asked me to pass along to you, the House of Fourteen, that there is no need for you to intervene in the Thad Reinhart situation. It is under control, and we need no help."

"I am sure you are correct," Hester DeVries began in a calm voice. "However, pooling our resources might be for the best. The Dragon Elite's numbers aren't what they once were and fighting such a formidable force; well, it could destroy you all. We can offer assistance." She held out her hand, indicating Liv and the others standing at Sophia's back. "How about the help of our Warriors?"

"That won't be necessary," Sophia said at once. "Thank you for the offer, but as world adjudicators, we prefer to handle this situation on our own."

"This is ridiculous!" Lorenzo exclaimed. "You are going to start a war we can't control or extinguish."

"No," Sophia fired. "We are going to prevent a war."

"What if," Bianca began slowly, looking between the various council members, "I know we haven't discussed this, but what if we invited the Dragon Elite to have a place on the council? It's just an idea, but maybe then they would be more willing to share their plans and have our input."

There was a collective murmur from the Councilors.

"We would decline such an invitation," Sophia interrupted, making all of them go silent.

"But you haven't even brought the request to your leader," Lorenzo argued.

"I don't need to," Sophia said with conviction. "The Dragon Elite does not work for the House of Fourteen. We do not need a place on the council. Although our numbers are small, it is important you recognize the hierarchy that was set up long ago. The Dragon Elite might have been gone for a long time, but we are back now, and we rank above the House of Fourteen and every other magical organization."

"With all due respect—" Lorenzo began once again.

Sophia rolled her eyes. "Would you stop saying that phrase since you absolutely intend disrespect by arguing with me?"

Lorenzo's mouth hung open for a moment, his eyes wide.

"Now," Sophia continued, "the Dragon Elite will deal with Thad Reinhart. We will reinstate order and take back our roles as adjudicators. This situation brewing worldwide is crucial to reset the stage."

This caused a great deal of chatter around the room. Sophia paused. She had just been making things up, but this sounded perfect. Hiker had allowed Thad to start these global events because how better to debut in this century as adjudicators? It hadn't been planned, but it made sense.

The Dragon Elite could have intervened in tons of small events to earn back their title, but it wouldn't have been as impactful. When they settled this dispute by putting out the fires of impending wars and taking Thad down, there would be no question they were the supreme authority.

All governments worldwide would endorse them as world adjudicators once more.

Haro Takahashi leaned forward. "I hope what you say is correct, Sophia. The world needs the Dragon Elite back in power."

"I understand you declining the position on the council," Raina Ludwig said, glancing down the bench at Bianca. "After further thought, that's like us inviting Father Time to have a vote when his authority surpasses ours. I apologize for any offense the offer caused."

Sophia nodded, surprised at how she'd played things. She always thought having a seat on the council as a dragonrider would be in everyone's best interest. If the Dragon Elite were going to come back into power, they had to claim their position, ranking above all.

CHAPTER ONE HUNDRED FOURTEEN

"That was freaking awesome!" Liv exclaimed as they walked to John's electronics repair shop. "You socked those jerks who were trying to get all up in your business."

Sophia blushed, pushing her hair behind her ears. "Clark doubts we have the Thad situation under control."

Liv rolled her eyes. "Good. Let him underestimate you. Let the council. That's for the best. That way, when you crush things, they will be that much more impressed. I usually like to put myself at a serious disadvantage before I claim the decisive victory no one saw coming. It's way more satisfying to see everyone's face then."

"The council has good reason to doubt us," Sophia confessed. "I mean, I respect Hiker, but I don't know if he can stand up to his brother when the time comes."

"Well, you didn't let them see that concern, which is crucial," Liv declared.

"Yeah, it was sort of a 'fake it until you feel it' thing," Sophia admitted.

Liv shook her head. "No, not at all. You were right to decline a position on the council. That would have made the dragonriders their equal, and you're not. You were also correct not to divulge your plans for Thad Reinhart. It's not their business. We preside over magical affairs and the Dragon Elite over mortal ones. The council has to find their place, and you did a good job of putting them there."

Sophia's nose twitched. "Well, honestly, between you and me, I couldn't have told them about our plans to deal with Thad since we don't have any. I'm hoping Alicia can help me. Otherwise, we might be screwed."

Liv offered her an encouraging expression. "If anyone can help you locate that magitech-wielding madman, it's Alicia. She's been working on it nonstop, which is why your 3D printer still isn't ready."

Sophia laughed. "I'm okay with that, and happy to have the help." Remembering the gift from Wilder, she smiled. "Oh, guess what I got for Christmas?"

"What?" Liv asked.

Liv clapped her hands to her chest when Sophia told her. "A man after my own heart. If he had given you chocolate or a gift card, I would have said to kick him to the curb, but a grappling hook? He's a keeper."

Sophia shook her head. "It's not like that. It was just a gift, and probably only because I was the one who pushed for Christmas to happen at the Castle. I gave him a fork."

With a laugh, Liv said, "Oh, that's perfect. Are you going to teach him how to use it?"

"Get out of my head," Sophia replied. "That's what I promised him. In return, he's supposed to teach me how to use the grappling hook."

Liv waved her off. "Oh, you don't need training. It's like this: you point and shoot, then get hauled off your butt. You're going to love it."

Sophia gave her an affectionate smile. "You think there was ever a potential for us to have normal jobs and not ones where grappling hooks were a part of our routine?"

"Not a chance," Liv said, striding into the electronics shop.

Pickles, the Jack Russell terrier, greeted them by barking while he danced around their feet in excitement.

Sophia leaned down and gave the dog a quick pet before smiling at Alicia, who was working at a nearby station.

"Good timing," the scientist said, screwing something into the back of a small silver disc. "I was just finishing up the tracking device."

"Oh!" Sophia exclaimed. "You were able to create something?"

Alicia turned the small object over. It resembled a compass, although there were a lot more symbols on it other than just north, south, east, and west. "I think so, although it still needs to be calibrated. And..." Her face fell with concern.

"What?" Sophia asked, sensing the hesitation.

"Well, this device can find great sources of magitech," Alicia explained. "Which will lead you to possible locations for this Thad Reinhart."

"But it could also lead us in the wrong direction," Sophia guessed.

The scientist nodded. "What you'd need to ensure it sends you in the right direction is some sort of connection to the person you're trying to find. That way magitech takes a two-pronged approached. It first searches for high levels of magitech energy, then narrows them down based on DNA. I realize you probably don't have some hair samples of Thad lying around."

"Actually, what about blood from a really close relative?" Sophia asked.

Alicia's face brightened. "That could work, but how close? Like, distant cousin would get you close, but probably not enough."

"Would twin brother work?" Sophia asked.

Alicia slipped the compass-like device into a small velvet pouch and handed it to Sophia. "Yes, that's perfect, actually. Have this twin brother follow the instructions I've included in the pouch to connect the device to Thad. If done correctly, it will take up to two days to activate."

"I hope you have that kind of time," Liv said, giving Sophia an uncertain expression.

She nodded. "We've allowed it all to go on this long. Another few days won't change much." She hoped she was right.

"Okay, that's good news," Alicia said, digging into a toolbox on the workstation. "I have something else for you, too."

Liv rubbed her hands together. "Isn't she great? Always supplying us with magitech gadgets? Last month she made me a device that puts people to sleep at the click of a button."

Alicia smiled. "Just don't use it on me and we're good."

"I'd love it if you used it on me," Sophia shared. "Falling asleep is difficult these days."

"Well, when you have the mission of saving the world, even counting sheep doesn't calm one's mind," Liv related.

"Especially if the sheep are all atheists," Sophia joked, earning confused expressions from the other two ladies. "Anyway, you have something for me?"

Alicia nodded, handing her a small black box. "That is a frequency regulator. I won't bore you with the details but—"

"Will you bore me with the details later?" Liv asked, eyeing the device with interest. Sophia's older sister had loved mortal electronics since the beginning, which parlayed into her initial career working at the electronics store for John Caraway. Later, when she had her magic unlocked and became a Warrior for the House of Fourteen, it was only natural for her interests to make her a magitech nut.

"You bet," Alicia answered before returning her attention to Sophia. "Now, this device can be your best friend or worst enemy, depending on how you use it."

"I'm intrigued," Liv said, leaning forward.

"If you're reliant on any magitech, then this will undermine your efforts," Alicia explained. "Fortunately, the compass I gave you won't be tampered with by you using this. However, if you are using any other magitech, it will make it ineffective."

"But the point is it will also bring down any of Thad Reinhart's magitech, right?" Sophia asked.

"That's the idea," Alicia agreed. "It sends out a frequency that should take the electronics offline, but depending on its level of power, it might just knock it out for a brief period. Hopefully, that's enough time to get you through a security measure or give you a way to figure out a strategy for combat."

Sophia eyed the device, holding it affectionately. "It's the best advantage we could ask for at this point since we have no idea what we're facing."

Liv clapped a solid hand on her shoulder, giving her sister a sturdy expression. "You may not know what you're facing, but I feel sorrier for the opposing side because they have no idea what's coming for them. You'll knock them out, Soph."

CHAPTER ONE HUNDRED FIFTEEN

"Point and shoot?" Wilder questioned. "That's what she said?"

Sophia nodded. "Yeah, Liv said there wasn't really anything to using the grappling hook. Just prepare to get hauled off my butt."

Wilder laughed. "Yeah, but if you don't know what you're doing, you can get hauled in all the wrong places."

The pair stood next to a rock wall on the far side of the Expanse, the Castle a backdrop to the training session. He patted his midsection. "When that grappling hook attaches to its target, you want to be prepared. If your core isn't engaged, the ride is going to be a bit uncomfortable, and the landing might rearrange your face, which would be a shame. It's key you're ready before you shoot. And then when it anchors, be ready and also when you land."

"Engage my core," Sophia repeated. "Cool, I can do that. It's like doing Pilates."

"What?" Wilder questioned.

"You know, Pilates?" she repeated. "The exercises you do on a reformer machine?"

He shook his head. "Is that a type of magic? What kind of spells does it call for?"

Sophia laughed. "Yoga pants and breath control. And no, it's not magic, unless having good posture and lean muscles is magic."

"It might be," Wilder pronounced. He positioned himself behind her, angling the hand holding the grappling hook at the rock wall. "Now, you want to be very precise with your aim, but also account for wind, temperature, air density, and any other factors that could throw it off."

"So, it's like golfing?" Sophia asked.

"Are all your references sports-related?" he questioned.

"Not all of them," she answered. "Sometimes they are pop culture, especially when I'm talking to Hiker because he doesn't get them and they make him angry."

"Angrier," Wilder corrected.

"Right," Sophia said, sandwiched in Wilder's arms as he held her hands with the grappling hook steady.

"Now, when you're ready, point and shoot," Wilder instructed.

"Engage core, account for variables, and get ready for a wild ride," Sophia said, listing the lessons she'd learned about grappling hooks.

He stood back and released her. "Oh, no. This is a wild ride. When you use that grappling hook, you're on your own."

"Ha-ha," she said, shaking her head at him. "That was an awful joke."

His dimples surfaced as he shrugged. "I make no apologies for bad jokes."

Sophia looked back over her shoulder at him, aware she wasn't focused on her target. "You really should." Then she pressed the trigger, holding steady as the grappling hook shot toward the wall. Not even turning around, she smiled as it hit its target and tugged her up to the top of the rock structure. When she neared it, Sophia turned and stuck her feet up to lock her into place just as she connected with the wall.

With a triumphant feeling pounding in her heart, she glanced down at Wilder with a proud smile. "How was that?"

"It was good, but you could have done it without showing off so much," he said.

"No, I couldn't have," she retorted.

When Sophia had lowered back down to the ground, Wilder showed her a few more techniques for using the grappling hook. "Now, after this whole Thad business, we'll have to take a break from your training for a bit."

"Because?" she questioned.

"Because I have to step away for a little while," he admitted, averting his eyes.

"Step away?" she asked. "That's what you have to do when you need to pop out for a cup of coffee or to run to the post office, but I get the impression there's more to this field trip you're planning."

"It's a mission for Subner," Wilder said in a low voice.

"Oh," she said with interest, putting her fist under her chin and regarding him with intense curiosity. "Let's share secrets."

He shook his head. "You know I can't. Subner asked for total confidentially with this one."

"But what if you need help?" Sophia questioned.

"From an eighteen-year-old dragonrider?" Wilder questioned with great skepticism.

Sophia scoffed. "How many days did you spend battling the dingoes in the Australian Outback?"

He sighed. "All of the days."

"Yeah, so don't underestimate youth," she said.

Wilder brushed long strands of hair off his shoulder rather dramatically. "Or beauty."

"Well, I won't pressure you about this secret mission with Subner," Sophia stated. "Hopefully, I'm nearing the end of my training anyway."

"You are definitely close to earning your wings as a rider and making things official," Wilder agreed. "You should know training never ends for us. Hiker is adamant about that." He pushed out his chest and straightened, doing his best Hiker Wallace impression. "The world doesn't stop, and neither should we. Always be better than you were and the best you can be."

Sophia laughed, but honestly, she respected a motto like that. Hiker Wallace shouldn't be underestimated, and she hoped all his years of training would soon pay off for them. Earth was relying on it.

CHAPTER ONE HUNDRED SIXTEEN

S ophia was returning from training with Wilder when she spotted Quiet, once more suspiciously scampering across the Expanse, looking over his shoulder like he was worried he was being followed. Again, he was headed toward a large cluster of rocks by the Pond.

Having left Wilder on his own to do something mysterious he wouldn't elaborate on, Sophia found herself alone and in a perfect position to follow the gnome and find out once and for all what he was hiding. It was obvious everyone at the Gullington had their secrets, and Sophia's job was apparently to be a detective, unearthing them all.

She crouched and turned on her stealth mode so she could follow the groundskeeper. Moving soundlessly across the Expanse, she cleared the space easily, not spotted by Quiet.

He glanced over his shoulder in the opposite direction of where she was stationed before hurrying toward the rocks. She was so close. Finally, she'd see what he was up to.

"BRRRINGGGG!"

The ring of Sophia's cellphone echoed across the grounds, making birds scatter from the field. Of course, the gnome turned with a scowl on his face, alerted to her presence.

Sophia blushed as she pulled the phone from her cloak pocket. It continued to ring, a rude sound that had not only given her away but was incessant and annoying.

"Hey," she said, putting the device to her ear, not recognizing the number. That was typical for magitech phones. Often those who didn't have her number could get it by using one.

"Hey there, cousin," said a voice on the other end of the line.

Not aware of any cousins out in the world, Sophia frowned. "Cousin? Who is this?"

"Don't you recognize my voice?" the person asked, and right then, Sophia did. She also knew this person wasn't related to her. They weren't even the same species. Or on the same wavelength.

"Hey, King Rudolf," she said mock-cheerfully. "How's it going? Did you lock yourself in a bathroom stall again? Maybe call Liv to get you out this time."

"I'm in a bathroom stall, but I can get out if I want to...I think," he replied. "Anyway, I'm just calling you to say the triplets are on their way, and I need you here pronto."

"Oh," she said, excitement filling her. "I'm thrilled you thought of me. I can't wait to meet your babies, but I'm actually on the brink of trying to stop a world war."

"That sounds like it can wait," Rudolf argued.

"You do understand what a world war is, right?" she questioned.

"You said 'brink,'" Rudolf reasoned. "That sounds like you have some time. Wait until all chaos spills over the waterfall and crashes to the bottom. That's when you swoop in. Don't you know anything about being a hero?"

Sophia shook her head. "Apparently, I don't."

"Well, I've been doing this for many, many centuries, so trust my advice," Rudolf yelled over a loud flushing sound. "Anyway, get here. I want you to meet my four children."

"Triplets," Sophia corrected. "You're having triplets."

"Exactly," he agreed. "Which is why I need you here. There will be one baby for each of us to hold while Serena rests after childbirth, which isn't a piece of cake, according to Bermuda Laurens. I'm guessing it's more like a walk in the park. Anyway, I've called Liv and Rory and now you. That means there will be a baby for each of us to care for, so get over here now."

"Okay," Sophia said, not having the heart to explain to Rudolf he was only having three children and didn't really need her since it felt good to be needed by someone. For a girl who only had two blood relatives in the world, it was nice to have so many people who felt like family. It just proved to Sophia that sometimes you have the family you were born to, and sometimes you have the family you choose.

CHAPTER ONE HUNDRED SEVENTEEN

"How did he take it?" Sophia asked when Liv returned from the delivery room, a speculative expression on her face.

She nodded. "The king of the fae seems relieved he's only having three babies."

Rory, the giant, shook his head. "You couldn't have told him this information prior to now?"

Liv laughed. "I didn't see you pony up any information to him."

Rory, whose subdued nature was a stark contrast to Liv's eccentric one, merely grunted. He was like Sophia's Hiker. She annoyed the Viking like Liv did Rory. It was as if it gave their life meaning to irritate a large grown man.

Maddy, Rory's girlfriend, had been called in to help with the birth since giants were considered very pragmatic on such occasions. It had to do with their magic being connected to the Earth. This left Sophia, Liv, and Rory ample time to stare blankly at each other.

The timing of the births couldn't have been better for Sophia to take some time off. She'd given Hiker the compass from Alicia, and that had started the forty-eight hour time period. She was hoping by the time she returned to the Gullington, the compass would be pointing them toward Thad Reinhart.

She could tell Hiker had mixed feelings about the whole thing. It had to be strange for him to be on the brink of confronting a great evil he was tied to. But he was the only one who could, and the time was quickly approaching. Worldwide events had heated up in the last twelve hours, tensions mounting between countries. War was inevitable for many.

"They are here!" Rudolf exclaimed, running from the labor and delivery room. He engulfed Liv in a hug and then Rory, who looked repulsed by the gesture, and then finally Sophia.

"They are healthy and have all eleven toes!" Rudolf declared.

"Eleven?" Liv questioned.

Rory shook his head. "All fae are born with eleven toes, but the weakest of them falls off later on."

Sophia grimaced. "That's so bizarre."

"The babies are healthy, though?" Liv asked, appearing sentimental. "That's great news, Rudolf."

"Yeah, and we can go through to the nursery in just a minute and hold them," he explained, but then tucked his chin and leaned forward, cupping his mouth. "I'm going to warn you, they are awful-looking."

Liv's eyes slid to Sophia and she had a cautious expression on her face. "Do fae children look like monsters when they are born?"

Rory shook his head.

"Oh, yes, they do," Rudolf argued. "Their faces are all pinched and red, and they look like old men. It's like they were crammed in a tiny compartment for a long time."

"So weird," Sophia said with no inflection.

"They don't do much," Rudolf said, leading them to another set of doors and looking over his shoulder at them. "Bermuda says they will probably just sleep for a long time."

"What were you expecting?" Liv dared to ask.

He shrugged, opening the door. "I had planned a snowshoeing excursion, as well as some paddle boarding for next week, but they apparently can't walk for like a year. I question that, though. Is it that they can't, or they aren't trying hard enough?"

"Maybe with that extra toe, they'll defy the odds," Sophia offered.

Three bassinets were lined up in a room adjacent to the birthing facility. In each of the beds was a tiny baby with a hat on its head, all wrapped up. All that could be seen were pinched red faces.

"Please allow me to introduce you to my girls," Rudolf said proudly.

"They are all girls?" Liv asked, sounding excited.

Rudolf nodded. "Yeah, although they can change their mind at any point. But for now, we'll refer to them as girls."

He picked up the first one, who had a round face and wide eyes and her hand in her mouth. "This one is my firstborn and she is hungrier than most, according to Bermuda. She's a Capricorn, and we named her Captain Morgan." He handed the bundle to Liv, who hesitated at first, but after some trials, she slipped her hands around the baby and cuddled her to her chest.

"Hi, Morgan," she said, a strange tenderness taking residence on her face. "I'm your godmother, and I promise to teach you everything your parents haven't picked up through sheer experience. I'm going to keep you alive, little one."

Rudolf watched this exchange with affection before turning his attention to the middle bassinet. He picked up a bundle that was longer than the other two. This child's face was slender, although red.

"And now, may I present my second child, who Bermuda says came out the wrong way, but that's better than not coming out at all. She's a Taurus named Captain Silver."

"How is it she's a Taurus if they were all born on the same day of the same month?" Liv asked, bouncing her baby.

Rudolf shook his head as he handed the baby to Rory, who seemed quite natural holding the bundle. "It's a decision they make. Our zodiacs don't choose us, we choose them."

"That's inherently false," Sophia said, watching as Rory thoughtfully gazed down at the baby and made her coo.

Rudolf pivoted and pulled the third baby from the last bed. "And here is my last-born baby, who Bermuda said didn't want to come out. She's stubborn, clever, and probably my favorite. Please meet Captain

Kirk." He laid the baby in Sophia's arms, and for never having held a child before, she found the experience to be quite natural. The baby cuddled into her, its warmth a welcome sensation in a world where Sophia was used to so much cold.

"I don't think you're supposed to have favorites yet," Liv offered, gazing down at her baby with affection.

Rudolf waved her off, dismissing her comment. "Of course, I am. That's how I pit them against one another, so they work harder to achieve their father's approval, which never comes."

"Smart parenting," Rory said. "That won't fail."

Rudolf was absolutely giddy, bouncing between the three holding his children, commenting on their different characteristics, or making assumptions about their political affiliations.

He came around to Sophia and peered over her shoulder, fondly regarding the baby in her arms, who was fast asleep.

"If there is a world war coming, Sophia, will you do everything possible to stop it?" Rudolf asked, his voice suddenly serious. "I brought these girls into the world. They are quite possibly the first half-fae and half-mortal children ever. I want a legacy for them that is deserving of their greatness. I want them to rule in a world that is appreciative of their uniqueness. And I want them to thrive on an Earth that is both beautiful and conducive to their growth. Will you help me to secure that future for the Captains?"

As looney as King Rudolf Sweetwater always was, he was also one of the best people Sophia had the fortune of meeting. He might get a lot of things wrong, but he got many more right, and the three brand new halflings in the nursery were part of that. King Rudolf was someone worth knowing and protecting, and his girls were reason enough to ensure war didn't take over the Earth.

"Yes, Ru," Sophia answered thoughtfully, handing Captain Kirk back to her father. "I'll go fight the bad guys so one day these girls will know a peaceful Earth."

CHAPTER ONE HUNDRED
EIGHTEEN

When Sophia returned to the Gullington, her heart was full of love and a need to protect future generations. And because her life had to be ironic, she was greeted by screaming upon entering the Castle.

"We've got to act now!" Hiker yelled from his office.

Sophia hurried up the stairs to the second story, rushing into his office to find a similar scene as before. Mama Jamba was laid out on the couch, still watching movies, and Hiker was pacing.

"I know that, Hiker," Mama Jamba stated. "The situation has been horrible since the beginning. I'm glad you're finally taking note of it."

He looked at the magitech device Sophia had given him. "The compass still isn't registering Thad's location."

"It will," Mama Jamba said in her drawn-out accent. "When it's time."

"Mama!" he boomed, throwing his hand at a television screen in the corner. "The reports are saying countries are moving into position. Armies are gearing up. Within the day, shots are supposed to be fired, all because of this fake need for resources and power Thad has brainwashed them with. He's pitted those with pitchforks against those with torches and told them they are each other's enemy."

Mama Jamba nodded calmly, pulling a warm afghan up to her chin and cuddling it. "Yes, that's exactly what he's done. He wants the world's population to take each other out, and in the process, kill the Earth. And he might be successful." She toggled her head back and forth. "But he also might not."

The two hadn't noticed Sophia lurking in the doorway. When she cleared her throat, they both turned their attention to her.

"You're back," Hiker said.

"Yes, sir," she answered. "Is everything…"

He shook his head. "No, it's not okay, but hopefully, it will be. Get ready to mobilize. The others are also preparing. I want you to be ready to go at a moment's notice. As soon as this thing you've given me shows Thad's location and facility, we're off."

Sophia nodded, adrenaline suddenly coursing through her veins. They were almost to it. The moment had almost come. And it was no greater for anyone than Hiker Wallace. Soon his moment of reckoning would be upon them. For Sophia, she wasn't sure whether he'd redeem himself from all those centuries ago when he let Thad get away or if he'd repeat the past.

CHAPTER ONE HUNDRED NINETEEN

Everyone was silent, on the verge of panic when they all seemed to get a phone call from within.

Mama Jamba hiccupped like she'd swallowed something the wrong way and pressed her hand to her mouth. Hiker's eyes fell distant, the way Sophia imagined hers did when Lunis spoke in her head. Then her dragon did speak.

I think you better come here and see this, Lunis said, his tone tense.

What is it? Sophia asked.

It's better if you see this on your own rather than hear it from me, Lunis insisted. *But bring Hiker.*

He's getting a message from Bell right now, I think, Sophia replied.

Yes, that seems about right, Lunis stated.

Sophia's and Hiker's eyes met, and they shared a foreboding expression.

Okay, we are on our way, Sophia told the dragon. *But first, is everything okay?*

"Okay" is always relative, Soph, he explained. *There's status quo, and then there's the precipitance to evolution, and then there's the opposite of all that. I hope we're somewhere in the middle, but only time will tell.*

Sophia and Hiker crossed the Expanse in silence. They hadn't said a word to each other when they left the Castle, both knowing their dragons had communicated similar messages.

As they neared the Cave, the tension mounted in Sophia's chest. She had to take three steps to one of Hiker's. She moved faster than him, so it worked out.

When they were at the bottom of the mountain that housed the Cave, they both halted.

"I've never been up to the Cave," Sophia admitted.

Hiker shook his head. "Me either. But if the dragons are asking us to enter, this is big."

"And Bell didn't tell you what it was about?" Sophia questioned, knowing his dragon had spoken in his head at the same time Lunis had in her mind.

"No, she said I had to see it in person," he stated.

Sophia nodded. "Same with Lunis." She motioned to the rock wall. "We can climb or use my awesome grappling hook."

To her surprise, Hiker rolled his eyes. "Awesome grappling hook, obviously."

She nodded and pulled it off her belt.

The Cave had never had humans in it. Sophia had seen it in Lunis' mind when she'd scried his visions. However, no person had ever stepped foot in the Cave, which had been the home of dragons since the beginning of the Gullington, the beginning of the Dragon Elite.

It felt like stepping onto a brand-new uninhabited planet when Sophia entered the Cave. Hiker seemed to share her anxiety. The dragons, if they felt anything about the trespassing, didn't show it.

Sophia knew with her first glance at Lunis that something was devastatingly wrong. It gave her little chance to notice the details of the Cave. It was nondescript, as she knew from scrying. There were cold, dark walls and little light. The ground was hard and unforgiving, as Lunis had often told her. In the corner were the shimmering dragon eggs she and Evan had recovered from one of Thad's facilities, but unlike the last time she'd seen them, they weren't shimmering.

CHAPTER ONE HUNDRED TWENTY

Sophia rushed over and knelt beside the five dragons who surrounded the eggs nestled in the corner. Hiker didn't follow.

She glanced at him, and her heart broke.

Sophia almost didn't have to look at the eggs to know what had happened. It was plainly written all over Hiker Wallace's face.

They had gone bad.

She pulled her gaze around to the five eggs and looked them over.

That's when she noticed cracks running down their sides and saw they were shrinking in on themselves. They were withering away.

"What happened?" she asked Lunis, sidling up next to him.

He shook his head. *We don't know.*

They could have always been bad, Coral answered, sitting next to Lunis.

It was strange to Sophia that the dragons all sitting around the eggs seemed more like housecats than large reptiles. Maybe it was just the significance of the moment.

"Lunis came from this batch," Sophia argued.

We all came from the same batch, Bell stated. *It's just that we were separated.*

One thousand eggs, Tala said stoically.

"And the very last five are dead," Hiker stated, sounding more like a zombie than himself. He ambled forward robotically, his eyes on the eggs. "The last of the dragons. Our very last hope. It's gone."

Sophia felt emotion welling up in her, but she refused to let it out in front of ancient dragons and the oldest rider. Instead, she swallowed. "But still, sir, a few remain."

He shook his head, pulling his gaze away as he turned for the entrance. "What does that matter anymore? There are only a handful of us left, and we are hardly enough. Our numbers were always our strong point."

"That's wrong," Sophia declared, not sure where her words were coming from. "Our power has always been in our unity. Mortals are powerful because of their grasp on magic. Elves with water. Gnomes, their ability with fire. And giants own the Earth. But only one race has ever dared to pair their grasp of wind and magic with that of the dragon. We are magicians, and we were chosen to ride. There is no lost hope as long as one of us breathes in this world."

Sophia took a step forward. "Sir, I'm breathing. Are you?"

She watched as Hiker's back rose and fell, the stress of the moment getting to him. Finally, he turned, a sober look in his eyes. He nodded. "Yes, Sophia. I'm breathing too."

She pointed behind her. "So are these dragons. They may be all that's left, but they are enough for us to win at least one more battle. One more war. Will you lead us into it?"

Hiker pulled in a breath, seeming on the verge of answering, but something pulsed in his pocket. He tensed and retrieved the compass. His eyes widened before he brought his gaze up.

"I know where Thad is," he said in a hushed voice.

"But are you ready?" she asked, feeling the dragons at her back, their strength fueling her in a way she'd never felt before.

He lowered the compass and nodded, his eyes darting to the dead eggs before landing on Sophia. "Unlike before, I have nothing to lose and everything to gain."

CHAPTER ONE HUNDRED TWENTY-ONE

Even after hiking around the Expanse for several hours, Sophia was having trouble processing what she'd just learned about the dragon eggs. Yes, there were only five before. That had given the riders a little hope the Dragon Elite would be what it once was, although no one voiced it aloud. Having five eggs was better than nothing.

They knew because Mae Ling had confirmed it, that these were the last five remaining eggs in the world. Knowing they would never hatch and there would never be another new dragon was devastating no matter how Sophia tried to spin it. Yes, there were still five dragons left in the world, and barring tragedy, they could live a thousand or more years. But after that, the age of the dragons would be gone. The Dragon Elite would be no more. The world adjudicators would be done.

Sophia tried to console herself with the fact Lunis came from that batch of eggs, and at least he hatched. Who knew why the dragon eggs went bad? The dragons had speculated it might have been the approaching war. It was triggering all sorts of things worldwide.

Bermuda thought the war was the reason King Rudolf Sweetwater's children were born when they were. Apparently, global consciousness was affected by the events Thad had put into motion, and it had far-reaching effects.

Still consumed with these thoughts, Sophia trudged up the stairs to the Castle, hoping to get a proper night's rest. Tomorrow the war was coming. The Dragon Elite would ride out together for the first time in centuries.

Sophia wasn't overwhelmed by what would come next, but she was preoccupied with it. That was why she didn't hear Mama Jamba call to her as she walked past Hiker's office.

The suit of armor stationed in the corridor stepped out from the wall and pointed at Sophia's back. Not as surprised as she should have been that empty armor was walking around by itself, she glanced over her shoulder, realizing the Castle was trying to communicate with her.

"Get your hiney in here, darling," Mama Jamba called from the open office.

"Oh, right," Sophia said, turning back to the suit of armor and nodding. "Thanks."

Pivoting, she hurried back the way she'd come. She'd just thanked an empty suit of armor for giving her directions. "My life is so weird."

"It will only get weirder," Mama Jamba said, still stationed on Hiker's couch. He was absent from his office, probably helping the dragons to dispose of the bad eggs.

Mother Nature appeared refreshed in comparison to her recent appearance. There were no wadded up tissues scattered around her, and she'd changed into a fresh pink velour tracksuit. Her silver hair was neatly arranged, and her feet were covered in sparkling Ugg boots that matched her outfit.

"I'm guessing you know about..." Sophia's voice trailed away.

Mama Jamba nodded and patted the space beside her on the couch. "Of course, I do, my dear. You must be taking this hard."

Sophia took the spot beside Mother Nature and nodded. "Did you always know they were going to spoil?"

Mama pulled in a breath and clasped her hands over her midsection. "The thing is, there isn't really such thing as destiny, and yet there is."

Sophia hung her head. "That doesn't make any sense."

Mama Jamba nodded. "And yet, that's the way life goes."

"Why does life have to be so complicated?" Sophia asked.

"Because there are no absolutes," Mama Jamba stated. "I made most of the rules. Papa made quite a few as well. And we made them, so they were never hard and fast. Each one can be broken if you know the secret, but…" She winked at Sophia, a twinkle in her bright blue eyes. "We don't give up our secrets easily."

"No, I wouldn't think you would," Sophia offered.

"So," Mama Jamba continued, "the eggs were meant to hatch, but things changed. And now they're spoiled. There is destiny, and it can always shift."

"Then it's not destiny," Sophia argued.

Mama Jamba agreed. "I understand how confusing this is, this game of semantics if you will. You're destined for certain things, and you will fulfill that destiny, most likely. But if you leave this room and an axe falls on you, then you won't."

"Well, the Castle has tried to kill me before," Sophia muttered.

Mama Jamba laughed. "It was simply trying to steer you in the direction it desired. My point is, events change what was destined. And now the eggs won't hatch."

"And that's the end of dragons," Sophia said.

"Not quite." Mama Jamba patted her leg. "We still have you."

"I finished the meditative portion of my training," Sophia said. "Does that mean I'm done? Do I have my wings?"

Mama Jamba smiled. "Almost. I knew you'd wrap it up quickly, and I'm grateful you're almost there. However, you have one last thing to do before you officially pass."

"Travel to another planet?" Sophia asked. "Survive a walkabout in the Australian Outback? Not kill Hiker after he throws away my provisions and demands I hike ten miles? Oh, wait, I've already done all those things."

The laugh that spilled from Mama Jamba's mouth was absolutely enchanting. It was the sound of the wind rustling willow branches. "Actually, the last task you must complete to finish training isn't something you can go out and do."

"Seems about right," Sophia said dryly.

"Instead, you're waiting for an opportunity," Mama Jamba continued. "To earn your wings, you must show a true act of comradery."

"How do I do that?" Sophia asked.

The old woman shook her head. "That will be for you to determine. I will say that if you go out looking for a way, it won't count. When we try to be nice, we're using the wrong motivation. When it comes from the purest part of the heart and we express love because it calls to us, then that is magic."

"A true act of comradery…" Sophia mused, her eyes looking without seeing.

"Yes, because that's the biggest part of being with the Dragon Elite," Mama Jamba explained. "They protect the world because they value life, and no lives are more important to my Elite than the other riders'."

"So I have to show an act of comradery to one of the riders," Sophia stated.

"Again, it has to be authentic and unplanned," Mama Jamba warned.

"I did tell you I didn't murder Hiker even though he was all but begging me to, right?" Sophia joked.

"I appreciate that, but I'm afraid that won't do." Mama patted her leg once more. "You'll figure it out, my dear. Or you won't and it will take you several years to complete your training, like Evan."

"But you told me completing the training is crucial," Sophia argued, remembering how adamant the woman had been about it.

"Indeed, I did, and it is. But so were a lot of other things that haven't happened in history," she explained. "Unfortunately, bad things happen, and usually that's a result of other things *not* happening. If you don't complete your training in time, I fear for this world, but I already do, so it's just more of the same."

Sophia fell quiet for a moment, trying not to feel overwhelmed by all this. After a moment, she pointed to the television screen before them on the table in front of the couch. "Are you done with sad movies?"

The television was blank, showing just static.

Mama Jamba smiled good-naturedly as she nodded. "Yes. How about you and I watch something that will make you laugh? You seem like you could use it."

"I could," Sophia related. "What do you want to watch?"

"Well, I don't know," Mama Jamba said, yarn and a crochet hook appearing in her hands. She immediately went to work making something. She held it up. "For one of King Rudolf's triplets."

"Oh, wow, they get a baby blanket from Mother Nature? Is it because their father is the king of the fae?"

"Everyone gets something from me," Mama Jamba answered. "They just don't always know it. This is because the triplets are unique."

"Because they are halflings?" Sophia asked.

In response, Mother Nature bobbed her head. "And other reasons, too, but no spoilers for you."

"And destiny could change," Sophia added.

Indicating the screen, Mama Jamba said, "Now, pick something to watch. You probably know all the hip new shows all the kids are watching? Is there something on Prime or Netflix I need to see?"

Sophia blinked at the woman. "Why do you not know everything? I'm confused by how this works."

"As you should be. It's very confusing. I know most things, but not everything. Like Papa Creola, I see the future, but not all of it. I can control many things, but only under the right circumstances, and all of that is subject to change if certain rules are broken."

"Wow," Sophia said, shaking her head. "Okay, well, how about some Trey Kennedy?"

"Oh, he's delightful," Mama Jamba stated at once.

"You've seen his YouTube channel?" Sophia asked.

Mother Nature shook her head. "No, I just know everyone."

"Right," Sophia said, pointing at the television and making YouTube pop up on the screen.

"Now, what does he do?" Mama Jamba asked, continuing to crochet the blanket.

"He does these spoofs where he makes fun of people: single girls, middle schoolers, white people, adults, millennials, people in the winter, moms. You know, that sort of thing?" Sophia explained. "It's like the stereotypical behavior we all are prone to, but he calls it out, making it funny."

"Oh, something like how moms be like 'Kids, get mommy one of her Dove dark chocolates,' or 'What is this Sea World? How is there so much water outside the tub?' or 'How do I send a G-I-F?' or 'Good morning, or should I say, good afternoon. Someone slept well,' or 'Put your coat on and take your other one. You never know,' or 'How was your pool party? Were the girls wearing appropriate swimsuits?'"

Sophia peeled back, giving Mama Jamba a look of astonishment. "Yeah, that was pretty much the episode on moms verbatim."

Mama Jamba scrunched her shoulders, looking proud. "I gave him some of my best jokes. Love that kid."

CHAPTER ONE HUNDRED TWENTY-TWO

Sophia sat atop Lunis, her fingers on the reins and her attention on Hiker Wallace as he did what he did best—pace. He strode in front of the line of dragons on the Expanse, thinking. She'd grown accustomed to seeing him pace. Fret. Worry away his thoughts.

She looked around, taking in the green hills and capturing the picture around her. It was unlike anything she'd ever seen, but she hoped to see it more often in the future. Four dragons with their riders atop them stood at the ready. In front of them, Hiker, the leader of the Dragon Elite, paced along the Expanse, his red dragon standing nobly at his back.

On the far side next to Evan stood Ainsley and Quiet, serious expressions on both their faces.

These five riders were all that remained of the Dragon Elite. After a thousand years and some odd, there were only five left with dragons. And then there was Thad Reinhart, the worst of the worst and the one they had to take down.

He didn't have a dragon. Thad had something worse. He had perfected magitech and turned it into his dragon. Sophia knew planes and jets enhanced with magitech and all other things related to the modern world would come at her that day. It would be the worst battle she'd ever endured.

As she looked at Wilder atop Simi on her right, she nodded. Mahkah sat upon Tala on her left, and he gave her confidence. They were all the Earth had, and it had to be enough.

Hiker paced some more before halting. Clearing his throat, he looked at his riders.

"I haven't always been the leader you wanted," he began. "But I have always tried to be the one you needed. I looked out for the dangers, but I missed them because I didn't know they were within me. Thad is my problem. He is the result of what I couldn't finish."

Hiker seemed on the verge of having a moment as he sped up, moving faster with his words, almost like he was still pacing in his thoughts.

"I have been a dragonrider since before any of you were born, but I've learned our years mean nothing." His eyes darted to Sophia. "I've learned wisdom comes from listening." His gaze darted to Mahkah. "I've learned experience comes from sacrifice." His eyes moved to Wilder. "I've learned positions come to those who go through hell and back." And finally, his eyes went to Evan. "And I've learned ingenuity comes to those who challenge the world around them."

He moved until he was right in front of Bell. "You all have stayed by me, some of you longer than others, showing your loyalty. That has always been appreciated. I know you're waiting for the fight. It is here and it wants us, and it will not be done until we are done. Men… riders," he corrected. "We have spent a long time waiting to be needed, and our time is here."

Hiker mounted his dragon in an easy series of movements that brought him up on the large red magical creature.

"I can't thank you enough for staying true to me," he stated, holding Bell's reins. "However, I have one more request, and it's probably the hardest one yet."

Hiker looked each of them in the eye before gazing at Bell. "If all else fails, if I don't succeed, elect a leader of the Dragon Elite who will keep you honest until the end."

"That's your request?" Ainsley asked, holding up a basket. "I have muffins. Does anyone want muffins for the journey?"

Hiker shook his head. "Would you get out of here, woman? We are having a moment."

Ainsley pointed at Quiet standing close by. "He said it was all right to interrupt and your speech was drivel and I should offer muffins to soften the boring part."

Hiker shook his head. "I'm trying to rally my men. People. Riders."

She shook her head. "No, you're boring them. If I was giving a speech, it would go something like—"

"You're fired, Ainsley," Hiker said flatly.

She bowed. "It is about time, sir. I've been waiting for this moment. I'll see you when you return."

He nodded. "See you later."

She turned and headed for the Castle in the distance.

Quiet also muttered something before ambling off, leaving the riders and their leader staring around blankly.

Sophia sensed they were all waiting for that "Braveheart" moment, and they might not get it. She smiled at Hiker and mouthed the words, "You've got this."

He smiled. Tightening his hands on the reins, he led his dragon in front of them. Bell moved with unique grace, striding back and forth as if she were pacing like her rider.

"I'm sorry if I have faltered," Hiker began, his voice stronger than before. "But follow me into battle, and we will not fail. I will fight Thad. You will take down his arsenal. And we will show our rule once more over this Earth. Even if we are the last of the dragonriders, we will be the very best this planet has ever known."

CHAPTER ONE HUNDRED TWENTY-THREE

The dragons rose, their wings flapping in perfect unison. Hiker was in the lead, directing his riders outside the Barrier, where he'd open a portal close to Thad's facility.

The Dragon Elite rode in formation, Evan and Sophia bringing up the rear. The sun was just rising over the Gullington, but where they were headed, it would still be night, which was important for their plan.

In truth, none of them knew exactly what they'd face. They could have taken time to do reconnaissance on the area, but Hiker had said it was time to act. There would be weapons. Fighting. Resistance. They were aware of that, and it was as much preparation as they needed.

Sophia had never ridden among the other riders like this, watching the tails of the dragons stream behind them in the wind. She felt a rush of emotion, her mind trailing back to ancient memories that weren't hers. In a flash, she saw Hiker riding next to Adam, the wind ripping through their hair and beards as they raced through a torrential rainstorm. She saw battles where intertwined dragons plummeted toward the ground. She saw the first rider, Alexander Conerly, flying over a clear blue ocean.

It's the chi of the dragon, Lunis said in her head. *It's connecting you to the memories of other riders like I am often connected to the collective consciousness of dragons.*

Wow, I didn't realize that was possible, Sophia said.

Anything is possible, Lunis said simply. *You're embarking on a pivotal adventure, and this is your first time to ride alongside the Dragon Elite. It's triggered memories of your own.*

Sophia was speechless, feeling the ancient winds the riders who came before her had felt. She felt the power of the dragons around her, a collective power that sent out a frequency unlike anything she'd known.

At that moment, she was connected to the past and the present of the Dragon Elite. The power of her own flowed around like the wind, and she made peace with the element that had always made her shrink in on herself.

She felt the blast of cold and didn't even consider hunching over to avoid the wind. Instead, Sophia straightened on Lunis, drinking in the breeze and holding her face high. She braced her shoulders and rode into the wind alongside the other Dragon Elite, for the first time feeling like one of them.

CHAPTER ONE HUNDRED TWENTY-FOUR

S ophia was the last to come through the portal, coasting in over the flat and sprawling city of Dallas, Texas.

The skyline was lit up, blotting out the stars. The moon hung overhead, a giant full orb high in the Texas sky.

Did you know it was a full moon? Sophia asked her dragon, having been too preoccupied recently to have made note of such things.

Of course, I did, Lunis replied. *I can feel them approach.*

That will make things interesting tonight, Sophia offered.

It will give me certain advantages, Lunis stated. *I'm both strongest and most vulnerable on the full moon.*

How is that possible?

That's how it is with most things, he explained. *A bodybuilder bulks up to be stronger, but it also makes them a bigger target.*

Right, Sophia replied. *If you turn on your supersize skills, we'll have benefits, but you'll be a larger target.*

Exactly.

The pollution that hung over the city was a stark contrast to the clean air Sophia was used to in the Gullington. The city of Dallas was filled with rows of cookie-cutter houses and roads, planned out on a mass scale. Buildings and bright lights stretched around the highways, where traffic moved sluggishly along, commuters headed home after a long workday.

Hiker spun the compass in his hand, and a confused expression appeared in his eyes. He pointed to Sophia and waved her forward.

"Why her, sir?" Evan complained from beside her.

"Because," Hiker yelled.

Sophia clenched her heels tighter to Lunis as he sped up and navigated between Mahkah and Wilder. The pair slowed, making room for her as she pulled up next to the leader of the Dragon Elite.

"The compass shows we're right on top of his facility," Hiker explained to her, the wind tangling his words. She made them out, thanks to her enhanced senses.

Sophia glanced down to find the city had abruptly stopped. Pastures dotted with trees spread out in front of them. It was possible Thad Reinhart lived in a modest cabin on a farm on the outskirts of the city, but knowing what she did about the man, it seemed unlikely. This compass wasn't just taking them to Thad Reinhart. It was also drawing them to a huge source of magitech energy.

A mostly empty series of pastures definitely wasn't the spot for magitech power. Yes, magical power, but to have magitech, there *had* to be technology. There was no getting around that.

"Did Thad know about the Barrier at the Gullington?" Sophia asked.

A perplexed expression crossed Hiker's face. "Well, of course. Early on, I tried to recruit him for the Dragon Elite, shortly after I magnetized to Bell and him to Ember. I thought being a rider might change him." He shook his head, obviously disappointed. "I was naïve then."

Sophia withdrew the frequency disk Alicia had given her from her pocket. "I think it's possible Thad created something similar to what we have at the Gullington."

"The Barrier," Hiker stated. "So his facility can't be seen or found by those who aren't welcome."

"And they also wouldn't be able to enter," Sophia said, slowing the dragon.

Hiker followed suit, as did the other riders at their backs, until they were all hovering over the field, the dragons flapping their wings to keep them aloft.

"If that's the case, how are we going to get in there?" Hiker asked.

"The Barrier keeps out anyone who isn't a Dragon Elite or serving them," Sophia explained. "However, Thad couldn't have the same parameters, I don't think. His would be controlled by magitech."

She set the controls on the frequency disk the way Alicia had shown her. Hiker watched curiously.

"If this works, sir, it will only bring down the security for a moment," Sophia explained. "That will be our chance to slip through. If it doesn't work, we have to find another way."

He nodded. "Then let's hope it works."

Sophia turned a dial on the disk and held her breath as the red meter on the front rose, showing it powering up and disturbing outside magitech frequencies. It wasn't choosey according to Alicia, so it would put all magitech offline for a brief period. The longer it was on, the more it could do, but stronger devices would resist after a short time.

It was lucky for the Dragon Elite they weren't reliant on magitech; otherwise, it could bring them down too. The compass was magitech, but it had already gotten them to their destination. Now they had to pull the disguise off of the facility.

"Here we go," Sophia said, watching as the meter rose all the way.

Hiker searched the area below them, his eyes anxious.

She flicked her eyes from the meter to the dark pastures, worried it wouldn't work.

Then, like Christmas lights flickering on for the first time in a season, a giant base materialized below them, spreading out a great distance.

Hiker let out a sound of shock. "For the love of the angels!"

CHAPTER ONE HUNDRED TWENTY-FIVE

The main headquarters of Thad Reinhart's enterprises wasn't like the Chainley facility Sophia and Lunis had visited, where they'd freed the slaves. That was tiny compared to this.

This was like a small city or a large military base. The tarmac stretched on, surrounded by lakes and irrigation ditches. Dotting the asphalt were dozens of jets, 747 planes, tanks, army jeeps mounted with guns, and semi-trucks. On the north end of the facility were multiple buildings and large warehouses, and in the center was an impressive fifty-story skyscraper. Without magitech, there was little way Thad Reinhart could have shielded this place.

The Gullington was hidden, but that was by an ancient and mysterious power fueled by whatever controlled the Castle. The House of Fourteen was similar, but it was fueled by the power of the founding families.

As far as Sophia knew, Thad Reinhart didn't have access to that level of magic. Technology was his strong point, and he'd fused it with magic to create a very impressive arsenal of magitech and security measures.

The base flickered below them like a lightbulb about to burn out.

"We have to go now," Sophia urged, waving those behind her forward.

Hiker sent Bell into a nosedive, and her large form took on the shape of a missile as it raced toward the ground. The others followed as the barrier to the military base began to fade. They had to get through before it did since Sophia wasn't sure she could get it to come back using the frequency disk. Bringing it down for this long had been a stroke of luck since whatever fueled it had to be a huge source of energy.

Alicia had also advised Sophia that magitech was intuitive and learned. A really advanced system taken offline by something will patch itself until it figures out how to troubleshoot the problem for the future.

Alicia had explained this to her to caution Sophia not to use the frequency disk too often. If she did, then when she really needed it, it might not work. For example, use it to bring down a helicopter, and it might be ineffective on the fighter jets they fought later.

The Dragon Elite raced toward the base. When Sophia slipped through the magitech barrier, she felt a force like static electricity run over her and Lunis. She halted in the air beside Hiker after they were all through the barrier.

The force field seemed to have affected them all. Hiker's long blond hair was sticking straight up like he'd had a balloon rubbed all over it.

Sophia laughed, relieved by having made it to their destination.

"What are you laughing at?" Hiker asked, sitting nobly upon his ancient dragon.

She pointed at his hair, which was reaching for the clouds. "You look funny."

CHAPTER ONE HUNDRED
TWENTY-SIX

W ith an annoyed glare, Hiker ran his hands through his hair, making it calm down once more. "You should see yours if you think mine looks funny."

Sophia could feel her hair wiggling all around her like it was possessed.

The other riders pulled up next to them, Wilder's head of brown hair also crazy from the static electricity.

"Anyone else keep shocking their dragon?" Evan asked, sidling up next to Mahkah.

I think the question you have to ask yourself, Lunis began, *is why does your dragon keep shocking you?*

Simi nodded, smiling at Lunis. *Yeah, I absorbed all of the electrical force I could so as not to jolt my rider.*

Me too, Tala admitted.

Evan bent and gazed at Coral. "Are you shocking me on purpose?"

Maybe? his dragon answered.

Hiker, who was not paying attention to this exchange, had his attention hinged on the military base below them. It had appeared to be mostly quiet at this time in the evening.

Sophia had actually thought it would be easy to drop in and scout around the place. Things were quickly changing below as fighter pilots ran to their jets and soldiers were deployed to the tanks and jeeps. They had triggered an alarm when they came through the barrier, and they were about to have a fight on their hands.

"We came to fight, though," Sophia said mostly to herself.

"That we did," Hiker replied, watching with keen interest as things quickly took shape on the ground.

Men in uniform scattered quickly, more spilling from the large adjacent buildings. There were a few dozen of them. She didn't have to remind herself there were only five of them. But they had dragons, and they had each other. It had to be enough.

Sophia was looking at Hiker, waiting for his orders as his jaw flexed and an expression of pure vengeance she'd never seen flickered in his eyes. Following his gaze, she saw what had caused the bitter expression.

A man in a black suit with a bald head and a face covered in scars had come out of the largest warehouse. Her enhanced vision studied the details of the man on the ground, who was different from the others racing towards aircraft or vehicles. She recognized his confidence. It was much like that of the man next to her. However, there was something so inherently evil about the man it radiated from even that distance.

He narrowed his gaze on the five dragonriders.

Thad Reinhart knew they were there. It was time for battle.

CHAPTER ONE HUNDRED TWENTY-SEVEN

Sophia cut her eyes to Hiker as he stayed locked on his twin brother on the ground. She watched him for signs of defeat. Everything centered on Hiker Wallace remaining confident in this battle. If he didn't, everything was lost. All the wars Thad Reinhart had instigated would commence. All the things they didn't want to come to pass would sprint forward. Hiker had to be what stopped his brother in order to stop everything that would destroy the planet.

The pair stared at each other for a long minute before Thad Reinhart pivoted sharply and strode back to the building he'd come from and disappeared. On the ground, the jets and vehicles were deploying. The fight was coming.

Drawing in a breath, Hiker dispersed orders at once. "We first have to take down the most vital offensive forces." He pointed to the ground where a large plane was sitting on the tarmac, a ground crew quickly fueling it. "That right there has something aboard it Thad doesn't want to be compromised."

"How do you know, sir?" Evan asked.

Hiker glanced back at him. "I know. Thad isn't used to me being close. He wasn't guarded just now, and I spied enough."

Indicating the jets taking off, Hiker said, "Mahkah and Wilder, you immobilize the small aircraft." He pointed at the tanks and jeeps moving into position. "Evan, you will draw the ground transport over to the water on the far edge. From there, you'll know what to do."

"Drown those frockers," Evan sang.

Sophia laughed, remembering Coral was aligned with water. That also reminded her of the others' elements. Simi was connected to the wind and Tala to the Earth. She wasn't sure how that would come into play or if it would, but she hoped they used every advantage they had in this fight.

Finally, when she thought Hiker had forgotten about her, he turned his attention to Sophia. "That plane. Thad referred to it in his mind as a 747. I want you and Lunis to take it down. Don't let whatever is aboard leave this facility."

She nodded, feeling the weight of great responsibility on her and Lunis' shoulders. "Yes, sir."

He leaned forward. "And my job will be to draw my brother out as only I can."

"How will you do that, sir?" Evan asked.

Hiker didn't give him a look of annoyance as Sophia would have expected. Instead, he drew a breath and sat up straighter. "It won't be hard. I don't know what Thad has, but he's excited to show it off to me. I think it is only a matter of time before my brother comes out of hiding, and I will be ready."

Sophia desperately hoped Hiker was right, and he was finally ready to face his twin.

CHAPTER ONE HUNDRED TWENTY-EIGHT

Because Wilder and Mahkah had a few dozen decades together, they shared a unique communication style.

He knew Mahkah would handle the aircraft being deployed, while Wilder was in charge of those already in the air.

The jets took off before turning around and coming in his and Simi's direction. He patted his dragon, encouraging her as they entered into their first real twenty-first-century battle.

Jets weren't something Wilder was familiar with. However, he was going to venture that they didn't know how to react to a dragon and rider. Most importantly, the jets had no idea what aces the dragonriders had up their sleeves.

Six jets roared in their direction, quickly approaching.

Wilder drew a breath, feeling his dragon suck in the wind like she was swallowing it and funneling it into a reserve. It was rare he and Simi had an opportunity to use their elemental skill. Actually, it had been forever.

This was their first real battle.

Long-awaited and with high stakes.

Most of the jets and aircraft were still on the ground, Mahkah observed, directing Tala over them.

He'd only have one chance to strike. After that, Tala would be depleted. He would have to channel all his power into one move instead of splitting it up. The key was to keep the other aircraft from taking off.

Unfortunately, the 747 with the important cargo was too far away for Mahkah to affect. Sophia would have to handle that, although he was uncertain how the young dragonrider would do it. Still, that wasn't his assignment.

Taking a risk he hoped paid off, Mahkah landed Tala in front of the aircraft gearing up for takeoff, earning curious expressions from their pilots.

Standing in front of a bunch of magitech jets wasn't a move anyone expected. They also didn't know what was coming next or that there was no escaping it.

Letting out a carefree scream, Evan held his hands above his head as Coral sailed past the ground transports. She flicked her tail back and forth, intentionally knocking into the jeeps and semi-trucks, hoping to enrage the drivers.

The vehicles teetered to one side and then the other before landing back on their wheels.

Evan could have had Coral knock them over completely, but where would the fun be in that? This was a game of cat and mouse for him.

The first step was to get them to follow. Evan turned his dragon around and headed for the water in the distance that surrounded the base. It was probably to help with perimeter control, but in this instance, it was hopefully going to take down the vehicles confined to the ground.

Evan turned to look over his shoulder, a smile unfurling on his face.

He knew how to antagonize, and in this case, it had worked.
The vehicles were following.

Take down a 747, Sophia said to Lunis.

No, problem, he replied. *I don't think I can in this current form, but if we go after them now, we get it before it takes off.*

And what then? she questioned. *You're going to chew its tires off so it can't get off the ground?*

You realize I'm not a Labrador, right? he fired back.

As awesome as you are in your current form, there's not a hell of a lot of damage we can do, even with how badass you are, she replied.

So I have to shift, he stated.

And by that time, the 747 will be in the air.

Not a problem, Lunis asserted with confidence. *Just get ready for a seat change. The saddle you're in is about to come unglued.*

CHAPTER ONE HUNDRED TWENTY-NINE

Watching his riders spring into action was by far the most thrilling thing Hiker Wallace had seen in a hundred years. No, two hundred. No, in all his life.

He had led many a battle. He had been at the center of some of the most important fights that changed history. That had saved countries. And yet, watching four lone riders move into position to take down magitech that outnumbered them was exhilarating. It was also terrifying.

He knew Mahkah had experience, and that would aid the rider as he took down the ground transports. Wilder was the bravest of his riders, and he had no doubt he could handle the aircraft. Evan? Well, he was the loose cannon, and Hiker could only hope his first real battle wouldn't be his last.

Then there was Sophia Beaufont. She was a surprise at every turn, doing things he never expected.

Hiker wasn't sure why he'd assigned her to the 747. It was what was left to be assigned, and she was the wild card—the one who used strategy over power.

If anything brought down that plane, it would be Sophia Beaufont and Lunis.

He believed that, but only half-heartedly, which was why when the blue dragon transformed with the moon at his back, Hiker thought he was hallucinating.

"Oh, angels above," he gasped, grabbing his beard as his eyes widened in astonishment.

"For the love of all that's holy," Wilder yelled, his lungs emptying of air as he watched Lunis transform in the distance.

He knew little about Sophia Beaufont and her dragon, and now he saw that they had kept the best secret at bay.

"Rock on, you amazing woman," Wilder said as the jets released their first round at him and Simi. "Now it's my turn to be badass."

Mahkah had suspected what Lunis' gift would be, but watching something like that before his very eyes went beyond magic. It spoke of the greatness that was Sophia and her dragon.

Dragons were controlled by elements, which was amazing in itself. That meant that like Hiker, they were stronger in the sun. Or like Thad, that fire fueled them. All of them had a unique advantage, but doing what Lunis had just done was the stuff of legends.

It was the kind of thing that in Mahkah's long life made this moment, in the midst of thousands of others, stand out.

He could live the rest of his life seeing only the spectacular, and he would never see anything like what he just witnessed.

"Woot! Woot!" Evan cheered as he watched Lunis transform from a medium-sized dragon the size of a small recreational vehicle into something as large as the plane he was going after.

He'd first seen this stunt when they were rescuing the dragon eggs, and it had been thrilling to witness then. Watching the other riders react was much more entertaining.

CHAPTER ONE HUNDRED THIRTY

The missiles raced toward Wilder, unrelenting as they targeted him and his dragon.

He yawned, pretending the whole affair was boring him to death. When the missiles were fifty yards away, he simply waved his hand as if shooing away a fly.

And just like that, the winds changed direction in front of him, sweeping the weapons back around and turning on those who had launched them.

The expressions on the pilots' faces as they realized their attacks were quickly rushing back in their direction was intoxicating.

Wilder cheered as the wind did his bidding.

The hum of the motors racing toward Mahkah was enough to make him want to take flight on Tala. He was not accustomed to this world and its technology. It would take time for him to wrap his mind around how things worked now.

And yet, he stayed frozen in place as the menacing vehicles raced in his direction, ready to take flight, their weapons at the ready.

Mahkah waited until they were close, knowing this would only work if he timed it absolutely right. Unfortunately for him and Tala, the planes' projectiles had a much greater range than his.

Shots were fired at him, and they were forced to take flight to avoid a collision. Darting away from attacks became his focus as Tala soared back and forth.

We must get back on the ground, he urged his dragon.

And we will, she promised, diving for the dusty Earth below. It was both a risky place to be and the only one where they stood a chance of defeating their enemy.

"This is how we play," Evan said, sending Coral into the air as the vehicles progressed in his direction, having taken the bait.

A tank lowered its gun, pointing it at them. The jeep, stocked with its own weapons, roared as it approached.

They were close, but not quite close enough.

Evan had to do another lap, hoping to get the guys with the big guns to continue to pursue.

However, his luck had run out, and soon the shots started, raining all around him and making Coral divert off course to avoid being struck. Several blasts bypassed her wings, nearly scorching them.

They circled back around, diving close to the largest basin of water that surrounded the perimeter.

The tank and jeeps were close now. Almost close enough.

Evan had one chance. After that, his secret would be out. That was why Coral hovered just over the surface of the water, enticing their enemy as he cackled, a sound that always encouraged others to play with him.

He hoped it worked this time.

The saddle had broken off Lunis and fallen to the Earth below. Sophia now stood on her dragon's back, her sword in one hand and her other hand out for balance.

Lunis' transformation to his larger size had taken time. They'd lost the advantage on the 747, and it had taken flight, but Lunis was now faster than usual and quickly gained on the plane. Soon it would be outside the barrier, but not by much.

Somehow, someway they had to ground that plane before it got close to the city. Not only did they not know what was on board, but they also couldn't risk damaging it in case it was highly explosive.

CHAPTER ONE HUNDRED THIRTY-ONE

The attacks sent to knock out Wilder connected with the jets after they had been launched. The planes exploded, great balls of fire that lit the sky and rained back down on the tarmac, creating more explosions around the facility.

Many landed on other vehicles, and huge sparks shot up as the domino effect continued.

Wilder darted around new attacks sent by jets that had taken off after the others. They had obviously missed the first show.

He and Simi had one more in them. That was it, and then they'd be done with the wind.

Wilder circled around, grateful for the ease with which Simi soared, her excitement to twirl around attacks and through plumes of smoke thrilling.

For their first battle, this was one for the memory book. He glanced toward where Sophia and Lunis were quickly racing after a huge plane. Somehow, he felt none of this would have happened if not for the girl riding the giant dragon.

Mahkah and Tala landed with a heavy thud, far less graceful than usual. What followed was of much more concern for the aircraft preparing to take off. The ground rumbled under their feet, but Tala didn't move.

Even when the Earth split under the dragon's feet, she didn't move. Instead, her eyes flashed red as a crack shot in the direction of the magitech planes, making them falter toward the ravine that was quickly opening and sending them sliding sideways.

Some spilled straight into the canyon, falling toward the middle of the Earth. Others simply toppled to the side, losing their precious balance.

"That's the thing about us all," Mahkah said in a hushed voice, mostly to himself. "We stand upright until something more powerful knocks us over."

When the ground vehicles were almost at the water's edge, Evan flew over them before spinning around and racing back toward the water. He needed to be on the other side of it if he didn't want to be taken down by his dragon's attack. However, they were firing now, and that was changing the whole flow of his fight.

"Hey, stay off the hair," he said, ducking and covering his head as something whizzed by his head.

He didn't know what all these fancy machines did or shot, only that they needed to be taken down.

Twice he and Coral had to swerve to avoid becoming casualties. To both their relief, they made it over the water before they were pulverized.

Maybe the men in the vehicles thought they'd retreated to safety. Maybe they thought they'd given up. The heavy smoke in the air from the various other fights made it hard to see everything.

Evan noticed the vehicles starting to retreat, which wouldn't work for this attack at all. He encouraged Coral to open her mouth and send them a message to make them back up.

The dragon sent a huge plume of fire at the tanks and jeeps. It blasted over the tops of their windshields, which were apparently fire-proof. The important thing was, it made them pause.

"Oh, did you all get a burnie?" Evan called to his enemies. "No problem. We'll cool you off with some water."

He raised his hands, and following the movement, a huge wave of water rose out of the basin in front of them, coming up for fifty yards on either side. The wall rose up until it was even with the dragon and rider hovering above the surface, also fifty yards up. And then, like starting a race, Evan dropped his arms, and the water fell too, crashing to the ground and flooding the vehicles threatening to take them down.

How do we take it down? Sophia asked as they raced after the 747.

Magic, Lunis answered.

She shook her head. *We can't use fire or deadly force. We need to ground that sucker, but the only way I can think of is to gently encourage it back down.*

Well, the good thing is that I'm a big cuddly bear, Lunis said, spreading out his giant arms as he shot forward, moving so fast it made Sophia's teeth hurt. Still, she wasn't deterred by the blast of cold wind that made her eyes water. She didn't feel like she needed to be strapped in as they zoomed miles over the Earth's surface. She was anchored to Lunis like she was a part of him—and in all honesty, she was.

They quickly gained on the 747 and took a higher position. Several times it tried to change course, but it was unable to outma-neuver them. Lunis was too fast and his movements were too stealthy.

When he overtook the plane, soaring overhead, the pilots had to know they were out of options.

Even if it was fueled by the strongest magitech known to man or woman, there was nothing that could hold it up when the next maneuver hit it.

Gently, Lunis lowered his front feet and placed them on the wings of the plane, lowering his body weight onto the aircraft. His back legs found the back end of the plane, and his claws hooked into place.

The engines sputtered, failing under the huge new burden. The pilots had no choice but to make an emergency landing. To Sophia's great relief, it was going to be just inside the borders of the facility, on the flooded ground where another takeoff would be unlikely.

CHAPTER ONE HUNDRED THIRTY-TWO

The Dragon Elite landed one by one around their leader on the roof of the skyscraper in the center of the base. Around them, devastation ensued. The base was flooding, thanks to Evan. A huge fault line had created a crack that split buildings, overturned planes, and created fires that were spreading. The winds Wilder had used to boomerang attacks had added to the destruction, and now the things they'd done were dominoing, quickly creating more damage as one thing started another.

The 747 was back on the ground, and with it, whatever it was carrying.

Sophia landed next to Hiker, her eyes on him as he stared at something in the distance.

"Good work," he said softly, knowing all his riders could hear him.

None of them answered as he urged his dragon toward the edge of the building.

Something was approaching, something that wasn't a jet plane or a helicopter or anything else they'd so far encountered.

For some reason, Sophia believed it was time for her and the guys to stand down. What came next was Hiker's battle.

As if sensing her thoughts, Hiker turned back and looked at his men and Sophia and drew a breath. "I trust you'll have my back, but hopefully, you won't need to. What comes next is Thad."

They all nodded at their leader, but their attention was stolen by what rose over the side of the skyscraper. It was unlike anything Sophia had ever seen or even conceived.

It was incredible in design. It was alive and also not. It was horribly wrong and also ingenious. And most importantly, it was possibly going to be the end of the Dragon Elite.

CHAPTER ONE HUNDRED THIRTY-THREE

A dragon with Thad Reinhart on its back rose into view above the skyscraper on top of which they all stood, but this was unlike any dragon Sophia had ever seen.

It was unlike any dragon ever.

Ember, Thad's dragon, wasn't dead. That much was clear now.

The dragon Thad Reinhart rode was half-real, her orange body reflecting the fires and lights all around them. But where one of her wings flapped normally, the other made a crunching noise as the machinery worked to keep her aloft. One of her red eyes was real, and the other was a bulb that shone like a headlight. The dragon was an amalgamation of blood and vessels and mechanics.

Ember was the first cyborg dragon. She was magnificent, and also wrong in every way possible.

Dragons were meant to be magic. They were meant for the ethereal.

This dragon was nothing like where she came from.

That was evident in the way all the other dragons on the rooftop tensed.

"Hiker!" Thad yelled from atop his cyborg dragon, his scarred face making his mouth move strangely. "You found me."

Sophia saw Hiker's back tense as he tightened his hands on the reins. "Ember didn't die?" Astonishment overflowed in his tone. Thad had wanted this reveal, and evidenced by the laugh he let out, he'd gotten the reaction he'd been going for.

"Oh, no," Thad replied. "You thought Adam ended her. I thought so too, but I'm a fighter. You've been given everything your whole life, but I've fought for it, and I found a way to bring back my girl." He carefully stroked the dragon's face, which was mostly metal.

"How?" Hiker growled, running his eyes over the impossible beast hovering before them.

"Magitech, of course," Thad answered. "But more importantly, I used dragons. Why do you think they are almost extinct?"

"No!" Hiker yelled.

"Oh, yes," Thad replied, pleased with himself.

"How could you do this?" Hiker asked. "You know better than anyone how important dragons are, no matter what side you align with."

Thad shook his head. "You've always forgotten I have no side." He threw his hand out at his facility, which was full of chaos, fire, and water everywhere. "I don't even care that you've destroyed something I've worked so hard for. I'll build it again after I finish you and your riders. Should I take you all at once or one at a time? Either way, there's no getting away this time, Hiker. Ainsley isn't here to save you."

Sophia felt Wilder turn and look at her. He knew now. They all did. It would be hard for Hiker to hide the truth now, but that was the least of his worries. He had to survive this, and there was nothing Sophia could do to help.

The stage was set, and Hiker Wallace was the only warrior from the Dragon Elite allowed on it.

CHAPTER ONE HUNDRED THIRTY-FOUR

Bell's form seemed to grow as the dragon rushed forward to spring off the edge of the building. She flew toward the enemy.

Thad didn't take it easy on them, immediately firing the guns laced into Ember's wings.

Hiker ducked as the shots whizzed past them, bullets spraying everywhere, making the dragons on the rooftop scatter. Lunis rolled over, pinning Sophia to the surface. Thankfully he'd returned to his normal size and tented himself over her, deflecting the bullets with his tough hide.

Those bullets were meant to take out a human, not a dragon. That worried Sophia, and she pushed up from the ground, urging Lunis off her.

When she could see before her again, her heart leapt. Things weren't going well for Hiker. He was losing before the battle had even started.

One of Bell's wings had been hit, and she was favoring it as she tried to stay up. Hiker had his sword out and brandished it as his brother, who was higher in the air and looking down at him, laughing.

"You never got it, Hiker," Thad yelled down to him. "Good does not win. It never has."

"You're wrong!" Hiker screamed, a guttural ache in his voice.

"I'm not," Thad said in a low voice all of them could hear.

The leader of the Dragon Elite was one attack away from defeat. That much was obvious to all that were watching. And yet, the riders couldn't intervene. They simply watched as Hiker struggled to stay upright and Bell hurt. Any attacks they made were going to be hard to place. Bell was trying to make up the lost space, continuing to flap her wings.

"The thing about you, Hiker," Thad went on, "is that you were always meant to lose. You don't have what it takes. You never did, and now you'll lose with everyone watching, as you were meant to from the beginning. Goodbye, brother."

The cyborg dragon shot a blast at Hiker Wallace none of them could have averted, and it hit him in the chest. It knocked Bell over, making her roll head over feet.

The lucky part for the dragon and rider was they crashed on the roof of the skyscraper, where they tumbled one on top of the other until they were completely still.

CHAPTER ONE HUNDRED
THIRTY-FIVE

"Noooooo!" Sophia yelled, sliding off Lunis and trying to race forward. Wilder caught her arm and pulled her back.

"No," he whispered. "He's not out just yet. Have hope."

"But he is," she wailed, watching as Hiker Wallace, bloody and mostly broken, pushed up from his dragon, who was trying to fold her wing back.

The leader of the Dragon Elite staggered toward the edge of the building. Sophia worried he was so disoriented he'd simply walk over the side. Instead, he halted a few feet from the edge.

"Is this what you wanted?" Hiker held a finger out to his brother.

Thad laughed. "Of course. And now for the finishing blow."

He turned his cyborg dragon around like she was a piece of machinery. Sophia could have sworn she heard the dragon beeping as it backed up, like a pickup truck. Her imagination was taking over, trying to block out the events she was seeing. None of it seemed real. None of it seemed right. Good guys were supposed to win. The bad were supposed to fall. That's how it had to go.

"We have to help him!" Sophia yelled, trying to jerk out of Wilder's grasp.

He held her tight, not letting her go. "No, Soph. He has to do this on his own."

"If he doesn't, he will die," she whispered back. "Don't let him die."

"Soph, there's nothing to do."

They both looked up as the gun under Ember's magitech wing glowed, charging up to fire. It was aimed straight at Hiker, and it would end him. He was too disoriented, staggering around and trying to find his footing, to dodge anything. Bell was in no shape to fight either. Her wings were badly injured, and her body burned. Whatever had hit her wasn't something she would easily recover from.

Sophia felt into her pocket for the frequency disk. She brought her chin up, conviction in her eyes. "There's always something we can do to save those who matter. Please, Wild. Let me go."

She knew, and so did Wilder, that if he didn't let her go, she'd stay pinned. Sophia was the master of strategy, not strength.

He saw something in her that caused him to release her. His hands let up on her shoulders. He seemed torn, but he allowed her to pull away. "I hope you know what you're doing."

"I don't," she said to him as she backed away. "I never do, though. It's all instinct."

She turned and raced toward the only leader she'd ever known. The only one she'd wanted to follow. She wasn't letting Hiker go without a fight—even if he hated her for it.

CHAPTER ONE HUNDRED THIRTY-SIX

Before Thad Reinhart noticed her, Sophia ducked into the shadows of the rooftop, cast by Bell, who had crouched in her agony. She'd do anything to take the pain from the dragon, but there were more pressing matters to attend to.

Sophia rolled and dove until she was crouched just behind Hiker.

"What was that?" Thad asked, his voice barely audible over the hum of the guns about to deliver a five-hundred-year-old man's untimely death.

"Just a pain in the ass," Hiker answered, his eyes diving to the side as he glanced over his shoulder, seeing Sophia.

Thad apparently didn't think much of this reply. He simply grunted as his attention stayed focused on the guns charging.

Sophia didn't waste any time activating the frequency disk. The red meter started to build. She hoped it wasn't too late, and Ember's software hadn't figured out how to troubleshoot it after the first attempt.

The large man continued to sway in front of her. Sophia was afraid Hiker would tumble over the side of the building before she could help him. She used the last thing she had remaining—her words.

"Sir," she said in a whisper only he could hear, the roar of the charging gun too loud for Thad.

Hiker tensed and listened.

"You are better than him. You are stronger. And we have your back."

She glanced down to find the red meter all the way to the top. The device was ready.

"Now it's time for you to have your front," she said, looking back and finding Hiker Wallace's sword lying next to his injured dragon. She grabbed it just as the humming of the gun ceased.

"What?" Thad yelled as his dragon descended, losing elevation.

"Sir!" Sophia yelled, thrusting the sword into the air.

Hiker spun and grabbed it in a fluid motion that nearly stole her heart. He still had his grace, even injured. His speed and strength followed with a flash of perseverance in his eyes. Hiker Wallace wasn't done yet.

The frequency disk had taken effect. Fear flashed in Ember's eyes. It quickly spread to Thad Reinhart—panic taking over both dragon and rider.

The lights on the dragon dimmed. The humming dissipated. It's wings froze.

"What have you done?" Thad yelled, frantically searching his dragon for the cause of the problem.

The cyborg dragon was quickly losing height and beginning to spiral, her wings folding in, bringing her closer to the edge of the building. With Thad on her back, his face full of terror, Ember fell toward the skyscraper.

Her wing folded in, crushing into the roof as she dove face first into the hard surface. Ember teetered halfway on the edge of the building. Her rider was forced to the side, hanging mostly off. Thad's attention was on Ember. He was scrambling, trying to figure out how to keep her from falling over the side, plummeting to what would be certain death this time.

Hiker didn't hesitate. This time when his brother fell toward him, he brought his sword around and down, decisively ending the one man who had terrorized him since the beginning.

The scream that cut through the night air was full of pain and regret. Thad's face contorted with terror as Hiker shoved the sword deeper through his brother's abdomen, pinning him straight down to the surface of the roof, making his head hit the concrete hard. The man's hands reached for Hiker, but he was powerless to stop his twin from twisting the sword, making the wound even deadlier.

Hiker then picked up his boot and with a deliberate shove, he kicked at the side of the dragon, sending her out from beside Thad. The metal scraped the rooftop but it didn't stop the dragon that was dangerously teetering over the side. Nothing Ember could do would stop her from what happened next. And she seemed mostly paralyzed without magitech. Much like her rider, she was powerless. Thad was pinned to the roof as Ember was sent with a brute force across the distance.

The dragon's body slid over the edge and down the side of the building. Thad, seeming more dead than alive, reached longingly for his dragon, but she was gone. And soon he would be too as he stayed stuck to the rooftop by a single blade—blood everywhere.

Hiker Wallace stood on the roof, his breathing heavy and his balance wavering as he looked down at his brother, watching him take his final breath. Hiker didn't appear victorious as his enemy perished but he was alive, and the greatest battle of his life was over.

CHAPTER ONE HUNDRED THIRTY-SEVEN

The cold of the Gullington air was the most welcome thing Sophia had ever felt. She didn't remember the hands that pulled her through the portal.

She didn't remember how they got there. All she knew was that she and Lunis had at the last moment sent all their magical energy to Hiker Wallace to keep him from tumbling over the edge of the building when he was at his weakest, right after the death of his twin brother. He actually tumbled forward, but she had stopped it. Lunis had helped.

Now the bigger question was who had saved her. Brought her back.

She didn't know.

But somehow, she was staring at the leader of the Dragon Elite on the frozen ground of the Gullington, not wishing to be anywhere but Scotland.

CHAPTER ONE HUNDRED THIRTY-EIGHT

The next morning brought a headache unlike any Sophia had ever experienced. With it came the realization that the world was brand new.

She awoke in her bed in the Gullington, soft and comforting, with so many questions.

Sophia sat bolt upright to find Ainsley smiling at her.

"You did it, S. Beaufont," the housekeeper said.

"Do you mean, I saved Hiker Wallace?" she asked, curious.

The shapeshifter shook her head. "Oh, no. He's madder than hell. In five hundred years, I've never seen him this angry. I was saying you finally got the men to behave."

Sophia swung her feet over the side of the bed, confused. "Ains? What do you mean?"

The mischievous housekeeper had her robe at the ready and held it out for her. "Find out for yourself, S. Beaufont."

Sophia stood, her feet faltering under her from tiredness unlike any she'd ever known. She slid her arms into the robe and shrugged it onto her shoulders.

The housekeeper led her out of her room, making her press her eyes shut like it was a strange birthday party, although Sophia had been born in the summer, not the winter. Spring would be dawning soon, she realized.

With a care that made Sophia's heart tighten, Ainsley led her down the steps to the foyer. When Sophia was at the bottom, the house-keeper said, "Open up."

Sophia Beaufont opened her eyes to find something she'd never imagined.

CHAPTER ONE HUNDRED THIRTY-NINE

Standing before Sophia Beaufont, the first female dragonrider in the Dragon Elite, were four polished men, ready to impress.

They were the sight she hadn't seen when she'd first entered the Castle, and they were every bit as perfect.

Sophia loved them for everything they were and everything they were trying to be to impress her.

She stood looking ridiculous in her pajamas and glared at Evan, Mahkah, Wilder, and Hiker as they nudged each other to stand straighter, look better, be more polished.

"Hey," she said to the four men before her.

"Hey," they all said in unison, sounding like a bunch of bumbling idiots, although she had to admit they didn't look like it.

Evan looked nice in his black suit. Regal, almost.

Mahkah was sophisticated, which matched his demeanor.

And Wilder? Well, he was more than nice, but more on that later.

As for Hiker, he was alive. For Sophia, that was all that mattered.

She went straight to the leader of the Dragon Elite with a wide grin on her face. "You made it," she said, knowing better than to offer a hug.

He shook his head as if she had offered such a thing. "I told you not to help me."

"Deal with it, old man," she retorted.

He lowered his chin, offering her kind eyes. "I wouldn't be here if not for you. It wasn't anything short of sacrifice that saved me, and it was you.

"I just didn't want Evan to be our leader," she answered with a laugh.

"Dude," Evan called, "I can hear you."

Hiker grabbed her hand and pulled her off to the side. "I can't thank you enough. There is little that divides us from life and death, I've found. It's usually just a well-placed friend. Thanks for being mine."

"Anytime, sir."

CHAPTER ONE HUNDRED FORTY

Spring was coming; Sophia could feel it. Somehow a warm breeze had appeared, and she had grown accustomed to it during her recent journeys.

She stood on the Expanse, feeling the breeze on her back. She was glad Thad was dead and the wars he'd started were over. She knew more battles were waiting to be waged. And then there was the end of dragonriders.

No one was ready to deal with that. Sophia knew she had to move on.

Sophia took one step toward the Pond and then another.

Each seemed to lead somewhere, although she wasn't sure why. She didn't even know where she was going when her feet led her to the other side of the Castle. It was where the Expanse met the Pond, which was a strange place to find oneself. But here she was, with an ache in her heart and the blue of the water spreading before her.

And then she saw what she had been looking for without knowing it.

Quiet.

The gnome poked his head out of a cave and withdrew it again.

She thought about ignoring him, but then he looked out again and glanced straight at her, and his eyes connected with her as he said, "Hey, you!"

Sophia's feet carried her to him.

CHAPTER ONE HUNDRED FORTY-ONE

The door to the cave was mostly closed.

Sophia held her breath, not understanding why her heart was beating rapidly, or why she felt like she was on the edge of something great.

She was just catching Quiet in an act of mischief.

When she pulled back the great stone door to this mysterious cave, she got it.

Sophia knew, and then she didn't. She soaked it all in, disbelieving, before she ran for the Castle, fetching Mom and Dad. Or in this case, Mama Jamba and Hiker Wallace, the only parents the girl had ever known.

CHAPTER ONE HUNDRED FORTY-TWO

Hiker Wallace slowed before they entered the cave as if he knew what they'd see, but he didn't. There was no way.

He covered his mouth. "Soph, what is this? What do you need to show me?"

She retreated back into the cave, waving him forward and encouraging him to follow. "I don't know, sir. I mean, not entirely, but I'm sure we'll get an explanation."

He hadn't said much about the rescue, not really. What he hadn't said was still evident in his eyes, and now he seemed reluctant in a different way. He was whole and broken at the same time. Hiker Wallace had finished his brother, the biggest threat he'd ever known, yet that was accompanied by the idea that his kind—the dragonriders —were done.

"Just trust me, sir," she said, sidling up to the cave door she'd just found. Before she could finish her sentence, she saw Quiet in the distance, and for some reason, she knew there was nothing else to say.

All questions were gone as she pushed open the cave door.

Hiker Wallace's awe was equal to hers and he gasped.

CHAPTER ONE HUNDRED FORTY-THREE

One thousand dragon eggs, full of potential, sparkled at Hiker Wallace and Sophia Beaufont as they entered the cave curated by the great Quiet, the groundskeeper for the Gullington.

They gaped at a sight most would never see.

"How?" Hiker asked after a long moment.

"Because," Mama Jamba answered from a distant corner where no one expected her to be standing, "she's Sophia Beaufont, and she completed her training."

"What?" Sophia asked since that was the only question in her mind.

"My dear, haven't you wondered what Quiet has been doing?" Mama Jamba asked.

"Every day," Sophia answered.

"He's been starting the seeds of sacred new beginnings," Mama Jamba stated, kneeling and cupping an egg.

"I don't understand," Sophia argued. "I thought the eggs were all gone."

"They were," Mama Jamba explained. "But that was from the first rider. There were always supposed to be two."

"Her?" Hiker asked, pointing at Sophia and looking around, perplexed.

"That's right," Mama answered. "The first rider came about when the first and only dragon landed on Earth. An experiment of sorts. That union with the first male rider spawned one thousand eggs—the first set. Then I decided, with the angels, that we'd have more riders, but I had no idea how to have more until now. It was Sophia who spawned the idea and this batch of one thousand eggs."

"If the first male rider got one thousand eggs..." Sophia said to herself.

"Then the first female also gets a thousand," Mama Jamba agreed. Mother Nature cupped her hands. "This is my gift to you—your eggs. Know that some will be good, and some will be bad. They are yours and not yours. That's how it works when you're a mother. You own your children, but you don't."

Sophia nodded obediently, looking at Hiker for direction. He was still the leader of the Dragon Elite, and that was how it was meant to be for as long as time, as far as she was concerned.

Finally, Sophia looked at Mother Nature and smiled with gratitude. "I promise to take care of them for all time, Mama."

She patted her side. "I think they will take care of you, but whatever, my love."

CHAPTER ONE HUNDRED FORTY-FOUR

The atmosphere in the Castle was different when Sophia returned after discovering the eggs. Hiker admitted to telling the guys about them.

But there was something else to it.

There was potential pouring up from the creaks in the floor, Sophia felt. She also had the distinct impression she was being watched. She glanced around the entrance hall, feeling strangely disoriented from the weight of everything.

She wasn't sure why but she turned to find Quiet smiling at her in a way she couldn't explain. The gnome stood in the shadows with a glint in his eyes.

She thought he might murder her or crown her at any moment with the strange looks he was giving her.

Sophia wanted to ask him about the eggs. Thank him. But then an arm hooked around her shoulder and she was swept away, her attention stolen.

"The thing about Quiet is," Wilder began steering her in the direction of the Valentine's Day feast, "he has a crush on you because you've been leading him on."

Sophia slapped him. "I have not."

"Well, of course, you have," Wilder argued. "You are available, we have no one like you, and you're all batting your eyelashes at him."

"There's no way to look at him without batting my eyelashes," Sophia argued.

He nodded. "Thanks for taking my literal point. You're good at that."

She shook her head, deciding to abandon talking to commoners like Wilder. That brought her to talking to Mama Jamba, who gave her a considering look as she approached.

"So, you knew about the eggs?" Sophia asked, taking a bite of a heart-shaped cookie. "That was the business with the training, wasn't it?"

"Oh, my dear, you don't think you've figured me out by now?" Mama Jamba asked coyly.

"No, I wouldn't dream of it," Sophia answered.

"Anyway, so you're happy here? At the Gullington?" Mama Jamba asked, grabbing Sophia's hands and holding them tight with great intent. "That's the biggest question, and the only one I can't answer for you."

Sophia didn't know how to answer for a moment, feeling a strange draw toward Mother Nature rather than the Castle. Then she decided it didn't matter. It was all the same.

"I'm more than happy. This is my forever home," Sophia finally answered.

Her thoughts ran over her like a waterfall. These people were her family. Her chosen family. Evan might annoy her. Quiet intrigued. Mahkah was an enigma. No one made her laugh like Wilder. And then there was Ainsley, who she needed to help, although she wasn't sure why or if it would matter. There was no one she respected more than Hiker. These people, all the Dragon Elite had left, were her family.

Familia est Sempiternum.

One day, the family would grow. The thousand dragon eggs nestled in the cave by the Pond guaranteed that. There would be more dragons one day, and with that would come the potential of new riders.

The Dragon Elite weren't done. Not by a long shot.

In a way, they were just getting started.

Sophia looked around the dining hall, smiling as everyone cheered, grateful for the celebration.

These people at the Gullington were all her family.

And Sophia Beaufont was going to do whatever was needed to protect them all from now on.

SARAH'S AUTHOR NOTES
JANUARY 25, 2019

Thank you so much for reading. Your support of the Liv Beaufont series and this one has been life changing. Thank you! Seriously! Thank you.

Right before writing this book, I went and spent a week in Scotland. I'd been wanting to so since the 20Booksto50K conference in Edinburgh. However, I had a series of life complications that prevented that from happening. My cat was mauled by a coyote. My daughter needed me home. And I needed to be there. So I didn't go and I thought that was okay. But the desire to see Scotland never left me...

And then I wrote a bunch of books. And then I had to keep a child alive. And then I went to Vegas for the main conference. And I got back and was like, damn it, I'm going to Scotland.

Here's the truth. I was burned out. I'd written 15 Liv and Sophia books in one year. I love those gals. They are Lydia, my daughter, and me. But writing nonstop is draining. I don't usually go out on the weekends I don't have my daughter. I wake up, go to Pilates, put back on my pajamas and then write for 12 hours. And then repeat.

So when I got back from Vegas and couldn't shake Scotland from my mind, the location for the Gullington, I didn't let it go. I did something I've never done and booked a spontaneous trip. I didn't really know anyone there. J.L. Hendricks was hanging there. RE Vance and lives there. But I didn't have a travel companion which is weird for me. I've never traveled alone internationally.

And it was incredible. It was a soulful trip where I learned how to be alone and make friends and realize I'm never alone no matter where I am.

I worried I wouldn't have anyone to eat with. That I wouldn't be able to navigate the city. That I'd be lonely. None of those things happened.

And I learned so much about Scotland which I hoped made this book richer for you. I hiked to the top of Arthur's Seat and pretended I was Sophia Beaufont. The skies were blue and the sun clearly shining. The Scotsman who led the way told me that it's rare to have a day like that in December in Edinburgh, but he's never been on that hike with a Cali girl.

When we got to the top the winds were so fierce he said he'd never experienced that in Scotland. Again, he'd never been with an LA girl— we make things happen (or at least I do). So there we were, on the top of a peak, the winds blowing our hair back and the sun shining. Talk about inspiration! We watched a storm move in, blowing across the North Sea. These are the things that fuel stories.

I pretended I was S. Beaufont riding on Lunis. The winds were so intense, the puddles had a current. The Scotsman, with a prideful look, told me about how the wind makes them stronger. They brace their shoulders and charge into it. You know that went into the book.

I found the Scots to be such sweet and lovely people. I got back saying, "Thank you. That's lovely. Cheers." I also took so much inspiration from the trip. This book is littered with things from that trip.

I can't tell you how much that trip refilled my inspirational vault. As writers we are constantly putting out creative stuff into the world, but it's important that we remember to refill our reserves. I soaked it all in. I fell in love with a country. I fell for the people. And I came home with stories unlike I ever thought I'd tell.

I was fortunate enough to make a friend with a native Scotsman and he taught me a lot. That's how I was able to discuss things like the Scots New Year in this book and their vernacular. I came back saying "quite" and "wee" a lot and also missing Edinburgh like crazy. I bought him a fork for Christmas. He bought me a gift card. We aren't Wilder and Sophia but we are entertaining nonetheless.

I always want to come home after a trip. Always. And yet, I felt like I left part of my heart in Scotland. Not entirely because of the people (although there was that). Because there had been something calling me there since before I started this series. And now it calls me back.

But I have so many places that demand my attention. I have so many stories to tell. So who knows if I'll go back. Only time.

Currently, I'm on a plane to Montana for a family reunion...in freaking January. Wish me luck. I hope not to freeze. Expect to see Sophia in the artic with Lunis. Lydia is so excited to see snow. I'm excited to take a break from the books because when I return, my focus is better. I love my characters and miss them when we take time apart, but we are richer for the break.

I love to travel. I love staying home and writing books you all enjoy. And more than anything, I love doing it with people I enjoy. Thanks MA for being awesome. Here's to another year of creating addictive stories together.

Now, it's his turn to tell you all about how I blamed him for the trip to Scotland to anyone who would listen. It couldn't be my idea so I told everyone that he "made" me do it.

Drops the mic and walks away.

MICHAEL'S AUTHOR NOTES
JANUARY 27, 2019

You know, TinyNinja™, as an adult you start to learn how to accept the blame of your choices, or the CREDIT when you do something fantastic.

You went to Scotland by yourself... that is pretty fantastic. So, I'll pick the mic up and give it back to you.

While you and I don't talk very much, Sarah - except on books and beats and covers - you have my admiration for what you have accomplished with Liv Beaufont and now S. Beaufont. Two sisters who are changing lives, not just those in the stories, but for you and her daughter.

Oh, and for those living in Scotland as you market their country to readers around the world.

(Truly, Edinburgh is a wonderful city and it deserves all of the attention we can give it. Not for Edinburgh, but rather in case we help a few readers decide to look into traveling to Scotland – it does fill up a soul quite well. And empty your pocketbook.

That might or might not be a comment on the prices or the fact their beer is plentiful. I'm not admitting which.)

Diary Entry - Week of Jan 26th to Feb 1st.

Thank you for everything...

Full stop.

We authors wouldn't be able to do so much in our lives without readers and we recognize it. While we provide escape, excitement and friends you (hopefully cherish, or hate) you provide us with the means to travel, eat, have a roof over our heads etc.

This past week, I'm still suffering.

Mark W. Stallings (successful businessman who sold his company to pursue a writing career full time in 2020 and 2021) texted me this week asking how 2020 was treating me. I responded, "Like her b#tch." I'm sorry, but 2020 is kicking my rear-end with this jet lag issue. I came back from Asia on Jan 12th and it is taking me two *weeks* to recover.

It has been horrible for sleep deprived me to function. I hate it (sleep deprivation.)

I'm not made for this type of abuse LOL. Write 10,000 words in a day? Ok. Fine. I can do it, I *don't like it* but I can do it. However, make me stay awake at odd times of the day, sleep when it is light outside, be wide awake in the quiet of the morning when there are only the zombies or partygoers moving? That's not me.

No, really. I was NEVER a partying type person. *I've never even been drunk.* I didn't go out and stay up until the morning regularly or call in sick to work.

In short, I had a pretty ho-hum life as a young adult. Well, in reality anyway.

As a reader I had a FANTASTIC life but that is another story for another time.

Now, because of 20Booksto50k™ I have travelled parts of the world, and because of LMBPN Publishing I have travelled other parts of the world every year. The absolute hardest part for me has not been the hotel rooms, foreign cities or even (for those that know me) the food in foreign countries.

No, *it's time changes and jetlag.*

I'm sure my parents wondered what was wrong with me as a high school kid. I would go to sleep at 9:30PM at night because I had to get up at oh-dark-thirty for school in Texas. Seriously, *why the hell do they have teenagers get up to start school so early?* Teenager bodies aren't made to get up early. It's a form of torture.

I bet it really has to do with getting kids out of the house.

So, that's a long-winded way of saying jetlag won last week. As of this morning, I think two things have helped me almost get over it.

I started walking to help lose weight (I have a menudo challenge (the soup, not the boy band) with my older brother Darryl... If I fail to drop 10% of my weight by June 30th, I must eat a bowl of menudo. While I eat more Mexican food than I eat hot dogs and hamburgers (or even steak), I have not found menudo very appetizing and I'm willing to move heaven and earth to lose the weight.)

So, last week I went to bed late due to exercising late (solved the problem of taking naps at 5:30pm) and when I did rest, I had better, deeper sleep.

I hope to wake up normally tomorrow.

PLEASE OH GOD LET ME WAKE UP NORMALLY TOMORROW!

Ad Aeternitatem,

Michael Anderle

ACKNOWLEDGMENTS
SARAH NOFFKE

I feel like I'm on the stage at the Oscars, accepting an award when I write my acknowledgments. I stand there, holding this award, my hands shaking and my words racing around in my mind. I'm not an actress for a reason. I'm a writer and talking to people in "real life" is hard. Not to mention a ton of people all at once.

I picture looking out at the audience and being blinded by spotlights and forgetting every word of the speech I memorized just in case I won. The speech would go like this and it's meant for all of you, not the guild. For the fans. The supporters. The people who are the reason I would ever stand on any stage, ever.

Okay, here we go. I clear my throat and smile, looking up at the camera, holding the little golden man. And then I begin:

This was never supposed to happen. I was never meant to publish a book and then another one. And then another. I was supposed to write in private and live a life that Henry David Thoreau called a life of "quiet desperation." I would always hope to share my books, but never bring myself to do it. And you would never read my words. But then, in a crazed moment of brashness, I did share my books and you all liked them. And because of that, I've never been the same. And here I am feeling grateful all just because...

That's why I'm here. Because of you. Thank you to my first readers. The ones who picked up those books that I didn't even outline and you still liked them. You messaged me and maybe you thought it was no big deal, but when your ego is new to the publishing world, it's a big deal.

I can't thank you readers enough. I've found that reading your reviews helps me to start a chapter when I'm stuck or lazy.

I really need to thank someone who has made this all possible and that's my father. I was going to quit. I can't tell you how many times I quit. But when I wasn't making it, he was the one who told me to not throw in the towel. "Give yourself a timeline," he suggested. If I didn't get to my goal by then, I'd quit. And apparently there was magic in that advice, because I'm still doing this. Dad, you're the pragmatic one, but when you believed in me enough to tell me to not quit, I knew I had to follow your advice.

And I thank all my friends who are constantly supporting me with thoughts of love and encouragement. Most don't read my books. I'm sort of self-deprecating, although I'm working on it and will be the first to tell my friends, "My books probably aren't for you." However, every now and then a friend surprises me and says, "I was up all night reading your books." It's always a total shock. But my point is, that even if they didn't read, I still have the best friends ever. Diane, you're my rock. And I love you, even though you will probably not read this.

Thank you to everyone at LMBPN. Those people are like family to me, although I'm not sure if they'll let me sleep on their couch. Well, who am I kidding? They totally will. Big thanks to Steve, Lynne, Mihaela, Kelly, Jen and the entire team. The JIT members are the best.

Huge thank you to the LMBPN Ladies group on Facebook. Micky, you're the best. And that group keeps me sane.

And a giant thank you to the betas for this series. Juergen you are my first reader and friend. Thanks for all the help. And thanks to Martin and Crystal for being some of the best people I know. What would I do without you? A huge thanks to the ARC team. Seriously, if it weren't for you all I might pass out before release day, wondering if anyone will like the book.

And with all my books, my final thank you goes to my lovely muse, Lydia. Oh sweet darling, I write these books for you, but ironically, I couldn't write them without you. You are my inspiration. My sounding board. And the reason that I want to succeed. I love you.

Thank you all! I'm sorry if I forgot anyone. Blame Michael. For no other reason than just because.

BOOKS BY SARAH NOFFKE

Sarah Noffke writes YA and NA science fiction, fantasy, paranormal and urban fantasy. In addition to being an author, she is a mother, podcaster and professor. Noffke holds a Masters of Management and teaches college business/writing courses. Most of her students have no idea that she toils away her hours crafting fictional characters. www.sarahnoffke.com

Check out other work by Sarah author here.

Ghost Squadron:

Formation #1:
   Kill the bad guys. Save the Galaxy. All in a hard day's work.
   After ten years of wandering the outer rim of the galaxy, Eddie Teach is a man without a purpose. He was one of the toughest pilots in the Federation, but now he's just a regular guy, getting into bar fights and making a difference wherever he can. It's not the same as flying a ship and saving colonies, but it'll have to do.
   That is, until General Lance Reynolds tracks Eddie down and offers him a job. There are bad people out there, plotting terrible

things, killing innocent people, and destroying entire colonies. **Someone has to stop them.**

Eddie, along with the genetically-enhanced combat pilot Julianna Fregin and her trusty E.I. named Pip, must recruit a diverse team of specialists, both human and alien. They'll need to master their new Q-Ship, one of the most powerful strike ships ever constructed. And finally, they'll have to stop a faceless enemy so powerful, it threatens to destroy the entire Federation.

All in a day's work, right?

Experience this exciting military sci-fi saga and the latest addition to the expanded Kurtherian Gambit Universe. If you're a fan of Mass Effect, Firefly, or Star Wars, you'll love this riveting new space opera.

NOTE: If cursing is a problem, then this might not be for you.

Check out the entire series here.

The Precious Galaxy Series:

Corruption #1

A new evil lurks in the darkness.

After an explosion, the crew of a battlecruiser mysteriously disappears.

Bailey and Lewis, complete strangers, find themselves suddenly onboard the damaged ship. Lewis hasn't worked a case in years, not since the final one broke his spirit and his bank account. The last thing Bailey remembers is preparing to take down a fugitive on Onyx Station.

Mysteries are harder to solve when there's no evidence left behind.

Bailey and Lewis don't know how they got onboard *Ricky Bobby* or why. However, they quickly learn that whatever was responsible for the explosion and disappearance of the crew is still on the ship.

Monsters are real and what this one can do changes everything.

The new team bands together to discover what happened and how to fight the monster lurking in the bottom of the battlecruiser.

Will they find the missing crew? Or will the monster end them all?

The Soul Stone Mage Series:

House of Enchanted #1:

The Kingdom of Virgo has lived in peace for thousands of years...until now.

The humans from Terran have always been real assholes to the witches of Virgo. Now a silent war is brewing, and the timing couldn't be worse. Princess Azure will soon be crowned queen of the Kingdom of Virgo.

In the Dark Forest a powerful potion-maker has been murdered.

Charmsgood was the only wizard who could stop a deadly virus plaguing Virgo. He also knew about the devastation the people from Terran had done to the forest.

Azure must protect her people. Mend the Dark Forest. Create alliances with savage beasts. No biggie, right?

But on coronation day everything changes. Princess Azure isn't who she thought she was and that's a big freaking problem.

Welcome to The Revelations of Oriceran. Check out the entire series here.

The Lucidites Series:

Awoken, #1:

Around the world humans are hallucinating after sleepless nights.

In a sterile, underground institute the forecasters keep reporting the same events.

And in the backwoods of Texas, a sixteen-year-old girl is about to be caught up in a fierce, ethereal battle.

Meet Roya Stark. She drowns every night in her dreams, spends her hours reading classic literature to avoid her family's ridicule, and is prone to premonitions—which are becoming more frequent. And now her dreams are filled with strangers offering to reveal what she has always wanted to know: Who is she? That's the question that haunts her, and she's about to find out. But will Roya live to regret learning the truth?

Stunned, #2

Revived, #3

The Reverians Series:

Defects, #1:

In the happy, clean community of Austin Valley, everything appears to be perfect. Seventeen-year-old Em Fuller, however, fears something is askew. Em is one of the new generation of Dream Travelers. For some reason, the gods have not seen fit to gift all of them with their expected special abilities. Em is a Defect—one of the unfortunate Dream Travelers not gifted with a psychic power. Desperate to do whatever it takes to earn her gift, she endures painful daily injections along with commands from her overbearing, loveless father. One of the few bright spots in her life is the return of a friend she had thought dead—but with his return comes the knowledge of a shocking, unforgivable truth. The society Em thought was protecting her has actually been betraying her, but she has no idea how to break away from its authority without hurting everyone she loves.

Rebels, #2

Warriors, #3

Vagabond Circus Series:

Suspended, #1:

When a stranger joins the cast of Vagabond Circus—a circus that is run by Dream Travelers and features real magic—mysterious events start happening. The once orderly grounds of the circus become riddled with hidden threats. And the ringmaster realizes not only are his circus and its magic at risk, but also his very life.

Vagabond Circus caters to the skeptics. Without skeptics, it would close its doors. This is because Vagabond Circus runs for two reasons and only two reasons: first and foremost to provide the lost and lonely Dream Travelers a place to be illustrious. And secondly, to show the nonbelievers that there's still magic in the world. If they believe, then they care, and if they care, then they don't destroy. They stop the small abuse that day-by-day breaks down humanity's spirit. If Vagabond Circus makes one skeptic believe in magic, then they halt the cycle, just a little bit. They allow a little more love into this world. That's Dr. Dave Raydon's mission. And that's why this ringmaster recruits. That's why he directs. That's why he puts on a show that makes people question their beliefs. He wants the world to believe in magic once again.

Paralyzed, #2
Released, #3

Ren Series:

Ren: The Man Behind the Monster, #1:
Born with the power to control minds, hypnotize others, and read thoughts, Ren Lewis, is certain of one thing: God made a mistake. No one should be born with so much power. A monster awoke in him the same year he received his gifts. At ten years old. A prepubescent boy with the ability to control others might merely abuse his powers, but Ren allowed it to corrupt him. And since he can have and do anything he wants, Ren should be happy. However, his journey teaches him that harboring so much power doesn't bring happiness, it steals it. Once this realization sets in, Ren makes up his mind to do the one thing that can bring his tortured soul some peace. He must kill the monster.

Note This book is NA and has strong language, violence and sexual references.

Ren: God's Little Monster, #2
Ren: The Monster Inside the Monster, #3
Ren: The Monster's Adventure, #3.5
Ren: The Monster's Death

Olento Research Series:

Alpha Wolf, #1:
Twelve men went missing.

Six months later they awake from drug-induced stupors to find themselves locked in a lab.

And on the night of a new moon, eleven of those men, possessed by new—and inhuman—powers, break out of their prison and race through the streets of Los Angeles until they disappear one by one into the night.

Olento Research wants its experiments back. Its CEO, Mika Lenna, will tear every city apart until he has his werewolves imprisoned once again. He didn't undertake a huge risk just to lose his would-be assassins.

However, the Lucidite Institute's main mission is to save the world from injustices. Now, it's Adelaide's job to find these mutated men and protect them and society, and fast. Already around the nation, wolflike men are being spotted. Attacks on innocent women are happening. And then, Adelaide realizes what her next step must be: She has to find the alpha wolf first. Only once she's located him can she stop whoever is behind this experiment to create wild beasts out of human beings.

Lone Wolf, #2
Rabid Wolf, #3
Bad Wolf, #4

BOOKS BY MICHAEL ANDERLE

For a complete list of books by Michael Anderle, please visit:

www.lmbpn.com/ma-books/

All LMBPN Audiobooks are Available at Audible.com and iTunes

To see all LMBPN audiobooks, including those written by Michael Anderle please visit:

www.lmbpn.com/audible

CONNECT WITH THE AUTHORS

Connect with Sarah and sign up for her email list here:

http://www.sarahnoffke.com/connect/

You can catch her podcast, LA Chicks, here:

http://lachicks.libsyn.com/

Connect with Michael Anderle and sign up for his email list here:

Website: http://lmbpn.com

Email List: http://lmbpn.com/email/

Facebook:
www.facebook.com/TheKurtherianGambitBooks

Printed in Great Britain
by Amazon